Extraordinary praise for Julia Amante
and Evenings at the Argentine Club

"Julia Amante has created an enchanting community to fall into, true-to-life characters to fall in love with, and a rich story that will fall directly onto readers' keeper shelves. Amante's tale is tantalizing tango for the imagination."

—Lynda Sandoval, award-winning author of *Unsettling* and *Who's Your Daddy?*

"An engaging story of family, community, and the love that binds it all together."

—*RT Book Reviews*

"Delightful and charming...A story interwoven with love, desire, conflict, secrets, and tradition."

—*Midwest Book Review*

"A story of family, culture, class, success, and love."

—*Booklist*

"A big, beautiful novel of love, family, and the close-knit community they inhabit. By turns touching, funny, tragic, and triumphant, it's the story of an endearing group of people in search of their own American dream."

—Susan Wiggs, *New York Times* bestselling author

Say You'll Be Mine

JULIA AMANTE

GRAND CENTRAL
PUBLISHING

NEW YORK   BOSTON

Grand Central Publishing
Hachette Book Group
237 Park Avenue
New York, NY 10017
www.HachetteBookGroup.com

First Edition: October 2011
10 9 8 7 6 5 4 3 2 1

Grand Central Publishing is a division of Hachette Book Group, Inc. The Grand Central Publishing name and logo is a trademark of Hachette Book Group, Inc.

Library of Congress Cataloging-in-Publication Data
Amante, Julia.
    Say you'll be mine / Julia Amante.—1st ed.
        p. cm.
    ISBN 978-0-446-58163-9
    1. Life change events—Fiction. 2. Foster mother—Fiction. 3. Motherhood—Fiction. 4. Domestic fiction. I. Title.
    PS3618.I567S29 2011
    813'.6—dc22
                                                           2011000853

To the two best mothers in the world.
My mother, Ana. My mother-in-law, Pat.
Through your love and your example, I know what a
perfect mother looks like. I strive, every day, to be more
like you. And I love you both with all my heart.

To my children, Marshall and Emily.
Without you my life was empty and I didn't even know it.
Thank you for letting me be your mother.

Acknowledgments

My deepest gratitude to my Comadres, who are my biggest supporters and are forever praising my work and recommending it to others. I love you all for encouraging me, but a hundred times more for your precious friendship.

My long-ago Argentine friends who probably remember the "Americana" who whirled into their lives one year in high school and became *one of them* before returning home to America. You all changed the way I perceive myself, and taught me about my culture. I've never forgotten you. I don't know if I ever said thank you, but gracias, Laura, Chelita, Claudia, Daniela, Stella, and the girls of Normal school.

A huge thank-you to my agent, Kevan Lyon, for reading and rereading many versions of this story. Kevan, on top of being a wonderful agent, you're a terrific person, and I'm grateful we had the opportunity to work together.

I want to thank Grand Central Publishing for hiring such wonderful editors, dedicated marketing staff, and brilliant Web techies with great advice for novice social network nongeeks like me. My editor, Selina McLemore—when you have a suggestion, I can't help but try to absorb every word you say, because I know that if I can, my book will shine. Latoya Smith, I'm so glad I've gotten to work more with you on this book. Your insights and contribution helped push the story to become everything I wanted it to be.

And lastly, I want to thank my husband, who has been my partner in this journey of parenthood. You're an amazing father! You are my Nick—without you, I wouldn't be half as good a mother. I love you.

Say You'll Be Mine

Chapter One

Gallegos Winery buzzed with a nervous energy unusual for a workplace filled with year-round sunshine, fragrant scents, and a serenity imposed by the very employees who worked here. The staff had gotten to work early, making sure that everything was as it should be—the offices organized, hot coffee placed in the boardroom, and the steel vats cleaned, shined, and checked for bacteria.

Isabel Gallegos, owner and CEO of Gallegos Winery, sat quietly in her office. Today she'd be leading a group of investors on a tour of the winery. If they liked what they saw, their lawyers might be able to talk sale of the business. She'd waited a long time for this moment, and now that it was here, she felt...not sadness exactly, but a heaviness in her heart.

The winery had meant so many things to her through the years. Hard work. Obligation. Bondage. But also it stood for accomplishment and legacy. The success of the winery was the one thing, more than any other, that defined who she was. Everything she had went into creating Gallegos and making sure it became a powerful, prosperous, vibrant part of the community. So letting it go, even though it's what she most wanted, was complex. Like leaving a marriage that had been comfortable even if it lacked love and passion. The end was welcomed, and yet she had to admit that some parts of the commitment would be missed.

The phone rang, two short bursts of sound, indicating the call came from her secretary Stephanie's private line. Isabel answered it.

"Isabel, they're here," Stephanie said.

"I'll be right there."

Gallegos Winery was worth millions. Isabel had made her now-deceased parents proud. If she was lucky, she'd be able to sell the business at a healthy profit. At least she could look at the money and know that she'd gotten, if nothing else, a financial reward from a business she felt had devoured her youth and drained the life from her soul.

She looked across her desk to a quote that was pinned to a bulletin board hanging on the wall:

CEO Dexter Yager of multibillion-dollar-a-year Yager Enterprises, Inc. once said, When a man starts on the road to success, he's an outlaw; he's a nut. When he starts to have a little success, then they say he's a little weird. When he's really achieved success—he's eccentric. They keep saying, 'This guy doesn't fit in!' So 90 percent of the people in America are trying to fit in with people who aren't makin' it.

Isabel reached across and yanked the Yager quote, which had made her feel better about being different—about being a woman in a man's business and being a Latina with an accent—and encouraged her to succeed. She crushed it in her fist and tossed it into the wastebasket. "Makin' it" held a price no one ever warned you about. The things you give up for financial success, you never get back. Though maybe, just maybe, she could recover one or two.

Isabel picked up a file containing data for the prospective buyers and left her office. She passed by the other offices on her way out of the L-shaped building.

In one corner was Nick Reeves's office. Gallegos's co-owner usually found every excuse to be out of the office, but today he sat behind his desk, dressed in a sharp suit—unusual for the wiry six-foot California native who was more at home outside in the sunshine. When he saw Isabel approaching, he stood and joined her in the hallway.

"Mind if I tag along?"

Surprised, not only that he'd come into work, but that he wanted to go with her to the meeting, Isabel gave a stiff nod and continued walking down the hall. "Fine."

"Gotta listen to the sales pitch one more time. No one can make a person fall in love with the vineyard like you can," he said with a smile as he joined her.

A lump formed at the base of Isabel's throat. Yes, she did have that talent, but she never could sell it to herself enough to love it like others did. "*Hopefully* one last time."

"Hopefully," he repeated.

She recognized that, for his own reasons, Nick would be just as grateful to be free of the business as she. "Congratulations on your engagement, by the way," she said, pausing at the exit. "I'm sorry I didn't make it to the celebration."

His gaze didn't linger on her long, and she couldn't read the expression in his deep-set, dark green eyes hidden below thick eyebrows. "I didn't really expect you to attend, Isabel. Invitations were sent out to everyone. Wouldn't have looked right to exclude you." He opened the door wide and stepped aside to let her walk past him. "We'd better get going."

"After all these years, you're worried about appearances?" she asked. Not waiting for an answer, she walked through the exit.

As they crossed the dirt path from their private offices overlooking the acres of vines and the production facility toward the public areas of the winery, Isabel tried not to think about the other night, sitting alone in her living room, a glass of white Zinfandel in one hand and Nick's damned invitation in the other. So many emotions had filled her. So many memories too.

But now was not the time to dredge that up. Shaking her head quickly, she put aside thoughts of Nick and instead focused on her presentation. They entered the public offices through the back doors and let Stephanie know they were ready to rock and roll. A group of five middle-aged men in gray and blue suits were then escorted to the boardroom, where Isabel Gallegos shook their hands enthusiastically and introduced her partner—and ex-husband—Nick Reeves.

They began their tour out at the vineyards.

"Do you know," Isabel said, weaving a story as they

walked along the vines, "that Argentine and Californian vines have a common beginning?"

The men followed, some with hands in their pockets, others clasping them behind their backs, and listened. Isabel paused and lifted a small twig from a vine. "Back in 1556, a Spanish priest called Juan Cidron arrived in Argentina with vine stalks that he planted with great care and tended until they grew and multiplied over acres and acres. We consider him Argentina's first winemaker. But the interesting thing is that *that* early Spanish-American grape variety is the same as the one introduced in California. Argentina's stalk is known as Criolla; California's is known as Mission."

Nick smiled and winked as he stood behind the businessmen, and for a moment, she saw the man he used to be before alcohol had ruined his life and their marriage. The happy, carefree guy with adorable dimples. Back then he'd had hair that fell boyishly over his forehead. Today, his black hair was cropped short, spiking on the top, making him look tougher, more athletic, more like a man in control. He'd recovered from his downhill spiral and for that she was glad. They'd moved on separately, but they still worked together, and sometimes a glimpse of the past would seep into the present, like now, and it would make time stand still.

Isabel smiled back, because they both knew the presentation was going well—a little enchantment was needed in these sales pitches, even if in actuality the vines in this valley had nothing whatsoever to do with Mission grapes. That didn't matter. These men didn't care if Argentine and Californian vines were similar, but they did care that *she* and her family knew wines.

"My family felt it was natural to expand the family business to California and then to actually transfer our expertise and history to American soil. When you buy Gallegos wines, you are buying history, culture, old-world finery fused to new-world quality, and state-of-the-art production."

She placed the twig in the hand of one gentleman, then continued the stroll through the vineyards, going into finer detail about the types of grapes and vines and explaining the early morning harvest procedures. She led them back to where the harvested grapes were crushed and juiced.

"The white grapes are deseeded and skinned, and we extract a clear juice when we crush them. With the red grapes we leave the skins. This gives the wine its red pigment and flavor as the tannins blend with the juice."

The tour continued into the fermentation room and then the barrel room, Isabel educating the group with every step. Some details were a bit on the biology class side—the process of converting sugar into ethanol and carbon dioxide, the metabolism of yeast. Other details were more romantic—perfect aging, softening and smoothing out the wine, and the art of blending flavors. "It's like making love, gentlemen. Like pleasing a perfect woman. Everything is in the touch. A master lover can make magic, as can a master winemaker with the creation of a complex wine that leaves the consumer satisfied, intrigued, and wanting more."

She didn't have to look at her audience to see the ecstasy on their faces. Her job was finished. She headed back to the boardroom with the men to discuss the actual dollars and cents of the business. Her lawyers were waiting with financial statements, and the reality of what it would take to become the new owners of Gallegos Wines.

Three hours later, the meeting concluded and Isabel was finally able to retreat to the privacy of her office, her longtime family attorney joining her. "Isabel, I have another matter to discuss with you."

She stretched the muscles of her tight back. "Can it wait, Allen? I'm tired."

"No, I'm sorry. It can't."

Isabel nodded once and sat behind her desk. "Okay. What is it?"

"This," he said, handing her a letter from an attorney in Argentina.

She looked it over quickly with a frown. What she was reading couldn't be correct. Her closest cousin, Brenda, had died in a devastating skiing accident caused by a weak slope that fractured while she and her husband, Andres, skied down the steep, unstable path in the mountains of Bariloche—a tourist outpost in the Patagonia. Once the fracture was instigated, the skiers who followed triggered a slide that caused the whole slope to avalanche. Brenda and Andres were unable to escape.

Bariloche had always held such fond memories. Hot chocolate, friends, a pristine winter wonderland at the end of the world where she had vacationed as a young teen. A winter paradise. Now, her cousin's gravesite.

"Oh my God," Isabel gasped in shock as the words on the page sank in. Brenda *died*. Isabel would never hear her voice or silly laugh again; she'd never receive another e-mail full of recipes when she knew Isabel didn't cook; she'd never be able to look into those big hazel eyes that they both shared and hug her good-bye. Tears sprang to Isabel's eyes. Brenda's face, with that bright smile full of perfect teeth, flashed in her memory, and Isabel felt like she couldn't breathe. She lowered the letter and covered her face with her hands, forcing herself to inhale deeply. Isabel prided herself on being able to master her emotions, but . . . Brenda? Why Brenda? She felt the beginning of a deep sob grow in her chest, and she took a deeper breath to stuff it back inside.

"Isabel," Allen said gently. "You need to keep reading."

She straightened behind her desk. Her hand shook as she continued to review the letter, until her eyes found the words *full custody*. Her cousin had entrusted her three children to Isabel's care. A second blow that added fear to a thick cloud of sadness.

"I don't understand," she whispered under her breath. "What does this mean about the children? I can't—"

"You're expected to travel to and stay in Argentina until the immigration paperwork is complete, then—"

"Wait. I'm sorry." She rubbed her temples and tried to control the tremble of her body. Travel? To claim them? The children? "I can't stay in Argentina. Especially now with the possible sale of the vineyard and winery."

"I know the timing isn't good. I agree. But, Isabel, this could get bogged down in paperwork for months. Years, if we don't handle it right. There will be countless forms to fill out before the children can be transferred to your care. Then you'll have to deal with our immigration procedures through the embassy. This will be much easier to navigate considering the circumstances, but only if you're there demanding it get done. You'll contact your cousin's attorney when you get there and..."

Isabel had stopped listening. Her mind was trying to wrap itself around the horrifying fact that her cousin and her husband had chosen *her* as the guardian of their children. What did she know about kids? She was forty-six years old and had hardly ever been around anyone under the age of eighteen. She'd certainly never been responsible for their care. She didn't even have a pet. "Why? Why would she leave the kids to *me*?"

Allen leaned back in his chair and seemed to suppress a sigh. "Only you and your cousin can answer that question."

Her cousin. Beautiful, tall, a head full of long, brown curls. "Oh God." Tears welled up again. "I haven't seen the kids in five years, since my mom died and I went to be with my aunt for a few weeks. I was barely in any condition to pay much attention to them then. I'm a stranger to them."

Plus I don't want them.

Ashamed, Isabel quickly pushed away that thought. The children needed someone who could be strong. Right now they were with their grandmother, and that was probably the best place for them to stay. She'd fly to Argentina and take care of the legal paperwork to reassign guardianship to the kids' grandmother, then return in time to complete the sale of the winery. The company lawyers could manage the details for a few days until she returned.

She looked at the letter she gripped in her hands. Brenda couldn't have really wanted her to take her children. Keeping them with their grandmother was much more logical. Isabel would see to it that it happened. This was a good plan and the only one available to her at this point.

Nick rolled out of bed, glancing over his shoulder at his fiancée, Beth. Cute as could be, she slept curled on her side, her blond hair fanning across her face and falling over her bare shoulder. He was so lucky to have found her. After the divorce from Isabel ten years ago and the painful years that followed recovering from his alcohol addiction, he never thought he'd be happy again. Never thought he'd find another woman to love. But he had. And this time he wasn't going to mess it up, because Beth was perfect. Loving. Patient. Sweet. Pretty. Uncomplicated. Undemanding. She was happy barely getting by with her little shop in old town Temecula, renting bikes to tourists and selling artistic trinkets, dressed in a simple pair of shorts and tank top, with her hair in a ponytail. So unlike his ex-wife.

He stood, unable to sleep. His mind turning to Isabel now, he acknowledged that the day had gone well. Isabel did a fantastic job with the tour, and he had to admit that she looked amazing, like always. Her long hair pinned up, her flawless makeup making her look like a woman half her age. More than once, he'd caught the fascination in the prospective buyers' eyes. They liked what she'd said about the business, no doubt about it, but they also liked what they saw. Isabel, so much like her vineyards, had a sexy, extraordinary essence that surrounded her. It came out in the way she talked, the way she walked, the passion that had somehow implanted itself in her soul, and those around her couldn't help but be drawn in. So, after they had courted these buyers for months through phone calls and e-mails, they were all taking a serious step now that they'd met Ms. Gallegos.

In the kitchen, he made a thick ham sandwich with lots of mustard. And he took it outside in the cool night air. Pulling out a wrought-iron chair that scraped slightly on the tiled patio floor, he sat to eat. He stared out in the distance, unable to see the glimmering valley lights through the dense fog. Didn't matter. He knew what it looked like by heart. He'd been living in a small caretaker's home on the vineyard grounds since the divorce, and before that in the main house with Isabel and her parents. Half his life had been spent surrounded by organized rows of grapevines.

Although he looked forward to moving on, marrying Beth, starting a new life, he couldn't help feeling sad about leaving the vineyard. He loved it here. This had always been home. Having loved not only Isabel but also her parents, whom he considered his family as much as hers, he felt like he was losing the only place that had ever really comforted him. No matter how much he'd screwed up, in his marriage or at work, the little vineyard house had been a haven.

"Hey." Beth's voice came from near the sliding glass door. "What are you doing out here?"

"Got hungry. Couldn't sleep."

"Are you worried about the sale?"

"No."

She sat beside him and reached across to run her fingers through his short hair. Felt good to be touched. Beth always caressed him. With her hands, with her smile, with warmth that made him feel loved.

"What's wrong, then?" she asked.

He shrugged. "Nothing really. Just thinking. Go back to sleep. I'll be in in a few minutes."

"Nick, don't worry about the winery selling. And I told you, we don't have to wait—"

"Yes, we do. Once it's sold, I'll move out of here and we'll plan the wedding."

"You can move now. We don't have to wait."

Beth had her own apartment in town, but most of the time she stayed with him on the vineyard grounds. She'd mentioned before that he could move in with her, but he had his own home here, and it worked out better to live close to work. But he knew they couldn't live here after they were married. "I can't start a new life until I'm free of this one. I've explained this to you."

"I know, but—"

He rose from his seat and leaned in to kiss her. "Be patient just a little longer. I need to do it this way. Okay?"

"Of course it's okay. I love you, Nick. You know that."

Yes, he did. He took her hand. "And that's why I want everything to be perfect. Once this is all gone, I can concentrate on making our life exactly the way it should be. Let's go back to bed."

Rather than worry Beth with his irrational fear about leaving this cocoon, he carried her to bed and made love to her.

Chapter Two

The next morning Isabel had an early meeting with her staff. She explained her upcoming absence as a family emergency. "I'll only be a phone call away." Stephanie and Doug, her public relations manager, would be in charge. No one mentioned that her choice was a slap in the face to Nick. They understood her reasons. Even Nick understood. After making a financially damaging error during his drinking days that took Isabel and her father an entire year to repair, Nick lost his position as CFO. He couldn't work with money, and he couldn't work with the wine itself for obvious reasons, so instead he supervised staff. Sometimes he worked in packing operations or helped out the harvest techs, even cleaning barrels and harvesting grapes. He worked—hard. But he really had no official responsibilities. His job title, president of operations, was something her father gave him to try to make Nick feel like he mattered.

Regardless, when Isabel was gone, he was *not* in charge.

As the meeting ended and everyone filed out, Nick stayed behind. "Question, Nick?" she asked as she lifted her pen and straightened her papers.

"Just curious about what's really going on. What's serious enough to make you leave the country now?"

She gazed at him from across the long conference table, considered offering a stock response, avoiding the question. He wouldn't challenge her, she knew. But as she stared at him, she couldn't do it. Nick was still like family. Her parents had loved him like a son, so much so that they had left him part of the business even though she'd begged them not to. And, of course, she'd loved him once too. He'd been more than a husband; he'd been her best friend, and she would have shared all her worries and problems with him in the past. Woke him in the middle of the night. Cried on his shoulder. But that had been a long time ago.

"My cousin Brenda, from Argentina, died. I've got to go make sure her children are cared for."

"Brenda?" he asked, and frowned. "Oh hell."

"Yes. Hell."

"How? What happened? She was so young."

"Skiing accident. I don't know much yet."

"So . . . what are you going to do? Travel to—"

"I'd like to ignore it all and let Brenda's more immediate family handle this, but . . ."

"She doesn't have anyone," he muttered.

"No. Well, her mother, but she's in her seventies and . . . when I talked to her this morning, she was a mess."

"I bet."

Her aunt had sounded vacant and numb. Perhaps she'd been medicated. She admitted to having broken down completely the day it happened. "Brenda died a week ago, and I didn't even get a phone call. My aunt was so distraught and she had to deal with the kids and...well, thank God the family attorney stepped in. I'm thinking maybe I can hire a nanny for them. Give my aunt some help."

Nick frowned, a look that turned dark, even accusatory.

"What?" she snapped.

"Hire a nanny? You and Brenda were more like sisters. I would have thought..." His voice grew deep and quiet, incredulous. "Didn't she have a will? Did she leave any indication of what she wanted?"

"It's complicated."

He stood and turned his back on her. She stared at his back as he looked out the window. Knowing Nick, there was more he wanted to say, but how could he? Where her personal life was concerned, he didn't have a say anymore.

"When are you leaving?" he asked without facing her.

"Tomorrow."

He dropped his hands into his pockets and faced her. "What can I do?"

"Nothing. There's nothing anyone can do. It's a tragedy."

"I'm sorry. Are you okay?"

Tears threatened to spring to her eyes, and she fought to hold them back. She didn't want to cry in front of him. She'd broken down when her father died, and he'd held her and comforted her and it had almost been too much to bear. "Okay?" She clasped her hands together and stared down at her fingers, trying to summon anger. Anger was better than sadness. "She and my aunt were all the family I had left," she said, her voice losing its hardness, unable to maintain the pretense and hide the pain.

"Isabel." He took a step toward her.

She stood and took a defensive step back. "And I didn't need this problem right now when the sale of the winery hangs in the balance." She drew a breath. Better. Her control was coming back. No wild emotion. Much better.

He stopped his approach, apparently realizing that she wouldn't welcome any tenderness from him. "Don't worry about this place. Just think about your family right now and do what's right."

"I'll do what's necessary. And I'll be back as soon as I can. If anything comes up, call me and I'll fly back immediately."

When she looked at him, she saw that his gaze had returned to its earlier hardness. Suddenly she remembered all the cruel things he'd said to her at the end of their marriage. The words were still etched in her heart. *A heartless, cold bitch that he wished he'd never met*. And even more painful, how grateful he was that they'd never had children. He'd been angry and probably drunk, but those words still cut deep, more so now, when she feared they might be a little true. But he didn't say anything hurtful now.

He said, "Right," and "Have a good trip," and turned away.

As he walked out the door, Isabel collapsed into a chair and dropped her head into her hands. Pain consumed her from the inside out. Her head pounded and her back ached. She wanted to go after Nick and apologize for being that cold bitch she played so well. Tell him that it wasn't really who she had become. That her heart could still bleed and that it was doing so now from every open sore. But instead she closed her eyes and re-membered when it had been easy to ask him for what she wanted. When they were younger and their dreams had been ahead of them.

Footsteps alerted her that someone had walked back into the boardroom. Before Isabel could alter her de-jected appearance, Stephanie said, "Sorry, Isabel. I came back to clean up. I didn't mean to intrude."

Isabel shook her head. "It's okay. I was just thinking of a past long gone." She rubbed her hands up and down her face one more time, as if it would wipe away her memories.

Stephanie offered a sympathetic look. "Missing your parents?"

"No." She sighed. "I mean, I always do, of course, but that's not it."

Stephanie waited for more.

Isabel was too drained to mask her feelings, and tears blurred her vision. "All my life, I've tried to do the right thing, be there for everyone that needed me, and . . . here I am without a soul I can reach out to."

"Isabel, you have—"

But she sniffed and stood. "Listen to me. Pathetic. Thank you, Stephanie. I'll call you as soon as I get to Ar-gentina."

Stephanie nodded with a look of sympathy in her eyes. "Take care of yourself, and have a good trip."

Not likely. "I will."

* * *

Nick stalked across the vineyard to his home. The anger boiling inside him had made him want to pound something. Damn it! Damn *her!* He was used to her treating *him* like he was insignificant, but to act that way about children—her own family—what the hell was wrong with that woman? She would turn her back on those kids in a heartbeat if she could figure out how. He knew she would, because she didn't have a heart.

And he was angry at himself, because part of him wanted her to do just that. Anything that stood in the way of a successful sale of the vineyard was bad. Wasn't it? Anything that continued to keep him bound to the business and to her was hell. What if she ended up having to spend weeks or months in Argentina? What if this jeopardized the impending sale? Then what?

But immediately he was filled with guilt for his selfish thoughts. He knew what it felt like to grow up without loving parents. He'd never known his father, and his mother had been a raging alcoholic who'd ended up dying young. He didn't wish that pain on any kid. And here were three who were related to Isabel and needed to be rescued. Isabel would have to step up to the job. And he had to offer whatever support he could. Help her so she could focus on working and getting the vineyard sold. This was what they both wanted. He muffled the voice inside his head that called him a liar. He *did* want to move on. Even if he was afraid.

He entered his small home feeling calmer. Sadness stirring in his heart to replace anger. Nick sat on the hardwood floor thinking about the look in Isabel's always-expressive hazel eyes when she said she had no family left. Damn, that had broken his heart. Even after all they'd been through, he'd wanted to say she had *him*. But she didn't.

That was the problem with their continued working relationship. He had never become free of her. When her parents had granted him part ownership of the business upon their death, he'd been stunned. Grateful, but stunned. He knew that it was their hope that if he stuck around, he and Isabel would one day work things out and get back together. They never understood their daughter and that there was no changing her mind.

What it had done was bind them together in a way that made it impossible to move on. He saw her every day at work in her sexy power suit and three-inch heels. Sensed her subtle moods, which she tried so hard to mask. Heard the strain in her voice when she was frustrated, the hardness when she was angry, the velvet smoothness when she spoke of the vineyard with a love and pride she probably didn't even know was there. But unfortunately, the worst part was that her pain and struggles still affected him. He still wanted to protect her when she hurt. Even though she hated his guts and would have fired him and tossed him out on his ass like he deserved if it hadn't been for her parents.

He groaned and leaned his head back, closing his eyes. Protecting Isabel must be written into his DNA. Even when he'd been deep inside the fog of alcoholism, he'd wanted nothing but to protect her. Even from himself. He'd even fantasized about dying, figuring it would be the end of her problems.

He imagined that one day she'd get the call that her husband had died. Maybe gotten run over by a car as he stumbled stupidly out of a bar. Or stabbed in a bar fight. Or drank so much his liver exploded. He'd spent hours fantasizing about his death. How it would happen. How they would notify Isabel. How she'd feel a wash of relief inside but would do the right thing and give him a proper burial. Sick. He'd been truly sick.

They were ridiculous scenarios anyway. No one would have stabbed him in a bar—he was too well liked. And he wasn't a fighter, so it wasn't like someone would suddenly attack him. And a car wasn't likely to run him over since he rarely walked the streets when he was drinking. And he hadn't really wanted to die even if everyone told him repeatedly that he was killing himself with booze. No, what he'd wanted was to save Isabel from having to hurt anymore because of him. Just like he wanted to do now.

But it had finally come to him that there was only one way to stop hurting her, and that was to stop drinking and grant her the divorce she wanted. He'd done both, but not alone. Isabel had saved him. Even after divorcing him, she'd put him through treatments, helped him get clean, stood by him every step of the way. Slept in a chair beside his bed while he vomited and went through withdrawals so severe he thought he'd really die. But he'd lived, and he owed Isabel his life. He slid down onto his back on the cool wooden floor and cursed. The woman hated him, resented the hell out of him for still being around, and yet she'd stood by him when he'd needed her most. How could he ever turn his back on her?

His front door opened and Beth walked in. "Nick?"

He thought of the children Isabel was going to go see in Argentina. And damn it, he knew what he had to do. "In here."

He heard her close the door and come around the corner. "What are you doing on the floor?" She walked to the living room.

A sharp pain deep in his gut made him pull himself up to the couch. He drew in a deep breath to keep his emotions in check. But when he glanced at Beth, he lost it and dropped his head back, letting the tears squeeze out of his closed eyes. The pain and guilt over all he'd done and what he was about to do poured out of him.

"My God, Nick. What's wrong?"

He sniffed and wiped his eyes with the heels of his hands. "I'm sorry. Sit down. We need to talk."

"You're scaring me."

He reached for her and they sat side by side on the couch. "Isabel's cousin Brenda was in an accident."

Beth frowned.

"She died."

"I'm sorry. Were you . . . close to her?"

"No, but . . . you know Isabel's family was like my family." He'd had no real family until he'd met Isabel, and then he'd realized what he'd been missing. Parents who truly loved their daughter, who worried about her and sacrificed for her as much as she did for them. Family stuck together. "Beth, there's more." He explained that Brenda had left behind three children and that he wanted to travel with Isabel to Argentina to make arrangements for their care.

"But why? She's not asking you to, is she?"

"No, she isn't. This is something I need to do for her."

Beth looked away, a touch of irritation evident on her face. "There's always something you feel you need to do for her."

"That's not true."

Beth stood and walked away from him. "When her mother died and then her father a few months later, I understood. They were your family too. But she can deal with this alone."

"I don't think she can. There are kids involved."

"I know you two wanted to have—"

"I have to make sure she's okay, that this doesn't tear her apart."

Beth stared at him with her arms crossed and her body stiff. "You're still in love with her. You're never going to move on, are you, Nick?"

"That's not true," he said, standing and holding Beth's shoulders gently. "I love *you*."

"You may love me, but not like you love her."

Could he argue with that? "It's different, sure."

"Nick, I told you I'd wait for you. That if it took a year or two or even three more to sell the winery and get married I'd be patient. Because when that day came, you'd finally leave here and I'd have you to myself. But I won't put up with my future husband still being in love with his ex-wife."

"I'm not." He sighed. "I care about her. I owe her my life. Don't you understand? I'd be dead today if it wasn't for Isabel and Mom and Pop. I can't turn my back on her when she needs me."

"Ever? For the rest of your life you're going to run to her side when she has a problem?"

"No." He dropped his hands. His cozy living room suddenly felt too small. Beth didn't understand. He'd known Isabel for twenty-six years. The first six he'd been crazy about her, but all she'd wanted was to get the winery established for her parents and to take off to build her own career away from the family business. Then he'd finally convinced her to marry him, and it had been a ten-year disaster. Only the last ten while they'd been apart, as he'd cleaned up and learned who he really was with the help of treatment groups, had he realized what a mess he'd made of her life. Little by little, he'd tried to make it up to her. And he realized that standing by her now was most likely the last and most important thing he could do for her.

"Nick, this isn't your problem. Don't go with her."

"Beth...I'm...going."

Without another word, Beth stepped back and picked up her purse from the couch.

"Please don't leave, Beth. Try to understand. I'm doing this for us too." He stepped in front of her path, hoping she'd walk into his arms the way she had so many times in the past.

But she lifted her chin and pinned him with her clear blue eyes. "You have a choice to make. It's past time. Me or her."

"I choose *you*. You're the one I'm going to marry. You're my future."

"Not if you can't let go of your past." She walked around him and left.

Nick didn't try to stop her. She'd come around. She'd see that he was right. That a real man didn't let family down. Isabel was family. And those children were too. He had to help Isabel figure out what to do with them. He wasn't holding on to his past. If he didn't help Isabel, this could delay the sale of the winery and that wouldn't be good for anyone. Then he'd come back and move in with Beth. Even if the winery didn't sell right way, he'd leave. He'd do that for Beth.

Chapter Three

❧

*I*sabel never enjoyed flying, but she wasn't one of those people who dreaded all the added security and delays. This was part of the reality of flying these days, so she endured it with dispassion.

However, when she saw Nick splayed out on a chair by the gate, with his eyes closed, she almost lost her sedate control. She slammed her carry-on beside his chair and took a seat next to him.

He opened his forest-green eyes and a slow grin grew on his mouth.

"What the *hell* are you doing here, Nick?"

"Linda booked me a ticket." His assistant. "I certainly didn't need to stay around the office."

"I specifically told you I didn't want you to go when you called last night." He'd made the crazy offer and she'd told him no and hung up on him. Of course, that twenty-second conversation had kept her up for hours wondering why he'd made the offer.

He shrugged. "I'd like to see Mom and Pop's country again. And they would have wanted me to go."

"I can't deal with you—"

"You won't have to."

"Nick—"

He stood and grabbed hold of her elbow, pulling her

to her feet and getting in her space. "Let's be honest with each other. This trip could tear you apart, Isabel." He stared at her in stone-cold seriousness. "And I will be there for you to lean on. I promise you."

Isabel blinked away tears. "I don't want to lean on you. I don't want you in my life at all."

"You think I want to be?"

She honestly didn't know. Sometimes she wondered. He'd chosen to hang around when he could have left years ago, especially after her parents died and there was no one to beg him to stay. "I can handle this on my own. I don't need you."

"You can handle this? By doing what? Turning your back on orphans?"

"I'm not turning my back on anyone." She glanced at the other passengers waiting for their flights; they were watching or at least listening to them with somewhat-disguised interest, and she wished Nick would leave her alone and go home. The stress of all this was getting to her. She wasn't eating, wasn't sleeping. Coffee and sugar were sustaining her, but it wasn't enough to give her energy to deal with Nick.

"No, that's not your style. You'll make sure everyone is okay. You'll *manage* the situation. Then you'll go on with your own agenda so you don't have to deal with your real feelings."

What the hell did he know about her real feelings? While they were married, he could barely deal with his own feelings, let alone hers. She yanked her arm back. "If by agenda you mean to get back here as soon as possible to complete the sale of the business, you're damned right that's what's going to happen."

"I know that's want you want and plan to do." He shook his head. "My guess is that you won't be able to, Isabel."

"I'll make everything work out well for everyone." She grabbed her bag to move to the opposite side of the waiting area. He could do what he wanted as long as it was not near her. "That's what I always do."

He took her bag from her hands and pulled her aside, as if finally noticing that they were creating a scene. "Let's cut the bullshit," he said when he had her by a sidewall, away from sitting passengers and others hurriedly rolling their carry-ons to their gate. "I can turn around and go home, no sweat, but when you get down there and are faced with the fact that you've now become an instant mom, then what?"

"I am *not* going to become anyone's mother." Her stomach began to clench.

He lowered her bag beside him and faced her again. "Do you honestly expect me to believe Brenda wanted her children left with some nanny, a stranger? I know your family better than that." Nick blew out a breath, and when he spoke next, his voice was softer. "Listen to me. You *wanted* to be a mom. I *know* how much you wanted to become a mother, Isa—"

"Shut up." A sob was gathering in her throat.

"I won't. This time, I won't. Because if you think this is going to be a simple deal you're going to go down there and close, you're fooling yourself. It's my future, too, we're talking about, and I want to know what you're going to do."

"I don't *know*," she said between clenched teeth and moist eyes. "Whatever I do, it won't impact you."

"Everything you do impacts me."

She met and held his gaze. There was nothing she could do about her cousin dying, but damn it, if it was an inconvenience for him, then too damn bad. She felt like curling up in a ball and crying for a week. What was he worried about exactly? That she might decide to stay and mother the kids and delay the sale of the business? That he wouldn't get his share of the money fast enough? "I'll do what I can to make sure your life doesn't have any ripples in it, Nick."

He cursed and moved closer. "This isn't about me. It's about you. I know you're in pain and you won't ask for a shoulder to cry on—"

"Not yours."

"Then whose?"

She didn't know.

He hesitated, then added, "And I know Brenda's children will remind you of the babies we never had."

She shook her head. "Just stop."

"Do you think I've forgotten for one day what you went through?"

Bile rose in her throat. "Oh, God. I'm going to be sick."

"Just because you've buried it all and refused to deal with what it did to you—to us—doesn't mean it's not all in there somewhere." He tapped beneath her collarbone. "And I'm afraid it will come out in Argentina and you'll be alone."

She shook her head, wanting to shake him away.

He gazed at her, pain and regret in his eyes, and that made her stomach flip again, her coffee from this morning seeming to burn the lining and choke her.

"I couldn't do anything about our baby," he said, and the words began to fade behind a loud ringing in her ears and the sudden loud noise of hundreds of people, wheels rolling on tile, and airport announcements. "I couldn't be there for you back then. But I want to be here for you now," he continued.

She pushed past him and rushed into the bathroom, where she dropped to her knees to vomit into the toilet. Holding herself up as much as possible, trying not to touch the public bowl, she let it all out of her system. She wiped at the perspiration on her forehead with the palm of her hand. Damn it.

Damn Nick. Like she wasn't already under enough stress. She didn't need this. And yet as crazy as it was, here was the reason her parents loved him so much— the reason they'd treated him like a son, even naming him in their will. Because he *had* been there for her. Miscarriage after miscarriage, and even one birth that almost provided them with a daughter, had finally caused enough damage to end any hope of her ever conceiving again. He'd been there for all of it. That had been the end of their dream of becoming parents. And she tried never to think about it. Obviously Nick still did. Or maybe it was these kids in Argentina reminding him of what they'd wanted to build together.

She stood and wiped her lips with toilet tissue. Out by the sink, she splashed water on her face and rinsed her mouth. Finding a mint in her purse, she unwrapped it and ate it. She'd get through this. Nick wouldn't be needed this time around. But he was going to travel with her, so she'd better accept it. He was going. And it would be okay.

He was outside when she came out of the bathroom. "I'm sorry."

"I don't know what you think you're going to accomplish by coming along. I don't plan to have a nervous breakdown and lose all focus."

"I *can't* let you go alone."

"You can."

"Isabel, I know how you feel. About me. But now that Mom and Pop are gone, I'm all you've got left. Give me a chance to help."

As frightening as it was to admit, he was right. She had no one. The winery had consumed her entire life. She had few friends and no family. "Let's go."

Isabel and Nick checked into the luxurious Park Hyatt in Buenos Aires when they arrived. The first time she'd had the money to stay in this hotel, she'd done so just because she could—amazed by her success in America and what money could buy. Comparable to the Ritz-Carlton in Los Angeles or the Waldorf-Astoria in New York City, the Park Hyatt in the heart of the Recoleta neighborhood was pure indulgence. But that was then; now she stayed here for convenience—she knew where it was and what to expect, and it was fully equipped if she needed to use their business service. This time she wasn't even interested in a stroll through the lobby and corridors to admire the paintings of local artists.

In the morning, she would contact Brenda's attorney and see what she had to do to legally transfer custodial rights to her aunt. Then she and Nick could fly to the province of Mendoza to actually meet with her family.

Before entering her hotel room, she gazed at Nick. "Thank you for flying with me. It was…comforting to have company."

Most of the flight he'd read a book, but during meals or while the in-flight movie played and the cabin was dark, he'd chatted. Just talked about nothing in particular. Old Town and friends he'd made close to Beth's store. A car show he'd gone to recently. Movies he'd seen lately. Even a video game he'd bought and couldn't conquer. She'd listened, finding it hard not to stare at him as if she didn't know him. Back home, they didn't talk unless it was about the winery, and even then she usually just asked how things were going or gave him an order. She had no idea what he did with his spare time, who his friends were, or what movies he watched. Thankfully, with all his chatter, he'd managed to keep her mind off Brenda and the pain that was sure to come her way in Mendoza.

Nick nodded. "You're welcome." Then he walked over from his adjoining door and placed a hand on her back. "I know you're scared. But you're like our old resilient grapevines. Somehow you fight your way through bad weather, survive, and come out stronger."

Despite how distant they'd grown, they always seemed to share the most difficult moments together. "Yes, well, Nick, eventually even the strongest vines have had enough and they give up."

"Well, that's why we're there to till the soil just right and tend to them until they recover. Nothing and no one gives up at Gallegos."

Her father had said almost exactly the same thing

many times about the business and about their marriage. Her eyes filled with tears. She'd disappointed him by giving up on Nick. And she even sort of disappointed herself. But she couldn't take any more. His drinking, his irresponsibility, the damned feeling of failure she felt every time she looked at him. She'd given up. "I'm very tired," she said.

"Good night, then." He stepped back.

"Good night." She entered her room. Emotionally and physically exhausted, she collapsed onto the bed.

The next morning, after waiting around for way too long for a ride to the lawyer's office, they were finally on the way. The delay wasn't because there weren't a million cabs in the city honking and maneuvering around traffic in search of passengers, but because the attorney, Dr. Nelsen Vermuelen, insisted on sending his private car. He was the one who had notified her of her cousin's death and about the intended guardianship. When she called him to let him know she was in Buenos Aires, he immediately volunteered to take care of her transportation.

And now they were making their way through the capital center. She'd always loved this city for being sophisticated and elegant in a way that most cities in America weren't. Maybe it was the European architecture or the music of melodic voices in the buzzing streets among the honking horns. Whatever it was, her spirits managed to lift during the short drive.

But once in the office building, the tension inside her reappeared. She and Nick were escorted into Nelsen Vermuelen's simple office.

"Welcome," he said. "And I'm sorry for your loss."

"Thank you," Isabel said, taking his hand. She and Nick then took a seat where he indicated, across from his desk.

Behind his mahogany desk, Dr. Vermuelen opened his file. "Ms. Gallegos, this is an interesting case. Delicate, because you are no longer an Argentine citizen."

"Let's uncomplicate it. I plan to transfer custody to my aunt, the children's grandmother. I'm in no position to raise them," she explained.

He eyed her curiously. "Mr. and Mrs. Garcia named you. You are, in fact, their legal guardian already. The only question is your citizenship status. Do you plan to live here?"

"Of course not. And I know what Brenda said she wanted. But she never discussed this with me."

"Most people don't think they're ever going to actually need their appointed guardians. It doesn't surprise me that she didn't remember to tell you."

"Just a small detail she forgot to mention."

"And since she has left you as their legal guardian, you may take custody while all the legal paperwork is finished. If you don't plan to live in Argentina, then I assume you will want to take the children back to the U.S.?"

"Like I explained, I don't plan to take custody. My aunt is the logical caretaker."

"Has she agreed?"

"I haven't spoken with her yet. Tomorrow I fly out to see her."

Studying her, he offered, "You should allow me to proceed as if you are to be the primary guardian. Just in case your aunt is unable to take responsibility."

"She's going to have to—I can't do it."

Dr. Vermuelen gazed at Nick, his thick eyebrows rising high on his forehead as if appealing for his intervention.

Nick looked down to his lap, clearly unhappy. He hadn't brought up the topic of the children again. She wondered if he and Beth had discussed having a few of their own.

"And if she should . . . expire before they are of age? Custody will again revert to you," the lawyer continued.

"I'll deal with that when the time comes."

"Very well." He closed the file. "Please keep in contact with me. If that is what you both decide to do, you'll have to come back and finalize that agreement legally, and we'll have to petition the courts."

Isabel again shook his hand and thanked him. Nick did the same. On the way to the car, he placed a hand on her lower back. "Are you okay?"

"Fine," she said. "Did you think I couldn't do that?"

The driver opened the door for Isabel and she got inside. Nick let himself in on the opposite side. "Are you under the impression that I *want* you to refuse custody?"

"Don't you? Isn't that what you came to make sure I do?"

His eyebrows went up in a look of genuine surprise. "Why is it so hard for you to believe I came to support whatever you decide to do?"

She shrugged and looked out the window at the city buzzing past her. Among the government buildings and office skyscrapers were outdoor cafés where people sat at tables under colorful umbrellas, enjoying the morning as if life was meant to be savored even in fast-paced Buenos Aires. This could have been her life, she thought with a crazy, vacant sensation settling inside her, as if she were a puzzle with a few missing pieces.

"Besides," he said, "it's how you're going to feel when you realize what you've done that I came here to help you face."

She turned to give him a sharp look.

The lawyer business finished, they went back to the hotel to gather their things and then head for Mendoza to see Tía Dominga and the children. To face the sad truth that these kids had lost their parents and were waiting for her to come make things better. Usually she was the problem-solver, the one with all the answers, but she had to admit to herself that this time, she was lost.

Chapter Four

*F*ireflies. They always reminded Isabel of spring nights in Mendoza. She used to love watching them blink on and off around the low piquillín creosote bushes that separated the single-story homes from the sidewalk as she strolled to the bus stop in the evenings. Her friends had had parties almost every weekend. They would get together about eight at night to barbecue, drink, smoke, gossip, play cards. Sometime in the night, the boys would show up, and they would all hang out in the front yard until dawn.

As the cab drove down the familiar streets to her aunt's house, Isabel longed for the lightheartedness of the young teen girl she used to be. Life had been simple and full of promise. Isabel wondered what happened when a woman hit her forties and fifties—did it have to be a time to simply look back and weigh successes and failures, or couldn't some of that optimism of youth be recaptured to continue to dream?

She and Nick got out of the cab. Isabel paid the fare. Voices of neighborhood children laughing and calling out to each other in that pretty, singsong Spanish echoed from somewhere down the block. The smell of barbe-cued beef immediately told her she was home. Nothing reminded Isabel more of Argentina than a grilled asado.

It scented the air differently than the typical hamburgers and hot dogs popular in America. Maybe it was in the cuts of beef that were cooked or the type of charcoal used—or maybe it was just her imagination. But like an unexpected gift, she accepted the familiar sounds and smells as a soothing native welcome to Mendoza. Unlike Buenos Aires, this mountainous province gave her a sublime stir inside of having arrived home, as if by simply stepping onto the ground where she was born she was reconnected to herself. Mendoza, with its dry weather and Andes Mountains, was very much like California. She looked out in the distance, unable to see the snowcapped tips, and mentally shook her head. No, these mountains dwarfed the tail end of the Sierra Nevadas and the coastal ranges of California.

Then she saw a couple of fireflies on her aunt's potted bush in the front yard. She stared at them. In mid-September, Argentina was at the start of its spring season, the opposite of what they were enjoying in California. Mesmerized by the fireflies, she asked herself, "How does the light go out?"

Nick frowned. "What?"

She hadn't realized that she'd spoken out loud. "The light. On the fireflies."

"Cool," he said. "Really cool."

"I used to think they were magical, but then I learned it's just a chemical reaction that creates the light. But what makes it stop, I wonder."

He stared at the bush. "Life," he said with a shrug. "Life makes it go out."

Isabel gazed at him, lost in his words.

Suddenly the door to her aunt's house flew open, and the elderly woman called out to her with a rush of emotion. "Oh, Isabel, you're finally here. Look at you. I can't believe it." She ambled her way over, having to slightly drag a tired right leg. She threw her arms around Isabel's shoulders.

Isabel bent down to hug the soft, warm body of the woman who looked so much like her mother. "Hola, Tía." She'd missed her. Oh, God, how she'd missed her aunt, and she hadn't realized it until this very second. Isabel held her tightly for a long time. "I'm so sorry, Tía." She knew what it felt like to lose a parent, but she couldn't imagine the pain of losing a child.

Tía Dominga hugged her tighter and cried a little. Together, they grieved. It seemed so unreal that Brenda was gone. Her younger cousin. Tía Dominga's only child. Life could be so unfair. Finally, her aunt pulled back and noticed Nick.

"This is my . . . Remember Nick?" Isabel asked.

"Of course. Querido, it's so good to see you." Shyly, she pulled him in for a kiss on both cheeks.

Nick spoke Spanish, which he'd learned in college and perfected by speaking to Isabel's parents. Since her aunt didn't understand any English, she was glad he hadn't lost his ability to communicate in her native language. He expressed his condolences beautifully, leaving Isabel with a lump in her throat.

Tía Dominga called for them to come inside. "The children are in the bedroom watching television," she explained. "They aren't well, as you can imagine."

Isabel nodded as she followed her aunt into the

small house, where she was assaulted by familiar cooking smells and tired furnishings that hadn't changed in over thirty years. *Things never change in this country*, she thought. That brought both comfort and sadness. In order for anything to progress, it had to change. But selfishly she enjoyed returning to a part of her life that was always the same as she'd left it.

"Every day is just another reminder that their lives will never be the same," Tía Dominga said, continuing her lament on the mental state of the kids.

"They probably don't remember me," Isabel said, standing in the middle of the living room with her ex-husband by her side, trying to process this surreal moment.

"Of course they remember you. Brenda talked about you all the time." She opened the blinds to let more light into the room. The warm rays of the sun seemed to dance through the slats, bursting into the sad house as if it had been waiting for the opportunity to be invited inside. Immediately warmth filled the room with a gentle peacefulness.

Isabel smiled, dropping her purse off her shoulder onto the couch, beginning to feel more comfortable. Her aunt looked like she'd aged considerably since Isabel had last seen her, and that pained Isabel, reminding her that she'd made no effort to keep in touch after the death of her mother. For some reason, seeing her aunt so alive made it even harder to accept that both her parents were gone. "I thought about Brenda often too," Isabel said, trying to stay focused on the present.

"Isabel, I hope you'll treat my grandchildren like your own. Brenda chose you because—"

"Tía, I don't plan to take them away from you." She placed both hands gently on her aunt's shoulders. She wanted to set her mind at ease immediately.

Her aunt stopped talking and stared at Isabel with her mouth open. "What do you mean?"

"The most logical place for them to live is here, with you. So don't you worry about losing them. That's not going to happen."

"No, but—" Tía Dominga shook her head and placed her hand over Isabel's.

"I'll make sure you have full custody. And I'll help any way I can. I'll pay for their education. Get them tutors. Get you help, if you need it. I'll do anything I can to—"

"Isabel," Tía Dominga interrupted. "You don't understand. I cannot care for three young children. I'm old, and tired, and have too many health problems. I love them, and because of that I know it would not be in their best interest to have me as their mother."

Isabel drew a breath and tried to reason with her aunt, the way she did with clients. She pulled her hands free and straightened her back. "That's why I've volunteered to get you help."

"Um." Nick cleared his throat and pointed to a door.

Her three young cousins were peeking out of the bedroom.

Tía Dominga turned to face them. "Vamos, vamos," she said. "If you're going to hide and peek, you might as well come out and see your cousin Isabel."

The oldest girl, Sandra, walked out. "We weren't hiding. We just didn't know if you wanted us out here yet," she said in a grown-up tone.

"Sandra is ten," Tía Dominga said.

Isabel smiled, noticing how much Sandra looked like Brenda, especially her eyes and heart-shaped face. But her hair was different, falling in light brown waves, but no curls like when she was younger. "Last I saw her, she was five. You've grown into such a pretty girl." She reached out hesitantly and embraced the young girl.

Sandra offered the required kiss on the cheek.

Next was Adelmo, who was eight. As he was pushed forward by his grandmother and warned to behave, Isabel figured he was a typical boy and told her not to force him. He slipped out of the older woman's hold, kicked her shin, and ran outside yelling, "I'm not living with her."

"Oh my." Isabel hurried to her aunt's side and helped her sit down. How dare he kick his grandmother! "Are you okay?"

She nodded, flinching, looking sad as she massaged the pain in her leg.

The youngest, Julieta, timidly wrapped her arms around her grandmother to try to soothe her. Julieta was the only child Isabel had never met. She was four. Isabel reached across and caressed the little one's curls. *Here* were Brenda's curls. Isabel had always told Brenda she was lucky to be able to wake up and shake her hair loose with her fingers and look gorgeous. Brenda had laughed good-naturedly, like always, accepting a compliment and turning it around to tell Isabel she had nothing to envy. Isabel hoped Julieta didn't lose the curls when she got older, as Sandra apparently had. Her grandmother pulled Julieta into her arms, and Isabel had this crazy urge to do the same—to hold something of Brenda's in her arms.

With a sigh, Isabel stood and glanced at Nick.

Nick shrugged. "I'll be right back." He walked out the door Adelmo had run out.

"He misses my mom," Sandra said in her brother's defense.

"I know." Then she added, "I'm so sorry."

Sandra nodded. "I'm sure you are. You didn't expect to get stuck with us."

"No, that's not what I meant." Isabel felt so inept at this. She smiled even though she didn't feel like it. "Your mother and I loved hanging out together when I lived here. We shared so many good times. She loved parties. Did you know that?"

Sandra frowned. "Not really."

"She did. I still remember her fiesta de quince. Your grandmother went all out renting a hall, and we danced all night until daybreak. I was eighteen, but if feels like just yesterday."

"Remember her high school graduation party right here in this house?" Tía Dominga asked.

Isabel gazed at her aunt. The lines of grief around her mouth softened with these happy memories. "Oh, how could I forget? The house was bulging with people. I don't know how you allowed her to invite so many people, Tía."

Tía Dominga grew pensive. "I couldn't say no, and she didn't want anyone to feel left out. You know how she was. She met you once and you were her friend forever."

"It was so much fun." Isabel remembered, sad that she had to go so far back to think of a time she'd celebrated something with Brenda. "And after that I left for America." And things were never the same.

"I think my mom wished you hadn't," Sandra said. "But she told me you were too smart to stay here. Maybe that's why she wanted us to live with you, so we'd be smart too."

"Do you want to live with me?"

"I want what my mother wanted."

Isabel nodded, glad to know where she stood, at least with Sandra. She turned to gaze out the door. Nick sat beside Adelmo on a broken wooden fence. They were both chatting. This was going to be more difficult than she thought.

That night in their hotel, Isabel needed a drink. But of course she couldn't drink with Nick around, and it wasn't what she really wanted anyway. She wanted to unwind. So she suggested a swim in the pool instead. From the chaise longue, she watched Nick swim back and forth in the warm night air, almost hypnotizing her. Finally he stopped and hung over the edge. He rested his chin on his well-chiseled arms and studied her.

"What did you talk to Adelmo about?" she asked.

"Soccer. Dogs. Mendoza. Argentina. The U.S."

She got up and went to sit at the edge of the pool, dipping her legs into the water beside Nick. "He didn't mention his feelings about me?"

"No." His eyes lowered to her legs, then out into the darkness of the flower-scented bushes and palms.

"I'm too old for this. I don't want to take on this responsibility."

His gaze stayed fixed in the distance. "You've got it whether you want it or not."

"When do I get to lead my own life?" She knew she sounded selfish and petty under the circumstances, but it was what she truly felt. She'd sacrificed her dreams for her parents. She didn't want to waste any more of her life doing what other people expected her to do.

Nick placed a hand on her thigh. Cold water dripped down the sides and made her shiver. Or maybe it was his touch. Her entire body stiffened. His eyes met hers. He swallowed. "I'll help you," he said.

"Help me how?"

"To raise them."

She made a move to get up, but he placed a second hand on her other leg and held her in place.

"You're insane," she said.

"No. I was a lousy husband. A loser, maybe. A drunk, definitely. But I'm none of those things anymore and I can help you. I *want* to help you."

"Why?"

"You need me. . . . *They* need *us*."

Isabel shook her head. "They don't need *us*. There *is* no us."

"There's always been an us. You divorced me and you were right to do it, but that didn't change the pieces of you and me that are interwoven together. There *is* an us. And you need someone to help you with this, Isabel. You can't walk away from it—you know that."

She didn't need him. And she didn't need *children*.

She stared into his passionate eyes for a few moments, then pushed his hands off her and stood. Damn it, she wasn't responsible for her cousin's family. "I've got a plan. I'm going to follow it."

"You can't."

"Yes, I can. And I will," she said, gathering her towel, flip-flops, and hotel key.

"Isabel!"

She turned to look at him, standing by the edge of the pool, submerged in water to his waist.

"You're not as cold as you pretend to be."

"Go to hell, Nick. It's not a matter of being cold. I'm doing the right thing. Do you really think those kids deserve to be raised by the two of us?"

He swallowed as he stared at her without an answer.

"What will you do, come visit them on the weekends? Play visiting dad? And what will you tell your new *wife*? Did you forget about the fiancée you promised to marry?"

"No." His voice grew deep and thick. "She'll understand."

Isabel laughed. "Get real, Nick. You've never been responsible for anyone but yourself, and you didn't even do that well. You..." Hell, why was she tormenting him? "You mean well. I'm sorry."

"No, please, yell at me. You never did. You even divorced me politely."

She closed her eyes and shook her head. "I'm going to bed."

He thrust himself out of the pool and stood dripping wet in front of her. "Why didn't you ever fight back? All the horrible, cruel things I said to you, why did you take it?"

"I don't like to fight."

"You should have slapped me."

She shook her head again. And lose control? What good would that have done?

"I never meant any of it. I was a bastard and you didn't deserve it."

"Nick, I—"

"I wish to God we'd had babies, and I never should have said I was glad we couldn't have them. I didn't mean it. You would have made a great mother."

A huge lump grew in her throat and she couldn't respond. With tears in her eyes, she turned away. Somehow it was easier to believe he thought of her as a cold, insensitive monster rather than the hurt, devastated woman she'd actually been. She'd been stronger than he'd been. She'd had to be. Every setback just drove him deeper into alcoholism. If she'd broken down, too, who would have run the business? Who would others have leaned on?

"I'll stay in the pool a while longer," he called after her.

"Okay." She went back to her room and opened her liquor cabinet. Maybe Nick had the right idea after all— just numb yourself until you no longer cared about anything.

"Shit," she said, and slammed the liquor cabinet closed. Tears burned her eyes. "What the hell am I going to do?"

"I can't believe you kicked Abuela last night," Sandra scolded Adelmo as he kicked his soccer ball against the backyard wall. "You better be good when Isabel comes over today."

Abuela had gotten them up early, given them breakfast, made them bathe, and, with an admonition not to get dirty, sent them outside to play until Isabel got here. Julieta spun round and round on a Sit 'n Spin.

"Did you see that woman? They better have both my legs amputated before I go live with her. I'll kick them all a million times if they try to force me to live with her."

Sandra looked like she wanted to cry. She cried a lot lately when she thought no one noticed, but he heard her and pretended he didn't.

"You know what the lawyer said. Mami chose Isabel." Sandra tried to reason with him.

"Mami must have had too much wine when she made that choice."

"Adelmo!"

Julieta stopped spinning and walked unsteadily toward them. "I think I'm going to throw up."

Adelmo caught his ball and smiled. "Can you hold it until Cousin Isabel gets here, Julie?" He crouched down and patted Julieta's back. "Sit on her lap and then let it all come out right on her chest. Can you do that?"

Julieta nodded.

Sandra rolled her eyes. "Julieta, don't listen to him."

"Why not?" she asked. "Adelmo said we shouldn't like her."

"Don't listen to him."

"I can scream really loud in her ear," she said to Adelmo.

Adelmo nodded enthusiastically, loving the fact that

his baby sister looked up to him and wanted to make him happy. "Good girl, Julie. You do that."

"No," Sandra said firmly.

Adelmo tossed the ball into the air and head-butted it against the wall. "Let me know when you see her, Julie. I'll aim this ball right at her stomach. Maybe she'll throw up with you."

Sandra took Julieta's hand. "Let's go wait inside." She paused and stared at him. "It's not her fault, Adelmo."

But he didn't want to hear it. As far as he was concerned, it was everyone's fault that his parents were gone. "She doesn't want us."

"Maybe we can change her mind."

He frowned and brushed his hair off his forehead. The hot sun made his head warm, and his grandmother made him wash it until it shined, but nothing was actually bright in their lives right now. Everything was dull and empty, so he rubbed his dirty hand on his hair. "Or we could make her life miserable and she'll leave us alone."

Sandra seemed to consider this. "What good will it do to chase away the only person who might be able to give us a home again? Abuela explained that she couldn't take care of us forever, remember?"

Scowling, he refused to answer her question.

"Besides, we have to do what Mami wanted. We owe her that much."

But Adelmo gazed at Sandra and wondered if maybe she wanted to go with Isabel. Their cousin was different than their mother. She dressed great and smelled great, and she was rich and lived in America. Sandra probably *wanted* to like her. But he didn't. He couldn't.

When he didn't respond, Sandra took Julieta inside and left Adelmo outside with his soccer ball. In a flash of rage, he kicked the ball as hard as he could, and it bounced off the wall and disappeared behind him. He *hated* Isabel because she wasn't their mother. She could go back to her stupid America and leave him alone, because he wasn't going to live with her no matter what anyone said.

Chapter Five

❧

*I*sabel caught a taxi to her aunt's house the next morning, no closer to having a solution than she was the day before. Tía Dominga planned a day at San Martín Park for the kids and Isabel to get to know one another, thinking wisely that perhaps meeting in a neutral environment might make everyone involved more at ease. Nick stayed at the hotel. When she knocked on his door in the morning, he'd been on the phone with Beth. Looking and acting irritated, like he was still upset with her, he indicated he preferred she go without him and continued his phone conversation.

So she'd gone alone, which suited her fine.

Parque San Martín, the largest urban park in Argentina, was more than a park, both in actuality and in Isabel's memories. With its lake, outdoor arena, zoo, theater, and acres of grass and walking trails, it offered something for everyone. Isabel had visited it on hundreds of occasions with friends. Finding an old ash tree to sit under, they brought sweet factura pastries and a backpack with the necessary items to prepare a good mate—the yerba tea, the bombilla or metal straw, the hollow gourd that would be filled with the strong yerba and sugar, and a thermos full of hot water. Shaded by the canopy of dark green leaves for a couple of hours, they'd laughed and talked incessantly. Those had been simple days that really did feel like a million years ago. Still, the memory brought a smile to her heart, softening the edginess that had become a part of her personality.

Without meaning to, she'd changed in America. She'd forced herself to become focused and determined. Not that she hadn't been before, but the difference was that in order to succeed with the winery, she'd obsessed about work and had left time for nothing else. A small part of her wanted to look up her old high school and college friends and see how their lives had turned out. But the time wasn't right now, with her aunt and cousins in mourning. The only friend she kept in contact with and planned to call was Rosa Calvo. And for her own sanity, she'd call her soon, because Rosa was the only one Isabel could talk to about her mixed-up feelings regarding honoring Brenda's wishes.

Passing through one of the main iron gates to the park, Isabel admired their bold ornamental condor and coat of Mendoza at its crown. Seeing them again touched off a bit of pride for her native province. Every year, Vendimia, the national wine harvest celebration, was held here in the open-air stadium. Families attended together to honor the main commerce of Mendoza. If you lived in this area, you either worked for the wine-production industry, knew someone who worked for it, or were a proud Mendozino wanting to pay tribute to those who harvested. Besides, Vendimia was just plain fun. Lots of food, music, and celebration—a day to spend with friends and family.

As she strolled along the lake and lush garden walks,

Isabel was free to pretend so many years hadn't flown past since those Vendimia celebrations. It made her feel young again, which was nice, since lately she'd begun to feel so old.

The kids didn't appear to show much enthusiasm for the park or for being out in the sunshine. Tía Dominga bought them a churro, maybe in hopes that the sweet treat might pacify them or soothe their grief. Though surely she knew that nothing external could alleviate deep sorrow. Isabel, working from the same desperation, offered them a ride on the boats. They refused and she didn't force the issue.

"Why didn't Brenda take the kids on vacation with her?"

"Andres wanted her to relax for a week without the children. She didn't want to leave them, but I was happy to spend time with them alone, so I told her not to be stupid and to go. Have fun with her husband. If only I could take that all back."

The children ran up ahead. Isabel watched them, wondering about fate. Was there a master plan, or was life just a collection of random occurrences? "You made the right decision. It was an accident. You can't live life in a bubble because something bad could happen."

"Eight skiers died that day and three were badly injured. Why did she have to be one of the ones to die, Isabel?" Her voice cracked.

Isabel didn't know why. And Tía Dominga didn't really expect an answer. "I've asked myself the same question. I also asked what she was thinking when she chose me as guardian. Maybe she chose me for financial reasons, for what I could provide for them, but I'm the wrong person, Tía."

"You're the only one, querida. I'm old. I'm going to die soon. Then they will have to endure another loss. No, you have to do it."

"I can't."

Tía Dominga caressed Isabel's arm with such tenderness. "But you will. They are yours already. Legally, those children belong to you." Her attention strayed back to where the children gathered by the lake. "Julieta, no. Not so close to the water." And she walked away to pull the four-year-old away from the edge of the lake, where she tried to poke a leaf with a stick, her short legs balancing unsteadily.

Isabel noticed how her aunt pulled the girl away from danger and warned her to stay back. Observing the scene, she realized that it would never have occurred to her that Julieta could fall into the water. Another example of what a terrible step-in parent she'd make. Her mothering antennas had never developed. At her age, they weren't likely to either.

Isabel treated them all to lunch at a lively confiteria— a café/restaurant. They served lightly grilled sandwiches on thin bread called carlitos with a plate of large steak fries. Isabel enjoyed the meal. It had been so long since she'd had Argentine food. Her guests barely seemed to notice what they ate. Adelmo drank two Cokes and spilled the last one on Isabel's lap. Tía Dominga lectured him about being more careful, but Isabel had a feeling he'd done it on purpose. Still, she told him it was fine and let him be. Finally, she took them back home.

When she got to the hotel, she called Allen, her attorney. "What the hell am I going to do? Everyone acts like my taking the children is a done deal legally. Don't I have any say here?"

"I suppose if you refuse to take them, they would become wards of the state. The grandmother would step up then. You just have to play hardball if you're determined not to take responsibility for them."

"Great." Discouraged, she walked out to her balcony to enjoy the view. Life was slower here, which allowed people to savor not only the sweetness, but the bitterness too. And sometimes you needed time for both. Argentines were good at delving into melancholy and contemplation. People took long walks, read the newspaper outside while drinking their mate in the middle of the afternoon. There was a lack of tension in the air. And some of hers faded as she stood outside breathing in the fresh air.

God, why had she ever left? Because while they were in college together, Nick had convinced her and her parents that they could do so much better in America, that was why. Most excited had been her father. She never should have agreed to any of it. She'd given up her country and her future. And for what?

Her cell rang and she reached in her shorts pocket and retrieved it.

"Isabel, you're here and still haven't come to see me? Be here in twenty minutes and I'll forgive you." Then the line went dead.

Isabel smiled. Rosa—instantly, she couldn't wait to see her.

* * *

Isabel still might not have a clue about what to do with the kids, but maybe she didn't have to decide today. She grabbed her purse, left the hotel, and called a cab. She and Rosa had grown up together, attended the same schools, vacationed together as teens, and shared dreams that had been complete opposites of each other. Rosa wanted to get married and have a family with Franco, her high school sweetheart. And she had. Isabel wanted to leave landlocked Mendoza for the coast. She wanted to be a marine biologist and work with the animals of the Patagonia—to live a romantic, free, minimalist life surrounded by nature. She hadn't.

In less than twenty minutes, Isabel rang the buzzerlike doorbell and waited, tamping down anticipation. Although they spoke on the phone often, she hadn't actually seen her friend in five years. Rosa opened the door and screamed. Immediately, she threw her arms around Isabel, laughing and crying and bouncing with excitement.

Isabel laughed and wiped away a tear or two herself.

"I've been waiting for you to call, Isabel. I'm so sorry about Brenda."

Isabel didn't say a word. Staring into Rosa's eyes, she didn't have to.

"Well, come in, come in, so we can relax and chat."

Isabel followed Rosa through her living room, to the balcony with a view that took her breath away every time she saw it. Rosa's house was situated on a hill that climbed easily, almost unnoticeably. And from the balcony, the entire valley spread out for them to enjoy.

Rosa hurried to the kitchen to fetch a pitcher of sangria, which she set on the black wrought-iron table. With a hand on her hip and a smile on her lips, she stared at Isabel. "You know, it's disgusting. You look younger and more beautiful every time I see you."

Isabel laughed. "Thanks. You look wonderful, too, Rosa."

"Sure, after giving birth to three youth-draining creatures and putting up with them day after day, I look like a princess."

"How are your kids? They handle the divorce okay?"

"Of course not. They hated me. And Franco was immature and difficult, like always. He'll never change. He did everything he could to get the children on 'his side,' but after living with him for a while, they started to see what I had put up with all these years and how I got all my gray hairs."

She didn't have gray hair at all. Her boys were probably in their early twenties and her daughter in her late teens, but children in Argentina lived with their parents until they got married. Sometimes even *after* they were married. "Are they still living with Franco?"

"Well, the boys live with their father, but they come see me once a week, thank God—so I can feed them. And Alisa is studying at an international business college in Buenos Aires. I didn't want her to go so far, but that's what she really wanted. She asked if it would be okay to move in with some friends out there. You know how these young pibas are now; they want to act like the Americans. What could I do? I said yes."

Isabel accepted a glass of sangria, enjoying the sweet

citrus wine, the fresh air, and the happy complaints from her friend. The woman loved her family, and her life, despite the divorce. Marriage and family were what she'd always wanted. Unlike Isabel, who had placed a husband and children very low on the priority list. Had Nick sensed that? Had God punished her with multiple miscarriages because he, too, knew she wouldn't be there for them like she should? Even though the husband part hadn't worked out, Isabel was sure Rosa wouldn't change a thing about what she'd chosen to do with her life.

Rosa sat across the table, putting her feet up. They sat in silence for a few moments.

"Life," Isabel said. "Just when you think you've got it figured out...Here I am sitting in Mendoza again."

"Just when you'd planned never to set foot on Argentine soil again."

"That was never the plan, Rosa." She sighed, feeling at peace. "I really don't mind. I just wish it was under different circumstances."

"Would you be here under different circumstances?"

Isabel gazed at Rosa and admitted, "No."

From behind her glass of sangria, Rosa raised an eyebrow as if to say, *See.* Though Rosa had a few more lines around her eyes and her skin looked more like thin leather than when she was twenty years old, she had the same expressions, the same mannerisms that Isabel remembered with love. Damn, she missed spending time with her.

"I'm a busy woman," Isabel said.

"Too busy to enjoy your life."

"Maybe. I've never had a choice."

"We all have choices, mi'jita."

Isabel shrugged. She hadn't. Helping her parents at the winery had been an obligation she hadn't chosen. Even if she'd enjoyed the building of the business, even if she'd been successful, it hadn't been what she'd *wanted* to waste her life doing. But her parents had needed her. Every time she thought maybe the time had come to move on, something had held her back. Nick. Her mother's stroke. The fire that consumed half of their crops. There was always a reason why she couldn't leave.

But Rosa knew that. No matter how much time passed that they didn't talk or see each other, they shared a camaraderie that was rare. They knew each other, deep inside at the core, and *that* time couldn't change.

"How long do you plan to stay?"

"As long as I need to resolve the custody issue."

"Did Brenda really leave them to you?"

"Can you believe it?"

"Honestly? No. What the hell was she thinking?"

"I don't know." Isabel looked out at the dark green trees standing majestically in the windless, perfect day, providing shade and privacy to the neighborhood. "I just don't know."

"How is your aunt holding up?"

"Good. I think she's holding it together for her grandchildren's sake. But she can't raise three little kids, Rosa."

"*That,*" she said, "was probably what your cousin was thinking."

"But I'm selfish, and ignorant about children, and—"

"Busy," Rosa supplied, pointing at her with her index finger. "Don't forget busy."

"I am. I'm never home." She spent all her time at the office, and when she walked across the grounds to her house, it was to sleep.

Rosa smiled as if she knew a secret Isabel didn't. Then she put the glass down. "What do you say we go get something stronger? Come on. Let's go for a walk."

Like they had so many times in their youth, they walked the same streets and chatted. Homes looked more run-down, and there were more cars parked in the street—it seemed more people drove these days. But otherwise not much had changed. When Rosa's parents died, they left her the house. That's the way it was done in Argentina—people were born and died in the same house generation after generation. One day Rosa's kids would get the house.

Bodegas peppered the tranquil town, and Rosa pulled her into one that offered taste tests.

"I remember going through these things as teens and getting blasted," Isabel said.

They laughed. Isabel had never been a big drinker. Growing up in a winery where the product was available everywhere took the magic out of alcohol. In reality, since the legal drinking age of eighteen was never enforced or monitored by parent or police, teens could drink whenever they wanted. But most of the time they chose not to. No taboo, no problem.

Still, there had been times when, just for fun, she and Rosa and other friends had overindulged.

They took the tour and tasted a dozen different varieties. Isabel didn't taste wine like a tourist, however. She'd been in the business too long. She evaluated the

blends, seeking out the unique notes, marveling at the
fruitiness of some and wondering what they did to
achieve the complex flavors in others. By the end of the
second bodega tour, her head had begun to spin.

In the late, still-warm afternoon, they strolled the
now-busier streets, feeling relaxed and dazed. Memories
of running through some of these same streets as a child
made her smile. Children have a different kind of freedom in Argentina than they do in America. No one thinks
anything of a child playing in the streets until the wee
hours of the morning or taking the bus alone to a city
park—or, like she had, to the movie theater downtown.
As long as she did well in school, her free time had been
her own to do with as she chose.

She wondered how Brenda's children would adapt to
life in America. And immediately she chased away that
thought. They weren't going to have to adapt. She wasn't
taking them back with her.

Rosa pulled her into another family-owned bodega,
where the smell of various grape blends hit them immediately. Upon entering, Isabel inhaled deeply.

"You know, it's too bad, if your family could have
hung on through those tough years, you could have still
had your vineyard and winery here."

And the idea didn't make her cringe as it would have
years ago. If she was going to spend her life on a vineyard, it might as well have been in Argentina. Moving
away from everything she'd known had been a mistake.
Nick had made America sound so promising, so lucra-
tive, that both she and her parents had been enchanted
with the idea of selling the vineyard in Argentina and re-

opening in America. Nick had been a young, gorgeous American exchange student, and he seemed to represent the bright and easy future of America. She'd been taken in by his vision of success. And if she were honest, by the nights of hot sex under the stars.

Isabel believed she could help her parents establish themselves in America, then go on with her life. But what had her parents really gained by closing down the family business in Argentina only to reopen it in California, where they slaved away day and night—without the benefit of familiar surroundings or friends they loved? Of course, *she* was never supposed to slave away at Gallegos, she reminded herself. That had never been her intention. Her parents were supposed to have their dream and she hers. "Here or there, this has been my life," Isabel said as they headed outside and strolled through the fields of planted grape stalks.

"Last time you called, you said you were thinking of selling."

Isabel nodded. "Yep. Hopefully when I get home, the deal will be sealed."

"You going to miss it?"

She gazed at the lush green vines surrounded by rolling hills. No one could argue about the absolute beauty, the breathtaking perfection of a vineyard.

"Maybe a little?" Rosa prompted.

They walked through a door that had a sign for the barrel room. It was dark and cold inside. "Sure, about as much as a prisoner misses the bars on his cell."

Rosa headed to the tasting tables. "Oh, come now. I find it hard to think of you as a prisoner when you're surrounded by all this every day. And millions of dollars to boot."

Most people didn't understand what she felt. From the outside, it must look like her life was a fairy tale. The American dream. But no matter how luxurious a person's jail, if it trapped them and kept them from their true desires, from being the person they wanted to be, they were still no better off than a little hamster running on its wheel. Unable to escape. With no alternative but to hop back on and stay active, not thinking of what life would be like if they were free.

The woman behind the table offered Isabel a glass. Isabel shook her head. She had enough wine running through her veins to last her a lifetime.

From that bodega, they headed back to Rosa's home. "So what will you do without your family business?"

"Move to the beach. Volunteer at marine institutes."

"No moving to the Patagonia and cataloging penguins anymore?"

Maybe once she became free of the business she would then travel to the Patagonia and explore. Imagine what her life might have been had she been able to pursue her dreams. But nothing serious. "I'm too old for that."

"Nonsense. Jacques Cousteau kept working until he was an old man."

"I know, but I don't want that anymore. I'm not a marine biologist, and I'm not going to become one now. I just want to relax, enjoy being free of business obligations. Donate some of my money to marine centers and help out doing what I can in my spare time, if I feel like it. I just want to be free, you know what I mean?" She was talking mostly to herself. Rosa was listening, of course, but Isabel barely noticed. Her mind wandered. "I want to sit on a beach and stare at the ocean for hours and hear nothing but the sound of the waves and seagulls. I want peace. I want a little part of that world that has enchanted me since I was a child."

Rosa nodded without bringing up the children and asking how they would fit into that picture. Because they both knew they didn't. And that made her stomach turn on itself, because if she didn't take this last opportunity to fulfill her dream, she knew it would never come again. Like George in *It's a Wonderful Life*, she'd be forever stuck and never live the life she felt she was born to live. People watched that movie every Christmas and saw a happy ending. She watched it and felt a stabbing pain for George and for herself. She knew what it felt like to postpone your dreams again and again to meet your obligations. Sure, he had a nice family and great friends, but he lost his destiny.

She wasn't going to lose hers.

Chapter Six

I sabel searched the pockets of her purse for the key to get into her hotel room. She had drunk too much and wasn't feeling at all normal. The door opened next door and Nick peeked out. Noticing her, he opened the door wider and leaned on the doorjamb. "You've been gone all day."

"Sorry," she said, even though she wasn't obligated to check in with him.

"You saw the kids?"

She frowned. That had been this morning. A lifetime ago.

"Have you been drinking?" He shook his head. "Stupid question. I know when someone's drunk."

"I'm not drunk."

He stepped forward and reached into her purse, pulling out her key. He swiped it and unlocked the door.

"Thank you." She stepped inside, happy to see a bed.

Nick followed her into the room and closed the door. "Did you eat anything with the booze?"

"I went to see a friend and we toured the wineries. I'm fine." She sat on the bed and moaned with contentment.

He stared at her. "Beth agrees with you that I need to butt out of your life and not encourage you to bring the children home."

Isabel didn't want to discuss the kids tonight, and she didn't give a damn what Beth thought. Of course she didn't want Nick involved in her life. Why would she? "Mmm."

"But you're both wrong."

She met his very sober stare and thought it funny that she was the one with completely unclear thoughts and he stood there looking strong and in control.

"What's so funny?" he asked when she laughed.

She shook her head. "My friend Rosa kept telling me how lucky I was. That she'd give anything to have a house with children in it again. But do you know how scary that sounds to me?"

He stepped forward and bent down until he was eye level with her. "Yeah."

"I wish I could walk away from this, Nick. I wish I could say to hell with all of them, that it's not my problem. But . . . I can't."

He stretched out an arm and touched her back, gently, pulling her into an embrace. She allowed herself to be held and allowed tears to fall.

"It's going to be okay." He sighed and held her, rubbing her back.

But she felt trapped again. Defeated. She pulled out of his arms and lay back on the bed. She curled onto her side and closed her eyes. The last thing she remembered was Nick pulling a blanket out of the closet and covering her with it.

Tía Dominga called her the next morning, letting her know she was expected for lunch. She found the "invitation" amusing, not being accustomed to receiving orders back home. But in Argentina, she wasn't an important executive or a valuable community player. And to her aunt, she was really no more than a kid, which amused her even more.

Isabel had planned to spend the day with Tía Dominga and her cousins anyway, but she played off the invitation as a great idea. When she and Nick arrived, Tía Dominga immediately handed her a nylon woven bag and told her to go to the corner bakery and pick up some French bread rolls. "Take Sandra with you," Tía Dominga ordered.

"Okay." Isabel smiled at Sandra. "Lead the way."

They walked along the narrow, irregular sidewalk, patterned with cracks. The smells from the open sewer mixed with the warm, muggy air. Sandra didn't seem to notice the stench. Those things hadn't fazed Isabel either at that age. She probably only noticed them now because she hadn't lived with them in such a long time.

"Is Nick your boyfriend?" Sandra asked as they strolled down the sidewalk.

Nick hadn't said a word this morning about last night. She was glad. Although she was minding less and less being vulnerable around him, she still didn't like crying and acting needy. After all, there was no point in starting to rely on Nick's shoulder when he was no longer hers. Glancing down at the child who was turning into a beautiful young lady, just like her mother, Isabel answered truthfully. "He's my ex-husband. We're still friends."

"Is that kind of weird?"

Isabel laughed. "Sometimes it is." Then she changed

the subject. "I remember running these types of errands for my mother," Isabel said, remembering her mother's early morning treks to each store. The bakery, the fruit and vegetable store, the meat market. Little commercial stores intermingled between neighborhood homes. There were no zoning laws to prohibit someone from opening a store on their property, so walking the neighborhood, her mother could usually get all her shopping done as well as her hair cut, nails done, and clothes mended and pressed.

"Yeah," Sandra muttered softly. "Me too."

Isabel's heart ached for the young girl. To lose a mother while so young was more than tragic. It went against everything that life promised. Someone to take care of you and guide you until you could stand on your own. To lose that meant to lose a part of your potential.

"Do you know," Isabel said, "that your mother and I used to get up early on Sunday mornings and meet at the bakery next to our church? We'd buy as many masas as we could afford, then go sit in the churchyard before anyone arrived and gossip."

Sandra offered a tentative smile. "What did you gossip about?"

Isabel shrugged. "Fat old Grandpa Tito and how many old ladies were bringing him treats since grandma had died."

Sandra smiled.

"And boys from school and the girls we hated."

Now the young girl laughed. "Here," she said, pointing to the bakery, which looked no larger, no more spectacular than the rest of the houses on the block. Sandra entered with the confidence and ritual of someone who was used to performing a daily chore.

"Hola, Sandra," said the woman behind the counter.

Sandra put in her order and the woman filled her nylon grocery bag. Isabel's mouth watered from the delicious scent of warm bread and sweet cakes. Isabel paid, and they were on their way. "Chau," Sandra said, throwing the word over her shoulder.

"I'm sure your grandmother loves having you with her," Isabel said, knowing that as difficult as it was to deal with Brenda's death, Tía Dominga must love the time with her grandkids.

"She's too old to deal with children," Sandra said. "That's why I help her out as much as I can."

Sandra's maturity was touching and admirable. "I'm sure she appreciates it."

"Wherever you decide we're going to live, it should be close to Grandma's house so we can check on her often."

Isabel gazed pensively at the top of the determined girl's head. "I'm not sure what we're going to do yet."

"What do you mean?"

"I mean, who's going to be caring for you. Where you're going to live."

Sandra frowned. "My mother chose you. We live where you say."

"I know, but... Sandra, I have a life in the United States."

Her eyes widened. "You mean you want us to move out of the country?"

"No." She drew a breath. "I wasn't... I mean..." She

forced a smile. "There's a lot to work out. Don't worry. Everything will...work out."

"My grandmother says that if my mother chose you, she knew what she was doing, and we should accept it."

Brenda had no idea what she was doing. She should have talked to Isabel about this. She should have asked. Prepared her, at least. Isabel didn't want to—couldn't— be angry with a woman who was no longer alive, but she wished that she could turn back the clock and insert a time, a phone call maybe, where Brenda and she spoke about the possibility of her taking responsibility of Sandra, Adelmo, and Julieta. If they could have discussed it, Isabel could have told Brenda the truth about how she felt. Maybe she would have accepted it if Brenda had explained her decision. Maybe she would have made more of an effort to get to know her young cousins, just in case. But none of that had happened. And the conversation that should have taken place between them was a vacant hole in their relationship now.

They walked the rest of the way in silence, Sandra only venturing to speak again once they reached Tía Dominga's home. "Cousin Isabel, I don't want to hurt your feelings, but we don't want to live with you."

"I guessed as much."

"But if it was my mother's wishes, we owe it to her to honor them." With that, the admirably mature Sandra walked away.

Isabel shook her head. She didn't know to whom she owed what anymore. Seemed like she always owed someone a piece of herself.

* * *

Tía Dominga had the table set, and she called the children to wash up and take a seat. Sandra and Julieta sat on either side of their grandmother. Adelmo was nowhere to be found.

They all began to eat after saying a quick prayer. Isabel glanced at Nick, wondering if anyone was going to question the missing child. The look on Nick's face told her he was equally confused.

"Tía Dominga, where's Adelmo?"

"Probably in the streets playing with friends."

Probably? That answer was completely unsatisfactory. If any of her employees had ever answered in such a poor way, she'd fire them. "Shouldn't we go call him or look for him?"

"Sandra already did before you got here."

"He wasn't at any of the places he usually goes," Sandra added.

They continued to eat. Isabel glanced from Sandra to Tía Dominga, then picked up her fork and knife and began to cut her meat, which was deliciously covered in chimichurri. But before bringing the food to her lips, she put the fork down. She couldn't eat. How could they be so relaxed about the kid being missing?

"Sandra," she said. "Let's go look for your brother."

Sandra gasped, astounded. "Now?"

Tía Dominga put her silverware down and wiped her lips. "He'll be back later. He spends a lot of time alone. He needs that right now."

Nick raised an eyebrow. "He does this a lot?"

Tía Dominga frowned. "Yes."

"Come on," he said, standing.

Instead, a knock at the door stopped them. "I'll get it," Isabel said. She opened the door thinking that it probably was not Adelmo since he wouldn't knock, but part of her hoped it might be.

But a dark-skinned man with shoulder-length, uncombed black hair stood on the other side of the door, unsmiling. "I'm Ramiro."

Isabel nodded. "How can I help you?"

"Ramiro Garcia," he clarified. "Andres's brother."

Isabel frowned. "I'm sorry, but—"

"I'm here for the chicos. They're my responsibility now."

Isabel's confusion deepened as she stared at this large, intimidating man. Andres's brother? Brenda's brother-in-law? "Come in," she said, allowing him to enter.

Tía Dominga looked up from the kitchen table. Immediately, before Isabel could tell her they had company, her color blanched. "What are you doing in my house?"

His expression softened. "Hola, señora. I heard about my brother and your daughter and . . . I'm here for the kids."

Sandra frowned and Julieta kept eating, too young to feel the tension that had Isabel suddenly on guard. What the hell did he mean he was here for the kids? Wasn't that sort of a bizarre thing to say?

"How dare you?" Tía Dominga asked, still irate. "Sin vergüenza, how dare you step foot in my house and ask about my grandchildren?"

"No offense, señora, but you cannot take care of them. I have property. Land. Space for children. I should and will provide what they need from now on."

She stood, bracing her hands on the table, her arms shaking from probably a combination of her weight and her age. "Your brother would roll over in his grave if he knew I even let you in the same room with his babies."

Ramiro looked contrite. "I'm their uncle. I have rights—"

"You have *no* right, you hear me?" she yelled, and came forward with more strength than Isabel had seen her exhibit in the last few days. "No right!" She pushed against his chest. "Get out!" She pushed again, and he stepped back toward the door.

Isabel watched with shock, afraid her aunt would have a heart attack or burst one of the veins bulging in her forehead.

"Leave and don't ever come back."

"Señora, don't make me call a lawyer."

"Don't make me call the police!"

Nick stepped forward, but Isabel gave him a stern look to stop him.

"Ramiro, let's talk. Outside, please," Isabel said.

He glanced at Isabel and nodded. They both stepped into the front yard.

A million thoughts and questions tumbled around in her head. "I'm not sure what's going on, but I didn't even know Andres had a brother."

"Well, he did—he does—and it's my duty to step in now. Their hijos are my responsibility and—"

"Actually they're mine." She stopped him. "Brenda and Andres appointed me their guardian."

He stared at her. "Who the hell are you?"

Same question she'd had about him. "I'm Brenda's cousin."

"Cousin! I'm those kids' uncle. Who do you think the courts will award them to?"

"Courts?" She pushed her hair away from her perspiration-covered forehead. She needed to get a handle on this situation, understand what was going on. "Look, my aunt is obviously upset and would like you to leave. Let's get together tomorrow for a cup of coffee somewhere and talk this out. I'm sure . . . we can come to some agreement."

He frowned and continued to stare. Finally, he nodded. "Meet me at Cafe Rossi in el centro. Three o'clock."

"Okay."

He stalked away, and Isabel watched this very large, angry man get into his old Ford pickup and leave. "What the hell was that?" she muttered, and returned to the house. Everyone talked to her at once.

"You told him never to come back, right? He's no good, Isabel. No good."

"Is he really my uncle?" Sandra asked.

"He's garbage," Tía Dominga said viciously.

Isabel sat beside her aunt, who was on the tired-looking couch, trying to calm down. "Okay, Tía."

"If he ever comes back, I'll call the police. And you have to take the children with you, Isabel. Soon, understand?"

No, she didn't understand. But she nodded and patted her aunt's back. She glanced up at Nick, who had a question in his worried eyes. "I'll take care of everything. Don't worry," she assured her aunt.

Tía Dominga kissed Isabel's face. "You're a good girl."

Nick cleared his throat and looked at Sandra. "What do you say we go find your brother now?"

Sandra looked from Nick to Isabel to her grandmother, then nodded. "Okay."

"Where could he be?" Nick asked as the three of them left the house.

"I don't know."

"Maybe a friend's house?" Isabel offered.

"He doesn't have any friends around here."

"Where does he have friends?" Isabel persisted.

"Well, in our old neighborhood he had lots of friends."

Isabel sent Nick a quick look, and he seemed to realize the same thing: the boy could have returned home.

"Lead the way," he said.

Because the kids' neighborhood was a distance away, they hailed a cab and headed to Brenda's condo.

"What the hell was that about back at your aunt's house?" Nick asked Isabel in English as they sat side by side in the cab.

Isabel didn't want to discuss this in front of Sandra, because all the kids spoke and understood some English. It was a required language for students to learn from the elementary grades on up. "Nothing. Maybe he's looking for money. I'll take care of it."

"That guy looked dangerous. I—"

"I'll take care of it," she said again in a tone she'd used often with him to end a conversation she didn't intend to have.

"But I'm here to take care of *you*, so we'll talk about this later."

She met his gaze, angry that he was pursuing this. But when it didn't appear that he was going to back down, a part of her was surprised and another reluctantly impressed. She *was* going to take care of Ramiro herself, but it touched her that he wanted to help and that he was worried about her.

She turned her attention to Sandra. "Have you been to your neighborhood since...you moved in with your grandmother?" Isabel asked as they approached the condo.

"No. Well, we've come to get a few things."

The taxi stopped and they got out. Sandra asked the neighborhood boys kicking a soccer ball around in the street if they'd seen Adelmo.

"Yeah," one of them said. "He went in there." The boy pointed to Brenda's condo.

They climbed the stairs to the third floor after getting the key from the building manager.

Sandra opened the door. Her hand shook. Isabel put a hand on the girl's shoulder. They walked into the dark living room that Brenda used partially as a dining room.

Nick strolled down the hall while Sandra looked around the living room with tears in her eyes. Her hand traced the back of the wicker love seat. Dust covered the dark green leaves of the fake plant on the coffee table. Sandra took it all in like a captive returning home and seeing her surroundings with new eyes.

Isabel had been to Brenda's home only once. Aside from knowing that this was where her cousin had spent so much time and feeling the same sadness that now al-

ways accompanied thoughts of Brenda, the condo itself
didn't have any power to deepen her sorrow. But she
understood that it wasn't the same for Sandra. This had
been her home. This was her mother and father's home.
"I know this is hard."

"I miss my mom and dad so much. It's not fair."

"No," Isabel said. "It's not."

"Why did this have to happen to us? My parents were
good people."

Isabel had asked that same question so many times.
Why had this happened? She'd also asked *Why me?* about
getting stuck with her young cousins and felt a rush of
shame for that. These children lost their parents—they'd
lost everything. She herself faced a little inconvenience.
She had no right to complain. "I wish I had an answer
for you, Sandra. It makes no sense to me either."

"My grandmother says God doesn't just take the bad.
He also takes the good. That he has his reasons and we
shouldn't question it." She narrowed her eyes and said
bitterly, "But I have a right to ask why."

Isabel nodded. Of course she did. Those damned plat-
itudes were unacceptable to her too. "And you have the
right to an answer. Maybe . . . one day it will come to
you."

"No, it won't. There can never be a reason I can accept for losing my mother."

Isabel caressed Sandra's face gently, wiping tears
away. "I'm with you, kid." She glanced in the direction
Nick had gone when she heard a voice that sounded like
Adelmo's. "Come on," she said, and coaxed Sandra down
the hall. But she stopped dead when she saw Adelmo sit-

ting on the hardwood floor playing with little cars around a huge, complex city he had built out of wooden blocks, multicolored LEGOs, and oddball toys.

Nick stood in the room with his hands in his pockets. "Truly awesome, man," he was saying.

"This one I got from a fair." He held up a car. "They had all kinds of German toys. It's a Mercedes-Benz racing car by Schuco. The man said it was very rare. My dad said we didn't have money, but then he surprised me when we got home. He put it on the center of the dining table. I was so excited."

Nick sat on the floor beside Adelmo. "Your dad sounds like he was a great guy."

"He was the best." His voice cracked. The room grew quiet.

"I wish I had had a dad like that," Nick finally said.

Adelmo angled his head. "You didn't have a good father?"

"I didn't have a father at all. He left me and my mom when I was like two."

"That sucks."

"Yeah, it did."

"But at least you had your mom."

Nick shrugged. "My mom was an alcoholic. She tried, but she couldn't handle things well."

Isabel listened, almost as interested as the boy. Nick didn't talk about his parents. Not to her. He must have in his Alcoholics Anonymous meetings, but as many times as she'd asked, he'd dodged the questions. *Never knew my dad. My mom was sick and died.* That was all he'd ever really said.

Sandra walked up and was about to interrupt, but Isabel put a hand on her arm and a finger to her lips to stop her.

"How did you do so well without good parents?"

"I didn't do well. I'm an alcoholic too."

Adelmo frowned. "You?"

He nodded. "I don't drink anymore, but I did for years and did some pretty bad things."

Adelmo listened with complete concentration.

"I wish I could have had a mom and dad like you had and maybe I wouldn't have become who I did."

"Yeah."

"But even though you don't have your parents with you anymore, you have all the good things they taught you. And you're lucky for another reason."

"What?" He didn't look convinced about being lucky.

"You have your grandmother and Isabel. And me."

Adelmo went back to pushing his cars around the play town. "I want my dad back."

"Yeah, but it's not going to happen."

Adelmo looked up sharply. Isabel, too, stiffened at the hard words.

"You've gotta deal with what is, Adelmo, or you'll become like me. Never willing to face reality. Your parents can't come back. You know that."

Adelmo's eyes filled with tears.

"But you have your memories of them, and that you'll never lose. You can have a good life still, but it's up to you." Nick reached across and patted the boy on his upper arm. "Give your cousin Isabel a chance."

Adelmo glanced at the door, his eyes connecting

with Isabel. Isabel hugged her arms around herself. Nick gazed at her over his shoulder, a warm look in his eyes.

"I want to live in my own house," he said, defiant and cold.

"I'm sorry, Adelmo. We can't live here," Isabel said.

His voice cracked. "Can I at least take my cars wherever we go?"

Her heart ached. She nodded as tears touched her eyes. "Yeah," she said. "You can take anything you'd like."

Adelmo started to pack his cars into a box.

Isabel met Nick's gaze and mouthed a thank-you. He gave her one nod and started to help the boy.

Isabel knew that this was the moment. This was the second when she decided that she didn't have a choice. Whether she wanted to or not, these heartbroken, lost children were her responsibility, and for the rest of her life she'd have to make sure they were taken care of. The only question left was, would they fly home with her, or did they actually have an uncle she could trust to raise and love them? Tomorrow she'd find out.

Nick and Isabel rode most of the way back to the hotel in silence. Nick hadn't shared with Isabel that Beth had told him, in her own way, to go to hell when he'd called her about bringing the kids back home and helping Isabel raise them. He'd tried to reason with her, tried to explain that they could still get married, could still have a great life. Lots of guys who had children got remarried, and it wasn't an issue. Beth had accused him of finding one more thing to tie himself to Isabel. According to her, since the winery would be gone soon, he'd chosen the kids as another way to stay connected to his ex-wife. He'd denied it and begged her to understand. She hadn't. And now that he sat beside Isabel after this emotional day, he was even more confused. Was Beth right? Was there something inside him that just didn't want to let go?

He reached over and took one of her hands. This seemed to pull her out of her own thoughts and she glanced at him.

"You were so great with Adelmo," she said, her voice barely above a whisper as if she were in awe. "So amazingly great."

"I see myself in that kid. Angry. Knowing life isn't fair and pissed off at the world." He gazed out the window at the darkness outside.

"He's going to need a man in his life. I . . . can't be that."

He tightened the hold on her hand. "Beth wants no part of me if I decide to help you raise your cousins."

"I'm not asking you to—"

"She accused me of"—he turned to face her, searching those large eyes that looked like liquid honey—"of still being in love with you and not wanting to let you go."

Isabel's gaze dropped. After a few moments, she noticed his hand holding hers and wiggled her fingers loose. "I'm sorry. I'll talk to her and tell her—"

"Tell her what? That she's wrong? How the hell do you know if she's wrong?"

Her eyes met his again. And the taxi stopped in front of the hotel. Nick paid the driver and Isabel got out and headed to the lobby. She stepped into the elevator without waiting for him, but he hurried inside before the doors closed. It began to move up.

"Isabel—"

"Don't. We are such old news. Don't try to revive it, Nick. We've managed to stay friends. Sort of. But that's all."

Being in Argentina where they met. Being alone with her. Seeing her away from the office, where she was always the boss and always right, gave him courage, made him bold in ways he didn't even recognize in himself anymore. But he stepped close to her and looked into her eyes. "Don't you wonder, just sometimes, now that the past is the past, what would happen if we just held each other, if we just made love to each other and forgave all the bullshit that happened, if it would finally heal the cracks in our hearts?"

The door to the elevator opened on their floor and he didn't move. She glanced over his shoulder at the open door. "Nick." She exhaled. "I don't wonder, no. I know nothing can heal all the pain you've caused me."

"I'm sorry. But I'm a new man. If Beth can see that, why can't you?"

"I know you too well." The door to the elevator closed, and it began moving down again. "Shit," she said, and pushed him away from her. "We could go right back up there and spend all night having sex, but sex will not heal the past." She shook her head unhappily. "And tomorrow morning nothing will have changed between us, except that you will have blown a chance to marry a woman who loves you like you deserve to be loved."

The door to the elevator opened at the lobby.

"Go, Nick. Move on with your life. Get a plane ticket home and forget about me."

He stared at her. Was she right?

She shook her head. "Just go." She pressed her hand to his chest and put pressure to make him walk out of the elevator.

He walked out backward but continued to stare at her. Another couple entered the elevator. "Excuse us," they said. "Going up?"

"Yes." Isabel nodded.

The elevator doors closed, and Nick stood in the lobby, staring at his reflection in the door. She was right. Beth was right. As always, he was the one who was wrong. He dropped his hands into his pockets and turned toward the exit to get some fresh air and think.

Chapter Seven

After spending the morning helping a friend make wine goblet charms to sell at the weekend street fair downtown, then rushing to her aerobics class, Rosa finally made it home and took a cool shower. She would prepare herself a salad to have with her leftover baked chicken from last night, then sit on the balcony and read all afternoon. But before she even made it to the kitchen, her doorbell rang.

"Isabel," she said, pleased to see her back so soon. "Just in time for lunch. Come in."

"Actually," Isabel said, glancing at her watch as she walked in, "it's almost two. Lunch is over. I thought we might go get a cup of coffee at a café."

"I can make coffee here. Come into the—"

"Do you know a guy named Ramiro Garcia?" Isabel blurted out of the blue, though Rosa knew that with Isabel, nothing was ever really out of the blue. If she was asking, there was a reason.

Ramiro Garcia. She hadn't heard that name in a long time. Where in the world had Isabel heard about him? "I don't *know* him, really. I know about him."

"Well, he made a sudden appearance at Tía Dominga's house yesterday, claiming that he's Andres's brother and that he's going to take custody of his nieces and nephew.

My aunt nearly killed him and herself trying to push him out the door. She was so upset."

Ignoring her grumbling stomach, Rosa motioned for Isabel to follow her into the living room. "Tell me what happened," she said, sitting on the sofa and tucking her legs underneath her.

"I'm not really sure what happened." Isabel didn't sit. "All I know is that if this guy is really Andres's brother and is willing to take custody of the kids, I should listen to him. This could solve everything."

Rosa shook her head. "You don't understand." Isabel had already been living in America when the whole love triangle thing happened between Brenda, Ramiro, and Andres. But their entire barrio knew about it. Brenda had dated them both but had married Andres. Andres was responsible and hardworking and won her heart. "Ramiro has always been trouble. A wild hellion, all through his twenties, who did what he wanted at the expense of others. But he had a soft spot for Brenda, and there was talk that Ramiro had never fallen out of love with her." Rosa filled Isabel in on the stories that floated around back then.

Isabel listened intently and seemed to process the history and evaluate it. Rosa expected her to say something, anything, except what she did.

"But that's ancient history." She shrugged, as if Rosa were ridiculous for bringing it up. "So what if he had the hots for Brenda? Maybe what he felt for her is part of the reason he wants to help out. I have to at least hear him out. Will you come with me to the café?"

Rosa wanted to slap some sense into her. "*No.* I don't think you should be talking to him at all."

"Why not? He's their uncle."

Maybe she hadn't been clear enough. Rosa tried again. "Isabel, Andres *hated* this man with such passion that he didn't speak to him. Andres even blamed Ramiro for stealing from their own mother. If Andres didn't trust him, how could you consider leaving Brenda's babies with him?"

"Because he's determined to raise them. So much so that he sort of threatened to fight this out in front of a judge." Isabel shook her head. "That would be a complete nightmare for me. I have to talk to him. He's not going to go away. Please, just come with me," Isabel coaxed Rosa. "I want a witness in case there's a question later about what we talked about."

"I think you're crazy," Rosa said, "but I'll go with you, because I know you and you've already decided you're going."

"Yes."

Isabel was making a mistake, but Rosa couldn't let her make it alone.

They met Ramiro at the café where he requested. Isabel noticed that he looked better than he had the day before. Cleaner. But he still had that long, dark hair and a strong, intimidating presence. He stood and shook her hand when she reached the table where he was drinking a cup of coffee. He glanced at Rosa and also shook her hand, his gaze lingering on Rosa a bit longer. She seemed to suppress a glare.

"Okay, Mr. Garcia, tell me what this is all about," Isabel began.

"Call me Ramiro. And I'm going to raise my brother's children."

His damned arrogance made her want to tell him that he'd raise them over her dead body, but she tried to be reasonable. She wasn't cut out to be a parent. Maybe he was. At least he'd be a good father figure for Adelmo, and from what she'd witnessed yesterday, he needed strong male guidance. "The way I hear it, Andres and you were not even speaking."

"I wanted to fix things with him." Ramiro drank some coffee. "Lots of times I tried to contact him. But he didn't want to give me a chance. He didn't want me around Brenda, probably. But he was stupid to be jealous."

Isabel didn't know what had really happened, but Brenda had never once mentioned Ramiro. If she'd been in love with another man, she would have said something, wouldn't she? Besides, she adored Andres. The few times Isabel had seen them together, Brenda couldn't do enough for her husband. "Perhaps Andres didn't feel you were a good influence on his children."

"Andres remembered the young boy. He never got to know me as a man. I've changed. I have a profitable farm. I work hard." He looked at Rosa as if to stress the fact to her too.

When the waiter showed up, Isabel ordered a cup of coffee and Rosa a Coke. "The issue now, Mr. Garcia, is that Brenda and Andres have appointed me as the legal caregiver in their will, not you."

"So we change that," he said matter-of-factly.

"No, we don't change it unless you show me that you will be a better parent than I."

Ramiro sat straighter and then leaned over the table. Any other woman would probably have backed up; Isabel held her ground.

"Let me explain something to you. I don't need to prove anything to *you*. I intend to fight for the children however long it takes, Mrs. Americanita. Months, years, I don't care. And in the end, I will win. I live in this country. I am a man. I have property for the children to live comfortably and money to educate them. What do you have?"

Millions, Isabel wanted to say, but that wasn't the point. She could *not* afford to get into a legal battle with this man. Months. *Years!* Living in this country, waiting to win custody of children she hadn't even wanted to raise, when there was an uncle who obviously wanted them? How logical was that?

"You'd never win, Ramiro," Rosa said. "We'd all testify against you, you bastard."

Isabel tried to settle all the thoughts jumbled in her head. And control the panic rising inside her. Damn it, she needed to return to California as soon as possible to finish the sale of the winery. She also didn't want Rosa to speak. Before Ramiro could say a word—he'd already turned his dark attention to Rosa—Isabel put up a hand between them. "This does not need to go to court, Ramiro," she said.

He glanced at her again and she continued. "We obviously both care what happens to the children. It would be best if we came to an agreement without involving outside people."

A smile grew slowly on his face as if he knew he

had her and she was ready to bargain. She'd seen that look on men's faces many times and it always frustrated her, because they knew and she knew that for whatever reason, she was at a disadvantage. "And what kind of agreement do you have in mind?"

Her disadvantage this time was that she just couldn't be stuck in Mendoza indefinitely. This had to be resolved. "Well, that depends. Are you leveling with me? Do you really have the best interest of the children in mind? Or are you, like others have told me, completely unstable and can't be trusted?"

He studied her. "Come to my place. My ranch. I can show you what I've done, the life I can give my nieces and nephew."

Isabel didn't want to break eye contact first, but she wished she could turn around and see the look on Rosa's face. "Let's go," she said.

"Now?" He looked surprised.

"Sure. Now."

Ramiro dropped some bills onto the table and stood. "Okay."

Now Isabel looked at Rosa and Rosa shook her head. But they followed Ramiro to his truck. They slid in beside him. Rosa sat between them. Isabel gazed out the window and questioned her own sanity. What was she doing? Brenda hadn't wanted this, so how could she even consider it? Maybe because she felt so completely inept at mothering. And maybe because at its core, it made sense for the children to stay in their own country with a man who was their uncle.

They drove out of the city, about forty-five minutes

into the countryside. Finally, he turned onto a long dirt road that ended at a beautiful one-story home. He parked in front of the house and jumped out, coming around to open Isabel's door. He helped her out and then offered to help Rosa, who refused to place her hand in his.

"Why so angry?" he asked.

"Because you haven't changed at all. Still taking advantage of situations and people at every opportunity."

"I'm trying to keep what I have left of my family. Those niños are my family, my blood."

Rosa turned away from him, but Isabel didn't miss the look of sadness in his eyes. It was the same look she was sure was in hers every time she thought of how everyone she loved was gone. Dead.

"I will show you my house." He walked ahead, unlocking and opening his front door, throwing it open so they could follow him inside.

He gave them a very male, very brusque tour. Kitchen, dining room, living room, bathroom, library.

"Library? Interesting. You read?" Rosa asked.

Isabel suppressed a smile.

But Ramiro went ahead and grinned, pausing at the threshold of the library with a look of satisfaction. "I do, as a matter of fact. After I finished law school, I started my collection of books I'd like to read."

Both Isabel and Rosa found it hard to mask their surprise. Ramiro was an attorney? Wonderful, just what she needed to hear.

"You're a lawyer?" Rosa asked in disbelief.

His smile vanished. "Practiced for a few years, then

decided I was better suited for life in the country. That's when I bought this. Now I raise cattle." He turned away. "My bedroom," he said, and kept walking past the masculine room done in modern dark woods and iron. "I have five extra rooms in this wing. The pibes will have their choice. Maybe I'll make one a media room. Kids like TV, video games, and those kinds of things." His eyes met Isabel's and softened. "I do, too, and it would be nice to have someone to share my things with."

Isabel had nothing to say to that.

"Where were *you* planning to have them live?" he asked.

She hadn't planned on living anywhere with them.

"Do you have a home large enough for two girls and a boy who will probably feel like two if he's anything like I was?" he pursued.

Her house was not suitable for children—not three, not one. "Large," she said.

"How about space for them to play outside? Horses for them to ride? A vegetable garden for them to enjoy? Schools and colleges in their own language and—"

"Point taken, okay? I get it."

Ramiro turned around and headed back to his living room. He asked them to take a seat on the sofa. "I turned my life around. Andres didn't want to see that, and that's okay, but I loved my brother. I loved my mother too. If she were still alive, she would have wanted me to take care of her grandchildren."

Isabel sat down. Rosa remained standing, her arms crossed. "Brenda's mother wants *me* to take care of *her* grandchildren," Isabel reminded him. If grandparents were the deciding vote, the scales were tipped in favor of Isabel.

"We can do it together, if you like. You're welcome to one of the rooms."

Isabel laughed. Another man willing to partner up with her to parent. "Right."

He shrugged. "I'm a simple man, and this is going to be my life until I die. I have room in my house and in my life for my family. Even you." He took a seat across from them on a lived-in-looking black recliner. One thing was for sure: He wasn't proposing anything illicit between them. No, he was telling her he'd even be willing to put up with her if it meant having the kids.

"This is something I can do for Andres and Brenda. And I did love her once. No matter what anyone thinks. She loved Andres. And she was right. He was the better man. But all that is over, and it doesn't matter. Only my nieces and nephew matter now."

Isabel believed that he was sincere. Maybe this was his way of doing something for Brenda and Andres that he was unable to do when they were alive. He certainly had more to offer in terms of time, shared culture, and child-friendly space than she did. And more importantly, he wanted the job. She didn't. That should count for a lot, shouldn't it?

"What do we do with the fact that I'm the responsible guardian?"

"You transfer custody to me. I accept."

Isabel leaned forward on the couch, resting her forearms on her knees. "How long would that take?"

"A few weeks, maybe two or three months at the

most. Legal paperwork takes time and there would be a brief court hearing."

"But I don't have that much time."

"Why not?" Time didn't appear to be something he ever worried about. His face remained impassive.

"I'm in the middle of an important business transaction. I own a winery in America. I'm selling it. I need to get back as soon as possible."

"Go and come back when the paperwork is ready to sign. The kids can live with me but remain legally in your care." He smiled. "They'd be visiting their uncle."

"You don't understand. My aunt doesn't want you to have them. She isn't going to make things easy for you or me."

"Isabel, you aren't seriously considering this?" Rosa stepped in between them after following their exchange like a tennis match.

Yes, she was. She ignored Rosa and stood, walking around her. "What do you think of this—I take them with me to America for, say, six months?"

"No."

"Hear me out. I'll agree to transfer custody in six months' time, sign all the paperwork before I leave. It can sit in bureaucratic red tape until I return. The kids can come to America with me for a while, which will please my aunt. I'll spend some time with them. This will give me the time I need to sell the winery and settle all business deals. Then I'll come back and tell my aunt that it didn't work out, and you and I will complete the custody paperwork. I'll stay as long as I need. In fact, I'll stay for a few weeks to help you out if necessary."

He considered her offer.

Rosa turned angrily to Isabel. "You're crazy. You can't do this. They're human beings, not wine bottles you can pass on to another owner."

"He's their uncle. You should have seen Sandra's curiosity the other day. And Adelmo doesn't want to live in America. He doesn't want to live with me. He needs a man to raise him," she reasoned.

"Isabel, this is wrong. You're making a deal with the devil."

Ramiro laughed and finally stood unhurriedly. "Rosita, I'm not that dangerous." He held out his hand. "See, no flames."

"Brenda wouldn't have wanted this," she said, the only one disturbed by a deal that made perfect sense to Isabel.

Ramiro reached across and adjusted Rosa's purse strap on her shoulder. "She would have—that's the interesting thing you all are missing. She never had a problem with me. She understood who I really was before anyone else did. Even before I did." He faced Isabel. "Okay, Americanita, you sign the documents to make me the legal guardian in six months, and you can take them on this little vacation. Agreed." He reached for Isabel's hand.

Isabel shook his hand, feeling a sense of relief and dread at the same time.

After Ramiro drove them back to town and dropped them off at Rosa's house, she closed the front door—a soft click that echoed in her quiet house. She stood beside the door and stared at Isabel without speaking.

"Thank you for going with—"

"Don't thank me," she said, her tone reflecting the anger on her face. "You've been gone a long time, but to have changed *this* much." Her hands swung up dramatically.

Isabel, too, felt herself growing upset, resentful about the expectations others had of her. "This has nothing to do with how much I've changed," she said coldly.

"You don't know that man."

"Neither do you," she threw back the words.

Rosa shook her head and walked closer. "You're making a decision that will affect the lives of—"

"Stop it!" she shouted. "This may seem selfish or—"

"Crazy, irresponsible—"

"But you have no right to judge me." And it hurt that Rosa was looking at her with such disappointment. It hurt that they were arguing.

"This isn't you." Rosa lowered the intensity of her voice. "You don't walk away from people you're supposed to love. Not you. Not my best friend."

"I came here to make sure they were taken care of. They have a family member who wants them and is able to provide guardianship. That's it; my part is over. I don't know those kids. We have no bond." She lifted her arms in desperation, and her voice cracked with frustration. "Rosa, I wanted to be a mother once, but that time is long gone."

"Oh, Isabel," Rosa said, shaking her head and gazing at her with lament.

Isabel blinked away tears. "I'd be a terrible mother at my age."

Rosa opened her arms to embrace Isabel. "You don't know what you're saying. Motherhood is such an amazing gift, and there's no switch that turns on and off with time."

Isabel rested the side of her head against Rosa's. She closed her eyes and hugged Rosa tightly.

"And even if I agree that I've never pictured you being a mom, you have so much to offer."

Isabel sniffed and wiped her eyes. Regaining her composure, she stepped back. "Not all women feel like you do, Rosa."

"I know that. But you don't have to *feel* like I do to step up and not turn over control to—"

"Their uncle."

"A stranger."

"*I'm* a stranger to them too. What difference does it make?" She shook her head. "Rosa, please, just try to understand. Please."

"Honey, I don't. And I don't agree with your decision. But I'll back you on it. If you're determined to do this, I'll sit back and watch you do it."

Isabel nodded. "Thank you."

Emotionally drained, Isabel returned to her hotel room to find Nick waiting for her. He sat on *her* bed watching TV. She closed the door and stood beside it. "You're still here."

"I'm still here."

"You aren't leaving?"

He stood. "Not without you and the kids."

He moved toward her and she toward him, and when

they were face-to-face, she fell against him. He wrapped his arms around her, lowering his lips to the top of her head. It felt so good to be in his arms. In Argentina, he seemed more like the man she had fallen in love with.

She let him hold her for a long time. Hell, maybe she'd even let him make love to her. She'd sold the children out; what did it matter if she slept with another woman's man? "I'm a horribly selfish person, Nick," she muttered.

"No, you're not."

She couldn't tell him about her meeting with Ramiro. After Rosa's reaction, she couldn't deal with Nick's too. "We need to get them passports and take them home. Will you help me?"

"Of course." He released her and she dropped onto the bed. "Were you really hoping I'd be gone?"

When she went to bed last night, she'd been proud of herself for sending him home to Beth, because it was the right thing to do. And she hadn't even checked in the morning to see if he was gone. She tried not to think about him and the appealing changes she'd noticed. "I was hoping...for your sake...that you would have listened to me, yes."

"For my sake?"

"Marrying Beth would be good for you. Moving on, moving out of the winery, would allow you to start fresh. Looking backward...at me...It was so bad the first time....It would be a mistake."

"Hmm, so you sent me away to protect me?" He gazed pensively at her. "And you're telling me you're selfish? That doesn't sound like a selfish gesture to me."

No, *that* wasn't. But she'd totally copped out on the issue of the children. And Rosa made her feel like she was as evil as Ramiro. But weren't they both doing the right thing?

"If you were selfish, you'd have brought me back to your room last night."

She smiled. "I didn't. And I didn't tonight either."

"I know. And I'm leaving. By the way, Beth told me it's over, and I think it is. I think it should be."

Not for the expectation of getting back together with her, she hoped. She truly wanted to be alone. Free of everyone. "Nick, I don't want you back," she said, not to be hurtful but to be honest and to make him understand where she stood. She was realizing that she still cared about him—actually, she'd always known that, but for a long time she'd been so hurt, so angry that it had been easier to hate him. But she'd never stopped caring about him. Still, she didn't want to repeat what was now painful history. They both needed to move forward, not backward.

He swallowed. His chin lifted. "I know."

"Then what are you doing? You're so close to being free. Free of the business. And of me."

He nodded. "Yep."

"Then how can you even consider extending what has to feel like a life sentence at Gallegos to be a step-in parent?"

"It's never felt like a life sentence to me. It's felt like home." That was all he said. Then he turned and left.

And Isabel's heart ached. She wasn't sure if it was falling apart or if the old wounds were finally closing.

Chapter Eight

The following week, Isabel traveled to Buenos Aires with her legal paperwork that stated that she was the guardian of the children. Her goal was to request their passports, but after standing in line for three hours, she was informed that she had no authority to take them out of the country.

"Pardon me," she said to the clerk, shaking a manila folder filled with paperwork. "I have complete authority over everything they do."

"Within the country, yes." Sitting behind a sheet of bulletproof glass, the woman appeared to stifle a yawn. The temperature in the room full of people had to be over eighty degrees.

"You don't understand. I don't live here. If I'm to care for them, they *must* travel to the U.S. with me."

"Miss, we have a five-year period where you must live in the country before you can take them out," the woman explained with forced patience. "All adoptions are the same. No exceptions." Ready to dismiss Isabel, she reached for a rubber stamp to indicate she'd done her job and another application had been processed.

"But I'm not adopting them. I'm...responsible for them. I..." Isabel tossed her arms up in the air, completely frustrated. "I can't live here for five years. I have a business to run. What am I supposed to do with the kids?"

The woman shook her head stupidly. "I do not know."

Isabel returned to her hotel room and called two people—Dr. Vermuelen, Tía Dominga's lawyer, and Ramiro Garcia—venting and demanding they both take care of whatever needed to be done to allow her the right to take the children home. "I'm in the middle of business negotiations. I can't stay here much longer. How ridiculous to tell me I'm responsible for these kids, yet I'm unable to get them passports or take them home."

"Don't worry, Ms. Gallegos," Vermuelen said. "We'll get it all straightened out. Even if it takes a little time."

"I don't have time."

"I'll do everything I can, as quickly as I can. Come to my office tomorrow and I'll try to have an answer for you."

Ramiro took a more proactive approach. He flew to Buenos Aires immediately. A few hours later he knocked on her hotel room door.

"Let's go to dinner," he said.

She wasn't hungry, but she didn't exactly want to invite him into her room.

He took her to Calle Florida in downtown. The glitter and buzz of the Buenos Aires nightlife was a different world completely from the peacefulness of Mendoza and his ranch, yet he seemed comfortable walking down the busy and fashionable pedestrian shopping street. He led her to a parrilla, which was an Argentine steak house.

Once they were seated, each holding a glass of wine, he asked for her to go over the problem again.

She explained what she'd been told.

"I have some contacts. I can help. Don't worry," he said.

"Well, I am worried."

"Trust me, you'll leave when you need to. I'll make sure it happens." And his confidence made her believe him. She liked people who got things done.

He ordered a parrilla for both of them to share. This wasn't actually as macho as it sounded. All parrillas were basically the same and consisted of a mixed grill with a little of everything. Chicken. Spicy sausage. Narrow strips of ribs. Flank steak. A mixture of exotic innards that most non-Argentines would probably wrinkle their noses at first glance.

"So, you're selling your winery, huh?" He pulled out a cigarette.

"Do you have to smoke?"

He shrugged and put it back.

"Cigarette smoke is bad for children," she reminded him, and reached for a piece of bread. "You should consider quitting if you're going to raise them."

He grinned. "Tell me about the winery."

"Not much to tell. We had a vineyard in Mendoza, and when we moved to California, we bought some land and planted some vines and started a business." Isabel swirled the wine in the deep, wide bowl of her glass, almost without thinking, the practice being automatic.

"Sounds simple."

"It was hard work." It took years before the vines produced grapes they could use. Years to establish a market. Years.

He nodded. "The Americanos like your wine?"

"They seem to." Isabel eased the glass aside without tasting the deep red wine. "Tell me about you and Brenda."

"No."

She raised an eyebrow. "No?"

The food arrived on a sizzling grill. And he began serving her and himself.

"Tell me about your friend Rosa," he countered.

"Why?"

"She's cute."

Isabel laughed. "Don't bother. She doesn't like you. Now, what happened with Brenda? How did you meet?"

"At a boliche." A dance club.

"Hmm. She never mentioned you." Isabel tried the food, and the beef practically melted in her mouth.

"We went to the same college, were part of the same graduating class. We all tended to head to the same club, so that's where we met. Danced a few times. Brenda needed to explore her dark side." He grinned devilishly. Though Isabel had never been attracted to the dangerous gladiator type, she could see what Brenda might have seen in him at one time.

"What's Rosa's story?" he asked.

"She was married to a nice guy, but he was immature and she got tired of him and divorced him." Isabel added some salad to her plate. "What happened after the dances between you and Brenda?"

"I took Brenda home, she met Andres, and decided she liked him better."

"How long did you date?"

"Not long."

"Did you . . . ? Never mind."

He gazed at her without comment. Then looked at his food and got busy cutting. "I was sort of wild and slightly crazy. That didn't bother her, because it was like she could see right through all that macho stuff to the real person. We spent a lot of time talking.

"Then things got serious between Brenda and Andres. He was older, serious, and focused on the future and on her. Andres and I had a fight. He didn't get that she wanted him, not me. He accused me of stealing from my mom. I left home. Never saw Brenda again. Though she wrote me a letter and left it with my mom, basically telling me she believed in me and wished me well."

Isabel gazed at him. There was so much she didn't know about her cousin. So much she now wished she'd kept up with. But, hell, she'd been busy trying to get the business established in America at the time. They were broke and desperate—afraid they might fail. "Did you love her?"

"Not the way you mean. Wasn't in me at the time. But she was a special girl."

"Yes, she was."

They sat in silence in the dimly lit grill full of happy Porteños enjoying the Buenos Aires nightlife, talking, laughing, and eating. But both Isabel and Ramiro had stopped eating.

"So, what are my chances with Rosa?" he asked finally.

Isabel laughed. Ramiro had a certain charm about him, and she was suddenly feeling very good about their arrangement with the children. He would make a strong parent, able to control them. Yet, he had a sense of humor, which made her think he'd be able to deal with problems without overreacting. Best of all, even though her aunt and apparently Andres thought differently, Ramiro was honorable. Feeling it his duty to take responsibility for the children, he was doing everything in his power to meet that obligation. This was more than she could say for herself.

"Tomorrow I'm meeting with my attorney here in Buenos Aires, the one who has been handling the guardianship transfer. I guess it's a good thing you're here. We should take care of the legal paperwork between us."

"Good idea."

They finished their dinner and he walked her back to the hotel. Without much of a good-bye, he told her he'd pick her up in the morning and left.

In the morning, they met Vermuelen at his office. Isabel explained that she would be assigning permanent custody to Ramiro Garcia. Ramiro explained that she had to legally accept guardianship; then she would later be able to reassign custody. If she simply declined, the children would become wards of the court. "I'll have custody for the next six months, at which time Mr. Garcia, the children's uncle, will become their permanent legal guardian. I need you to draw up the paperwork."

"And you're sure that this is the agreement you wish to make?" Vermuelen asked.

"She's sure," Ramiro said.

"I was speaking to Ms. Gallegos."

"I'm sure."

"And actually I was thinking about the passport issue last night. This will make things easier," Ramiro said. "The children will simply travel on a tourist visa. You're not petitioning for them to live permanently in America. You just want them to visit."

Isabel widened her eyes in surprise. He *was* brilliant. "How fast can you speed the process through?"

"A week? Maybe two," Ramiro said.

She had no option but to hold tight. The frustrating bureaucracy in Argentina made Isabel want to scream, but luckily with these men on her side it wouldn't be so bad.

She and Ramiro signed the paperwork needed for the guardianship transfer, which would be approved by a judge in a few months; then she flew back to Mendoza to wait.

The slower pace of life in Argentina certainly wasn't something Isabel would ever get used to, but she felt the tension that always pulsed just behind her mind ease. The pressure of having somewhere to go, something to do, someone to please was suddenly missing from her life. She made her daily phone calls to the office and was assured that things were in order. No problems.

As they sat around in her aunt's courtyard drinking mate and eating sinfully fatty facturas with dulce de leche and drizzled icing, she almost felt guilty. Not only because of the sugar in the delicious pastries, but also because she was doing nothing. Wasting time, letting the hours slip by as she watched the children. Adelmo and Sandra played some Nintendo games that she'd purchased for them when she'd gone to the city to shop a few days earlier. Julieta played with some Barbie dolls on the cool tile floor. Her aunt stared at them as if trying to memorize every precious expression, every glint in their eyes.

Isabel fanned herself lazily. The day was unusually warm. "Tía, why do you think my taking the children to America is a good idea?"

"What?" Her question seemed to pull Tía Dominga out of her thoughts. "What, querida?" she asked again. "You want another mate?" She reached for the unique hourglass-shaped mate full of the strong green tea and refilled it with hot water from the kettle. She spooned in a bit of sugar and let it all settle, the air bubbles disappearing, before handing it back.

Isabel accepted it and frowned. "I still wonder if they wouldn't be better off here with you or their uncle." Not brave enough to come right out and tell Tía Dominga her plan, she thought she would test the waters.

But Tía Dominga gaped at her as if the suggestion were completely preposterous. "I told you that man is no good. Don't even think of him."

"But Brenda cared for him once."

"She was young and impulsive. But she made the right choice in the end. Andres was a good man. And he didn't want to have anything to do with his brother. There was a reason for that. He knew what that boy was really like."

"Maybe. But people change, and maybe Andres didn't give him a chance to grow up. Maybe we should give him the opportunity Andres didn't. After all, he's no longer a boy."

"Absolutely not." She shook her head and stood. She wore a loose, dark blue dress with white flowers, sort of like a Hawaiian muumuu. She picked up a watering can and filled it, then began to water the house plants that covered her patio. "People don't really change."

Isabel sighed. For some reason, she thought of Nick. He'd changed. And hadn't she? For the better or for the worse, she didn't know. Placing the mate down untouched on a small glass table, she watched her aunt sympathetically. "On the small chance that this man really *did* change or mature, it would be a shame if the kids didn't get to know a blood relative just because of an old feud."

"Isabelita, I know you mean well." She watered a beautiful leafy hanging plant. "But don't pursue this." She moved to the faucet and refilled the watering can. "*You're* their family now. And you're enough."

No, she wasn't. She was one person. One inexperienced person at that. Isabel wasn't sure how she was going to break her decision to her aunt. Obviously, it wouldn't be now. She wasn't ready to hear it anyway; she wasn't ready to accept Ramiro. For Tía Dominga's grandchildren's sake, Isabel hoped she would eventually. She stood and took the can from her aunt and finished watering the plants. "You're my family and I love you. Do you know that?"

"I love you, too, nena," Tía Dominga said. "And I'm very fond of that ex-husband of yours. I haven't asked, but what made him fly down with you?"

"I don't know," Isabel said truthfully. She put the watering can back on the shelf beside the faucet where Tía Dominga kept her gardening tools neatly organized.

"My sister never gave up hope that you and he would work through your differences." She shook her head, then plopped back on her white garden rocker. "Pobrecita," she said as if a tragedy had befallen Isabel's mother. "She suffered right along with the two of you. She wanted you to have babies together."

"Tía." Isabel placed a hand on Tía Dominga's shoulder and then knelt beside her and looked into her dark eyes. "Let's not bring that up. It didn't happen. And actually I did quite well without babies, so it all worked out for the best."

She went back to her seat and caught Sandra's watchful eye. Isabel wasn't sure what the dark glance meant. It lasted only a second; then the girl looked back at the TV, pretending that she hadn't been listening.

Nick entered the patio. He'd been inside watching TV. "So," he said, "anyone getting hungry?"

The kids mumbled no under their breaths. Tía Dominga motioned him to have a seat and enjoy some of the pastries. He did. Then with a satisfied smile, he raised his face to the sun shining through the trees. "What a great life," he said. "I love this country. I never should have convinced you to leave, Isabel. We might have been happy here."

Isabel had had that very thought too many times while

struggling to make it in America. But now she felt her impatience coming back. The need to do something burned to a fever pitch. She stood. "It's been a week. I'm going to call the lawyer and see if he's made any progress with the kids' visas."

Nick watched her walk into the house and knew that her lack of real connection to the winery was getting to her. Isabel was too much of a control freak to accept that she wasn't there, on top of every aspect of the business.

He glanced at Tía Dominga and caught her staring at him, watching how he couldn't keep his eyes off Isabel, even after all these years.

"My niece is strong, but she has a soft side too," she said, as if he didn't know everything that made Isabel tick.

He smiled. "Not when it comes to me."

"Niño, you didn't come all this way to accept that, did you?"

"Oh, I accept it. I deserve it, trust me."

"Hmm," she said, picking up a book and settling herself deeper into her chair. "And as stubborn and strong as she is, she let you follow her all the way to Argentina."

"She didn't. I invited myself."

"Hmm," Tía Dominga said again.

He'd been persistent, persuasive maybe, but he knew that if Isabel really hadn't wanted him to come with her, he wouldn't be here today. And as each day passed, she seemed less resistant to his presence. "Okay, you're right," he said. He stood and went in search of her. As he walked into the living room, Isabel got off the phone.

She placed the phone in her purse and looked at him. "No information yet," she said.

"How about a run?" he asked, knowing she needed to release some of that nervous, restless energy.

"A run?"

"Yeah, you want to go for a jog?" Back in the States, he often saw her returning home in the early morning in a pair of shorts and a sport top, her hair in a ponytail, and less than an hour later dressed to perfection in a suit as she walked to the office in those crazy heels.

She appeared to want to resist, but she nodded. "Good idea. Let's go back to the hotel and change."

They started their jog through Parque Independencia, which was a small park across the street from the hotel. Then they turned onto Rivadavia, weaving through quiet residential neighborhoods. Getting into a good rhythm, they ran about twenty blocks before they hit Parque General San Martín. Sweat poured off Nick's body, but it felt good. He hadn't been kidding when he'd stated how content he was in Argentina. He loved the pace of life, the food, and the people. He was plain happier. "Should we turn back?" he asked.

"If you want, we can run through part of the park, then go back," she said, looking like she didn't want the run to end.

He'd have to rest before heading back, but he was doing good now. "Let's go." They crossed the park, following the walking paths under the old trees. Getting a second wind, he turned toward Avenida del Libertador, which ran by the college building where he'd studied as an exchange student.

"Stop," he said, bending down and stretching the backs of his legs and breathing deeply. "Our school."

Isabel wiped her face with the sleeve of her shirt, walking in place. "Yep." She nodded. "This was it."

"Come on." He started to climb the stairs to the front door.

"What are you doing? We can't go in."

"Why not? I need to use the bathroom and could use a break." She was no longer breathing heavily, but Nick's heart still drummed hard against his chest. If they didn't stop and get a drink of water, he would probably pass out. He walked inside. School wasn't in session, but a few students were roaming the grounds.

He made his way to their old history classroom.

"We shouldn't be here," she said.

"This is great!" He strolled around the desks, then sat where he remembered sitting as a student.

Isabel wiped her forehead, then placed her hands on her hips and looked around the plain room with blank yellowish walls. She'd been supersmart and so damned cute when they were students that he'd barely been able to concentrate on his work.

"Bring back good memories?" he asked.

She shrugged. "It was school."

"No, it was great! I had such a good time here." He ran his hands up and down the desk, remembering those days so long ago when he'd thought himself invincible.

She sat at a desk beside him. "You barely did any studying, so what are you talking about?"

He angled his head. "Who's talking about studying? Guess I was thinking more of the after-school activities."

Shaking her head, but with a look of amusement, she said, "Nick, you've always been impossible. Life is just a big party to you."

"It wasn't me. It was you Argentine girls who were all over me."

She smirked. "You were from America. We were stupidly in awe."

He leaned forward on the desk. "But I was interested in only one girl," he said with a boyhood flirtation that he hadn't directed at his tough ex-wife in ages.

Expecting her to turn to ice and walk away, he was surprised when she didn't. Maybe she was finally relaxed or the endorphins had kicked in and mellowed her.

She shook her head and gave him a "get serious" look. "You flirted with all us gullible girls." She stood. "And I was the most gullible of all. Come on, I need a drink of water."

Standing and stretching, he called after her, "You've always been too smart to be gullible."

"I was young and innocent." She continued to make her way out of the room.

"Smart," he called. "And cute. That's why I was hooked the second I saw you." But she'd already walked out of the classroom. Chuckling, he went after her.

They were stopped on the way to the drinking fountains and bathrooms by a custodian.

"We used to study here," Isabel explained. "We stopped by to . . . reminisce."

The custodian smiled. "But I can't have you wandering the halls. I'm sorry."

"Can we get a drink of water and use the bathroom?"

The custodian nodded. "Quickly, then you have to go."

Nick didn't want to leave quickly. He wanted to stop time, maybe even to reverse time.

But Isabel promised and soon they were back on the street, jogging toward the hotel.

Their feet pounded the pavement, and his heart pounded to a rhythm of the past. What would it take to start again and go back in time to be the young dreamers they once had been? Was it possible? Could he get back everything he'd lost?

Nick really didn't know the answers to these questions, but he did know that it was way past time he found out.

Chapter Nine

Nick seemed to barely make it back to the hotel. He had to stop about three times to catch his breath and massage his legs.

"I'm sorry," she said. "This was too much for you. Do you want to catch a cab?"

"No," he'd said. "I can do it." And he'd kept going.

He limped into the hotel and leaned on the elevator wall as they traveled up, his eyes closed.

"Are you okay?" she asked.

"Oh, yeah," he said, his eyes opening just enough to let her see the dark green that she'd always thought perfectly matched the vine leaves on their property. Then he smiled lazily. "Though I may not be able to walk tomorrow."

"Maybe you should go sit in the Jacuzzi for a while?"

The elevator announced the arrival to their floor. "Join me?" he asked.

"I think I just want to take a shower."

"Jacuzzi first?"

She didn't really want to sit in the Jacuzzi, but considering he'd about killed himself to keep up with her on the run, she nodded. "Okay, meet you down there in ten minutes."

Splashing some cold water on her face in her bathroom felt *so* good. Taking a fluffy hand towel, she wiped her flushed face and looked in the mirror. The run felt great, but she had a feeling Nick wouldn't be the only one who was going to be sore in the morning. She hadn't run this much in about a month. But she'd had a great time. Seeing her university again had been fun.

The face in the mirror definitely showed signs of aging, but today she didn't feel the heaviness of the last twenty years. For a little while, she had been back in that classroom, reliving that idyllic time and the year she met Nick. Millions of times, when he had stumbled around work drunk or when they had another fight, she had remembered her college years bitterly. Meeting Nick had changed her whole life—had ruined her life, she told herself. But today she remembered it differently. He had been irresistible and he'd made her feel special. He'd made her happy.

Shaking her head, she put the towel down and went to find her swimsuit. Nick had been trouble from the beginning, with his sexy, lazy smile and carefree personality, and she had probably known it deep inside, but she hadn't cared. His crazy American ways of not following rules, of drinking heavily, of doing what he pleased and not worrying about consequences had only attracted her more. *So you have only yourself to blame for everything that came after.* Still, it felt great to go back in time today to before they'd both messed up so badly. A whisper in her heart told her that it could have turned out so differently, if they had...listened to each other? Because back then, everything had clicked.

Dressed in her swimsuit, she slipped on a cover-up to

head back downstairs and join Nick in the Jacuzzi, where he was already soaking.

"So," he said as she took a seat across from him, "I've been thinking of something I want to do before we leave, and I want to see what you think."

Without meaning to, she stiffened. What did he want to do? He was so close and half naked, and her mind was fuzzy from exercise and being overheated. "I'm listening."

"Well, you know how much Adelmo likes soccer."

Adelmo? "Soccer?"

"Yeah, he loves soccer. What do you think about taking him and the girls to a game? I checked the Godoy Cruz schedule, and they play Boca Juniors in two days."

Isabel started laughing. "You want to go to a soccer game? That's it?"

He smiled and gazed at her strangely as if wondering why she was laughing. "Yeah. That's it. What do you think?"

"I think ... it's a great idea."

"Really?"

"Yes, really. I think it would be fun. Now can we go to the pool? I can't handle this heat one second longer."

Seated in Estadio Feliciano Gambarte, Adelmo held a choripan, a sausage sandwich, in one hand and a horn in the other. He wore the team's royal blue shirt and a crazy fuzzy hat on his head. He alternated between bites of sausage sandwich and yelling at the team at the top of his lungs until the veins in his neck bulged. Julieta stayed with Tía Dominga, who rightfully felt she was too young to enjoy the game, but Sandra joined the crowd in their boisterous cheering whenever the players came close to scoring.

Isabel sipped on a soda and watched the game and the rowdy fans, including the ones she'd brought with her.

"Not enjoying it?" Nick asked, sitting beside her.

"It's great," she said.

He laughed. "Doesn't look like you're having much fun."

But before she could answer, the crowd went crazy as one of the Godoy Cruz players neared the goal and kicked the ball. After a momentary breath that everyone seemed to take at once, the stadium erupted into cheers, wild horns, and screams as Mendoza's team scored.

Adelmo blew his horn excitedly as he jumped up and down. He high-fived Nick and Sandra and pretty much ignored Isabel.

Nick took his seat again, laughing. "This kid is great."

Isabel wasn't so sure. Adelmo sort of scared her. He seemed wild and uncontrollable.

After a couple of hours, the kids were screamed out and stuffed with junk food. Godoy Cruz won, and everyone was all smiles.

"You made their day," she said to Nick as they flowed out of the stadium with the crowd.

"I thought they'd like it. Thanks for coming."

"It was fun. I haven't been to a soccer game in . . . well, since college."

"Me neither." He rested an arm behind her back. "But visiting Argentina and not going to a soccer game is like going to New York City and not going to see the Yankees. You just have to."

She didn't know about that, but it certainly got your blood pumping. "We should have visited more often when Mami and Papi were alive, and done more things like this."

"They visited a lot. You didn't."

"*We* didn't," Isabel corrected.

"Damn fools we've been, haven't we?"

Isabel laughed. "Yes." It wouldn't have killed her to take a break every once in a while, but for so long the winery hadn't made money, and when it finally did, it became such a time-consuming business that she didn't have time to take a vacation. "Hey, Nick?"

They reached the long line of people waiting to catch a cab. "What?"

"You know when we were at the university the other day, and you were talking about how much you'd enjoyed the attention you got from the girls in class?"

He chuckled. "Yeah?"

"Why did you pick me?"

He seemed surprised by the question. "Well..." He glanced at the children, busily talking among themselves, Adelmo reliving the game and Sandra trying to add a word every once in a while. Nick leaned in close and whispered, "You were hot."

"Come on, I'm serious," Isabel said, not smiling.

He straightened and dropped all teasing from his voice. "You were everything I wasn't. Smart, motivated. You had dreams and ideas and you made me want to be a part of them. You made me want to be a better person." He shrugged. "I liked the way you looked at me like I mattered. No one had ever done that before." He looked away and his Adam's apple moved up and down. The teasing look came back into his eyes. "And you slept with me."

Isabel could tell he was trying to lighten the conversation, and she went along with it. "Yes, I did. I thought you'd leave when the semester was over and I'd never see you again, but still, I couldn't help myself."

Nick grinned, apparently pleased with her response. "That was something else I liked about you. You were willing to try anything."

"Funny," she said. "That's what I liked about you." Their turn to take the next cab arrived, and they climbed inside with Adelmo and Sandra.

Isabel stared at Nick's profile. "I think I would have been more like you if I had stayed in Argentina and done my own thing," she said.

But Nick shook his head. "Isabel, even back then you weren't really like me. If you had stayed here, you would have been a kick-ass marine biologist with one hundred percent focus on your job. That's just who you are, and actually, *that* was what I liked best about you." He winked. "Although the other thing I mentioned was damned good too."

Isabel smiled.

"Why the questions?"

"I guess I'm trying to figure out when I changed. When I stopped being that college girl and became me."

His gaze softened, and he looked at her like he used to when he'd been so infatuated with her, and it made Isabel feel exposed in a very pleasant, intimate way. "You really haven't changed." He ran a finger down her bare arm. "Just grew a tougher skin to protect yourself from assholes like me."

Her entire body flushed from the gentle touch. "I'm not going to say you weren't an asshole," she said, then smiled. "But it wasn't entirely your fault."

And he was no longer an asshole. She promised herself to try to forgive him for everything she'd been holding inside her for so many years. It was over. All of that was over, and maybe they could both move on and stay friends.

It was the first week of October, and the day finally arrived for them to leave. Isabel, Nick, and Rosa went to Tía Dominga's house to help the kids pack. Sandra and Julieta were easy, but Adelmo decided to lock himself in the bathroom and not pack.

"Querido," Tía Dominga said. "Please, come out."

"I'm not packing. I'm not moving," he shouted through the door.

"You have to," she said. "Now come out. Be a good boy."

Isabel and Rosa waited along with Tía Dominga for him to unlock the door, but it remained shut.

"Adelmo," Isabel tried. "This isn't helping. Why don't you come out so we can talk?"

He refused to respond to Isabel at all. At least with Tía Dominga he would shout back.

She glanced at Nick, who sat on the couch watching the three of them try to convince one small boy to do what he absolutely didn't want to do. Isabel frowned. "Do you want to give it a try?"

Nick smiled. "No, it's too much fun watching him control the three of you."

Rosa snorted. She banged on the bathroom door so hard that even Isabel jumped. "You get out of that bathroom right now, young man, and pack your suitcase. Or else I'm packing it for you, and you're getting what I say you're getting."

Adelmo didn't respond.

Rosa hit the door one more time. "You have five seconds to open this door. One...two...three...four..."

The door jerked open and Adelmo glared at Rosa. "What do you care? You're not going to America," he shouted.

"If I get to five, I'll pack clothes and no toys. Am I packing or are you?"

He stomped to the bedroom the children shared in Tía Dominga's house.

Rosa stood tall, very proud of herself.

Nick clapped. "That's a woman I wouldn't want to mess with."

"I raised two boys. No sweat."

Once all three suitcases were packed and the kids were outside playing, Isabel sat with a sigh of relief on the bed that used to belong to Brenda.

"The good thing about all this is that I'll probably see you more often." Rosa sat beside her, the old bed creaking in protest.

"Don't count on it."

"Mala," Rosa said, and stuck her tongue out at her friend.

Isabel chuckled. "I'm kidding. I'll be back just as soon as the business sells. And then I'll make regular visits to see my little cousins, so, yes, you'll see me more often."

"That's good. Though you could just keep the chicos and not come back."

"No, I couldn't even if I wanted to. Ramiro and I signed custody paperwork in Buenos Aires."

"I wish you hadn't done that," Rosa said, shaking her head in lament.

Isabel wanted Rosa to understand. "It's going to work out fine. Those children are not supposed to live in the U.S. This is their country. And he is their uncle."

"I'm not going to argue with you. You made your decision. I don't like it, but you've got my support. Just let me know if I can do anything to help."

"Ramiro might need some help. He seemed interested in you, you know." Isabel angled her head to catch a glimpse of her friend's reaction.

"He can go to hell."

With a teasing smile, Isabel poked Rosa. "A younger, sexy man might be just what you need to celebrate your new life as a single, available woman with all her kids out of the house."

"Stop talking nonsense and let's get these bags outside and call a cab." She stood, not seeming to consider the possibility even as a joke.

"Good idea," Isabel said, dropping all talk of Ramiro.

They headed out of the room and Isabel paused. "Rosa?"

"Hmm?"

"Why am I so sad? It's like I don't want to go home

all of a sudden. The past few weeks have been nice, and for a short while I remembered who I used to be."

"Yeah?"

"Yeah."

"Maybe there's hope for you, after all." Rosa smiled and hooked an arm around Isabel's shoulder.

In a heartbreaking exchange of hugs and kisses, the children said good-bye to their grandmother. "Cuidate, mi amor, portate bien, nunca te olvides que te quiero," she said in between kisses and hugs. "Take care of yourselves, my loves, be good, never forget that I love you."

"We'll be back to visit you soon," Isabel promised her aunt, whose face was stained with tears.

Tía Dominga cradled Isabel's face in her hands. "You take care of them and love them, Isabelita. That's all I ask."

Isabel nodded. "They'll have whatever they need."

"They need love."

Isabel wanted to promise that she'd love them. She was already fond of them, and she had resigned herself to the obligation of her guardianship—at least temporarily. But she was starting to feel like a fraud knowing that she didn't plan to make a real home for them. With regret, she hugged her aunt tightly. "Don't worry, Tía."

The children cried. They didn't want to be taken away from all they'd ever known. How could she blame them? When she left Argentina, she'd been an adult and it had been her choice. "You'll love it in America," she promised, even though the second she said it, she realized it was a stupid thing to say.

"*This* is our home," Adelmo said, standing stiffly beside his grandmother. If he didn't bolt, they'd be lucky.

"He means that though we're sure it's great there, we love our country," Sandra translated.

"I understand," Isabel assured them.

"As soon as I'm an adult, I'm coming back," Adelmo promised.

Isabel wanted to tell him he wouldn't have to wait that long, but she couldn't offer that solace just yet.

Julieta simply sat on Nick's lap sucking her thumb, a regression that her pediatrician assured them would go away.

Not wanting to draw out the moment any longer, Isabel loaded them all into the taxi that would take them to the airport to catch the international flight home. Larger personal belongings would be shipped to California later, she promised them, though it wouldn't really be necessary. She'd buy them anything they needed, and they'd be back home before they missed their things too much. For now they each took one suitcase with clothes and a few toys.

Once they boarded the airplane, their sadness diminished slightly as they grew excited about the ride. This was the first time they'd been on a plane. They were given the royal treatment in their first-class seats, with personal choices of movies to watch and ice-cream sundaes with their favorite topping. Anything they requested was brought to them. Before takeoff, Isabel called Stephanie and asked her to prepare the house that she'd shared with her parents on the winery grounds, since it was not child-friendly. She hadn't bothered to change anything in the house, even though her parents had been gone a long time. Of course, she'd donated their clothes and some personal items to charity, but all the furnishings and design of the house were identical. Now she'd finally have to move some of those items out to make room for the kids. That was a good thing. When the winery sold, she'd have to empty the house anyway, so why not start now?

Once they were in the air, she sat quietly looking out at the blackness of the sky from the small airplane window. She'd meant what she'd told Rosa about getting in touch with who she'd been—the young girl who'd sat in that classroom with Nick, excited about learning and about life's possibilities. This made her even more determined to recapture at least a little of that old self. Once the winery was gone and her temporary obligation to the kids was over, she was going to live the life she should have lived years ago.

For now, she was glad to be going home, though worried. Scared. But still glad to return to her business and make sure what needed to be done got done.

Nick picked up a sleeping Julieta, who sat between them, and moved into her seat. "What are you thinking?"

Sleepy eyed, she turned her attention to him. "Nothing." For the past few hours, she'd practically ignored them. Luckily, the older children entertained themselves with snacks and movies. And little Julieta played games with Nick until she fell asleep.

"You know, if you interact with them a little more, it might make it easier."

"I interact with them."

Nick stared at her. "Yes, you do. But I wonder..."

She raised an eyebrow and waited to hear what he wondered. The hum of the airplane filled the silence when he didn't finish his sentence.

"Just remember you can count on me. I'm willing to help you as much as you need."

Isabel swallowed, touched by all the kindness he'd shown her lately. "Okay." But the idea that he thought he could help her raise three needy young children, that he thought she actually planned to raise them, was simply ridiculous.

"I mean it. These last few weeks. I hope...I think we've grown closer."

They had. But that didn't change her plans to sell the winery and lead her own life.

"I just don't want things to go back to how it was between us before we left."

"I'm not sure what you mean."

He pointed at her. "That's what I mean. I can see you shutting down. Don't do that."

"I'm not shutting down, Nick. I'm just thinking about work and what has to be done in the next few months."

"Just remember that you don't have to keep everything locked inside you. I'm here. If you're worried or scared about how you're going to deal with all this, let me know. I'm willing to ease a little of the pressure."

"I appreciate that, really." She looked back out her window. But she didn't feel any pressure. She wished she could open up and tell him what she actually felt: eager to sell the winery and get on with her life; anxious for this setback to be over. But she couldn't really voice those feelings. And besides, she couldn't count on him to help her with the children, even for the short-term. It wouldn't be fair. She had no intention of getting that close to Nick again. And when the business sold and she took the kids back to Argentina where they belonged, Isabel planned to move into a small house by the beach, alone. No Nick. No problems.

Chapter Ten

The plane landed about midafternoon. Even though they'd been flying all night, with the time change it would soon be evening again. And in America, October put them in the fall rather than the warm spring they'd just left. Days were shorter, which meant evenings came early. Thankfully, Nick had driven his Chevy Avalanche to the airport rather than one of his little sports cars, so they all climbed into his truck for the ride home.

Arriving at the vineyard brought back a mixture of feelings. One of the most vivid memories Isabel had was of her mother. Every time they pulled onto the property, her mother would sigh as they drove up the long paved path, vineyards on both sides. She'd say, "I can almost pretend that I'm back home when we make that turn."

The vineyard would forever remind Isabel of her parents. This was their life. Their love. Their passion.

"Looks like home," Sandra said.

Isabel glanced at the young girl beside her in the truck. "It's been my home practically since the day we moved to America."

"Now it will be ours?"

"No." When Sandra frowned, Isabel added, "I'll be selling the business soon."

"Because of us?"

"No." They pulled off the dirt road, the tires grasping the parking lot asphalt securely and allowing the truck to glide into the back lot, where the offices were located. "I just want to move on to something else."

Sandra acted like she understood, but Isabel knew she didn't. It took living a whole life full of work and family, demands and pressures to fathom the need to move on.

"You can park in my spot," she told Nick. A parking space reserved for her specifically—she wondered how much longer it would be before someone else was entitled to park here. A possessiveness she didn't know she felt made her shrug away the question as the car turned off.

"Let's grab our things and make our way to my place. It's down the path a bit," Isabel said.

Nick's small home was on the opposite end of the vineyard. Hers was on a little hill closer to the offices. "You want me to follow you up?" he asked.

"Of course not. Go home. We'll be fine."

He took his suitcase. "Okay. You guys get some rest," he said to the kids. "I'll see you tomorrow."

She watched him walk away, a pang of regret tugging at her heart now that they were home and the friendship they'd shared in Argentina was coming to an end. Without letting herself linger on thoughts of the two of them, she turned to the kids. "This way."

When they got to the house that her mother always facetiously referred to as "my little cottage," Sandra gasped. "You live here?"

It was no little cottage. The house was a work of art designed by an architect according to her father's wishes for a home that would celebrate the Spanish heritage of the area. What had once truly been a small, two-bedroom house with rotted wood siding sitting on acres of vacant land was now a spectacular adobe estate with grand arches and balconies that overlooked a courtyard covered with flowers and fountains and green rows of grapevines.

The three of them followed with curiosity gleaming in their eyes. She wondered what was going through their minds. If they wanted to know more about her now that they were forced to live with her? How much should she share? Should she volunteer information?

"Yes. This is home." Isabel opened her front door, and everything was exactly the same as she'd left it.

They walked around. Adelmo nodded. "Not bad. Small but cozy."

Isabel smiled. The boy had a good sense of humor. Then he saw the one extravagance her father had allowed her to have. The wall separating the living room and Isabel's private home office was actually a floor-to-ceiling aquarium.

"Wow," he said. The girls ran to his side, and they stared wide-eyed with smiles on their faces.

Isabel gazed at her old fishy friends swimming in and out of algae or sleeping behind coral.

"Look at that one!" Julieta pointed excitedly at the Fu Manchu lionfish.

"Interesting-looking, isn't he?" Isabel said. "He's a lionfish."

Julieta giggled. "He doesn't look like a lion."

"Well, he's a predator like a land lion. His spines are

poisonous. But this one isn't too bad. He likes to hide in the rocks and doesn't bother other fishes much."

"What's that one?" Adelmo asked.

"That's called a raccoon butterfly fish."

They spent a few minutes identifying the different species and talking about how cool they all were. Isabel enjoyed sharing her love of sea life with them, and it was great to see the look of wonder in their eyes. How fulfilling it must be to be a marine educator and lead groups of students on ocean tours every day.

"What are you going to do with this aquarium when you move, Isabel?" Sandra asked.

"I'll have to leave it. It's part of the house." This had been her home for years. Though she wanted to sell the winery, she lamented having to leave her home. Who would move in? The corporate partners who would purchase the winery probably had their own homes. They wouldn't be interested in the house. They might use it as a guesthouse. Even though her heart ached at losing her personal refuge, where she'd hidden away from the stress of business and dreamed of a different life, she'd find something just as nice close to the ocean.

"The fish too?"

"Probably. We'll see," Isabel said. "You know, it's funny...my parents fought me on putting in this aquarium, but they loved it once they saw it. Maybe the new owners will as well."

"Too bad I didn't get to meet your parents," Sandra said, picking up a framed picture that Isabel kept on a bookcase beside the aquarium of her mother, father, and herself. "This is my grandmother's sister?"

Isabel smiled, finding that the question touched her deeply for some reason. "Yes." Maybe it was the way that she phrased it, or the fact that she brought up her mother, but at this moment she felt a close bond with Sandra. With all three kids.

"I need to go to the bathroom," Julieta said, pulling Isabel's attention back to the other two. "I'll take you." She grabbed Julieta's hand and turned to Sandra. "I need to clean a lot of things out of here before I sell the business. Maybe you all can help me."

They all nodded.

"Good." Isabel took Julieta to the bathroom.

When she returned, Adelmo was sitting on her sofa and bouncing slightly up and down. "You didn't have far to go for your afternoon siesta," he said. "You work close to your house."

"People don't take siestas in this country." It had been so long since she'd heard someone talk about a siesta.

"No?" he said, and jumped to his feet. "My father wouldn't have liked it here. He *loved* to come home for a siesta."

"My father didn't either when he first moved to this country." Isabel locked the front door even though there was little need since the gates were locked at the entrance and no one could reach the cottage. "He moved here because Nick convinced him it was a smart idea, but the first couple of years he regretted it, I think." They'd planted the vines. They had no grapes. No income. They were buying grapes from other vineyards and trying to build their accounts. Their savings were dwindling and their stress level was high.

Adelmo shook his head and gazed at her like they had all lost their minds.

Sandra gave him a little shove.

"Hey, what'd you do that for?" He frowned.

"Just shut up."

"I didn't say anything."

"You were about to."

"How do you know? Think you can read my mind?"

Isabel wondered if kids bickered a lot. And was she supposed to stop it? Get involved? "Well, let's get you all settled in your rooms."

She'd asked Stephanie to move her things into her parents' old room so that Sandra could have her room. Julieta got the spare room, and Adelmo would sleep in the small den where her father used to sit in the evenings and read the newspaper. It had a TV, lots of books, and a computer. Isabel figured he'd like this room best.

Stephanie also arranged for dinner to be delivered to them from Pat & Oscars in town. So after they unpacked, they ate a tomato-fredo pasta bowl each and a great salad. Sitting around the table for the first time together made Isabel realize how little they had to say to each other. A weighty silence settled between them, and the kids picked at their food, or stared at the fish, or yawned. Maybe they were too tired to eat. She was, so she collected the dishes before they finished.

Sandra took a shower and then went right to sleep. Adelmo asked to watch TV, so she let him. And Julieta needed to be held. She cried and Isabel felt immediate, intense panic rise in the pit of her stomach. What in the world did one do with crying children?

She took her hand. "Shhh, it's okay. I know it's not the same as your house. But I'm sure you'll learn to like it." She walked her to her bedroom. "See how nice it is? Cute bed. Big room."

"I want my mommy," Julieta wailed.

"Oh God, help me," Isabel said, looking around the room for something to distract the girl. When nothing was available, she picked her up and sat with her in bed. "Shhh, Julieta. Come on, work with me." She caressed her curly hair and pulled her quivering body close to her own. "I know I'm not Mommy, but I'm going to try really hard to take good care of you, okay?"

"But I want Mommy."

"I know, baby. I know." She kissed the top of Julieta's warm head. "I think Mommy is in heaven watching you right now. She's saying, 'Julieta, there's nothing to cry about. Your cousin Isabel will take care of you.'"

"But I want Mommy to take care of me." She sniffed.

"I'm sure she wishes she could. And that she could hug you like I am," Isabel said with a catch in her voice. She knew how to handle declining sales, grape crops that didn't yield what had been expected, dissatisfied customers, but she didn't know how to give this child the only thing she desperately needed—her mother.

Julieta squeezed in tighter.

Isabel continued to hold her and rocked her gently until she eventually fell asleep; even Isabel almost dozed off. But she was able to slip out of Julieta's hold and out of the room. She glanced into the den and saw Adelmo still watching TV. She turned away and collapsed into her bed. This was going to be hard work.

* * *

A strange poke and shaking drew Isabel out of an uneasy, dream-filled sleep. She rolled over with a moan.

"Cousin Isabel." A tiny, high-pitched voice with tears accompanied the poking this time.

Isabel sat up quickly, startled. She blinked in the darkness and saw the small figure beside her bed. "Julieta?"

"I'm scared."

God, she was so tired. "Honey, scared of what?"

"I don't know."

"Well, there's nothing to be scared of. Go back to sleep, okay?" She patted her on the head, then dropped back under her blankets, lovely, warm sleep returning.

A whimper started, followed by a quick staccato of little sobs, almost as if she were trembling. Isabel immediately sat up again. "No, Julieta, don't start that again." She wasn't sure what to do. "Come here." She pulled the little girl close, intent on having her sit for a moment so she could reassure her that there was nothing to fear. But Julieta didn't just sit; she climbed into Isabel's bed and cuddled beside her, her tears subsiding.

Isabel glanced down at the curly head pressed to her breast. She sighed. "Feeling better?"

"Mmm," she said, and slid down until she lay on the bed.

"Ah." Julieta didn't think she was going to sleep here, did she? In *her* bed? Touching Julieta's hair, she pulled it back away from her tear-stained face. Her eyes were closed and she looked comforted and...asleep.

Isabel dropped down on her back. Dear Lord, was this what she had to look forward to for however long it took to sell the winery? Being woken up in the middle of the night? Losing not only her waking hours, but also her bed at night?

She rolled to the side, facing Julieta, who breathed deeply now. She pulled the blankets across to cover her. Poor thing. First night in a new house with a cousin she barely knew. *Oh, Brenda, there had to be someone better than me.*

"I'm frightened, too, Julieta," she whispered. Not right away, but eventually, she fell back asleep.

Morning wasn't much better. A TV blared early, and when Isabel dragged herself to the living room, she saw three kids watching cartoons. Blankets and pillows were strewn all over the lush, white carpeting, wrappers and drink containers from McDonald's beside them. Toys were scattered on the couch and on the floor, trapping Adelmo's cars in gridlock as they circled the living room.

She stared, unbelieving. How could these kids make such a mess in such a short amount of time? Nick slept on the floor with them. When had he gotten here?

Rubbing her forehead with her fingertips, she turned around. Coffee. Strong coffee. Thankfully, Stephanie had restocked the kitchen with essentials. She found the filters, pulled one out, and poured the grounds thickly inside. She loaded the reservoir with water and pushed the button to get the coffeepot working. As it began to percolate and hiss, Nick came around and sat on the bar stool.

"Hey," he said. "I got them McDonald's. Got you a sandwich too."

She shook her head and held her stomach in disgust. "Thank you but coffee is all I need."

"Rough night?"

"Julieta came to sleep with me."

"She told me."

"Do you think she'll do that often?"

"Don't know."

"And I think we need a rule about eating at the table."

"Oh." He looked over his shoulder at the mess on the floor. "Right."

"And keeping toys in their rooms."

He smiled and scratched the back of his mussed hair. "Anything else?"

"No TV, and silence is probably too much to ask for, so I guess no, nothing else."

"I'll go tell them to clean up."

She reached for a coffee cup. "Thanks."

"Yep." He stood. "You have plans for today?"

"Plans?" She took a drink of her dark, strong coffee and moaned, closing her eyes. "Oh, this is perfect."

When she opened her eyes, Nick was staring as if mesmerized.

"Sorry," she said. "Why did you ask about plans?"

"Well, I thought I'd take them out this morning. To give them something to do."

"Great idea," she said immediately. She needed to unpack and get her mind straight, and she'd do that much easier without the children around. In fact, the first thing she needed to do was check in with Stephanie. No doubt she had meetings to attend in relation to the sale of Gallegos.

"Maybe I'll take them to the Wild Animal Park. Get some fresh air. Burn some energy. Run around a bit. Kids need that," Nick continued.

How did he know what kids needed? Not that Isabel was in a mood to argue the point at the moment.

"Good." She nodded. "Perfect." Then she paused. "Can you watch all three at once?"

"I'll keep them right by my side."

"Watch Julieta carefully."

"I will."

"And make sure nothing frightens her, please."

He smiled as he turned away, as if her worries were ludicrous.

She sipped her coffee and thought that Nick had much more nerve than she did. She didn't feel comfortable even watching them alone within these walls, much less in a public place like a zoo.

Groaning, she wondered how she was ever going to make this work.

Chapter Eleven

Rosa hated that the kids were grown and out of the house. She hated to be divorced. Never did she imagine that her marriage would fall apart the way it did. All she'd ever wanted was to fall in love and live happily ever after. But it had never really been happy, if she were honest with herself. Passionate for a while, then when that faded, it had just been her caring for a big kid. And one day she simply decided she couldn't and didn't want to be a man's mother anymore.

Of course, knowing that she needed to move on and actually moving on were two different matters. Some things were harder to accept than others. For example, no one coming home for dinner every night after years of having a household of hungry mouths to feed created an emptiness inside her and a sad loneliness she didn't want to explore. But the last thing she wanted was to have a pity party for herself. She'd made the decision to let her marriage go, and she had to live with the choice.

When her son Nicolas called asking if she had a toolbox with different types of screwdrivers that he could borrow, she immediately volunteered to bring it over. Anything to have contact with her sons and to feel useful again.

Nicolas was such a hardworking boy. He agreed to

help a friend's father do repairs on his apartment building to earn extra cash. She was proud of her children. They'd all turned out to be responsible, loving young people. She and Franco had done a good job, considering they'd started a family when they'd been so immature and barely out of high school.

As she was combing through her hot storage room for tools that Franco might have left when he moved out, she decided to abandon the search and surprise her son with his very own toolbox. She grabbed her purse and caught a bus downtown to the large home improvement store that had opened up about three years ago. She still preferred the small family-owned ferreterías that were more prominent when she was younger. The owners of those small shops knew where everything was and the best tools to use to complete each job. In these large warehouses, she felt lost, but since this was close and the bus let her out a block away from the store, she went willingly.

Once inside, she lovingly picked out a red toolbox, one that was not too large but not too small. She chose not only screwdrivers, but also a mixture of tools for him to fill the toolbox. There wasn't much she could do for her boys anymore. Feed them, of course—they still needed good food. But this would be a nice surprise for him. Once she was satisfied with her selection, she got in line to check out.

"Rosa?"

She looked over her shoulder and saw *that man*, Ramiro, behind her. Of all the unpleasant people to run into. "Oh, hello."

He had a basket loaded with items she didn't recognize, and he looked like he'd come straight from the fields into the store. Judging by the odor emanating from his clothes, he'd likely been working with fertilizer. It figured that an overpowering smell of shit would come from him.

"Buying a few tools, I see."

"Yes, I am." She put her items on the belt as she reached the register. She paid and walked out without looking at him.

Ramiro paid for his purchase quickly and hurried after Rosa. He saw that she was headed to the bus stop. "Rosa, wait."

She stopped. "I'm sorry, didn't I say good-bye?"

"No, you didn't. Listen," he said, "would you like a ride. My truck is over—"

"No, thank you."

He reached for her toolbox. "Really, I'll carry this for you and give you a ride wherever you want."

She held on to the toolbox as if he were a thief trying to steal her purse. "I'm fine. I don't need help or a ride. Thank you." She frowned, gazing at him without asking what was bringing on this Good Samaritan behavior. "Good-bye, Ramiro."

"How about dinner?"

She gaped at him. "Dinner?"

"Yes. You don't need a ride or help, but everyone needs food. You eat, right?"

"Yes, but—"

"Great! Where can I pick you up?"

"I'm not going to dinner with you." Her face reddened in anger, and the pulse at the base of her throat began to throb.

"Oh." He grinned, because she looked flustered and confused. And cute. "You don't like me very much, do you?"

Rosa clenched her jaw and looked Ramiro squarely in the eye. "No."

"Why not?"

Rosa pointed her free hand accusingly at Ramiro. "You blackmailed my best friend into signing over custody of her children. Children that Brenda and Andres wanted *her* to raise. And for God knows what reason—"

"Because they're my brother's kids. They should live with me. Not in a foreign country with a woman they don't know and who doesn't give a shit about them." The words came out harsher than he wanted. He was trying to be charming, but damn it, she had no right to question his motives.

"And you do? Give a shit?" She dropped her arm back to her side.

He almost laughed, except that her attitude made him angry. "Yes, they're my family."

"I think," Rosa said slowly, shaking her head, "if you had any love for your brother, you would have respected his wishes. They chose Isabel for a reason, and though neither you nor I know why, *she* is supposed to be the one the children are destined to grow up with."

Not for the first time, Ramiro asked himself if he was insane for pursuing custody of three kids he didn't even know. He had tried telling himself to let it go. Andres, the asshole, never gave them a chance to reconcile their relationship. He was always jealous. Deep down, he didn't believe his wife chose him wholeheartedly. But she had.

Brenda hadn't loved Ramiro like she'd loved Andres. She'd been intrigued and the bad girl in her had wanted a good time. At least for a little while. But what they had hadn't been serious—had never been intimate. To hold a few dates against him for so many years had been stupid. But Andres had been cold and judgmental and...well, it didn't matter now.

He gazed at Rosa. "Maybe I don't love my brother at all. But his hijos are still my family. You probably don't know what it feels like to be alone, to go home to an empty house every day and have no family to visit, but it's awful."

Rosa's gaze softened, but then she looked away. "We all get what we deserve. If you don't have a family, there must be a reason."

Ramiro ran a hand over his face and tried to collect his thoughts. Rosa was pretty, and he'd wanted to make a good impression on her to clear his reputation. He wanted Isabel to feel good about the decision she made, and he wanted Sra. Dominga to realize that he meant well. Perhaps if they became friends, the children could visit her. It would be much better if they could all get along. But Rosa didn't appear to want to be his ally.

"The reason is that I didn't fight for the family I had back then. And I'm not making the same mistake again. I'll fight for my nieces and nephew. And though I'd prefer to be your friend, I'll fight you, too, if you try to get in my way."

Rosa lifted her chin and blinked. "I won't get in your way. Isabel made her decision."

"Yes, she did. I guess you did too." He took his cart to his truck and turned around to watch Rosa wait for the bus. *Too bad*, he thought. He would have liked to make dinner for her and to share some time with a nice woman. Too bad.

When Isabel and the kids faced each other alone the next day, without Nick, she had decided she would approach parenting with the same efficiency she used to run a business. If her strategies had helped her build a winery—a complex business—out of nothing, it could certainly help her parent three children for a while.

She ordered breakfast in and sat down to plan. She'd always been able to lead an organized life, because she was good at planning and scheduling.

"The first thing we have to do is get you guys enrolled in school," she said over coffee for herself and hot chocolate for them. If they were going to live with her for six months, they would have to go to school.

Sandra and Adelmo didn't look happy about that.

"We're going into my office today, and my secretary, Stephanie, will find you a good private school."

They stared at her dispassionately.

"Won't that be good?"

Adelmo shrugged. Sandra nodded. And Julieta announced that she was too young for school.

"You'll go to preschool. You'll learn to paint and write your letters and get to play with blocks and clay and things like that."

"I already know my letters and playing with blocks is for babies."

Note to self: Julieta is not a baby. "Of course. You'll learn to write paragraphs and computer programs, and you'll play with—"

"Puzzles?"

"There you go. Puzzles," Isabel said, tossing her arms up for emphasis.

Julieta grinned.

"*I'd* like to learn to write computer programs," Adelmo said.

Surprised that he'd volunteered anything, Isabel quickly turned her attention to him. "Would you?"

He shrugged. "Sure."

"Okay. We'll arrange for you to take computer classes. How about you, Sandra?"

"Just regular school is fine," she said without enthusiasm.

Out of the three, Isabel felt the most for Sandra. She was the oldest and always tried to be so strong and mature. "Well, let's get going. And you'll really have to behave when we get into the offices, okay?"

"Okay," Adelmo said, as if she were speaking only to him.

Sandra continued to scowl, and Julieta took Isabel's hand and skipped happily.

Awkwardly, she led them to the offices, where she was greeted with excitement and hugs. She introduced the children as her nieces and nephew, even though they were in fact second cousins.

To Stephanie, who knew the entire story, Isabel instructed, "You need to find them schools. Adelmo would like to learn about computers."

Stephanie took notes as they settled the children into one of the conference rooms. Isabel leaned on the arm of a chair and turned to look Sandra, Adelmo, and Julieta each in the eyes. "I'll be back. Stay with Stephanie and...I'll be back." She walked out of the room, breathing a sigh of relief. The rest of the morning she spent in meetings with lawyers. The realization that she really would be finished with the winery soon if it sold was mind-blowing. Would she recognize herself as someone other than Isabel Gallegos, president of Gallegos Wines?

After the meetings, she sat in the quiet of her office, only the hum of the light above making any sound. She thought of her old dreams and felt...old. No one began work on their lifelong dreams at almost fifty.

On impulse, she called a friend of hers who was a Realtor. "I want to buy a beach house. No, nothing big. A couple of rooms. Huntington Beach is fine. Perfect."

Through the years, Nick had built a collection of beautiful cars, from Land Rovers to the BMW M6 convertible he was washing when Beth came over. He paused and watched her get out of her car and walk across the sidewalk. Beautiful, patient, loving Beth. He should run to her, pick her up into his arms, and marry her today. What was he doing going down the same road with Isabel? Even Isabel thought he was crazy not to hightail it out of her life.

"The first time I saw you, you were driving an old sixty-seven Mustang, and it was gorgeous. Like you," she said when she reached him.

Nick smiled. She'd always accused him of being more beautiful than she was, which of course had made him laugh and playfully accuse *her* of being the best-looking. Theirs had been a gentle, sweet relationship, but it lacked... passion. "Wish I hadn't sold it. It was a great car."

A shadow of loss dulled her usual bright eyes. She was finished waiting for him, and they both knew it.

"Thank you for coming. Let me finish waxing this and then we can go for a drive." He quickly ran the buffing cloth along the surface of the car, bringing out a spectacular shine. She watched him. When he was finished, he put all his bottles and various rags into his plastic carrier, grabbed its handle, and put it away in the garage. Beth was waiting for him in his car when he returned.

"We don't need to go anywhere, Nick," she said. "Just say what you need to say."

He sat in his bucket seat and stared at the steering wheel, his fingers wrapping around it, tightening and loosening. "I don't know what to say."

"You love her. You want her back."

"Not really." He gazed at her. "I don't want her back. I want to get on with my life without her. But..."

"You still love her."

He reached for Beth's hand. "I'm sorry." She wasn't a lady who yelled or fought. While he'd been in Argentina, she'd said her piece, told him he was foolish, expressed her anger at him for making her waste so many years waiting for him. Now she looked resigned.

"Me too." Tears filled her eyes. "Do you really think she can make you happy this time? She hasn't changed."

"I don't know. But maybe having the family we both wanted, being parents to Brenda's kids, will make all five of us whole somehow. I want to try." Not that Isabel had given any indication that she wanted him back. In fact, she said she didn't. But maybe, in time, she'd come around. She'd been his wife. She'd rocked his world from the first instant he'd met her when she'd been so alive and ready for life. With her, he'd learned to look at the world differently, at what was possible, rather than as a curse he had to endure. Yes, he still loved her, and maybe she'd realize that she still loved him too.

Beth sniffed away tears and nodded. "Okay." She turned and gave him a long hug, and just as quickly, she turned away and flew out of the car. He watched her leave, feeling like the biggest asshole in the world. A fool. Because the truth was that Isabel had never loved him like he'd wanted to be loved. The passion and drive that attracted him to her was what kept her too preoccupied with other things to offer him anything but leftovers. And now he planned to serve her his heart on a platter all over again.

He started the car and headed to an Alcoholics Anonymous meeting. He didn't attend often, but he still went every once in a while and he volunteered to be a mentor when someone needed one. Having been sober for almost ten years now put him in a position to help others.

At the group meeting, he sat in the circle and listened to other people's stories. They were all versions of his own. Unique because each person ended up in this spot for different reasons. But he could relate to most of them. As they spoke about what they missed about drinking, he broodingly wished he could shake his head in a superior way and say he didn't know what they were talking about. But as one woman spoke about seeing the world through the alcoholic haze, he remembered the feeling all too well.

He remembered stumbling out of the Pala Casino, muffled bells and tinny music from the slot machines following him out. Leaving behind the happy voices that he pretended belonged to people who liked and approved of him. Warm air greeting him, fanning his face once outside as he wove a path to his car. Easing the seat back and staring out of his sunroof at the black sky that looked almost like velvet, he'd felt great. The party atmosphere made him feel less lonely. When it wasn't Pala, it was a bar in downtown San Diego or Orange County. Always far away. Always noisy. That's when he got the most drunk.

He drank in his office at Gallegos and at home too. But that consisted of a glass or two of wine, a few bottles of beer. Enough to give him a confidence, a bravado he seemed to lack otherwise.

He sat back and reminisced tonight. Afraid in a weird way that deciding to pursue a relationship with Isabel would somehow lead him back to the man he'd been then. But he shook away those thoughts. He'd never be that man again. He refused. As things wrapped up, he shared a cup of coffee with others and offered advice and encouragement. This was who he was now. Responsible. Someone others could lean on. Not perfect, but far enough removed from who he used to be to know that guy was gone for good.

Chapter Twelve

Life with children made for a different rhythm, Isabel thought as she pulled Julieta out of bed for the second time. "Honey, come on, put your shoes on."

Julieta lay on her back, moaning. "I'm tired."

Sandra paused at the door. "You have to put her shoes on for her, if you want them on."

Isabel looked over her shoulder at Sandra, who was already dressed and watching them.

"I'll do it." She walked inside and took little white sandals out of the closet.

Isabel got to her feet. "Thank you. Is your brother out of his room?"

"Probably not."

Isabel stepped around the girls and knocked on Adelmo's door. This slower pace called on her rarely practiced trait of patience. "Adelmo, are you dressed?"

"Almost," he called from the other side of the door.

"Can you hurry, please?"

She encouraged them to brush their hair and teeth, and they finally made it to breakfast. They all sat at the kitchen table and waited as Isabel prepared something. She wasn't a breakfast person, but growing children had to eat, so she took out an egg carton. She could make scrambled eggs. Easy enough. She cracked a half dozen into a pan and added salt and pepper. Some salsa would be nice, but no one knew what salsa was in Argentina, so she figured she'd skip it and add some cheese instead. They seemed to take forever to cook, probably because she was in a hurry. She moved the thick mixture around with a wooden spoon. Finally, when the glop seemed to have firmed up, she dished it out onto three plates and grated cheese on top.

Looking around for something else, she added a slice of bread. She wished she had bacon. She'd have to remember to buy some. She took the first two plates into the dining room, placed them on the table, and hurried back to get the last. The three kids stared at their plates. Just a hint of steam came from the eggs, but Isabel didn't think they were too hot to eat.

"Something wrong?" She poured milk for each of them.

Sandra made a face. "Thank you, Isabel, but we don't usually eat so much food for breakfast."

"You don't?" She didn't notice them complaining when Nick brought them fast food from McDonald's for breakfast. Kids—Argentine, American, didn't matter—all loved junk food.

"Just a cup of café con leche and a piece of bread is fine."

"Really?" She took a seat. "Aren't you a little young to drink coffee?" She tried to remember how old she was when she started drinking coffee, and couldn't. Heck, she'd always drunk coffee.

"My mom always served us coffee and bread like Sandra said," Adelmo agreed. He took the bread and began to eat it. "Thanks."

Sandra ate her bread as well.

Isabel returned to the kitchen and made them both a cup of coffee with lots of cream and sugar.

Isabel glanced at Julieta. "You don't drink coffee, do you?"

"I like the milk."

"Good."

"Can I have dulce de leche on my bread?"

"Don't have any. Sorry. You want honey?"

"Okay."

She got the honey from the kitchen and brought it back to the table. She watched the little girl happily eat her bread, and smiled.

Once she managed to get them fed, she loaded them into her Lexus, grateful that she'd chosen a sedan rather than a smaller, sportier style. As she buckled Julieta inside, she sighed. Dang it, she was so little. She needed a car seat or booster or whatever kids her age used. Having no option but to have her go without, she drove them to school and made a mental note to buy a car seat on her way back home.

Stephanie had found them each a perfect school for their age and academic level, but the problem was that Adelmo went to one school and the girls to another. By the time she became free of the morning domestic duties, it was after ten and she was exhausted.

She drove back home and sat in her office, savoring the quiet and trying to catch her breath. Waking up and facing three little expectant faces in the morning jump-started her in a way she found... terrifying. She was used to getting up early, working out, showering, and having her first cup of coffee at her desk as she reviewed the plans for the day.

Shaking her head, she turned on her computer and began to strategize the next phase of her life. But before she knew it, just when she got inspired, it was time to rush back to school and pick up the kids.

After a week of this, she called Stephanie. "I need help," she said.

Stephanie simply laughed.

"Is there such a thing as a domestic personal assistant?" She explained her dilemma.

"Honey, you need a full-time nanny. I'd be happy to hire one for you."

"Thanks, Steph." Everything Stephanie had been doing for the kids had been a huge favor; Isabel understood that. In the past, Isabel never asked Stephanie to run personal errands or to get involved in her private matters. Mostly because she didn't have a private life. Work *was* her life. "I owe you."

"No, you don't."

"Thank you. I'm drowning."

"Now you know what it's like to be a single mom."

Yes, she thought. She had a new appreciation for women who did this every day of their lives, juggling work and kids. How the hell did they do it?

Isabel hung up the phone and groaned when she noticed the time. "Wonderful." She got her car keys and headed to the schools.

* * *

School was very long in America. They had recess, lunch, then a second recess and classes in between. In Argentina, Adelmo was used to going to school in the morning session where the day ended when he went home for lunch. They had only one recess, when they played a quick game of soccer. It was fun. But here, at this school, all these breaks were boring.

Mrs. Hall, his third-grade teacher, asked a boy named Daniel to be his buddy and play with him, because she'd noticed him standing alone during recess.

Daniel made an annoyed face and said, "Come on."

Adelmo dropped his hands into his pockets and followed.

Out on the playground, Daniel ran to play with a group of his friends. Adelmo continued to walk toward them. He was in no hurry, and he didn't really care if they played with him or not. For now, he was following Mrs. Hall's order.

Daniel and four other boys stood around talking. As far as Adelmo could understand, they were discussing what to play. Then a couple of older boys walked up to them. Adelmo was pretty sure they were a couple of grades above them.

"What are we playing, Daniel? Did you get a ball?" one of the older guys, a fat boy with blond hair, asked.

"I got a basketball, but we don't want to play basketball." He pointed to Adelmo. "Mrs. Hall said he has to play with us."

The blond kid looked at Adelmo.

"This is my brother, Mark." He said each word slowly to Adelmo as if he were stupid.

"Why the heck are you talking like that?" Mark asked.

"He can't speak English," Daniel explained.

"No, I do," Adelmo said. In Argentina, at his school, they taught English from first grade. Of course, it wasn't a lot. But Mrs. Smith, who had studied English in America, in a state called Michigan, came in twice a week to teach them. So, he'd had three years of English, in first, second, and third grade. He didn't have a huge vocabulary, and it was difficult for him to understand most things people said, but he did speak some English. "I'm Adelmo," he said.

The boys all laughed.

"Elmo?" Mark said. "Like in Sesame Street?"

Again everyone laughed, and Adelmo didn't quite understand why.

"Hey, I have an idea," Mark said. "Let's have a little fun with him. Let's play dodgeball."

"But all I have is a basketball, and it's too hard," Daniel said.

Mark smiled. "That's right." He shoved Adelmo into the center of a circle that he told the other boys to make around him. "Ever play dodgeball, Elmo?"

"No," he said. "My name is Adelmo. Ah-del-mo."

"Yeah, whatever. We're going to throw the ball, like this." He took the ball and threw it at Adelmo. Adelmo caught it as quickly as he could.

"No, no, moron. Don't catch it. Dodge it."

Adelmo was about to walk away. He didn't understand what he was supposed to do, and he didn't want to mess up their game.

"Like this." He took the ball and threw it at Daniel. Daniel jumped out of the way quickly.

"Got it?"

Adelmo nodded.

Then they all made a circle again and started throwing the ball. He was able to move out of the way of the fast-flying ball about three times before it hit him hard on the left side of his back.

Mark picked the ball back up and threw it hard at Adelmo again. He was still recovering from the first hit and couldn't move out of the way. This time it hit him on the shoulder.

"Hey," Daniel said. "You're not playing right. Besides, his turn is over. You hit him, so it's your turn."

"Change of rules, Danny. Only he gets to be it. Get the ball, quick. Move," he shouted.

They threw the ball at Adelmo again.

"No more," Adelmo said, ready to get out of the circle.

But Mark and his older friend didn't stop throwing the ball, so Adelmo didn't have any option but to try to avoid getting hit. But he was getting tired and had been hit so many times on his legs, his back, and his chest that he wasn't as quick as he was the first minute or two playing this game. He wasn't sure he liked this stupid game either.

"Hey, boys!" One of the teachers blew a whistle and walked up to their circle.

"That ball is entirely too hard to play dodgeball with, and besides, you've tagged him many times. Right?"

"Sorry, Mrs. Nielsen." They immediately stopped the game. Then the bell rang and recess was over anyway. The boys all ran away. All except for Daniel.

Adelmo hurt all over. What a crazy game.

"You okay?" Daniel asked as they walked to their line, where the teacher was going to pick up their class.

Adelmo nodded even though he really wasn't okay. Still, if boys in America liked to play rough games like that, he didn't want them to think he was a wimp.

"Good, 'cause you can't tell on my brother to Mrs. Hall, or he'll beat you up. Got it?"

Adelmo frowned. "Tell Mrs. Hall what?"

"Nothing," Daniel said, and got in line.

Confused, Adelmo got in line too.

Sandra was particularly quiet on the drive home. Isabel kept glancing at her in the rearview mirror. The older girl didn't look happy.

"Anything wrong?" Isabel asked.

Sandra shook her head.

"I know it's been tough adjusting."

Sandra called her grandmother every day, and probably cried herself to sleep if the muffled sounds coming out of her bedroom at night were anything to go by. "Everything is different."

"Yes." Isabel nodded.

"I have no friends."

"You will. That takes time."

"The girls in my class make fun of me because my English is so poor."

"We'll get you a tutor." Isabel smiled into the rearview mirror as she spoke.

Sandra nodded but seemed even more depressed.

Isabel searched her mind for something to cheer her up and at the last moment pulled off the freeway and into a shopping mall. "You all need cell phones so I can get ahold of you, and you me. What do you say? Should we get some phones?"

This got an interested nod from all three kids. For a few moments, they seemed to forget the stresses of school and became involved in choosing the features and colors they liked best in their phones. Julieta thought it was the coolest thing in the world to be offered her very own phone.

Seeing the smiles on their faces brought Isabel her own brand of happiness. She wanted them to adapt, to hurt less, to be happy. And she wanted to be a good substitute for her cousin, at least for a little while. When they returned to Argentina, Ramiro would become the legal guardian, but she didn't intend to turn her back on them entirely. She still wanted to be part of their lives. She would establish college funds for them and visit at least once a year. She would call Ramiro and explain to him that she expected contact to continue. The kids were family. They were part of her life now, and she wanted to do a good job. But she just didn't know how yet.

They left the mall with three new phones.

"Tomorrow I've got a meeting with my lawyer and a Realtor," she said to Sandra, who sat on the passenger side now. "What do you say you come with me, and then we'll do something together, just the two of us."

Sandra seemed pleasantly surprised. "What about school?"

"Well, I guess you get a day off."

After only a week. Probably a bad idea. But maybe

Sandra needed more than book learning right now. Isabel was willing to give it a try.

After dropping Adelmo and Julieta off at school, Isabel and Sandra drove to the Realtor's office. He showed them three beach houses that matched what Isabel was looking for: *on* the beach, not just near it; small, no more than two bedrooms; and in perfect move-in condition. One home in Laguna Beach looked promising. Isabel could see herself living in it, getting up early in the mornings and going for a run, maybe a swim in the ocean. Then having breakfast and heading over to the Pacific Marine Mammal Center and volunteering to help injured sea lions. She'd smell like sun and salt and fish, and there wouldn't be a grapevine within miles.

She promised the Realtor she'd think it over and make a decision soon. Since her requirements were minimal, the home seemed perfectly acceptable, so why not take it?

Wrapping up this business by noon, she and Sandra went out to lunch at a little vegetarian place called The Stand. They sat under a shade tree and waited a few moments for someone to come take their order. Quickly, before she had the chance to enjoy the outdoor atmosphere, they were served.

"So you're going to buy that last place?" Sandra asked.

"Thinking of it, yes."

"Wow. The ocean is amazing. So immense and powerful and what do you call it when it makes you feel alive and like you can do anything?"

"Inspiring?"

"Inspiring, yes. I never would have imagined." Sandra ordered the same sandwich as Isabel, tomato, sprouts, onions, and avocado. But she took only one bite. She ate instead the plate of tortilla chips that Isabel didn't touch.

"I think so too. When I was your age, I used to dream about living and working close to the ocean."

Sandra dipped her chips in guacamole and listened.

"I used to go to the library and check out all the books I could find on sea life and the ocean. We had no Internet back then, so books and movies were all I had. Then I went to Mar del Plata and saw it in person and my heart felt like...like it had come home. I saved all my money to take trips to the sea whenever I could, and I promised myself that when I was older, I'd work to protect the oceans and the animals that lived in it."

"Why didn't you?"

Because life doesn't always give you what you want, she thought. But she smiled. "It wasn't as easy as I thought."

"But you came to America and made tons of money. You could have done it. I mean, you don't have kids or a husband. You could have, couldn't you?"

Isabel saw the enthusiasm and faith in the impossible in Sandra's eyes, and her heart lurched just a touch. She'd had the same naive belief that everything was possible when she was younger. "I didn't have children, but I did have my parents, who needed my help. So, I had to give up that dream. Some things just aren't meant to be, Sandra."

"My mom used to tell me anything was possible if I wanted it bad enough."

Probably because Isabel herself used to tell Brenda the very same thing. But if that were true, she'd be a marine biologist today. There was nothing she had wanted more. "Your mother was right. She wanted your father. And you kids. I think she got everything she ever wanted."

They both grew quiet.

"This beach house will allow me to have a little of what I wanted. I won't be out saving penguins on the coast of Argentina, but I'll get a taste of ocean life at least."

Sandra finished her chips and looked at her sandwich with distaste, then sighed and gazed at Isabel. "I think the beach is awesome." She stared at the surfers on the waves out in the distance across PCH. "I'd love to do that."

Sandra's words had the effect of touching someone and receiving an electrical shock; they zapped Isabel's interest, and she angled her head. "Would you?"

"Of course! How great would that be?"

"Well, I'll make you a deal." Isabel leaned across the table.

"What?"

"You order a sandwich that you actually like, and eat it, and I'll see about getting you surfing lessons."

"You're serious?" Sandra's eyes grew wide and she sat straight up in her booth.

"Very serious."

"Isabel, that would be . . . way cool, amazing, the most exciting thing to ever happen to me in my whole life."

Isabel smiled. The whole ten years of her life. "What kind of sandwich will it be?"

"Oh, I'll eat this one." She picked it up and plopped the avocados out, then the onions. And she ate the rest with a smile on her face.

Isabel decided that Sandra was the most perfect child in the world. Bright. Kind. Mature. Friendly. Had Brenda's great looks. She had everything going for her. And Isabel was going to make sure that she had every advantage in life. Everything that she herself hadn't had.

Chapter Thirteen

❧

*A*fter one last check of the fermentation tanks' temperature, Nick mentally signed himself off work and walked toward the cottage to see how Isabel was doing with the kids. He'd done his best to stay away unless she called and asked for help. But Isabel being Isabel hadn't, and probably wouldn't. When he saw her at the office and asked how she was doing, all she said was fine and that the children were in school. Julieta cried a little less. Adelmo seemed quiet and had caused no trouble. Sandra didn't like school. She would deliver the news briefly, then continue with whatever she was doing at the time.

But when he knocked on the door, she wasn't home. The kids were with a woman they said was their nanny, which after two weeks home shocked the hell out of him. Isabel had already managed to get them into school *and* hire a babysitter? So much for spending time with them and getting to know them. And so much for promising to let him help out.

Sandra and Adelmo were doing homework on the kitchen table. "What's with the nanny?" he asked.

"Isabel needed help so she could work more," Sandra said, looking up from her math.

Why hadn't she said anything? Nick leaned in and whispered, inclining his head toward the nanny. "What does she do?" The woman was sitting on the couch watching the channel eleven news.

Adelmo rolled his eyes. "Tells me to use an inside voice."

"She picks us up from school and watches us until Isabel comes home," Sandra amended.

Nick nodded. "Got it. Where's Julieta?"

"In her room," Adelmo said.

"Be right back." He peeked into her room and saw her playing with her dolls. He smiled and knocked on the open door.

"Hi, Nick," she said, getting up and giving him a hug.

He spent some time talking to her, then decided to go make some dinner. He told the nanny she could go home, which she seemed happy to do.

Then he headed to the kitchen.

"What are you doing?" Adelmo jumped up onto the bar stool and watched Nick stare into the pantry.

"Looking to see what I can make for dinner." He studied Isabel's meager items.

"You cook?"

He laughed. "Of course. I eat—that means I cook."

"My dad never cooked."

"Why not?" Nick gripped the edge of the bar, placing his weight on his arms as he paused to chat with the boy.

"Mom cooked."

"What if your mom couldn't or wasn't home?"

Adelmo twisted back and forth on the rotating bar stool. "We ate toast."

Nick made a face. "Not me. Not relying on a woman to cook for me. Not this dude."

Adelmo laughed.

Nice sound to hear. He seemed to be accepting his new life better than Nick had expected. "Go finish your homework and you can help me, if you want."

He shrugged. "Okay." Then he paused. "You know a game called dodgeball?"

"Sure," Nick said. "Do you play at school?"

He nodded. "I did one time but didn't like it because it hurt when the ball kept hitting me. The boys call me chicken-shit because I don't want to play."

"What do you mean the ball keeps hitting you? It can only hit you once, Adelmo; then you get out of the center. But if you don't want to play, then don't."

Adelmo explained how they'd played and how the boys had placed him in the center alone. Nick frowned as he remembered the rules of the game. It started with everyone but two people in the center of the circle, and as you were hit, you got out of the circle. The last one in the middle was the winner.

"Guess what, buddy. Those boys played a trick on you." He explained the rules.

Adelmo didn't look happy.

"Maybe you should play with other boys. Or tell them you want to play the game the right way."

Pensively, he nodded. "Thanks, Nick." He slid off the stool.

"Hey, Adelmo," Nick said. "Guys sometimes test the new kid, you know. Sort of like an initiation. Don't take it personally, okay?"

"Yeah, maybe you're right."

"But if they're really picking on you or you're scared, talk to a teacher."

Adelmo immediately stiffened. "I'm not scared."

Nick grinned. "All right. Well, go finish your school-work and get back in here to help me. I'm hungry."

In better spirits, Adelmo took off to the dining table. And Nick shook his head. Childhood was brutal.

By the time Isabel got home, it was well after nine. At about five in the afternoon, when it looked like she'd be late, she called her nanny's cell and was told that Nick had sent her home at four after she'd returned from picking the kids up from school. Surprised yet relieved, she let the worry about them slip to the back of her mind and focused on her work obligations. Park & Manning, the corporation interested in Gallegos, were still poring through financial records and deciding whether they wanted the winery. She'd contacted them upon her return home and had a friendly conversation with the CEO. He still seemed enthusiastic about the acquisition, but these things never happened quickly, so she tried to be patient. In the meantime, Isabel continued to run her business as she always had. Like an orchestra leader, she had to make sure every department—marketing, sales, production, harvesting, technology, personnel—worked in harmony to produce an excellent final product. Depending on the season, some areas of the business took more time than others, but because she insisted on having input in every aspect of her company, she was always swamped with work.

But now that she was home, she was curious about how Nick had done. Looking comfortable on the couch in front of the television, he glanced at her as she stepped into sight.

"Hi," she said, wondering what to say, even though *What are you doing in my house?* was the first thing that popped into her mind. "This is a pleasant surprise." She put her briefcase down.

At the sound of her voice, Julieta came running out of her bedroom.

"Tía," she squealed, and ran to give Isabel a hug. Isabel hugged her close, then lifted her into her arms. Her hair was moist and she smelled clean and wonderful. Dora the Explorer jammies were on. "Where were you?" she asked.

"Working. Didn't mean to come home so late. I'm sorry."

"My homework is all done."

Isabel grinned. "Really? That's great. And you've had a bath."

Julieta nodded with an adorable smile.

"Now it's story and bedtime, isn't it?" Past her bedtime, actually.

She nodded again. "I waited for you."

Isabel put her down. "Go to your room and I'll be right there."

She ran to Nick and gave him a hug before hurrying to her room. Isabel watched her, knowing she missed her parents—she still cried at night—but she had an amazing kidlike capacity to accept what was. Isabel wished she had that ability.

Even though she was exhausted and starved, she followed Julieta to her bedroom. Julieta had already chosen a book and sat on her bed eagerly awaiting her story. Isabel sat beside her, and Julieta cuddled close, practically on her lap.

"I like when you read to me," Julieta said.

Isabel wrapped an arm around the little girl. "I like reading to you. Did Mommy read to you too?"

Julieta furrowed her brow like she was thinking. "No."

That surprised Isabel.

"But she kissed me good night and tucked me in," Julieta added brightly.

"Well, that's a relief."

Julieta laughed, and Isabel's heart filled with warmth as she wondered if it was possible to love someone so quickly.

"Okay, let's see what we've got here. The teddy bear book again?"

Nodding enthusiastically, Julieta helped to turn the first page. "I like this one."

Isabel figured rereading the same books probably helped her with her English. So she read as animatedly as she could and smiled when Julieta jumped in on sections she already knew by heart.

When the book was over, Julieta moaned and begged for a second book. Isabel almost gave in because she didn't want the special bedtime moments to end either. Holding Julieta close and listening to her sweet voice and cute giggles was addictive. And to think she might never have met this little girl.

As always, her feelings about enjoying her time with Brenda's children were mixed. She never forgot that it should be Brenda sharing these special moments.

"It's late, Julieta. Only one story tonight."

"But, please."

"Sorry." She stood. "Tomorrow, I'll be home earlier and we'll read two. Okay?"

"Promise?"

Isabel turned on the night-light, turned off the room light, and tucked her tightly under her blankets. "Promise."

Julieta wrapped her arms around Isabel's neck. "Thanks, Tía."

A butterfly kiss grazed her cheek.

Isabel disentangled herself and stood, wanting to distance herself from the emotional feelings this girl who now called her *Aunt* awoke. "Good night."

"One more hug?"

Isabel gazed down and with the look on little Julieta's face, she knew she was a goner. She bent down and ran her fingers through Julieta's hair. Julieta tossed an arm around Isabel's shoulder and closed her eyes. Isabel sat on the floor and caressed the girl's scalp, playing with her hair until she fell asleep. Isabel watched her sleep for a few extra minutes, then finally got up and left.

She peeked in on Sandra, who told her all about making a new friend at school. She seemed happy. Then lastly she knocked on Adelmo's door.

"Hi," he said, standing at the threshold of his bedroom, the door barely open.

"Hi. Good day today?"

He shrugged.

"No?"

"Some boys in school pushed me because I didn't

want to play a game, but no big deal. Do I have to go to sleep now?"

"That would be a good idea. But who pushed you?"

"Just some boys." He shrugged. "I'm not going to play with them anymore."

"Probably a smart idea." She didn't pursue the issue, figuring all boys pushed and shoved. Wasn't that what boys did? Besides, he didn't seem particularly bothered by it, and he seemed smart enough to play with nicer kids.

"Okay. Good night." He started to close the door, and since she had nothing left to say, she stepped back and returned to the living room.

"I warmed up your dinner," Nick said from the couch, pointing to the kitchen table.

"Oh." He cooked for her? "Thank you."

She sat and pulled the lid off her plate. A delicious filet of salmon, mashed potatoes, and steamed vegetables lay underneath. Simple and perfect.

Her stomach growled and her mouth watered. "This looks so good. I didn't eat lunch today. You made this?"

He stood and walked around the couch to sit across from her at the table. His lazy smile under the dim lights pulled her attention away from her plate. "Hope you still like fish?" he asked.

For an Argentine raised on a diet heavy in beef, seafood was always a treat that she welcomed. "Love it."

"The kids didn't care for it much, but they ate it."

"Good. Thanks for making dinner."

"Mmm-hmm."

"And for getting them showered and ready for bed."

She held her fork in her hand but continued to look at him a little longer. He continually surprised her lately.

"No problem." His eyes were at half-mast. "Now that you're home, I'm going to get going. Heading to the gym. Gotta stay in shape."

Without meaning to, she checked him out. He'd regained his fantastic body, which he'd lost during his heavy drinking days. Age and alcohol had made his sleek muscles disappear back then. He'd gotten thin except for a belly that had grown past his rib cage, but no more. He was now firm and muscular, and looked damned good.

Caught staring, she cleared her throat. "You look tired."

"So do you." He winked. "Enjoy your dinner and get some sleep."

"Thanks, Nick. For stopping by and...all of this."

"Anytime. I'm happy to help."

He left and she ate the flaky, honey-flavored salmon; the creamy potatoes, perfectly buttered with a hint of garlic; and vegetables with nothing on them except the individual flavors of the carrots and broccoli seeping into her mouth. Nick must be pulling her leg. He couldn't have made this. As she finished, her stomach full, she sighed. How was it that in a house full of people she felt so alone tonight? Crazy.

Chapter Fourteen

A week later, Nick planned a trip to a pumpkin patch. When he suggested it, Isabel agreed immediately. Mostly because it got the children out of the house, but also because they liked him so much and enjoyed seeing him. Once they got to the immense dirt lot blocked off with walls of hay, they had a blast.

"I never saw squashes this big," Adelmo said, kicking up straw as he walked along the path to the entrance.

Isabel smiled. "They're a special kind of squash, called a pumpkin."

"Remember we saw them in that movie?" Sandra said, pointing out the title of an American movie they'd seen while living in Argentina.

Nick led them past the gate and paused at the entrance to pay their ticket fee. He pulled out his wallet and grinned. "Five, please," he said.

The young woman in the little wooden booth at the entrance was cute. She smiled at Nick as she gave him a rundown of what there was to do and see, making flirty jokes and going on longer than she needed to. He took the tickets and thanked her with that brilliant smile of his. Isabel turned away.

They made their way up and down the aisles of pumpkins of various sizes. Julieta got dramatically excited when she saw pigs and goats, her eyes widening and her lips forming an O. Her little body practically vibrated.

"Do you want to pet them?" Nick asked.

"Do I!" She jumped up and down and took his hand.

He glanced at Isabel. "Want to go in with her?"

"You go right ahead," she said.

Nick glanced at the two older kids. Their eyes sparkled with interest, but they would not admit to wanting to pet the animals. "Come on," he said to them. "Keep me company."

Adelmo immediately followed. Sandra shrugged and acted like she might as well get it over with. Isabel stood at the gate, enjoying the look of pleasure on Julieta's face when she touched the wiry hair on the goat's back. The little girl had the most angelic face and the most tender, sweet voice Isabel had ever heard. Her hair felt like rings of goose-down feathers when she brushed it in the morning into little waves that immediately coiled back into their shape. Everything from her soft, pink skin to the wonder of her expressions melted Isabel's heart and reminded her of what a young little girl Julieta still was. A baby.

For the first time since coming home, she thought of Ramiro and his farm. The kids were going to love living on a farm. He had cows and chickens and probably other animals too. But a tug of regret squeezed her heart.

Julieta screamed when a goat pulled on her coat and lazily drew it into his mouth. Julieta tried to climb up Nick's leg in a desperate attempt to get away. Adelmo laughed and smacked her playfully on the back of her head. "Just chase him away." He eased the goat back with his knee and made a *shoosh* sound.

Nick picked her up and smiled as Julieta tried not to break into tears. "Goats eat everything they see. He doesn't want to hurt you."

She nodded, then looked over at Isabel with a pleading look for rescue. Isabel held out her arms, and Nick handed Julieta over. Isabel's heart expanded as she held the child close to her for just a few seconds. She placed Julieta down as Nick, Adelmo, and Sandra left the goats and pigs.

"What do you say we join the carving contest?" Nick led them across the dried fall leaves without waiting for a response. A tent was erected solely to allow those brave enough to carve their pumpkins on the spot to give it a try. He bought tickets for them all.

"I'll watch," Isabel said.

"Oh, come on," he said playfully. "Get your hands dirty."

"I'm fine." She stuck her hands into her coat pocket and stood to the side. The smell of fresh pumpkin filled the tent, making Isabel crave a slice of the pie made from the flesh off this wonderful "squash," as Adelmo called it. With lots of sweet whipped cream.

The kids dug right in, carving the top and pulling the guts out with their hands.

"Ewww." Julieta made a face and stuck her tongue out. "It feels yucky."

Nick moved her aside. "Yucky? Let's see." He stuck his big hands inside. "This feels like worms. No! Maggots inside a cold corpse."

Adelmo grinned. "And the seeds?"

"Seeds? Those are roaches that came to see what was left for them to claim."

Sandra and Julieta stared at him like he was nuts. Adelmo laughed and nodded.

Nick ended up having to help Julieta dig the seeds out and clean her pumpkin.

From the side, Isabel laughed; then she checked her watch. She still hoped to get a little work done this evening.

"Hey," Nick called out to her, wiping his hands on a paper towel that was provided. "For once, don't worry about the time."

"I'm not."

He walked over, a large grin on his face. "I saw you looking at your watch. Liar."

"Caught," she admitted. "I have a bit of work that I need to do."

He reached for her hand. "It'll still be there in the morning. But this day will be gone in just a few hours. Come on. When's the last time you carved a pumpkin?"

She shrugged. "I don't know. Never, I think. I was too old for that when I moved to this country."

He raised an eyebrow. "Then how can you resist?"

Good question. She let him lead her to the table. And rather than carving her own pumpkin, she helped Julieta with hers. Together, they made the cutest pumpkin in the whole batch. At least she thought so. And so did Julieta. Nick and her siblings also agreed that Julieta's was the best. Never having had brothers and sisters herself, Isabel was touched by the sweetness of the older siblings.

They all proudly carried their pumpkins to Nick's truck.

"Do we have to go now?" Adelmo asked.

Isabel was tempted to check her watch again, but she resisted. "Nope, we haven't gone on the hay ride yet."

"Oh boy!" he said, running back inside. Sandra took Julieta's hand and led her toward the hay wagons.

Isabel walked beside Nick. "How am I doing?"

"I'm proud of you," he said. The evening was cool, yet he didn't wear a coat.

She laughed. "I'm proud of you too. You're great with kids, Nick. I'm sorry you didn't get a chance at parenthood when we were married."

He walked with his hands in his pockets, the only hint that he might be a bit cold. "Thanks for giving me the chance to give it a try now."

Breathing in the fresh hay-scented air, she shook her head. "I didn't. You took the role without asking me if I was okay with it."

He frowned and gave her a sideways look. "I didn't mean to push myself on you."

"That's okay. Believe me, I didn't realize how much I'd need you." They walked through the chain-link fence, back into the pumpkin patch. In the distance, young boys and girls giggled and yelled as they ran round the hay bales and bounced on bouncers. "And I don't mean just with the children."

"No need to thank me. Making up for past sins."

"Forget about the past. It's over," she said. All the resentment. All the anger. She wanted it gone. They were different people now. That had become evident to her in the past few weeks.

They reached the hay wagon, and Nick bought tickets. They all climbed on. Isabel sat between Julieta and Nick. "And I'm sorry for all the times I didn't want you around."

He reached for her hand. "No one did."

"My parents did. They always did."

Tears touched his eyes. "I must have been the biggest disappointment ever to them."

She squeezed his fingers. "No. They knew that one day—" Her voice caught. "One day, you'd come out of it. I'm the one who didn't believe it."

He leaned over and dropped a kiss on the side of her face. Innocent and sweet. But as he held her hand and laughed with the children he'd agreed to help her raise, she had completely inappropriate feelings stir within her.

And she checked her watch. She had to get back to her office.

Adelmo leaned against a tree during recess and watched the other students play, bored to death. He wondered if all schools in America were this boring. After more than a month, he didn't seem to understand that much more English either. He had never been a brain or anything, but now he felt stupid. Before the bell rang, he went to get a drink of water.

Three boys circled him, and one pushed him aside. Mark, and his jerk friends who always pushed.

"Che," he said. "What you doing?"

"Getting some water. What does it look like?" Mark said.

"I'm not finished." He stood beside the drinking fountain, stiff and ready to push his way back in.

"Yes, you are. You moved aside. And can't you speak English?"

"Yes," Adelmo answered. He *was* speaking English.

"So, what was your name again? Adogshit?"

The boys laughed.

Adelmo smiled, not really sure what was so funny. "Adelmo," he corrected.

"That's what I said—Adogshit. Are you like from Mexico or something?"

"Me? No." Adelmo shook his head. "Argentina, you know, South America."

They looked at each other and laughed. "Yeah, whatever. Another stupid Spanish kid," he said, bending over the drinking fountain.

Adelmo frowned. Who was he calling stupid? "Hey, stupid are Americans. You know nothing. We have good schools."

"You don't have shit," one of the other boys said. "That's why you all come to our country."

It was frustrating to catch some words and not others. "We have better schools, play better soccer, and I speak English. You don't speak Spanish," Adelmo said proudly, with a smile.

"Shut up," Mark said. "Why would we want to speak Spanish?"

He'd had it trying to talk to these guys. They were rude and didn't want to be his friend, so why was he bothering? "You, shut up," he said, and turned away to go stand by the tree again.

But he was shoved hard from behind and almost fell on his face. The three other boys laughed. Adelmo got instantly hot, his face flaming. He turned back and as they were laughing, he socked Mark in the stomach, making him gasp for air as he bent over.

"Hey, you jerk," one of the other two said.

"That's to teach you. You don't push me," he said. He expected the confrontation to be over, but Mark threw himself at Adelmo and started punching him all over. He got Adelmo right on the mouth and cut his lip.

As Adelmo wiped at the blood, the kid's knee got him in the ribs and a screaming pain shot up his side. At that point, Adelmo stopped thinking. He started fighting back—hitting and punching. Even when Mark no longer returned the blows, Adelmo kept hitting the stupid boy. He hated him, hated this school, hated that he had to live in this ridiculous country. And that hate poured out of him until an adult pulled him off Mark.

She yelled a bunch of things he didn't bother to listen to or try to understand. He was about to hit the teacher, too, but instead allowed her to march him to the office. At least he was getting off the playground. Blood covered his face and his fingers, and his clothes were dirty and ripped. He didn't care.

"You sit right there, young man, until the nurse sees you; then you can explain to the principal why you shouldn't be expelled."

He stared down at his lap, wanting to cry. Tears filled his eyes, but he blinked them away. In Argentina, boys didn't cry.

The secretary from Adelmo's school called Isabel to notify her that Adelmo had been fighting and was in the principal's office. She was in Laguna Beach, trying to close the deal on the house, and couldn't pick him up right away, so she told the secretary to let him sit in the office until she got back. But apparently Nick had also been called as the second contact listed on Adelmo's emergency card.

When Isabel finally made it to the school, she found Nick sitting in the principal's office. She took a seat beside him, across from the principal. "Mr. Reeves has explained Adelmo's situation, and I understand and am sympathetic. However, I cannot condone fighting."

"Of course not," Isabel said, wondering what Nick had shared about Adelmo. The fact that he'd lost his parents? That he had no friends? That nothing was familiar to him?

"But the other kid was teasing him," Nick said. "Making fun of his English, pushing and hitting him, so he lost it."

"We'll talk to him," Isabel reassured the principal.

"We've contacted the other students' parents as well. But this will be Adelmo's only warning. The next time, I'll have to suspend him."

Nick stood. "Then maybe this isn't the right school for him."

"Nick," Isabel warned, and stood as well. "Thank you, Mr. Gardner. We understand and will make sure this doesn't happen again."

Nick stormed out of the office. Isabel followed.

In the administrative office where Adelmo sat waiting with his head down and his feet dangling off the chair, Nick tapped him on the shoulder. "Let's go."

Adelmo moved away from his touch.

"Come on. It's cool."

Adelmo glared at Nick, probably wondering if he was in trouble. Which he would be once Isabel figured out what it was she was supposed to do now with a child who fought.

"He can ride with me," she said.

"No." Nick shook his head. "We're going for a ride together."

Adelmo stood. He looked from Isabel to Nick and finally turned away from Isabel and they both left.

She stood alone for a few moments in the office. Slowly, she grew angrier and angrier about what had just happened. How dare he usurp her authority? These kids were *her* responsibility. Nick couldn't step in like that and just take over. She shook off her mixed feelings and headed to the office and then home.

Nick stopped the truck in the parking lot of a minigolf park with batting cages. Adelmo hadn't spoken since they'd left the school. "Come on," Nick said, and got out of the truck.

Adelmo looked around in confusion, but he got out too.

"Ever play baseball in Argentina?"

"No."

"Well, these are batting cages. Helps you work on your swing and connect with the ball." Three of the four cages were taken. Behind them were sounds of bats popping the balls into the air and occasionally hitting the chain-link fence.

Adelmo stood awkwardly beside the truck, gazing at

the batting cages with a frown on his bruised and cut face.

Nick's heart went out to the boy. "Let's give it a try."

Adelmo dragged along behind him without any enthusiasm. Nick paid for their tickets; then he chose a cage. He handed Adelmo a bat, but he shook his head.

"I'll teach you how."

"No," Adelmo said firmly.

Nick shrugged. Putting on a helmet and taking the bat, he went in himself. The balls began to shoot out at him and he started to hit them. One. Five. Fifteen. Thirty. "I never got to play Little League when I was a kid, because my mom didn't have money. But when I got older, I liked to come here and hit balls. Made me feel better." He stepped aside and looked back at Adelmo. "Stupid, huh?"

"No, I like to kick my soccer ball. After, you feel like really tired, but not so angry."

Nick understood that feeling exactly. That release of tension. That drained feeling one got after a good cry. Swinging his bat at the balls produced that same feeling. And he guessed that kicking the soccer ball did too.

"Soccer ball, huh? That works too." He grinned. "Interested in playing? On a team, I mean?"

"I don't know."

Balls kept shooting, and Nick ignored them. "I can sign you up."

"Why?"

Nick stopped the balls from shooting out and slapping the cushioned backrest, and placed a hand on the chain-link fence. He gazed at Adelmo through it. "Why not? You like to play."

"What do you care?"

"I guess I want to try to make you happy."

"Why?"

He shrugged. "Because I can. And you need a friend." He winked. "And so do I."

Adelmo blinked and wiped his eyes with the backs of his hands. "Let me try that."

Nick changed the speed of the pitches and handed Adelmo a bat. He showed him how to stand and indicated when to swing. The first pitch came and it flew too quickly. Adelmo swung and missed.

"Wow, that was fast." Adelmo's mood seemed to lift. He repositioned himself and focused on the next ball. Again he swung and missed. Adelmo cussed and waited, even more determined. This time he caught a corner of the ball and fouled it to the side, but at least he hit it. With a proud grin, he glanced at Nick.

"Way to go, buddy. Do it again." Nick watched Adelmo with a lump in his throat. He'd failed a lot in his life, but he wasn't going to fail this kid.

When Isabel got home and Nick and Adelmo weren't there, she got angry all over again. She picked up her cell and called Nick.

He answered.

"Where the hell are you?"

"We're having dinner. I took Adelmo to the batting cages, and we were both starving afterward."

"You took him to play? After we got called into the school office for his misbehavior?"

"He didn't misbehave. He *should* have knocked the

other kid on his ass. And the school better watch what they do or they're going to have a discrimination lawsuit on their hands."

Isabel placed her fingertips on her temple. God, she didn't need this. "Nick, we have to talk."

"Okay," he said cheerfully. "We'll be there in about an hour."

As she clicked the phone off, she drew a breath.

She ordered Chinese food for the girls. Mostly they talked among themselves and then went to their rooms to do their homework. Sandra helped Julieta with what she couldn't do on her own, but adding teddy bears together on her math sheet and writing letters wasn't all that difficult.

Nick and Adelmo came a while later, laughing and joking. Happy.

"Go take a bath, Adelmo," she said.

"Okay." He whistled as he walked down the hall. Isabel heard Sandra call him into her room.

Nick crossed his arms and leaned on the wall. "Go ahead. Lay into me."

"You think teaching him to fight is a good thing?"

"I'm not teaching him to fight. Seemed to be pretty good at it on his own."

She glared at him.

"Look, he's been through hell. He hates his school. Hates the boys, because they tease him. I'm supposed to punish him for trying to put an end to it all? Fuck that."

"Keep your voice down."

He reached for her hand, opened the door, and pulled her outside into the fresh, cool, November evening air.

She yanked her hand free. "How am *I* supposed to punish him after you've practically congratulated him for what he did?"

"You're *not* supposed to punish him. I told him to write a letter of apology to the principal, which he promised to do. And I told him he'd lose one of his privileges for a week." Nick stood in front of her, smelling like popcorn and crisp fresh air. "Your choice."

Speechless, she crossed her arms and frowned.

"He needs to be understood and loved. He needs us to be on his side, Isabel. Everything is new and scary for him, even if he tries to be tough."

"I know that." She resented that Nick felt he had to instruct her on how to deal with the kids. What made him any more qualified than she was? The way he'd taken over when he had no right to do so made her angry. But then, a huge part of her was glad that he'd handled it, and *that* made her even angrier. "But the children are my responsibility. My obligation to raise them the way I see fit. I don't want you to interfere again like you did today."

"They're not my responsibility or my *obligation*, Isabel. Sometimes people do things because they want to, not because they're supposed to."

Was that a slap in the face? She tried hard to control her temper.

He reached for her arms and uncrossed them. "I'm sorry. I didn't mean to upset you. But I didn't want you yelling at him the second you got him in your car."

"I wasn't going to yell at him."

"Or lecture." He gripped her arms harder and drew her closer. "Look, Isabel, I got into fights all the time at school. Guys called my mom names for being drunk and dirty. She didn't walk very steady, and sometimes she forgot to bathe. She just lost track of time."

In the semidarkness, she gazed into Nick's eyes. His hands were holding her in place so she couldn't turn away—not that she wanted to—all the while keeping her at a distance from his body.

"My mom always punished me when the school called. I couldn't tell her I was defending her. I know how shitty it feels when you think you have no one to turn to."

She studied Nick, her heart drumming hard in her chest. How very little she knew about his life prior to them meeting. Why hadn't he ever shared these pieces of himself when they were married? Maybe because he'd always been too drunk to remember any of it, or drunk enough to forget. Or had she been too preoccupied with the business and her parents to ever probe into his past? "Okay, Nick." She gave up. "He can turn to you. I don't really know what to say to him anyway."

"I don't either, but somehow I'm managing to connect with him and that makes me feel...great."

She looked into his warm eyes and handsome face, and suddenly all the anger and fight drained out of her. "That's because you *are* great. You've always been a loving person willing to give your time...give your heart. You're the ultimate good guy, Nick."

"You say that like it's a bad thing."

She shook her head.

He pulled her into a hard embrace. Awkwardly, she let her arms go around him as well and patted his back.

After a few moments, he released her and silently gazed at her. She blushed, unsure why. Maybe because she still felt his fingers on her skin.

He crossed the patio, walking away from her, going to his house.

She sighed and went back inside. Adelmo came back into the living room, unshowered. "Cousin Isabel?"

"Yes," she said.

He gave her a sheet of paper. "It's a letter of apology to you and one to the principal. Sandra helped me write it. I didn't mean to cause trouble. But those boys, they called me... Well, they're just so dumb. They don't know a thing about Argentina. But... I didn't mean to embarrass you."

"Honey," she said, looking him in the eyes and wishing for the hundredth time that Brenda was still alive, "you didn't embarrass me. But fighting doesn't solve anything. And you simply can't use your fists to make others see things your way. The school won't put up with it, and I can't either."

He nodded, looking down at the ground.

"But it's over." She reached across and touched his hair. "Go on and take your bath."

He nodded again and ran off.

She sighed. Tomorrow would be a new day.

Chapter Fifteen

❧

*T*hey gathered around the long conference table, the minutes on the clock ticking away, as everyone quietly waited for the owner of Gallegos Wines to make her grand entrance. Her investors and staff were nervous. Nick checked his watch discreetly, wondering what was holding up Isabel.

Dressed professionally in breathtaking autumn colors that made him want to perch himself on the hilltop below the late-afternoon sun and enjoy the flavors of Gallegos, she breezed in a few seconds later, completely composed as if she didn't realize she was late. But he knew that she was aware. Isabel was never late. Something with the kids must have set her behind.

"Good morning, everyone," she said.

"Thank you for understanding that I had to postpone this meeting. As Stephanie has probably explained, I was selfishly soaking up the heat of my birth country beside the fragrant vines on the foot of the Andes."

A small rumble of laughter came from the men at the table.

"You're making us extremely jealous," one of the potential buyers said with a smile.

She laughed. "The truth is that I had a family tragedy to deal with, so it wasn't strictly a pleasure trip, but I have enjoyed visiting the land where Gallegos began." Easily, she brought the conversation back to Gallegos.

After a few more words from Isabel, she passed the meeting over to the spokesperson of Park & Manning. "Well, Ms. Gallegos," he said. "After meeting with a team of consultants, we feel Gallegos wines are not as commercially popular as other wines."

Isabel drew a breath, and Nick could feel the tension just behind her voice. "But you've looked at our financial records and you know our specialty markets are strong. Not to mention the many recognitions our wines have earned locally. Best of show, best of class, and numerous gold medal distinctions. Our Cabernet Merlot was named best wine for the Southern California region at the California State Fair three years in a row."

Gallegos's CFO, Gerald Porter, broke in and argued consumer demands and price, and things that weren't Isabel's specialty. She sat back and waited.

Nick leaned forward. "We know there's a tendency toward standardization, but that leads to too many wines being identical to other wines. We happen to believe that wines should be an expression of their origins. The soil. Climate. Grape varieties."

"Yes, but they have to be commercially favored products," the other side argued. "No matter how many awards your wines earn, if they're not competitive in the market, we're limiting sales and consumer demand."

"We have a vintage for the casual consumer. Absolutely," Isabel said. "And we want our wine to be a good value. But we've also kept the small winery atmosphere for the wine enthusiast. We don't want to be Napa Valley. We're not."

They nodded and made notes. Then questions turned to their marketing people, followed by asking to review financial records again. The next two hours were more of the same. For the most part, Isabel sat back and simply let her people answer. Nick did the same.

Looking at plain numbers, they had to agree that Gallegos had steady growth and financial stability. They produced easily 700,000 cases a year, with Chardonnay and Sauvignon being their primary grapes.

They took a break, and when they returned, one of the men addressed Isabel. "Ms. Gallegos, how would you feel about staying on as a consultant and public figurehead for the next five years? After all, *you* are Gallegos."

Isabel's heart plummeted down to her stomach. Five years! She didn't want to be involved with Gallegos for another five years.

"We'll provide you with a salary, you'll keep your office, and you—"

"Gentlemen, in selling, the idea is not to be involved at all in the business."

Her advisors began shaking their heads violently. They obviously wanted her to consider their offer.

"My staff is excellent. They know everything, from harvesting to production to marketing. You won't need me."

"We disagree."

She bit her lower lip and thought. She wanted the sale to go through. "How about one year?"

Their spokesman laughed. "Are we bargaining?"

"I can see sticking around for a year, as a consultant only when needed. But after that, you won't need me."

They spoke among themselves and called a two-hour break, which she gladly agreed to. They left the conference room, and her staff stayed behind.

"Isabel, this is crazy. What are you doing? If they feel more comfortable having your name still attached to the winery, then hell yeah, you're staying on," Gerald said.

"Does selling mean anything to you all?"

"They just want your name attached to the business. You won't have to *do* anything."

Obviously tired, and with emotions strained, everyone spoke at once, arguing and debating what the best options were for the company.

"Either you stay on as a damned consultant or you stay on as the owner. Your choice," Gerald said plainly.

Of course he was right. If it came down to this being the deciding item in negotiations, of course she'd agree, but not to five years. She'd rather stay on and find other buyers. "Let's see what they decide."

She walked out of the boardroom. Nick stayed beside her, following her to her office.

"Damn it," she shouted, then collapsed into her chair.

"It might not be so bad."

"God I *hate* this place. I can't get away from it." Her hand shook and she looked pale.

"Have you eaten today?"

She felt light-headed. So many things were pulling her in so many directions that she felt she was going to burst. Between Nick, and her recent role as parent, and the sale of the winery, she couldn't take much more pressure. She closed her eyes and tried to tune out the world. "Leave me alone."

"I'll bring you a sandwich." He got up and left.

A bit later, she was startled awake by the ringing phone. Surprised that she'd fallen asleep, she reached for the phone.

"They're back," Stephanie said.

"Give me a sec, okay?" She stumbled to the bathroom and splashed a bit of cold water on her face. Her heart beat at double speed. This was it.

Nick, who sat on the couch, handed her a sandwich.

"No, thank you."

He picked up the phone. "Steph, we'll be there in ten minutes." Then he turned to Isabel. "Eat."

About to refuse again, she opened her mouth to speak but decided she was starved and took the sandwich. She ate at her desk and Nick watched her. "What do I do?" she asked.

"I'm with you no matter what."

"I can't stay on for five years as a consultant."

"We'll find other buyers."

Not anytime soon. She finished the sandwich. "Julieta was sick this morning." She went back to the bathroom and brushed her teeth.

"Did she stay home from preschool?"

"Yes, I was hoping to go check on her at lunch. Let's go do this and be done."

"Okay."

She paused before opening the door. "Thank you for the sandwich."

He smiled. "Thanks for eating it."

"All right, let's sell this place."

In the boardroom, she stared at the group of men

and women assembled. They laid out their terms, and Isabel listened. They had her down for three years as a consultant. Also, they wanted to replace key staff members, which made no sense since these were the people who had helped her make Gallegos a success. The purchase price was good. Some other issues were discussed among those in attendance. Park & Manning had plans to increase the size of the wine-production facility. They also wanted to turn Gallegos into a viticultural Disneyland, in her opinion, by building restaurants on the premises and opening up the winery to the public. They wanted to offer winemaking seminars and hold events like weddings. Even a timeline for building a wine country resort and spa was in their development plans. She listened with a mixture of horror and interest. Finally, the question came to her about her role, and she was prepared.

She demanded that jobs not be affected. "You won't have the same company without my people. You think keeping me on is the key, but it's not. They run the winery."

"Agreed."

"And I'll stay on as an active, working consultant for the year I agreed to, and of course will be available to your people if there's ever a real need after that, but not officially. You're welcome to list my name as a consultant for the next two years if you feel that helps, but I won't be available on the premises."

No one seemed happy. Even her own officers were shaking their heads. But after a little disgruntlement, they accepted her offer. The paperwork would be drawn up after the holidays, and they would sit down with legal representation to officially sign what they'd verbally agreed to at the meeting.

Isabel almost passed out with relief. The sale had been salvaged. She walked out of the office ecstatic but exhausted. "It's done," she said to Nick. "Can you believe it?"

He smiled, sadly she thought. "Congratulations. You were great."

"Thanks. I'm going to go see Julieta." She paused. "Want to come?"

He nodded. "I'll stop by later."

As promised, he dropped by but didn't stay long. Isabel sort of wished he had, finding that needing him wasn't terrible.

Wiping the sweat off his brow, Ramiro unloaded a sweet, two-year-old mini-motorcycle from the back of his pickup truck. A friend of his was selling it and he thought what the heck, the boy might like learning how to ride. He pushed the lightweight bike into his storage barn, which smelled of grease and oil from all the spare parts he kept in there to repair cars and tractors, and parked it next to his own. Standing back and looking at what he'd purchased, he questioned his sanity. These kinds of spur-of-the-moment decisions were what his brother had criticized him about. "You don't think," Andres had said often during their many arguments.

Ramiro had always shaken his head and grinned, but really had been more bothered about Andres's criticism than he would let on.

"You're irresponsible and impulsive and it always gets you into trouble," Andres had said as if condemning him. Sometimes Ramiro wondered if his being the bad boy helped Andres. After all, it allowed him to be the self-righteous family hero.

When Andres got on his case too much, Ramiro would walk away. He turned away now, from the memories and from the bikes. Inside his house, he poured himself a glass of water, then strolled to the bedrooms as he drank it down. He'd had the girls' bedrooms painted and bought flowery bedspreads for the beds. He'd put computers in each room. But that had been the extent of his purchases. When the chicos got here, he'd take them out to buy what they wanted. A bedroom had to reflect a person's personality, especially with kids.

He hadn't heard from Isabel since they all left. A small part of him worried about her not returning. Maybe he'd been stupid to let her take his nieces and nephew out of the country. But he had her signed agreement; he didn't have anything to worry about. Besides, she didn't really want them permanently; that much had been obvious.

Leaving his house, he decided to go pay a visit to Sra. Dominga. After six weeks, she was sure to have heard from her grandchildren, and he was curious what was going on. He climbed into his truck and left the ranch. It took him about thirty minutes to arrive at the grandmother's house. She was gardening in her front yard, bent over a section of orange lilies and light purple daisies. She moved around slowly, wiping at her forehead. Ramiro frowned and got out of the truck. At the slam of his door, she turned to look at him.

"What do *you* want?" she asked in a cold, sharp tone.

"Good afternoon," he said, ignoring her question. "Beautiful flowers."

She wiped her forehead again, and he noticed that she was breathing heavily.

"Are you okay, doña?"

"Go away. I'm just hot."

He reached out an arm, because she looked unsteady, but she smacked it away and swayed as she walked toward her front door.

"I'm leaving," he said. "But first, let me help you get a glass of water."

"I don't need your help."

The hell she didn't. She didn't look well, and it had nothing to do with her dislike of him. He opened her screen door and held it open for her.

She walked through the door, breathing unsteadily, her skin splotchy in spots and pale in others, and headed to her kitchen.

"Please, let me get you the water. Sit down and cool off. I insist."

She frowned but did as he suggested. Ramiro hurried to her kitchen, found the glasses, and filled one three-quarters of the way with water. He placed it in her hand and then took a seat across from her in the small living room.

She drank the water silently, and he watched and waited, trying to decide if he should call a doctor. The redness of her cheeks was easing and she seemed to have caught her breath.

Finally, she met his gaze. "Los chicos are gone, Ramiro."

"I know."

"Then why are you here?"

"I'm wondering how they are. Have you heard from them?"

She sent him a questioning look as if wondering if he really cared; then she sighed, resigned to his presence. "They're fine. They're adjusting. Isabel has enrolled them in school. Adelmo is playing soccer. Sandra is surfing. Surfing of all things. And Julieta..." Doña Dominga shook her head. "She's a baby, and I'm afraid that one day soon she won't remember Brenda at all."

Ramiro sympathized with Doña Dominga. Brenda was her only child, and she had been beautiful and perfect. That probably wasn't exactly true—no one was perfect— but it was the way he'd always thought of her. She'd been too perfect for him anyhow. No doubt, Brenda's mother also thought of her child in the same way.

Doña Dominga wiped her eyes and drank more water. "Have you visited the cemetery?"

"No."

"Why not? He was your brother."

"And he's gone."

Doña Dominga didn't approve. Story of his life.

"I still feel that sending the kids to live in another country with a woman they don't know was a huge mistake," he said.

Dominga stood with difficulty and waved away his concern. "It's what Brenda wanted, and Isabel is doing a good job." Yet she didn't dispute that it was a mistake. Ramiro found that interesting. He longed to say that just because Brenda wanted it didn't make it right, but he resisted.

Ramiro looked down at the scars on her old wooden floor, probably etched there many years ago. Changing people's minds was impossible, he knew that, but probably even more difficult to make an old woman who lost her child realize her daughter had made a mistake. He looked up again. "If Andres hadn't been so stubborn and had gotten to know me as an adult, he wouldn't have chosen Isabel. He would have picked me."

Dominga laughed. "Look at you, Ramiro. He would never have picked you."

He wore dirty work jeans and a black T-shirt. But his clothes didn't reflect who he was inside. "You don't know me."

"Basta. The decision's been made. I don't need to know you."

"But, señora—"

"Enough, Ramiro." She raised her voice. "Go now. Go," she repeated, firmer.

Outside the screen door, a voice called, "Señora Dominga? Are you all right?"

To his surprise, the screen door opened and Rosa walked in. And then, shocking him even more, she came at him, shaking a finger in his face. "What are you do-ing here? I can't believe you're here upsetting Brenda's mother. You bastard!"

"Nena, nena, calm down," Doña Dominga said. "He's not upsetting me." She sat down and breathed tiredly. "He helped me come inside, out of the sun. I forget I'm not as young as I once was, and I got overheated. Ramiro got me a drink of water."

"Oh," she said, glancing at him with uncertainty.

"I accept your apology," he said.

Turning away from him, she went to Doña Dominga's side. "You got overheated? Are you okay? Should I call a doctor?"

"Oh, goodness no. I'm fine. But maybe I'll take a cool shower and sit inside the rest of the day."

"Good idea. Can I bring you some dinner?"

"Please, Rosita, don't fuss over me. What brings you over anyway?"

"Isabel asked me to check on you and make sure you were okay. Now I'm not sure what to tell her."

"You tell her I'm just fine."

Rosa glanced at Ramiro; then, as if angry with herself, she frowned. Directing her attention back to Dominga, she said, "I brought you some fresh peaches from my tree." Rosa returned to the door and picked up a large bag stuffed with peaches.

Dominga brightened. "Oh, thank you. Goodness, I can't possibly eat that many, but I'll make some preserves."

Rosa looked pleased.

"Would you like some, Ramiro?" Dominga asked.

"Sure, I'd love some of Rosa's peaches." He smiled at her evil eye and reached into the bag and took a handful.

"I brought those for you," Rosa said to Dominga.

"Oh, querida, he can have a few." She carried the bag into the kitchen.

"You shouldn't be here," Rosa said as soon as Dominga left the room.

Was Rosa always so loyal and protective of the people

she loved? And was it that trait he found so attractive? He stepped back. "Neither should you; she's tired. Let's go."

She was about to argue, but when Dominga came back into the room, Rosa gave her a hug and said she'd check on her again in a day or two.

"You don't have to, but if you want to stop by for a jar of preserves, you're welcome to."

"Okay," she said.

"Ramiro," Dominga continued, the warmth she showed Rosa fading, "thank you for stopping by, but maybe you shouldn't do it again. We've said all there is to say to each other."

He wasn't going to argue with her, and besides, when the children came to live with him, *she'd* be the one looking for *him*. "And here I thought you were going to invite me to get a jar of preserves too."

"I'm sorry, Ramiro."

"Yes, me too," he said, and with a bow of his head walked out the door to leave her in peace.

About to get into his truck and drive away, he paused when Rosa walked out. He had a good mind to tell them all to go to hell. He didn't have to befriend them. Legally, he'd have the kids soon and they wouldn't be able to do a damn thing about it. But . . . they would want to see their grandmother. And he wasn't that much of a bastard that he'd say no.

He got out of his truck and called from across the hood, "Rosa."

She was about to head to the bus stop. "Yes."

"I'll give you a ride."

"We've been through this."

"Get in." He didn't wait for her to respond. He got back in and started the truck. If she didn't get in, she didn't get in. But a second later the passenger door opened and she slid inside.

"I know you think I'm a jerk. I'd rather not hear it again." He put the car into drive.

"She's not well, and I'd appreciate if you didn't come over to upset her."

"I came over to try to find out how the chicos were." He stopped at a stop sign and turned to look at her.

"What? Why are you staring at me?"

"I'm going to be the one with the pibes soon. I don't have to try to be nice to her. Or to you."

She blinked, understanding. "That's true."

"I'm trying to make this work. She's the grandmother. I'm the uncle. Why can't we all act like family and raise the kids together?"

"Ramiro—"

"Why?" he demanded loudly. "Because Brenda and Andres were complete idiots and sent their hijos out of the country to live with your best friend? That was insane and you know it."

"Maybe I better take the bus." She reached for the door handle.

"I got their rooms ready. I've looked into private schools. What else do I have to do to make you people stop thinking of me as a devil?" He wanted to slam his fist on the steering wheel, on anything, but he drew a breath and controlled himself.

"What do their rooms look like?"

He raised an eyebrow. "Want to see?"

Surprising him, she said, "Okay."

Before she could change her mind, he headed to his house.

They actually spoke about the weather and Godoy Cruz, the local soccer team, as if they were neighbors meeting at the corner bakery.

When he pulled into his ranch, he was feeling good again.

"I want them to decide how to decorate their rooms, but I had to start with something."

"Sure," she said.

He led her inside and down the hall. They strolled through the rooms, and he pointed out what he'd done. For Julieta's room, he'd bought a couple of dolls and stuffed animals. "What do you think?" He picked up a stuffed German shepherd and shook it.

"She's going to love it."

He smiled. "She's the one I'm the most worried about. She's a little girl, and what do I know about little girls?"

Rosa sighed. "I agree. Little girls need their mothers."

He sank onto the bed and tried not to look disappointed. "I know. But I can't help that."

"Too bad Isabel lives so far."

"Yes, too bad. I might have only asked for visitation rights if she were local." Rosa stood stiffly in place looking uncomfortable, so he stood. "Well, I'll do my best."

"It all looks great," she said. "Really, I'm glad you're taking this seriously. Children are a huge responsibility."

"I am." They walked back down the hall. "Can I make dinner for you?"

"Oh . . . no."

"It's no trouble. I have to cook for myself, then eat alone. I'd love the company."

"I don't think so, Ramiro. But thank you."

He shoved his hands into his jeans. "If I change and brush my hair, will you stay?"

She laughed. "No."

He nodded. "Okay." He pulled the keys out of his pocket. "Then let's go. You can make me dinner at your place." He opened the front door.

Rosa stayed where she was, sizing him up. Bad? Good? Were those the questions going through her mind? Or was she contemplating eating dinner alone at her place and realizing how unpleasant that was night after night?

"What can you cook?" she asked.

He held the door open. "A great barbecue chicken."

"I'll be the judge of how great it is," she said.

He smiled and closed the door. A truce. Good first step. Great. And maybe because he'd spent so many years in the company of temporary women, the possibility of becoming friends with Rosa, who was the complete opposite, pleased him.

All she had to do was accept that he'd be raising Andres's kids, and they'd get along just fine. He wasn't going to stand for anyone getting in the way. Ramiro didn't think of himself as an unreasonable man, but as he'd made clear to Isabel, he'd fight anyone and everyone to fulfill his duty to his brother. Rosa included.

Chapter Sixteen

*I*sabel watched Sandra struggle on her surfboard, but she was getting the hang of the thing. She loved the water and the waves. The early December morning was cold and overcast, and while Isabel wore a warm coat and boots, out there in the water, Sandra barely seemed to notice. Riding each wave until it petered out, she'd then paddle back out. She was practically a natural. Checking her watch, Isabel wondered how late she was going to be to the staff meeting.

Thirsty, Isabel walked to the refreshment stand and bought a bottle of water. Turning back toward the beach, she bumped into a man behind her. "Excuse me," she said.

"Isabel Gallegos?" the man asked.

She took in a middle-aged man in Dockers shorts and a Burberry T-shirt. Mismatch, but maybe he threw on the shorts for the beach. Not recognizing him, she said, "Yes?"

"Do you remember me?"

"I'm sorry, I don't. Should I?"

"You own Gallegos Wines, don't you?"

"Well, technically, yes, but not for long. I'm selling the business."

"Oh, what a shame. We did business together once."

Isabel frowned. "Did we?"

"I bought crates of wine bottles as gifts for our employees and clients for Christmas. I own a PR firm here in L.A. We loved Gallegos Wines."

Isabel's frown turned into a smile. "Thank you. The wines will still be available. Don't worry, I'm staying on as a consultant. So"—she motioned with her hand—"what are you doing here?"

"Doing a little PR for the surf school. You?"

"My . . . I brought a relative to take surfing lessons."

"Really?" He smiled. "Got a future surf bum in the family?"

"I'm encouraging her interests." She laughed. "And my own. I love the ocean. I am, in fact, hoping to retire in the area soon."

"You're too young to retire."

Nice compliment. "Well, I'm sure other opportunities will present themselves. They always do. Maybe I should get your card. I might need to hire a good public relations company when I decide what I'll be doing next."

"Of course." He pulled out a leather business card holder and handed her a card. "Alex Hewitt."

"Thank you, Mr. Hewitt."

"Alex."

Wet and smiling, Sandra ran up the beach with a surfboard tucked awkwardly under her arm. When she got close to Isabel, she put down the surfboard and excitedly began sharing how well she thought she did.

Alex smiled. "This is the surfing star?"

"This is Sandra," Isabel said.

He shook Sandra's hand as if she were a grown-up.

Then he reached for Isabel's hand. "Great to see you again. Best of luck in retirement," he said with a wink.

"Thank you." She watched his long stride as he walked away.

"He was nice," Sandra said.

"Hmm, very nice."

Sandra raised an eyebrow. "You think he's cute."

Isabel laughed. "What do you know about cute, young lady?" She placed an arm around her adorable little cousin and began making her way out to the parking lot.

"I know," she said, angling a mature look Isabel's way. "I'm not a kid." She picked up her surfboard.

"Oh, yes, you are."

"I'm going to be eleven in a couple of months."

"Oh, well, I'm sorry. That makes all the difference in the world."

Sandra laughed. "Anyway, I know he was cute. And he smiled at you a lot. And you're not married."

"And it's going to stay that way."

"Don't you even want to marry Nick?"

"God no." By the look Sandra gave her, she back-tracked. "I mean, we've been there and done that. I don't think of him in that way anymore."

"Maybe you should."

"Why?"

"I don't know." She shrugged.

They walked through the parking lot. "Yes, you do. Spit it out."

"Well, he's just so nice. And he's always with us. And it would be great to know he was always going to be around."

Isabel got into her Lexus and put on her sunglasses, even though it was overcast and dark clouds blocked all possible glare. "He'll always be around."

"Even if you marry someone else?"

"I'm not going to marry anyone else."

"Then why not marry Nick?"

"All right, that's enough," Isabel said, and laughed, even though she was getting irritated. She pulled her sunglasses off and turned in her seat to stare at the inquisitive girl. "Sandra? I do have a question, now that we're discussing these...sorts of things. I've been thinking. You have an uncle in Argentina, and...how would you feel about getting to know him better?"

"What do you mean? We live here now. And my grandmother said he's no good."

"Well, right now you're living here, but...if you were to go back to Argentina, you'd want to get to know him, wouldn't you? He's not a bad man."

"No?"

"He's your father's brother."

"So? You're my family now."

"I know, but I'm only your...How do you think of me?"

"Like an aunt, I guess. You loved my mom like a sister, right?"

"Yes. But I was her cousin and you're my *second* cousin."

"I know."

"Much more distant in the family tree than your uncle Ramiro," she explained, but at Sandra's look of disappointment, she added, "I mean, if you kids want to think of me as your aunt, then that's fine."

"We do."

"Okay." She stared at Sandra a few seconds longer. "I just don't want you thinking of Nick and me as your parents, honey, because...I mean, I'm not the mothering type, and..."

Sandra stared down at her fingers as she pushed them together and twisted them around.

"Never mind." Isabel put her sunglasses back on and patted Sandra's knee. "What if we go home, get changed, and go get our nails done?"

Her spirits perked up. "Really?"

"Sure. Let's get a complete makeover." The hell with her meeting. She'd call Stephanie and tell her to reschedule for tomorrow.

Christmas was a small event, just the five of them. However, the gifts were anything but small. She bought them video games and bicycles. Skateboards and laptops. Illogical, because they wouldn't have a chance to use any of it before they returned home, but she'd have it all shipped. Julieta didn't have enough space in her bedroom for the amount of toys both she and Nick ordered from Toys "R" Us. It took all morning to open presents, and they disappeared into their rooms to play afterward.

Nick sat on the floor, picking up wrapping paper, while Isabel warmed up their catered dinner and placed the food on the table.

"Hey, Isabel," he called.

"Yes?"

"Come here."

She licked her index finger where the creamy gravy

spilled from the side of the bowl. "What?" she asked as she moved around the couch.

"Here." He patted the floor beside him.

She frowned but did as he asked and sat down.

"I have to give you your gift."

"You didn't have to buy me anything."

He leaned closer and eased some of her loose hair behind her ear. "It's just a little something I hope you'll like."

Those intimate kinds of touches sent tingles of pleasurable discomfort throughout her body. She ignored it along with his intense gaze, and smiled. "Well, what is it?"

He retrieved a box that still sat under the tree and handed it to her wordlessly. She quietly unwrapped it, the ribbons falling away from the box, which had a smaller lid that sat on the box. She opened the lid, and inside was a photograph of the three children. Professionally taken, and beautifully framed.

As she stared down at it, a lump formed in her throat. They looked happy and carefree. This was the kind of picture Brenda herself would have sent. And Isabel would have smiled and put it aside without much thought. But she knew these kids now. Adelmo's cocky smile, Sandra's camera pose, and little Julieta's innocent grin full of love. They weren't just someone else's children. They were hers. And it made this picture all the more precious.

"Do you like it?"

Tears came to her eyes. "It's . . . perfect."

"Glad you think so." He placed a hand on her shoulder and smiled as he looked down at the framed photo. "They had a lot of fun taking it. I have a whole envelope of pictures to give you. I bought them all."

"What a wonderfully thoughtful gift, Nick. I..." She was at a loss for words. "Thank you for taking the time to do this." She caressed the frame delicately with her fingertips.

His hand moved from her shoulder to run through her hair. And her nervousness returned, because this was all so perfect. So intimate and homey, and wrong. She wanted to fall into his arms. And that *had* to be wrong. She looked up and caught his stare. His lips moved closer and closer to hers, and finally she reached up and hooked her hand behind his neck and pulled him toward her.

His lips closed on hers and moved smoothly in a practiced, mature kiss of a man who knew how to make a woman appreciate the closeness he could provide. He'd been extremely popular with the ladies before and after their divorce. His fingers tightened in her hair, and he closed his eyes and moaned as he deepened the kiss, mixing in a little edginess with the sweetness.

She kissed him back, testing the new feelings she'd been having for him. Testing the possibility, just like she did with new flavors of wine. The quality and character of young wines were difficult to evaluate in their infancy. This was why she hired professionals to determine and predict their aging potential. Her father had been an expert, a professional. He'd predicted late ripening for Nick, and he was right.

Expressing the tenderness that had grown at his daily

devotion to her cousin's children, and the selfless way he stood beside her, taking care of whatever needed to be done, Isabel gently caressed the nape of his neck. When Nick loved, he gave everything, and her heart expanded when she thought of how easily he'd accepted this imposition into his life. How he didn't even consider it an imposition. She yielded to the luxury of having his lips once again blend deliciously with hers and drew him closer.

Like their valley here in Temecula, named by the Pala Indians to mean "where the sun shines through the mist," warmth seeped into her soul from being this close to him. Their relationship seemed to be in constant evolution, and this was one more change.

He gently ended the kiss and leaned his forehead against hers. "Since the divorce, you've let me kiss you only once on the lips, and it was for show. For your parents, at that New Year's Eve party they threw for their clients."

"Well, there's no one here but the two of us this time," she whispered, wishing he'd move back to give her a little space before she did something really crazy and asked him to take this even further.

"So what's the excuse?" He lifted his head and gazed into her eyes.

"Would you like me to make one up?"

A sexy darkness simmered in the depths of his eyes. "No."

Good, because she didn't want to lie to him or herself—she'd wanted and needed that kiss, that was the truth, and she didn't want to pretend she didn't. "Thank you for the present," she said instead, bringing the attention back to the gift that had stirred such deep emotion within her.

"You're welcome."

"I didn't think to get you anything. And I should have. You've been so wonderful all these months."

"Isabel, all I've ever wanted was you."

"Nick," she said, easing to the side and shaking her head. "No." She put the frame back in the box. Wiping her lips, she quickly glanced at him. "No."

"Why not?"

"We're friends."

"So. That's good, isn't it?"

"Nick, I don't think you need any complications in your life. I know I don't."

"I love you, Isabel."

"I know." She shook her head. No man, not even Nick, would still be here if he didn't love her. No matter how much she'd tried to close her eyes to that fact, she couldn't anymore. Her ex-husband still loved her...and he shouldn't.

He looked almost apologetic. "Maybe you can love me back one day. If I do things right this time. If I—"

"I can't love you that way."

"Why not?"

Because they had too much history together and she was afraid it would repeat. Because she just couldn't take it if it did. Or maybe because she didn't want to try again. "I'm sorry."

He looked angry as he eased back and stuffed wrapping paper into plastic trash bags. But the anger faded into a look of disappointment. Then he drew a breath. "Just paint a big L on my forehead. It's what you think of me."

Her heart ached. "Nick, I don't want to hurt you. I do love you. Just not like that. Not anymore."

"Then what was that kiss about?"

"I don't know. This whole having kids around. It's all so domestic. And you're so...good looking," she ended lamely. "I got carried away with the moment."

He stared at her, then broke out into a grin. "Okay."

Okay? It actually wasn't okay. That kiss awakened too much inside her. She felt a surge of sexual need that had long been extinguished. She didn't date. Didn't have sex. And didn't want to feel these things. And she shouldn't have kissed him. It was unfair.

"I'm starving," he said.

"Call the kids. Everything's ready."

He leaned across and dropped a kiss on her cheek, looked into her eyes like he wanted to say something. But he turned away and left her alone.

When she glanced down the hall, Sandra stared back at her. With a look of disappointment, she turned away too. "Shit," Isabel said, wondering how much she'd seen and heard. Too much, obviously.

Chapter Seventeen

*H*e kissed her?" Adelmo said, full of shock and disgust.

Sandra dragged him and Julieta outside, which was okay since he was dying to try out his new skateboard, but then she kept talking and making him lose his concentration. He hadn't wanted to listen to her until she told him that Nick kissed Isabel.

"Yes, what are you so surprised about? They were married once," she said.

"But . . ." Adelmo wrinkled his nose. "Why would he kiss her?"

"Because it's Christmas," Julieta said from the spot on the grass where she'd decided to sit.

"Because he loves her," Sandra corrected, trying to make him understand as if he were dense or something. "Isabel is smart and pretty. Why wouldn't he love her?"

Adelmo shrugged. "I'm glad I didn't see it." He got back onto the skateboard and jumped, trying to make it flip and land back on its wheels. But it landed on its side and he almost fell.

Sandra sat on the grass beside Julieta with her knees bent and her elbows on her knees. Her hands held up her chin as she watched Adelmo, but instead of telling him how cool he looked, she kept talking about Isabel and Nick. "I told her she should marry him again, but she said no, and she told him no too."

"He even asked her to marry him?" Adelmo picked up the skateboard and placed it beside Sandra. He sat on the skateboard.

"No, he just wanted to keep kissing her, I think," Sandra said. "So how can we make her change her mind?"

"Why would we want her to change her mind? We should try to make *him* change *his* mind."

"Are you like completely brain-dead?"

"What?"

"You know how great Nick is. Don't you want him around forever?"

Adelmo frowned. "He's not going away. He likes being with us."

"But if Isabel marries him, he'll *have to* be around. He'll become in charge of us too."

That made sense. Adelmo smiled, because he liked the idea of Nick being his legal guardian. He'd never be like his dad, but Papi would have liked Nick. "Hey, yeah. But how do we make Isabel, you know, love him again?"

"We probably have to figure out why she stopped loving him."

"Probably because he drank too much wine," Adelmo said, kicking his heel on the grass and making bits of dirt spray up. "He told me he wasn't very nice back then."

"But he's fine now. She should marry him again."

"I don't know about that stuff." He stood and got back onto the skateboard. "Why don't you just tell her to marry him? She does whatever you want."

"I tried that."

He flipped the skateboard and landed back on exactly the way he wanted. "Yeah!"

Julieta stood and clapped her hands. "Good, Adelmo. You did it."

He roughed up her hair, glad someone appreciated his awesome moves. "So, what do you think, Julie? How do we make Nick and Isabel fall in love?"

"You don't, silly. She already does. When the prince kisses the princess, she falls in love with him."

Adelmo laughed.

But Sandra stood, all excited. "Hey, maybe she has a point. Maybe Isabel really is already in love with him."

"Now you've really lost it, Sandra," Adelmo said. "You believe in princes and princesses too?"

"No, but maybe all we really have to do is wait. And make sure they get to spend a lot of time together. And stay out of their way. What do you say? Will you guys help?"

Julieta nodded, and Adelmo agreed. What did he have to lose?

"You're sure about this?" Isabel asked Stephanie for the tenth time. "I can't believe they invited themselves to your house. I'm so sorry."

"Will you stop worrying? My munchkins are excited about the sleepover and about sharing our traditional Disneyland outing with your kiddos."

"I'm not worried. It's just that five kids...You're not doing this because you work for me and want me to give you a raise before the business changes hands, are you?"

Stephanie gasped. "How did you guess?"

Isabel smiled. "All right, then. I'll see you on Monday." She had a skeleton crew at the office between Christmas and New Year's. Things were pretty much closed down. And Stephanie always took the whole week off. Taking Sandra, Adelmo, and Julieta even for part of her week off was way beyond kind. They would be with Stephanie for two days. Two days. To herself. The way it used to be. But as she watched them play in Stephanie's backyard, a feeling of loneliness began to slowly creep to the surface. The house would feel empty without them.

In an hour, she had an appointment for a massage at her favorite spa, out by the vineyard. Putting the kids out of her mind, she drove toward Temecula. She checked into the spa and tried to relax as she received her treatment. But relaxing her body and quieting her mind were two separate things. Her mind wouldn't cooperate. Then she entered the steam room and closed her eyes.

Crazy. Her life was crazy. She'd been avoiding Nick for the last couple of days. And he'd avoided her. Had she been too cold? Too mean? She shouldn't have kissed him—that she knew. Or maybe she should have. Maybe she should just stop fighting this phantom relationship that had been brewing lately. He'd always loved her. Probably had never stopped. Would it really be that bad to accept that he was the man she was destined to be with forever?

She cursed and left the steam room. Taking a quick shower, she drove to the winery. Ignoring the offices, she headed out to *her* spot—a small gazebo she had built on the edge of the vineyard. On one side she could see the valley of grapevines, and on the other, the city. One side was always what pulled her toward her roots and kept her trapped; the other offered escape if she dared to run. Christmas lights just started to come on.

She felt tears run down her face. "Why am I crying?" she asked herself. This was the one spot where she could talk to herself. In another year, she'd have no right whatsoever to step foot on this property. And she wondered if she'd made a mistake.

Her parents had slaved to build this business. *She* had slaved to create the winery her parents wanted. And she would be giving it all up. Was she a fool?

Her thoughts returned to Nick. When they first met at the university, he'd approached her as he would have any woman: He'd flirted, asked her out, and hoped to get lucky. She'd accepted a date, and they'd gone out for a drink. Somehow they'd ended up strolling downtown window shopping and had had so much fun just talking that neither one of them had thought to treat their night out as a cheap date.

They'd become friends. Calling each other about tough teachers and tests that had been difficult or easy. Going out for drinks or dinner. Sharing nothing more than friendship. But at some point, she knew Nick wanted more. A relationship. And she didn't. She wasn't sure why. He was absolutely gorgeous. Sweet. Funny. But there was this lack of ambition, this acceptance of life as it came that turned her off. Isabel was a go-getter, and Nick, well, Nick was happy to barely get by. Happy to be in Argentina, kicking back, barely passing his classes. She'd made an unconscious—or maybe a very conscious—decision not to fall in love with him. In lust, yes. They were young and sex was new and exciting. If only it had remained that simple.

But once he convinced her and her family to move to America and became so involved in the business, she came to depend on him. Like now. And she'd married him, without ever really asking if she loved him.

She sighed, tucking her legs up to her chest. She watched the night roll in. Christmas lights shined down in the valley. The little bits of color were so beautiful. This was what her life lacked—these tiny sprinkles of color that made everything worthwhile. Could she open herself up to that kind of sparkle? Or had she become like Nick, too willing to accept that there were some things in life she just wasn't entitled to?

Isabel walked into the house. She almost felt like walking right back out. It was quiet like when her parents first died. But she entered because she had nowhere else to go. Nick sat on the living room couch.

"Well, hi," she said. "What are you doing here?" She frowned.

He put a book down. "Did they get off okay?"

She nodded.

"I bet they were excited."

"Yes." She sat on the opposite side of the couch, the memory of that kiss fresh in her mind.

"Are you worried?"

"No. They'll be fine."

He stared at her.

She gazed at him.

He reached across to the the coffee table and picked

up an envelope. "I thought we'd take advantage of the empty house to go catch a movie." He handed the envelope to her. "I expected you home earlier, though. I think we've missed it."

She pulled tickets out of the envelope. He'd bought them movie tickets. She'd been moping and dreading coming home to an empty house, and he'd planned to spend the night doing something she'd like. "Let's go." She stood.

"But we missed the show."

"If we hurry, we can catch the last one."

He stood, pleased. "Okay." He followed her out the front door.

Isabel loved movies. Well-made movies engaged your senses and emotions in a way that she had always found magical. Sound and music, scenery, and moving characters. To be taken to other worlds and to be able to experience others' lives. Hollywood made you believe in the impossible. Movies had been her first introduction to America, and she loved them. So why had it been over ten years since she'd gone to see one?

When she and Nick left the theater, they strolled across the shopping center to his car. With all the time he'd spent drunk, he never once got behind the wheel while intoxicated. Usually he called her. And when she refused to respond anymore, he called others or slept in his car. So he had managed to hold on to his license, and with some of the money her parents had given him, he'd built a collection of beautiful cars.

Tonight he'd brought his BMW M6 convertible. She

sank into the butter-soft leather seat and moaned. "Where are you storing all your vehicles?"

"They're still on the winery grounds. No one's asked me to move them, but I know I'll have to soon." He plugged in his iPod and blasted classic Led Zeppelin through the car speakers.

Isabel winced.

"Too loud?"

"Just a bit."

He grinned. "Hungry?"

"Yes, but it's too late to eat."

He scoffed. "Says who? You wouldn't even have any popcorn at the movies. You've got to learn to live a little, Isabel."

He drove a couple of blocks from the shopping center, stopping at a twenty-four-hour diner. "Remember when we didn't have more than five bucks to our name and we'd order a three ninety-nine breakfast and share it?" He turned off the engine, and the inside of the car became dark and quiet.

Isabel remembered. Those times weren't so bad. "I bet the waitresses hated us."

He chuckled deep in his chest. "Let's leave a huge tip tonight."

She smiled. "How much?"

"What do you have?"

"On me?" She shrugged. "Thirty or forty dollars."

"I've got about a couple hundred. Can I leave it all?"

He was crazy. "It's your money."

"Hell, all the money I have is yours, Isabel. I know that."

Not true. He'd worked at the winery since day one. He'd earned his salary. And the inheritance that her parents left him was his to do with as he pleased. "If it makes you happy to leave a huge tip, I think you should."

"Let's go." He got out and waited for her. They strolled side by side for a late-night bite to eat.

The smell of coffee and food when they walked into the restaurant made her stomach grumble. Just the thought of cutting into a stack of fluffy pancakes smothered in maple syrup at this late hour should be enough to make her turn right around and go home. But her figure be damned, she was hungry and planned to indulge.

Scattered mostly to one side of the restaurant, a few couples and one family with little ones occupied the shiny red vinyl booths and tables. They were shown to a corner booth, which was as isolated as you could get in a chain restaurant intended to move people in and out as quickly as possible.

"This was a good idea. Going out, I mean," she said, feeling strangely free to be out doing nothing for a change.

He leaned back in his seat. "Yep, but I've got a confession to make."

She stiffened. "What?"

"It was sort of Adelmo's idea."

"Adelmo?"

Nick chuckled. "Yeah, he surprised me too. He told me that I should take you out for a movie 'or something,' because you work so hard and don't have any friends, and that if I was a real friend, I'd take you out to have fun."

Isabel laughed. "Since when does he worry about me having fun?"

Nick kept his soft gaze on her. "I decided he was right."

"Well, thank you both. I had a lot of fun."

They sat and waited for menus. Conversation wasn't exactly flowing. Nick reached across to a neighboring table and grabbed an empty, amber-tinged, plastic water glass.

"What are you—"

"Got a quarter?"

"What?"

"A quarter."

"Yes," she said. "But..."

He held out a hand.

She rolled her eyes and reached for her purse. Shaking a quarter loose from her wallet, she handed it to him.

He placed it on the table, turned the glass over on it, and smiled. "Now get the quarter out without touching the glass."

For a second, she stared at him. What the hell? "I can't," she said logically.

"Sure you can."

"No," she repeated. "I can't."

"All you have to do is pull the quarter through the table."

She laughed. "Right."

"I can do it. Watch," he said. Then he reached underneath, straining and grunting with real concentration. "If you just remember from physics class that nothing is really solid..." His brows and forehead wrinkled and his face turned red in his act to make the coin drop through the table. "That the physical world is just an illusion."

She watched with amusement.

"And if you really want the quarter to come through..." He worked it a few seconds longer, then finally smiled, his facial features relaxing. "Got it."

He pulled his hand out from under the table, and in it he had the quarter.

"Cute," she said.

"What?"

"That's not my quarter. You had another one in your hand."

"It's the same quarter."

"Okay, Nick. Whatever."

"What? It is. Look," he said. "If this isn't your quarter, then yours should still be under that glass, right?"

"Right."

"Okay, pick it up. See for yourself," he said, sounding completely confident in his challenge.

She eyed him skeptically and watched him as she cautiously reached for the glass. She lifted it slowly, half expecting something horrible to jump out at her. Even though that was silly, of course.

But when she lifted the glass, the quarter was still there just as she'd expected. She cocked her eyebrow. "Well?"

He reached across the table and picked up the quarter. "Got it." He smiled. "I told you I could get it out without touching the glass."

And she laughed. He got her. She shook her head. "Dirty trick."

He shrugged. "Won quite a few beers with that trick."

"Wonderful."

"Got a lot of funny ones but you have to be drunk to appreciate them."

The waitress showed up with their menus, which they took, thanked her, and began to look over their choices as she moved on to the next table.

"I'd forgotten how much fun it could be to hang out with you, Nick."

He offered a lazy, sort of sad smile. "I wasn't much fun for a while there, I know. But tonight has been cool."

"Yes."

"You weren't much fun either, Isabel."

She put her menu down, trying not to be offended. "You're right. I got caught up in building the business, and most of the time I was unhappy because I saw the years disappearing and I wasn't doing what I really wanted to do."

"No, you were doing what your parents wanted and what I wanted, and we all knew you would have been happier out of that business suit and high heels, but . . . maybe we never should have gotten married."

She shrugged and picked the menu back up. "Well, we did. And I was a terrible wife."

Her menu came back down, this time because he eased it down. "That's not true."

"It is. I didn't want the winery and I didn't want to be married. And you started drinking because I made you just as miserable as I was. You were trying to escape. It was my fault." She said this without much emotion. Facts were facts, and they both knew them. At this point it was in the past and it didn't matter.

He gazed into her eyes, then blinked and sighed. "Do you know that I had my first drink when I was ten? Just to see what my mom liked so much about it." He looked at the empty space over her shoulder. "It was from a bottle of apricot brandy. It was great. I didn't care for beer much. But wine coolers, rum and Coke, all the sweet liquors she kept in the house—those were great." His gaze returned to her face. "As a teen, I'd get drunk on the weekends mostly. By the time you met me, I drank daily."

She didn't say a word, just listened. Her heart thudded heavily in her chest. She almost didn't want to know any of this. But he was finally opening up. Finally letting that poison out. And she didn't dare speak or flinch.

"I drank before I went to class. Afterward. At night before bed. But I was in control," he continued. He reached for his glass of water and rolled it back and forth in his large hands. His eyebrows furrowed and he looked tense.

Out of the corner of her eye, she noticed the waitress making her way to their table. She sent her a gesture that told her to wait, and the woman turned toward another table.

"At least I thought I was in control. Until . . . it became too much. Your miscarriages and the whole baby thing. You looked at me like you hated me. Isabel, I realized I wasn't in control of anything. I was just like my mom. I was barely getting by. I had nothing and I'd always have nothing. I had no one . . . but you. And I . . . couldn't make you happy. My whole world just started to crumble. I didn't give a shit about anything anymore. But none of it was your fault. It was all my fault."

She drew a breath and held his gaze. She had this sick feeling in her stomach—a heaviness and an emptiness. Or maybe it was in her heart. How had she failed to see the pain he'd been going through? She reached for her water glass and drank until there was nothing left but ice. She hadn't failed to see it. But she'd been submerged in her own hell, her own drama and pain. And for years she'd told herself that Nick's drinking was no big deal. She'd lied to herself as much as he'd lied to himself. "Oh, Nick," she whispered. "You stupid jerk."

He lifted an eyebrow in surprise.

"It was never your job to make me happy."

"But I wanted to. I wanted to pretend that once you married me, all your other dreams wouldn't matter. That *I* would be enough."

"I'm sorry," she said.

He shook his head. "No, don't be. How the hell were you going to be happy knowing you'd married an irresponsible drunk?"

"Nick—"

"No, don't deny it. I spent years admitting this to myself."

She sought his gaze. "Even if you had been the most amazing husband in the world, I wouldn't have been happy. I didn't want to be married. To anyone."

He nodded. "I know. Something else I pretended wasn't true. Because I wanted you."

But she didn't have to marry him. She didn't have to run the winery for her parents. She'd chosen to do all that, then blamed everyone else for her unhappiness. She'd been wrong to let others decide what she should do. She placed her hand over his where his fingers still grasped his glass. "I married you because my parents loved you so much, and you loved me so much, and I thought 'why not?' That's a hell of a reason to marry someone, isn't it? It was completely unfair to you."

He released his glass of water and gripped her fingers. "We were both unfair to each other."

"Doesn't it seem like life just sort of snowballs and you start going down one road and pretty soon you realize it's too late to turn back, that you have to keep going, because you've left yourself no other option?" She shook her head, not waiting for his answer. "None of it was your fault or mine, any more than Brenda and Andres dying is anyone's fault. Bad things happen all the time. And people make bad decisions, maybe for good reasons, but they're still bad decisions."

He squeezed her fingers. "I'm finished making bad decisions and hiding from the truth. No more snowballs for me. What about you?"

She smiled. "Same here." At least she was trying to reach that place where everything just felt right. Where she wasn't making decisions based on other people's expectations and needs. Had she gotten there completely? No. But she was close. She was almost finished with the winery. She was preparing to move close to the ocean like she'd always wanted.

Nick had it figured out. He was finished hiding inside the bottles of wine, and he finally looked happy.

"It only took us twenty-six years to get back on track," she said, thinking about when they left Argentina full of plans and dreams. Back then everything seemed possible, sort of like it did right now. It was almost like the ten horrible years of marriage and ten years as a divorced couple didn't exist anymore. Or at least, it didn't matter.

He leaned back again, looking drained. "This time it's all going to come out right."

She was a little surprised to hear him sound so confident. "I hope so, Nick."

"It has to." He shrugged. "We aren't going to get another chance."

Those words remained in her head all the way home. This was absolutely her last chance to be who she wanted to be. And she had to be careful not to make any mistakes. When she got home, she called Stephanie to make sure the kids had gone to bed all right.

They were all still awake, playing and giggling with Stephanie's brood in their bedrooms.

Isabel spoke to each of the kids. And they immediately asked to speak to Nick when she told them he was there. She handed him the phone and sat quietly on the couch, leaning her tired head on her arm.

When he clicked off communication, he smiled. "What?"

"Nothing."

"You're looking at me funny."

"Am I?" She straightened. "I'm just grateful that you're being so kind to the kids. I'll never be able to repay you for how wonderful you've been since Brenda died."

"Are you going to kiss me again?"

Her back stiffened and a bit of the warmth in her heart changed from tenderness to sexual awareness. "No."

"Damn," he said, full of lighthearted amusement. He stood. "Good night, then."

She reached out for his hand. "Good night."

He bent at the waist and planted a kiss on her forehead. "I'll see you soon."

Sometimes it was difficult to know when you were making a mistake. She'd made a mistake once by marrying Nick. Was she making another one by letting him go?

Chapter Eighteen

Rosa couldn't believe that she agreed to go out with Ramiro. Not only was he five years younger than she was, not only did he act like a child most of the time—which was disturbingly similar to what attracted and frustrated her about her ex-husband—and not only did she hate that he had conned Isabel into signing custody of the children over to him, but also he was reckless and impulsive and...made her want to be just as crazy.

When he arrived on his motorcycle to pick her up, she really became concerned with her sanity. She'd dressed in a flowing summer skirt and sandals. "What kind of man picks up a woman on a motorcycle?" she asked.

"I thought you'd like this better than my dirty truck."

He had a point.

"Get some jeans on. I'll wait."

Having second thoughts, she almost told him to forget the whole thing. She had no business dating a man like Ramiro. But she had nothing else to do tonight. She had nothing else to do most nights. And she could use a little fun. So she turned around and changed into a pair of jeans and closed shoes.

As she climbed on behind Ramiro, she gripped his shoulders. "Aren't you a little old to be riding around on something like this?"

He moved her hands down from his shoulders to wrap around his stomach. "Aren't you sort of young to have stopped living? Hold on." He started the motorcycle and off they went.

As he drove in and out of traffic, she had to hold on tight. Despite her fear, she felt an exhilaration as the wind blew her perfectly set hair back. Even the smell of the car exhaust didn't bother her much, because the clean smell of Ramiro and his warm body was really all she could concentrate on.

When he crossed the city and wove back into a neighborhood, she became confused. And when he stopped the motorcycle in someone's front yard, she really had no clue what was up.

"My friend invited us for lunch."

Their big date was at someone's home? Was he kidding? She'd expected something wild and crazy. A bar. Dancing. A parrilla out in the open. "Your friend?"

He took her hand and walked to the small house. A young couple welcomed them inside, where Ramiro introduced Rosa as his friend.

"You want to see them?" the woman, named Irene, asked him.

"Can we?"

"Sure, follow me."

She led them to her cozy backyard sanctuary encircled in the privacy of large leafed plants. There, next to a professionally built brick barbecue grill, was a box, full of tan and white little puppies. The mother, with distended nipples, lay on the patio soaking up the sun.

Ramiro crouched down beside the box of puppies and grinned. "Look at them. They're so small."

Irene leaned in toward the box to take a closer look. "They're growing. You can take them home in about five weeks."

"Come see," Ramiro said to Rosa.

Rosa moved closer. Curled into sleeping crescents, eight bunched-up puppies almost filled the box.

"I'm going to take three. One for each kid. What do you think?"

Rosa stared at his profile. Today he was clean and well dressed, his long hair tied back. All the hardness seemed to have disappeared. How could any man look hard when he was smiling down at a box of puppies? "I think it's a nice idea."

"Chicos love dogs, right?"

"I don't know. Most do, I guess. But they're a lot of work. Are you sure you want three?"

"Can't have one dog for three pibes." He stood and smiled.

Rosa wasn't sure about him. Something told her he really had no clue what parenthood was going to be like. He thought it was just a matter of preparing a few rooms and buying a few things. He didn't realize how difficult dealing with individual personalities was going to be. Dealing with hurt feelings, or anger over their situation, or teen issues that would be there sooner than he expected. She'd been through it all, but she'd had her kids from birth and learned to adjust a little at a time. He was going to get three growing children all at once. His arrogant, impulsive decision was sure to backfire, and she doubted he knew what was coming his way.

Yet, he was so sweet and enthusiastic that she couldn't help but become a fan of his.

"I made milanesas con pure," Irene said. "Vamos a comer."

Rosa enjoyed Ramiro's friends. Irene was a student, getting her law degree. Her husband worked as a state engineer. Rosa wondered why Andres had refused to leave the door open to Ramiro. No matter what the past, he'd managed to turn himself around. If these friends were any indication of who he chose to hang out with, Ramiro was not the man Doña Dominga believed him to be.

After enjoying dinner with a couple of bottles of wine, they left. He took her home, and she invited him inside.

"Sit down," she said as she walked into the kitchen to make a pot of coffee.

He leaned an arm on the doorjamb, his hand resting on his head. "Rosa, you're so sexy," he said.

She laughed, started the coffee, and turned to look at him. Leaning on the counter, she crossed her arms. "Who are you, and what are you doing in my house talking nonsense?"

"It's not nonsense. You're beautiful."

He was the one who was attractive beyond the norm. "Sit down. We'll have some coffee; then you need to go."

He walked over to her and placed his hands on each side of her, on the counter. His strong body brought with it enough heat to make her flush. She met his piercing stare. And when he lowered his head and touched his lips to hers, she didn't dare move. Without touching more than her lips, he made her heart leap out of control and her breath catch in her throat.

Then he growled like the barbarian that he was and pressed his body against hers, letting her know there was no escape. She kissed him back, matching him in intensity and heat. Her hands gripped the back of his shirt, fisting the material until her knuckles went numb. Finally, needing to breathe, she pulled away from his thick, sexy lips and dropped her head back. He continued to kiss down her neck.

"No," she said hoarsely.

"Porque no, Rosita."

She let go of his clothes and eased her hands to his chest. "Step back. I'm a mother of three children, and only recently divorced."

He chuckled deeply. "Is that supposed to turn me off?"

"It's supposed to make you realize that I have responsibilities and I haven't dated since before I married my ex-husband. I don't know what I'm doing."

He raised an eyebrow. "Felt like you knew what you were doing."

She touched the side of his face with the palm of her hand. He was provocatively sexy and complicated, and she wasn't supposed to like him, much less be attracted to him. But she was. "Let's have some coffee."

"Okay," he agreed.

They shared a cup of coffee, then another, then sat and watched TV together, side by side, until late into the night. She couldn't forget that she had a tightly wound, sexually primed male beside her, which made it difficult to relax. But he didn't pursue what he'd started in the kitchen. When it was time to turn the TV off, he kissed her good-bye sweetly before he left, and Rosa went to bed confused and exhilarated as if life were starting again, magically giving her a second chance.

Very much like a typical family on a Saturday morning, Isabel, Nick, and the kids drove to the soccer field. Nick signed Adelmo up to play soccer at the Temecula Valley Youth Soccer Association, and he had a game. Usually, Nick went with him to practices during the week, while the nanny drove Sandra to surfing lessons and Julieta to ballet class. But on the weekends, he took all three children to the games alone. Isabel stayed behind and worked or she drove to the beach house that she'd made an offer on and bought. It had to be furnished and decorated, and since this was going to be her retreat—her future life—she wanted to do it all herself.

But this Saturday morning as Adelmo was getting ready for his game, Nick knocked on the door to her home office. "Coming?" he asked.

"Where?"

"Adelmo's game."

"Oh." She looked away from the computer. "You can't go?"

"I can go, but I thought we might all go today. You've never seen him play. He's good."

She didn't dare say she wasn't interested. After all, he'd been going for weeks, doing her a big favor. If he wanted her to come along this time, she should. So, she dressed in some jeans and a sweater, and they all climbed into Nick's Land Rover.

The second Nick parked, Adelmo ran out of the car, hurrying to join the team. She watched the little boys all grouped by the color of their shirts. Various shades of black and brown heads and a few blond ones. Little men. Adelmo sure was. Both he and Sandra were mature beyond their years. Maybe kids who had to grow up quickly simply were. She had been.

Nick chuckled. "He's excited."

She strolled to the benches and bleachers where the parents were making themselves comfortable with blankets, special chairs with backrests that they adjusted onto the hard metal bench of the bleacher, and coolers full of drinks and food. They seemed to be camped out for the duration. Isabel took a seat on the cold metal, feeling out of place until Nick sat beside her and Sandra sat on the other side. Julieta climbed onto her lap without asking permission.

Isabel wrapped her arms around her and kissed the top of her head. Glancing at Sandra, then at Nick, she wondered if anything could ever be more perfect than this moment. Motherhood wasn't easy, and she'd had so much adjusting to do, but how amazing it would be to have this feeling the rest of her life, and really raise these precious human beings and watch them grow. Of course, it wasn't what she'd planned, and she had no business getting attached to any of this. It was all temporary, and actually, it was about time that she start making plans to get them back to Argentina where they belonged.

Once the game started, she got involved in the sport

and became absorbed tracking Adelmo. He played hard, running at full throttle and taking each goal by either side very seriously. She watched closely and wondered if he had always been such an intense, aggressive boy or if this was brought on by the changes in his life. She tried to remember things that Brenda had shared about him but couldn't think of a thing.

Every time one of the teams scored or came close, the parents went wild, screaming and cheering as if this were a Major League game. Of course, to them it was better than a professional sport—their kids were playing. And it *was* nice. Nothing like sitting outdoors on an early spring day, with the sun warm and bearable and the smells of cut grass in the air. Nothing like watching young athletes play a game with such passion. She vowed not to miss another of Adelmo's games.

On their drive home, Adelmo drank a Coke and ate a bag of chips that he was given as a snack. "You played well," she said.

He snickered. "Cousin Isabel, do you know anything about soccer?"

"Of course I do."

"You didn't seem to when we went to the game in Argentina."

"Just because I didn't scream and yell doesn't mean I didn't know what was happening on the field. Actually, I've gone to lots of soccer games, and watched them on TV. I grew up in Argentina, too, you know, and the kids from school were always challenging each other to a match or two."

"Oh yeah? We did too. In our barrio."

"When I was very young, I participated in those games. Then when I got older, I preferred other things. But I liked watching the boys play."

"Well, sometimes you don't seem like much of an Argentine."

She glanced back at the sweaty boy. "Why do you say that?"

"You just don't act like one."

"And how would I act if I were 'more Argentine'?"

He guzzled down more soda, then laughed. "I don't know." Then he pointed at her like he'd thought of something for her to do. "You'd cook."

"All Argentine women cook?"

"Yep. All of them."

"Interesting. I didn't know that."

"Well, maybe the ones who work in Buenos Aires don't," he amended.

She laughed, and Nick smiled as he drove.

"You're too busy doing your own thing, and you're not very motherly. And you don't drink mate, and you don't speak much Spanish."

"That's because I want you to learn English." She thought about his other complaints, because she was sure they were complaints. "Sorry about not being the motherly type. That might be more because I've never had children, not because I'm any less Argentine than you."

"But you left our country."

Somehow, she thought they'd finally reached the real question on his mind. "I didn't leave because I didn't want to be Argentine anymore, Adelmo."

"So why did you leave?"

"I guess I was an adventurer. I wanted to see something new and different. Experience more than life on a winery."

"It was my fault," Nick added. "I convinced her and her parents that they'd be more successful in America."

Adelmo nodded and put his empty Coke can in a cup holder.

"Sorry you had to leave when you didn't want to, Adelmo." She wondered if this was the perfect time to tell him he'd be going back soon. "I'm planning to take you back when—"

"Mostly I wish my parents were . . . still alive."

Her explanation died in her throat. "Me too," she said.

They drove home. When they got out of the car, Sandra and Julieta walked up ahead beside Nick. Adelmo walked beside Isabel to the house. "Thanks for watching my game. I was great today."

She laughed. "Yes, you were something." She fluffed his sticky hair. "And you need a shower."

"Do I have to?"

"Yes. Please."

He smiled and ran inside.

Isabel watched him go with a tiny lump in her throat. She was sure Adelmo would be glad to go back to Argentina. They all would be, wouldn't they? So why was she having such a difficult time telling them? Maybe it had something to do with the fact that she really didn't want to think of the day she'd have to fly them back to Argentina and leave them with Ramiro. She'd miss them, she realized. So it was better not to think about it just yet. She had time. One day soon, she'd let them know the good news.

Chapter Nineteen

The following week, when Isabel was working, Sandra called from school to ask if she could go surfing with some friends.

"Well," Isabel said as she filed away expense reports she'd been reviewing, "I'm not sure that's a good idea. You're still taking lessons. Are you good enough to go out on your own?"

"Of course," Sandra said. "I won't go too far. I know what I can do and what I can't. Don't worry. So, can I go?"

Why not? she thought, glad that Sandra had made a couple of friends who shared her interest. "Okay, do I need to pick you up?"

"No, I'll get a ride back home."

Isabel spent the day working, pausing only when Nick strolled into her office. He sat across from her.

"What's up?" She glanced up from a form on which she was noting down the sugar content of the grapes on the vines that she'd just measured with the refractometer.

"I was asked by the Temecula paper to write an article on the benefits of wine to health." His lips quirked to the side. "I think I'll do it, as long as they allow me to stress moderation and common sense. Okay with you?"

She thought about it for a few seconds. "I'm fine with

it. I mean, you're not going to go into the dangers of alcohol when you're representing—"

"No," he said. "They're looking at the opposite, how
red wine can prevent heart disease, lower blood pressure, aid in digestion—you know, the stuff studies always
mention. But I want to make it clear that this doesn't
mean drink a bottle a day."

"Good," she agreed. "Sounds perfect."

"All right." He stood. "Oh, Stephanie asked if she
could take the kids to the movies."

"Sure. Well, Adelmo and Julieta, yes, but Sandra decided to go surfing with friends."

Nick frowned. "Alone? Are you crazy?"

Isabel stood as well. She picked up a sheet of new labels she needed to approve. "I said she was going with
friends."

"She's ten."

"Yes."

He shook his head. "Forget it. How about I make you
dinner tonight?"

Wondering now if she'd made the wrong decision
about Sandra, she wanted to call her back and tell her
she couldn't go. But she'd be fine, wouldn't she? "You
don't have to."

"I don't mind. Better than cooking for just me."

She headed to the door. "Okay. And do you really
think I shouldn't have let Sandra go?"

He smiled and placed a hand on her shoulder. "She's ten."

"Shit." She shook her head and headed to Stephanie's
desk to give her the labels. "I don't know a damn thing
about children."

"Just say no," he called after her.

That was the solution to all her problems. She needed to learn to say no. No, no, no.

"Dinner at six," he said.

"Okay," she yelled back, checking her watch and realizing that was only two hours away. Dinner. Shit, she hadn't even had lunch.

When she got home, Nick had dinner waiting for her. The table set. A delicious aroma coming from the kitchen. Soft music playing.

He walked out of the kitchen. "You made it," he said.

She gazed at him. He was dressed casually but handsomely, like he was going to go out to a restaurant to eat. He approached her, slipping her purse off her shoulder.

"I'm sorry I'm late," she said.

He shrugged and smiled. "You're always late getting home. Thank God you don't have a long commute."

She smiled. "Smells great."

"It is." When she tried to pass by him, he reached down for both her hands and held them warmly in his. "Wait."

"What?"

He stepped closer to her, gazing into her eyes. "Just slow down a second." His eyes narrowed and focused on her lips. "You're always so busy. Just stop."

And everything did stop. Suddenly, she wasn't relieved to get home and eager to eat dinner; suddenly, she was aware of him standing just inches from her body.

Then he angled and lowered his head.

His lips were just about to touch hers when she took
a step back. "Nick, no."

"Shut up, Isabel. Just let this happen."

Her heart immediately began to pound. "Let what
happen?"

He walked forward, crowding her against the hallway
wall. "*It*. Us. Whatever it is that is happening."

"*Nothing* is happening." Then why was she actually
trembling?

"I'm not asking for promises—for forever, marriage,
any of that. I just need to see if...I'm crazy." His hands
slid up her arms and settled on her shoulders. "Or if
you're feeling what I've been feeling lately."

"The kids—"

"Are not here."

Isabel closed her eyes and rested her forehead on his
shoulder. What was he asking her to do?

Like a man who only wanted to comfort her and let
her know she was okay, he wrapped his arms around
her and pulled her close. "I see you every day, watch you
with the kids, like at the ballpark the other day, and pretend that I don't want to touch you, that I don't need to
hold you. But I do. And I need you to hold me back. Put
your arms around me."

She rolled her head from side to side. "Nick—"

"Isabel, for once do what I'm asking you to do."

Her arms slid around his waist and she released a
shaky breath. She needed this too. For years, so much
rested on her shoulders and she kept everything inside.
A rush of pent-up emotional pain brought tears to her
eyes, and she gripped him harder, her fingers clutching

the fabric of his shirt. For months he'd been exactly the kind of man she needed, and it felt great to have someone to lean on and not always have to be so strong.

He kissed her temple and caressed her back. When his lips touched the sensitive skin of her ear, her body flushed with heat, and her tears began to dry up. She closed her eyes tightly and tried to shut out the voice in her head that warned her not to let this happen—that they'd been through this and it had turned out badly.

His tongue traced the outside of her ear.

She moaned.

"Let's erase the past. Let's start over," he said against her lips.

Yes, part of her said. But she remembered that she *was* starting over, without him. Just like they'd talked about at the diner, she wasn't going to fall into things like she had in the past. Since her plans didn't include him, she eased her hands back to his chest, her palms on his hardened nipples. "I can't." Her voice was unsteady.

"Try."

"I can't," she said, louder and stronger.

Without warning, he picked her up and carried her to her bedroom, dropping her on the bed. "Try." He unbuttoned his shirt.

"Nick . . . I don't want to try."

"Then the hell with you, Isabel!" he shouted, surprising her. "I'm sick and tired of being in love with a woman who won't even try to love me back."

He turned to leave and she scrambled out of bed. "Wait."

"I've waited! All my life, I've waited. Maybe you just

don't have it in you. You're so damned good at pretending you don't have feelings that maybe you really can't love me or anyone else."

"I have feelings and desires and all those things." Her vision blurred with tears. "But, what do you expect me to do about them? You know my plans include selling this place and moving away to a beach house. Nowhere in my plans do I have 'sleep with Nick, date Nick, marry Nick.'"

"So why can't those plans change? And don't even mention my drinking or our marriage. I haven't had a drink in almost ten years, since our divorce. I'm not that guy anymore, Isabel. I'm a good man. And you know it."

She had her hair pinned behind her head, but it was coming loose, so she pushed the strands away from her face. "Of course I know it. But that doesn't mean I want to jump into a relationship with you again."

"We're already in a relationship. We've never stopped being in a relationship," he reasoned. "The question is do you want me in your bed as well as in the other parts of your life? Or should I go once and for all?"

This time she knew that if he walked out of the house, he was gone for good. She saw it in his eyes and heard the power in his voice. As she stared at his bare chest and sat back down on the edge of the bed, she arched an eyebrow as she admitted to herself that yes, she did. She wanted sex. Not sex—she wanted to make love to Nick. But she had to ask, just to make sure, "What if all I want is sex?"

He moved slowly and got onto the bed on his knees, gazing down at her with the look of a conqueror. There was that male look that told her he knew he'd won the negotiation. She ran her hands up and down his chest and allowed herself to want him and to feel every feeling that this touch triggered.

His crooked grin said it all. "I can live with that."

"Can you? Honestly? I won't promise anything permanent," she warned.

"Okay. I don't want promises you can't keep."

"I'm not even promising that I'd be willing to do this again."

"Okay." He lowered his body closer to hers.

"Okay?" She pushed on his chest. "This isn't okay. It's wrong."

"Isabel, we're both in our late forties. Who do you think will judge us?" He eased her back and stretched out above her.

"I'm actually responsible for three kids now. And need to be a role model."

"They love me," he whispered as he kissed her neck. "They won't mind if you do too."

"I didn't say I loved you."

He pulled her top off over her head. "Well, pretend you do. For a little while." He released her bra and stared at her breasts, his train of thought seemingly lost. "Sex between us was always damned good. I'd almost be willing to live without love, if you were willing to become my lover again."

She wanted to lower his head to her breasts. She wanted that so bad, but she gripped the back of his head and pulled on his hair. "I don't want to be your lover. We're just having sex once."

"Okay, just once. You're the boss."

She released the hold on his hair and caressed his head, his stubbled face, and pulled his lips to hers. They kissed hungrily, and all her doubts and questions were hidden behind the need they both had to be touched and loved.

His lips made their way across every curve of her body as he undressed her. They felt each pulse on the side of her neck, on the insides of her wrists, and between her legs as he tasted the heat he created inside her. Isabel closed her eyes, letting the pleasure of his touch dissolve any lingering doubt. Need and desire pulsed through her body, but there was too much heat, too quickly, and contrary to what she'd said, she didn't want this to be just sex.

She pulled him up, wanting to explore him as well. She ran her hands over the firm muscles of his chest, arms, and back, muscles which he had neglected for years during their marriage. Now, they were toned and solid. Finally, the man she'd met long ago in Argentina had returned. She dropped kisses on his chest where his heart beat strong. But unlike back then, she really knew him now, and she truly loved him, maybe for the first time ever.

He moaned as her hands traveled down his stomach and she took him in her hands. Lowering his head, he kissed her as she stroked him. Nick braced his arms, holding himself over her to let her touch and explore, but his arms shook. Finally he captured her hands and lifted them over her head. He fit himself between her legs, fluidly entering her body and they were joined.

Full of emotion and desire, Isabel arched her back and lost herself in the feel of his body against hers. When he moved inside her and above her, the precious intimacy that they'd shared so many times in the past flooded back and felt perfect. Natural. So magically ecstatic that she never wanted it to end.

And yet the intensity of their lovemaking escalated and the passion inside them both, magnified to a point that it had to end or she'd die. When it did, the pleasure left them wrapped in each other's arms even closer than when they were engaged in the act of lovemaking, and she sighed with satisfaction.

"Isabel," Nick whispered into her damp hair.

"Yeah?" Her eyes were closed, her face pressed against his chest.

"Nothing," he said, and kissed the top of her head.

She eased her head back and gazed sleepily at his face. "What?"

"Can I tell you I love you?"

"Yes."

He smiled. "I do."

"I love you too."

After enjoying a few minutes in each other's arms, while not trying to overanalyze what they'd done or what they'd said, Isabel began to move away.

"Where are you going?"

"The kids will be here soon," she said. "Besides, I'm hungry."

He rubbed his eyes and groaned.

"You were cooking when I got home."

"Yeah."

She stretched and got out of bed.

"I'll go get things ready."

Dressing in a loose pair of shorts and a T-shirt, she met him in the kitchen, where he was warming up the pots of food he'd made earlier.

She sat on a bar stool and watched him. "Need help?"

"Nope."

The microwave beeped and he took out a plate with small cabbage rolls and rice. Then he spooned some chilled cucumber salad beside the rice.

"This looks fantastic."

He placed the plate in front of her on the bar. "Thanks."

"Where did you learn to cook like this?"

"I dated a chef for about a year."

She bit into the cabbage roll and her taste buds came alive with a spicy flavor of garlic and some kind of hot sauce. "Mmm, these are amazing."

He came to sit beside her with his food.

"So you dated a chef." Crazy, they'd lived a few feet from each other, yet led completely different lives. They barely saw each other, avoided each other, actually. Before Beth came into his life, Isabel had no idea what he did or with whom.

Putting a forkful of food into his mouth, he nodded. "She used to buy Gallegos wines and recommend them to the restaurant where she worked."

Did she know this woman? Had it been long after their divorce? Did it matter? "She taught you well. This is very good."

He reached across and tucked some hair behind Isabel's ear. "Glad you like it."

"Did you plan all of this tonight?"

"You mean the part about getting you into bed?"

"Yes, that part." He knew that was what she was asking.

"No, but while I was making dinner, I thought about how crazy it was that we're playing house and neither one of us is asking, 'What next?'"

"And you decided that sex was next."

"Sex is always next." He grinned. "And I knew deep down, you wanted me."

She flicked a piece of cucumber at him.

He dodged it and laughed. But then he sobered. "And this time we're only doing what you want. I won't be another one of those snowballs in your life, okay? Whenever you want me gone, tell me and I'll leave."

She leaned across and kissed him. "You're going to make me cry. Stop being so sweet."

He shrugged. "I never want to make you feel trapped again."

"Shhh." Caressing his face, she eased back. "Right now, everything is perfect. Is it perfect for you?"

"You can't imagine how perfect."

"Yes, I can. Let's enjoy it."

They ate without further conversation, then cleaned up the kitchen together. Sandra arrived shortly afterward, then the other two kids about fifteen minutes later, sharing their moviegoing experience enthusiastically.

Isabel got them all ready for bed and came back to the living room when they were finally in their bedrooms. Nick was stretched out on the couch.

"I guess I'm going to turn in too," she said.

"Can I stay?"

"Not a good idea."

"Didn't think so." He stood and kissed her softly, ending with a lazy smile. "I meant what I said, you know. I'll never stand in the way of your dreams again. When you say we're done, we're done. No pressure."

She ran her fingertips along his lips. "Let's just see what happens."

"We don't have to repeat what happened tonight either."

Now she smiled. "Nick, I *want* to sleep with you again. I just don't want you to spend the night, while the kids are here."

"Got it." He headed to the front door, but paused before opening it. "This feels like a dream."

She gazed at him. Maybe it was.

"Why do I feel like it's all going to vanish when I wake up in the morning?" he asked.

"It's not." But wasn't it? Weren't the children going back to Argentina next month once she signed the finalized paperwork? Wasn't she going to move into the beach house? Weren't they going to leave the winery grounds and go on with their own separate lives? Suddenly, she didn't want any of that to happen, and she had an almost panic-filled need to go back in time and stop the wheels she'd set in motion.

Trying to control her breathing and the pounding of her heart, she told herself she didn't have to go back in time. She could simply call Ramiro and tell him she'd changed her mind. He'd understand. His nieces and nephew were happy. They were getting used to their new lives. She wanted to make it all work. For all of them. He'd understand. He'd have to.

With a good-night, Nick left, and Isabel curled up on the couch to wait for the perfect time to call Ramiro.

Ramiro sneezed and blew his nose. Damned cold. He lay back on the couch and closed his eyes. He groaned. He felt like he'd been on a weeklong wine-tasting tour. Dazed, sick to his stomach, weak.

The phone rang and it felt like someone had gonged a bell inside his head. It rang again. He reached for the stupid thing and clicked it on. "Hello," he barked.

"Ramiro? This is Isabel."

Isabel? Oh, right, from America. He sat up and tried to focus. "Hello." His voice was like gravel.

"How are you?"

"Fine. Well, I have a cold, but I *will* be fine."

"I'm sorry to hear you're not feeling well. Should I call at another time?"

"No. How are the kids?"

"Good. Great, actually. That's why I'm calling."

He listened.

"They're doing fantastic. Learning English, making friends, starting to really blossom as they get used to their new lives."

"They don't have new lives. They're on vacation," he said, getting annoyed at hearing how happy the kids were living with that woman. His head pounded harder.

"Right," Isabel said. "Look, Ramiro, I think maybe we made the wrong decision."

Now he kicked his legs over the side of the couch and sat completely upright, even though it made him dizzy. "Honey, we have a legal, binding agreement, not a decision. So think closely about what you're about to say."

"I know we have an agreement. I know that. But I'm calling to tell you from one relative to another that a new move might not be in their best interest. They're happy. They're adjusting. I was wrong and selfish when I made that deal with you, and now I'm thinking about *them.*"

He stood and held the back of his head so that it wouldn't split open. "Ms. Gallegos, don't fuck with me. I can get a lawyer in America tomorrow and have those kids back in Argentina where they belong before the week is over." Not that legal matters worked that fast, but what the hell did she know? "I can understand that you might be getting attached to them. That's great. I want you to maintain a close relationship with them. But they will be living in their own country with me. Now, when are you returning?"

Silence crackled over the phone line. "I'll be in touch," she said, and hung up.

Damn it! He clicked the phone off and dropped back onto the couch, groaning. He needed to feel better, and soon.

Isabel's hand trembled as she called Rosa. What was she going to do? She should have told the children from day one that their stay in America was only temporary, that they were only visiting her to make their grandmother happy. But she hadn't.

"Hola," Rosa answered her phone.

"It's me, Isabel," she said, failing to raise her voice above a whisper.

"Isabel! How are you?"

"I'm okay. I just spoke with Ramiro."

"He's turned out to be the biggest surprise ever, hasn't he?"

"What do you mean?"

"He's so prepared for those children. Buying them computers and talking to the schools where they're going to attend. I didn't expect any of the things he's done. We were so wrong about him."

Not what Isabel wanted to hear right now. "Oh. You sound pretty convinced."

"I tell you, Isabel, I was all wrong about him. Somehow, you made the right decision."

Her heart sank further. "I'm not so sure about that."

"Trust me, you did. They are going to be loved. And growing up on his ranch with all that gorgeous space and the new puppies he's actually getting for them. Honey, you have nothing to worry about."

Except her heart breaking. Still, if it truly was better for them to return to Argentina, then there was no question that she would live with missing them.

"And if he ever needs my help, I'll be there, Isabel," Rosa continued.

"You don't have to do that."

"I don't mind. You know how much I miss being a mother. I'd actually enjoy spending time with them. And, well, with Ramiro too."

This did surprise Isabel. "What do you mean?"

"For the first time in a long time, I feel attractive and wanted."

"Are you *dating* him?"

"I'm not sure what to call it. I'm seeing him. He showed me the preparations he's made, took me out to see the puppies, calls me to let me know when he's done something new, like check out the schools. And we always end up talking for hours."

Why did this feel like a betrayal? Isabel was the one who decided to trust Ramiro and pass on what she viewed as an unpleasant obligation to the man. Wasn't it good that he'd turned out to be so fantastic? And that even Rosa had fallen for him? If the kids were going to have any female influence in their lives, they couldn't do much better than Rosa. She was the perfect mother. Much better than she was. Adelmo's complaints were proof of that. She didn't cook, didn't go to soccer games, didn't do any of the motherly things that Rosa would do. "Is this getting serious enough that you'd consider marrying him?"

"No, absolutely not. I've been through that before. But...I'd definitely consider becoming more involved with him. I get hot just listening to that rough voice of his. Am I crazy?"

She sounded like a teenager. Excited and full of doubt. "No. No, falling in love is not crazy." She thought of the feelings she was having for Nick again. Feelings that were and should have stayed long dead but had been reawakened. Love was unpredictable.

"I'm not sure it's love. I'm just happy around him."

"And you deserve to be happy."

"So do you, Isabel. You're doing the right thing. You have nothing to feel guilty about."

Didn't she? "Okay. I've got to go."

They said good-bye, and Isabel sat in the dark think-ing for a long time. She couldn't bring herself to tell Rosa that she wanted to keep the kids, that she loved them and that a hole would be forever in her heart once they were gone.

Chapter Twenty

A moving crew packed all her parents' belongings that Isabel wanted to keep and delivered them to storage. A different company took items that she wanted in the beach house and moved them out of the winery grounds. Although the new owners were going to allow her to keep the house while she stayed on as a consultant, she wanted to mentally move out, and there was no better way to do that than to start putting personal items in the beach house.

At the same time, at work she became involved solving an issue with an Italian distributor. Not only did putting in fourteen-hour days keep her so busy that she didn't have time to talk to the kids about returning to Argentina, but it also managed to keep her from dealing with her own emotions.

While Isabel was in a meeting, Stephanie passed through a call from Sandra, and she took it quickly.

"I'm going surfing with friends, so I'll be home late," she announced.

Isabel's first instinct was to suggest that she ask rather than announce her plans. And secondly, after the last time, she'd decided it was a bad idea for her to go alone. Nick was right. "Why don't you wait until your lesson tomorrow?"

"Come on, Isabel. I have all my homework done. I'd be bored at home, and I could use the practice."

"Honey, I just don't want this to become a weekly thing."

"It won't."

Just say no, Nick had said. "Who are you going with?"

She named a couple of friends and their older siblings.

"Sandra, no. Not today, honey."

"What? Why not?"

"I'd rather you come home."

"Why? You're never there!"

"Look, I'll be there. Come home with the nanny today, please. No surfing."

"But, Isabel—"

"I'm not arguing about this, Sandra. Home."

Sandra clicked the phone off without another word.

"Damn it," she whispered. Being a parent rather than a buddy was so difficult.

Immediately, Isabel returned to her meeting. Then a couple of hours later, she invited her Italian visitors to enjoy a bottle of wine under the flower-covered trellis where Gallegos often had guests start their tour of the vineyard. The scenery was perfect and it created a peaceful ambiance.

"I can tell," one man said, "that your heart and soul are deeply rooted here on this land."

Isabel thought that a curious thing to say. "You feel the spirit of my parents. They brought all their passion from Argentina and planted it in this soil."

"Which is why your harvest yields an abundance of

precious fruit." He lifted his glass and sipped. "Delicious."

Isabel was pleased that they were pleased. She never stopped being proud of what they'd accomplished. Even though this wasn't how she'd imagined spending her life, she knew they'd managed to create something pretty terrific.

Her cell interrupted them. "Excuse me," she said.

"Ms. Gallegos?" asked a frantic voice.

"Yes."

"I'm April. Sandra came to the beach with my sister and me, and she caught a really crazy wave. I mean, it just flung her, and—"

"Is she okay?" Isabel cut in. "Is she hurt?"

"The ambulance took her to the hospital. That's why I'm calling. The board flew off and landed on her head. She was out a long time and—"

"What hospital?"

The girl rambled on a bit more until Isabel raised her voice and demanded she calm down.

"A problem?" one of her guests asked as she disconnected the call.

"Yes, I'm sorry. I have to go." She hurried to her car, her heels clicking almost as frantically as her heart. On the way, she called Nick to have him meet her at the hospital, trying not to break into tears.

Rushing inside the hospital, she hurried to get information. Sandra had been unconscious when the paramedics got to the beach. She'd been pulled out of the water by a lifeguard and other surfers, but she'd still gotten water in her lungs before being rescued.

Nick arrived with a scared look on his face, right before a doctor invited Isabel to walk with him to Sandra's room. "She has an ugly gash on the top of her head from the force of the surfboard."

"Okay," Isabel said, appreciating the warning.

"She also experienced a contusion to her spinal cord at the base of her neck," he said. "She probably experienced temporary paralysis, which is why she was tossed around and wasn't able to swim to the surface."

"Paralysis," Isabel repeated the word, a ripple of fear making her almost light-headed.

Nick gripped her arm and held her steady.

"Temporary," the doctor explained. "The cord was hit hard, but she didn't crush a vertebra, thankfully. I'm going to give her a neck brace to wear for about four weeks. She should recover quickly."

Nick smiled, exhaling with relief. "Thank God."

"You can see her." He walked inside, and Isabel and Nick followed.

Poor Sandra's hair had been shaved enough to allow for stitches. Her eyes barely opened.

Isabel held back tears. "Hey there, surfer chick. This wasn't where we agreed to meet tonight."

Sandra blinked. "I'm sorry."

Now tears filled Isabel's eyes. "Oh, baby, I'm the one who's sorry. I should make the time to take you surfing myself."

"Accident," she said.

Yes, accident. But it could have left her paralyzed or dead.

Nick reached across and took her hand. "You're going to be fine."

She nodded.

They sat with her until she fell asleep; then Nick took Isabel's hand and led her out of the room, where he pulled her into his arms. "Damn, your call scared the hell out of me. Are you okay?"

"Yes." She eased back. "But this is my fault. I was busy, and I should have known she'd go with her friends no matter what I said. I should have gone with them all."

Nick sighed and ran a hand through his short hair. "It was a freak accident. What could you have done? Even if you were there, you couldn't stop a wave from throwing her."

"The point is, Nick, that she's a little kid, and I was too damn busy to take her myself and see what those waves looked like."

He met her gaze. "You're new at this. So am I. We're going to make mistakes."

Rosa wouldn't have made that mistake, she thought. "I'll stay with her. Will you watch Adelmo and Julieta?"

"Sure."

She turned away and went to sit with Sandra. A parent was allowed to stay past visiting hours, so she watched her sleep most of the night. Who had she been kidding? Parenting wasn't her thing. Her cousin had chosen her as a guardian, not necessarily as a parent. She would make sure to provide for their care and to see that they never lacked anything for the rest of their lives. But they were going home as soon as Sandra was able to fly.

Not only did Ramiro have the legal right to demand she return with the kids, but that's where they belonged.

She'd only been fooling herself that it could be any other way.

Sandra came home two days later. Isabel took her to get a haircut. The hairstylist showed her how to style her hair to best hide the scar. Once her hair grew in again, it would look much better. Both Isabel and Sandra were happy about that.

Sandra wore her neck brace for a couple of weeks, and Adelmo thought it was the greatest thing. He kept telling her it was way cooler than the cast he'd had on his arm when he was in second grade. Sandra just rolled her eyes.

Four weeks after Sandra got out of the hospital, Isabel bought tickets for all of them to travel to Argentina. When she got home, she sat the children down in the living room to finally tell them what she should have said from day one.

"I have a surprise," she said as they gathered on the couch and waited to find out what she wanted.

Nick poured himself a glass of Coke and sat on the arm of the sofa.

She was on the edge of her chair, her hands clasped in front of her. "We're all going to Argentina next week," she announced, figuring it was the easiest place to start.

Adelmo's eyes got as big as soccer balls. "You mean it?"

She smiled. "Yes."

The kids all cheered, and she didn't want to continue with the rest of her announcement, because the rest of it wasn't as fun, but she had to. "I've decided that even though I've loved having you with me, Argentina is your home and it's where you'll be safest and happiest."

Sandra's smile faded. "What do you mean?"

They all stared at her with questions in their eyes, even Nick.

"You mean we're going to Argentina to *live?*" Adelmo asked.

"Yes."

"But I thought you didn't want to live there," he said.

"You'll be living with your uncle Ramiro, Adelmo. And I'll come visit you every month or so."

"Visit!" Sandra raised her voice. "This is because of what I did, isn't it? You don't want to be responsible for us because we're too much trouble."

Isabel drew a breath. She knew this was coming, and she deserved their anger.

Perhaps being truthful was unkind. Or maybe it would be unkind to continue to deny the truth. Either way, it had to be said. "I've always believed that caring for you three would be too much responsibility for me, Sandra. It had nothing to do with your accident. Look, your uncle has agreed—"

"My dad *hated* our uncle! Abuela said so."

"Well, your father was wrong."

Now Adelmo took offense. "My father was never wrong about anything," he said, his face dark and serious.

"This time he was. And so was your mother about me. I tried to fill her shoes, but I can't. I'm not able to be a good parent."

Sandra's eyes filled with tears, and with a look of pure

hatred, she ran out of the house and slammed the door. Adelmo followed. Julieta lowered her head and it was all Isabel could do not to drop to her knees and pull her into her arms.

Nick placed a hand on her shoulder. "Julieta, why don't you go to your room for a little bit, okay, kiddo?"

Once Julieta was gone, Nick stared at Isabel with his jaw set and his fists clenched. "What the hell are you doing?"

"I made a deal with Ramiro Garcia when I left Argentina that I would transfer permanent custody to him after the sale of the winery."

"What? Why?"

"Because I didn't want the kids." Honesty. Ugly as it was, she had to be honest.

He gave her a look of disgust. "But... why didn't you ever tell me?"

"I didn't think it was any of your business at first. Then... I guess I fell under the same illusion we all did, that we could be this happy family, and I put my deal with Ramiro out of my mind."

"But we *can* be a happy family."

"We can't."

"Why not?" His voice got higher as if he just couldn't comprehend what was happening.

"Nick, I just want to sell the winery and live a peaceful life without responsibilities. Without having to worry about children, and where they are, and if they might get hurt. I'm not cut out for that. They'll be better off without me."

His face softened momentarily as he absorbed her words. "Oh, Isabel. What have you done?"

She hugged her arms around her body and shrugged.

"And you agreed to that man's request? Some man you don't even know? Are you crazy?" Now the voice of anger was replacing the shock.

"He's their uncle."

"You don't *know* him."

"He's a nice person. I've kept in touch."

Nick turned around and ran a hand though his hair. "I can't believe you've done this. I can't *believe* it." He faced her again. "They've started to build a life here. You can't yank it all away from them, Isabel."

She didn't want to. She loved them. But damn it, she didn't have the legal right to keep the children anymore. And besides, they would grow up happier and safer in Argentina.

"This is the worst thing you've ever done. If you go through with this, Isabel, it's over between us. I mean it."

She drew a breath and tried not to cry. "It's done."

"Then so are we." Following the older kids' example, he walked out the front door.

Ramiro's cell phone vibrated inside his front right pocket as he rode back from rounding up his cattle. He slowed his horse and took the call.

"I'm bringing them back next week." It was Isabel. "But the sale of my business is still not complete. I can't stay."

He stopped the horse completely. Her voice, her promise, brought a jolt of adrenaline to his heart. Up until this moment, having children had been a fantasy. A theoretical notion. He took off his hat and wiped his forehead. Now the day he'd been planning for had finally come, and he took a moment to sit with it.

"Hello?" she said.

"I'm here. Do you want me to pick you up at the airport?"

"That would be helpful, yes."

"Okay. When?"

She gave him the date and time.

"How do the pibes feel about all this?"

"You suddenly care?"

He cursed. "If I didn't care about them, I wouldn't bother with any of this."

"They hate me right now. And they should. The agreement I made with you was selfish and despicable."

He hopped off the horse and looked up at the sky instinctively. Was his brother cursing him right now from above? Had he been despicable too? Had he taken advantage of this woman's confusion to do something impulsive and ... wrong? "I'll be there to pick you all up. Good-bye."

He clicked the phone off and gazed into the distance. Then he closed his eyes and drew a steadying breath. Thoughts filtered randomly through his mind. Questions. Doubts. But a recurring thought made him have to leave. Rosa. He needed her.

Without questioning his motives, he took the horse back to the stall, removed the saddle, and got him cleaned up, then got into his truck and left. Blindly, he drove to her home and knocked hard at her door. When she answered, he stared at her, his heart beating double time.

"What's wrong?" she asked.

He opened his mouth to speak but couldn't. Sweat made his hair stringy and it fell over his face.

She reached for his clammy hand and pulled him inside. "What's wrong?"

"Isabel is bringing the children back."

Rosa smiled. "That's wonderful . . . isn't it?"

"It's . . . crazy wonderful." He drew a shaky breath. "My brother's son and daughters."

"Yes."

"I've done so many irresponsible things in my life, Rosa. Is this another one?"

"Why would you think so?"

"Because I don't know anything about raising children. Did I do something stupidly selfish by convincing Isabel to let me raise them?"

Rosa brushed his hair back and traced her fingertips along his eyebrows and down his cheekbones. "Yes."

His eyebrows drew together. "Yes? Aren't you supposed to try to make me feel better?"

She smiled softly. "Maybe." She shrugged. "You were both stupidly selfish. But you know what?"

He placed his hands on her hips and pulled her closer. "What?"

"Your heart is in the right place, and you're going to be a good parent, Ramiro."

"I'm nervous as hell."

"Time to let that all go and do the best job you can."

He nodded. "I love you, you know that?"

She pushed more of his hair back and leaned against him. "Aren't you supposed to wait for me to say that first? Pretend I forced you to say it back?"

He shook his head. "We're not teenagers. I'm not going to play games with you."

Angling her head, she frowned. "You're not the game-playing kind of man, are you?"

"I used to be. But I don't want to risk losing you, Rosa. You're the kind of woman a man wants around forever."

She chuckled. "I tried forever. Forever turned out to be painfully long."

He lowered his head and kissed her. "I'll make all the promises then; you don't have to make any."

Smiling into his eyes, she didn't respond.

"Once the kids get here, I'll be busy. All my attention is going to be on them."

She nodded. "I hope so."

"But you'll be there in my heart, in my dreams."

She laughed. "Why don't you invite me over to help you out, and then I can step out of your dreams for a while."

He traded places with her and pressed her against a wall. "Rosa, if you want, you can come by every day."

She raised an eyebrow. "Every day?"

"Too much to ask?"

"Yes. But I love Isabel and I loved Brenda. And I'm starting to fall in love with you. I'd be more than willing to help out."

His mouth covered hers, and he lifted her into his arms and walked her into her bedroom, where he made love to her for the first time. In a crazy way, he felt his life was just starting. And if he was lucky, Rosa was going to be a big part of it. She was sweet and caring and loyal, and he needed a real family woman in his life.

And she needed more excitement and someone who would take her out of the house she'd been so used to serving others in. They were good for each other. Holding her closely in his arms, he fell asleep, dreaming of the future.

Chapter Twenty-One

Comfortably seated in first class, thousands of feet in the air, Isabel glanced at each of the three children, who were not speaking to her unless absolutely necessary. She closed her eyes and tried to sleep. This was a long flight. But the prospect of having to face her aunt, as well as getting the cold shoulder, added to her anxiety and she couldn't sleep.

Life was crazy. Each time she made this trip to Argentina or back to America, there seemed to be a momentous reason. To start a business, to pick up three orphaned children, to bring them back. The knot in her stomach wouldn't go away. It hadn't since she'd told them of her plans two weeks ago.

The truth was, she was worried. Would they really be okay? Would Ramiro know how to deal with Adelmo the way Nick did? The boy wasn't easy. In fact, he was great at being rebellious if he didn't like you. And what about Sandra? A preteen with a slew of potential issues that would confuse even her. Who would she talk to? Rosa, maybe. Isabel hoped so. Rosa had been through it all before, so she had a huge advantage over Isabel. If only Sandra would bond with her and trust her. Sadly, selfishly, Isabel didn't want to think of Sandra bonding with Rosa the way she had with her.

And then Julieta, who was so little and needed so much love. What was all this movement and uncertainty doing to her?

Isabel sighed. Being hated she could deal with; guilt and worry were harder. She picked up a magazine and tried to read. In a few hours, they would land and everything would turn out all right. She hoped.

Ramiro waited anxiously at the airport, Rosa by his side.

"Calm down," she told him. "The plane isn't going to get here any faster because you pace."

He cursed. "Let's go get a drink."

She walked beside him to the bar.

He ordered a beer. "You know my brother accused me of stealing from my mother."

"I heard."

He sat on the bar stool and stared at his drink. "My mom wanted to remodel her bathroom. She had this old furnace that heated the water in the house. It kept turning off. It was annoying because you could be taking a shower and all of a sudden the damned thing would go off and you'd get nothing but ice-cold water raining on you. And it was dangerous. All of a sudden you'd start smelling gas."

"That isn't good at all."

"No, and the rest of her bathroom was old too. The tile on the floor was cracked and pieces came loose. Everything needed to be changed. But she only had enough money to change the furnace." He shrugged. "I thought I could take that money and double it or triple it and get more of the bathroom done."

Rosa listened and he turned to face her. "I thought I would buy these old motorcycles, fix them up, and sell them at a profit. I knew I could do it. So, I took her money that she kept in a shoe box in her closet." He shrugged and drank some of his beer.

"So?" Rosa asked. "Did you sell the motorcycles and make money?"

"Not before my mom noticed the money missing and Andres went into a rage and accused me of stealing her money."

"That's too bad that it worked out that way, Ramiro."

"It was a stupid move. I couldn't have made enough money to pay everything that needed to be done. A stupid risk. I take stupid risks," he said.

She raised an eyebrow. "Maybe. But not everyone is cautious and conservative about life. Andres was. You weren't. Andres didn't end up a lawyer with a lot of property. He never left the province. He didn't have all the experiences that you've told me you had."

He grinned. "He ended up with Brenda."

"You might have, too, if you'd really wanted her."

He leaned across and kissed her. "I didn't." Then he sat back and checked his watch. "Plane should be landing. Let's get back."

Rosa put a hand over his. "I don't really think you're worried about doing a good job as a parent. You're so arrogant, you think you're good at everything." She smiled.

He smiled back. "Guilty." He drew a breath. "No. I just haven't changed all that much. I had to step in and do this, because the pibes are my family. But a big part of me still enjoys risky ventures and being unpredictable."

He stood and took her hand. "I might decide to kidnap you, move to the capital, open up a tango bar, and live on the banks of the Paraná River next year."

Rosa gave him a sympathetic look, maybe knowing that the scenario wouldn't be happening with children involved. His wild days were going to be over, or at least toned down. He couldn't drag a family off with him every time he got a new whim. "Don't worry, I'm too old for that crap," he said.

When the kids and Isabel passed through immigration and bag check, Ramiro's anxiety returned. The children barely looked at him. They said hello when Isabel prompted them to, but none smiled.

Isabel and Rosa hugged for a long time. Isabel looked close to tears.

"You must be tired after that long flight," he said.

The little one held on to Isabel's hand like it was her only hope for survival. The boy looked off in the distance. The older girl mumbled something about being tired after *two* flights—one to the capital and one to Mendoza.

"I rented a van that will fit all of us."

"Thank you, Ramiro," Isabel said.

Quietly, they walked to the parking lot. Only Rosa and Isabel spoke. The kids dragged behind.

"Play soccer?" Ramiro asked Adelmo.

He scowled and rolled his eyes. "Who doesn't?"

Lots of people, he thought. "I play on Saturdays with some friends."

But the boy didn't choose to continue the dialogue, so

Ramiro gave up and walked the rest of the way to the car without trying to engage any of them in conversation.

Ramiro drove them to Doña Dominga's house. They got out and took their bags from the back of the van.

"I'm going to ship all their things separately." Isabel stood beside the children on the sidewalk, looking elegant and professional even with obvious lack of sleep from the exhausting trip.

"That's good," he said. "I bet they got lots of nice things in California."

Isabel nodded. "Yes. Well"—she glanced toward the door and motioned to Sandra to go on to her grandmother's house—"give me a couple of days to explain all this to my aunt, and I'll call you when we're ready to make the move to your place."

"Take your time." He glanced at Rosa, then back at Isabel. "And if you need my help for anything else, call."

"I will."

Tía Dominga was moved to tears when she saw her grandbabies. She held them and rocked them back and forth for a long time. The children allowed themselves to be smothered. Julieta asked to be picked up, so Tía Dominga sat down and held her on her lap. "I missed you so much. All of you."

Sandra and Adelmo sat beside their grandmother and smiled.

"Look how big you've gotten, Adelmo. If your father could see you, how proud he'd be."

Adelmo nodded. "I bet I could score a goal on him now."

Tía Dominga laughed and Adelmo smiled.

"And, Sandra, is that makeup you're wearing?" She glanced at Isabel. "Are you crazy?"

Isabel wasn't sure what the proper age was for girls to wear makeup, and Sandra was so mature that when she'd asked, Isabel had agreed. "She looks beautiful."

"She looks beautiful without makeup. Little girls don't need that mess on their faces."

"I'll wash it off, Abu," Sandra volunteered. "Cousin Isabel just let me try it."

Is she defending me? Isabel wanted so much to hug Sandra. She couldn't be more like Brenda if she tried. Sweet and loyal and beautiful.

"Well, I made little sandwiches. Are you all hungry?" Tía Dominga asked.

They all ran into the kitchen, and they sat around the table to devour the sandwiches and lemonade. They spent the next few hours sharing all the things they'd been doing in America, and Tía Dominga listened with glistening eyes.

When they went to bed, she and Isabel shared a cup of café con leche and sat on the patio enjoying the beautiful fall weather. A cool but gentle breeze made them both return inside for a sweater.

"I wish you lived closer, Isabelita."

"Me too," she said, not wanting to jump into the news that she would have her grandchildren back for good.

"Has it been as difficult as you thought?"

Isabel drew a breath and then smiled. It had been humbling, and, yes, incredibly difficult. She had a new level of respect for parents. "I made so many mistakes in such a short time, Tía."

"They look happy."

"Yes." They seemed to be. "They're good kids and made it easy for me. But..." She tucked her legs up. "They've missed home and it's been a difficult adjustment."

"Of course. Getting used to a new way of life, a new language—even if they learned English here in school— it had to have been difficult."

"They're happy to be back."

Tía Dominga sipped her coffee and seemed to look right through Isabel. "Yes. Though Julieta told me she doesn't want to lose another mommy. Funny thing to say, don't you think?"

Isabel couldn't maintain eye contact.

"Is there something you want to tell me?"

Like her own mother, Tía Dominga was too perceptive. "Yes, but probably not tonight."

"You might as well. It won't be any easier tomorrow, mi amor."

Isabel knew she was right. She looked at her aunt. "I can't do it anymore, Tía."

"Isabel—"

"No, try to understand. Sandra almost died on a surfboard last month. I don't have the mothering instinct that most women do. I don't know when to say no and when to say yes. I shouldn't have let her go surfing unsupervised. She's too young. But...I was busy working and I thought she'd listen when I said no." She allowed tears of fear to flow the way they hadn't when it happened, and she dropped her head into her hands. "My God, she could have been paralyzed for life."

"Isabel."

"And there are so many dangers. America isn't like here. It's so easy to get involved in drugs, and kids grow up so fast. I shouldn't have allowed the makeup either, but she seemed so happy when I said yes." She sniffed. "I can be a good aunt...but not a mother. I can't do it."

"Isabel," Tía Dominga said softly.

"No, I've made up my mind. Ramiro Garcia will—"

"Ramiro!"

"I've agreed to let him raise them."

Now Tía Dominga gasped and stared at her with her mouth open. "Are you out of your mind? How can you think that he'll make a better parent than you?"

"He might not. But at least they will be living here in Argentina close to you. Going to Argentine schools. They'll be in a better environment, trust me."

"I did, and you're letting all of us down."

Isabel had spent all her life trying not to let anyone down, trying to make things all right for everyone. "I'm sorry." She turned away.

Tía Dominga called her back. Isabel stopped and braced herself for another onslaught of argumentative words. But her aunt just shook her head.

"I'm doing this because I love them, Tía."

Tía Dominga looked at her lap. "Then for God's sake think about what you're doing."

"I have," Isabel whispered, then turned and walked into the house. She came face-to-face with Sandra, who was holding a glass of water and standing in the living room.

"I'm sorry," Isabel said again, this time to Sandra.

"Just go home, Isabel. We'll be fine without you. We don't need your kind of love."

Isabel accepted the slap in the face. Maybe she even deserved it. She nodded. "No, you don't. But I do love you, Sandra."

Sandra walked past her to the patio, where she sat beside her grandmother, hooking an arm around her back. Isabel couldn't look away.

"What are you doing awake, honey?" Sandra's grandmother said.

"I can't sleep. Are you okay?"

"Yes." Tía Dominga smiled sadly. "I'm worried about you all. Isabel is a little confused, but she'll come around."

"No, she's not confused. She's right," Sandra said, surprising Isabel.

Tía Dominga looked at her with a frown, as if she also had a difficult time believing what she was hearing. Sandra probably didn't want to worry her grandmother. She might be angry at Isabel, but the girl had a heart of gold—always thinking about other people's feelings. "Isabel tried, but she wasn't a good mother. She works all the time, and she barely spends any time with us."

This pierced Isabel's heart, but Sandra glanced back inside the house, and knowing Isabel heard, she seemed to send a silent apologetic message her way.

Tía Dominga's frown deepened.

"I mean, she *did* spend time with us," Sandra amended. "But, well, to be honest, we want to come back home. I hated American schools, and Adelmo never wanted to leave in the first place."

Tía Dominga nodded and gazed at her sternly. "You'll be living with your father's brother if you return. On a farm."

Sandra didn't react. Only a momentary flash of horror appeared on her face, and then she quickly covered it with a smile. "A farm? Good," she said. "Isabel lives on a winery. There was absolutely nothing to do there. At least on a farm there are animals, right?"

Tía Dominga smiled back. "I think so."

"Don't worry about us. We didn't want to live with Isabel anyway. We only went because Mamá wanted it that way."

Tía Dominga hugged her tight. "Having you close again does make my heart fill with a selfish kind of happiness."

Sandra hugged her back and blinked rapidly. Isabel knew she was trying not to cry, and when they made eye contact, she wanted to go pull the girl she loved like her own daughter into *her* arms. But because she didn't have that right anymore, she turned away and went to Tía Dominga's bedroom.

Isabel tried to tell herself that Sandra loved her grandmother and that being in Argentina had to be comforting in some way even if she felt abandoned by Isabel. Out of all three children, she had been the closest to Sandra. She remembered seeing her as a five-year-old playing with Brenda, and she'd been so cute. Even before that, Brenda had sent pictures of Sandra and letters about her firstborn much more than she had the other two. Probably because she didn't have time to take as many pictures as she had with only one baby. Isabel had transferred some of the love she'd had for Brenda to Sandra, and she knew Sandra felt that closeness. Maybe she even felt that because of the love Isabel had for Brenda that she still had a piece of her mother in Isabel. She hated to destroy that illusion, the promise that she would have Isabel with her forever. It hurt so badly to inflict pain when they'd all had so much already.

Isabel opened a window in the bedroom to let some fresh air in. Tía Dominga sat alone on the patio now. Steps in the hallway told her Sandra had come back in. The girl paused by Isabel's door. "Aunt Isabel," she whispered through the slightly opened door.

"Come in," Isabel said.

"I just want to let you know that Grandma will be okay."

"So will you. Honey, your mom—"

"You know, Isabel, I wonder how my mom, who was always so right about everything, could have been wrong about you."

"She wasn't wrong, Sandra." Isabel dropped her head back and shook her head, closing her tired eyes. "Ugh, *I* was wrong. It was me." She met Sandra's gaze again. "I didn't have the faith in myself that she had in me. I'm sorry that I underestimated myself. But I loved your mother, and I know she would have been okay with your uncle Ramiro raising you."

"You loved my mother?"

"Very much. You know that."

"Then I really don't understand. How could you have loved my mother so much and us so little?"

Good question. How could she have loved Brenda so much and been so unwilling to raise her children? Only, now the opposite was true. "Actually, I love you, Julieta, and Adelmo more than I ever did your mother. Brenda was my cousin and my friend, but we led separate lives. You're—"

"Just your second cousins, I remember." Sandra turned away and left Isabel alone.

No, she thought. Family trees lie. Love isn't measured by the distance on a stupid branch of a tree. Love grows slowly at first, then exponentially with each smile, with each interaction—happy or sad—until you can't imagine not having that person in your life. Drawn out on a family tree, they might be distant cousins, but in her heart, Sandra, Adelmo, and Julieta were simply *her* children.

Chapter Twenty-Two

💕

Morning in the little household wasn't any better than it had been the night before. Over breakfast, no one spoke but rather had their bread and coffee in silence. Only the sounds of squeaky chairs and silverware touching plates and the wooden table filled the room. Finally, Isabel pushed her food away and cleared her throat. "I know you all think I'm a traitor and that I'm abandoning my responsibilities." She turned to look at each of them, including her aunt. "I admit that originally I had no interest in being a stand-in parent. I had my own plans and they were important. They're still important to me. But I'm glad we had a chance to get to know each other. I don't plan to walk out of your lives. However, I believe I'm making the right choice for your future and mine, and like it or not, it's the way it's going to be." She stood, placing her cloth napkin on the table and pretending that this little businesslike speech wasn't breaking her heart. "Tomorrow, I'll have Ramiro pick us up."

She was about to walk away from the table, but Julieta jumped up and wrapped her arms around Isabel's legs. Isabel glanced down at her curly head, thinking how wonderful and innocent childhood was, that you could lay your emotions out on the line so easily. Julieta hadn't yet experienced the pain of being so open. Isabel picked her up and carried her outside.

She sat with her on a garden bench. "Julieta, can I tell you a secret?"

Julieta nodded.

"I don't want to do this. I want to take you back home to America with me."

"Why don't you?"

"Because your uncle really wants you to live with him."

"I don't want to live with him."

"He has great horses and lots of fun animals that you're going to love, and he wants to share them with you."

She buried her face on Isabel's shoulder. "I don't want to see them, Isabel."

"Oh, baby." She hugged her and held her close, trying to memorize the feel of her. "Your uncle really wants you, just like I do. I was already lucky enough to have you for a little while. Now it's his turn. We want to give him a turn, right?"

"No."

Isabel smiled. "He was your daddy's brother. He loved your daddy and really wants a chance to be your uncle. If I promise to visit you all the time, will you try to live in his house and be happy?"

She squeezed Isabel harder. "I don't want you to go. Can you live there with us?"

Again, childhood simplicity. "I'll stay as long as you need me to."

She lifted her head and looked into Isabel's eyes. "Promise?"

"Yes, but it's not going to be forever, okay? You have to promise to try your hardest to get used to living in his house."

"Okay."

Ramiro, surprised but happy that Isabel called him so soon, drove out to pick up the children. From the doorway, Doña Dominga watched them load the suitcases back into the rented van. The look in her eyes tugged at his heart. He strolled across the yard.

"Buenos días," he said.

"There's nothing good about this. You're a snake, and just because you got your way for now, don't count on any support from me."

He dropped his hands into his pockets. "Okay." He squinted against the sun coming over the top of the roof.

"I thank God my daughter had the good sense to leave you when she did."

Ramiro nodded. "Me too."

Doña Dominga looked at him sharply. "Why? Why are you doing this? How can you raise three children? You're a man."

He fought a need to smile at the sexist comment and chalked it up to her age. But the corner of his lips twitched. "Which is why I'll need some help. Rosa has agreed to help. Isabel promised to visit often and send money if I need it, which I won't, but she can do what she likes for their future. If you were willing to—"

"I won't help you, so don't ask."

He swallowed. "Will you come visit them on my farm?"

"No."

"Okay." He looked over his shoulder at the pibes waiting by the van. "I'll bring them to see you. Okay?"

She called to them. "Come give me a kiss. Ramiro will bring you back on the weekend. Vamos."

He guessed that was his answer. The kids dutifully hugged their grandmother. They looked miserable. Isabel looked miserable. No one was happy. Frustrated, he turned away and got into the van. He rested his arm on the steering wheel and stared out the windshield. Why was doing the right thing so damned unpleasant?

Isabel climbed into the passenger seat. "I hope the offer of that extra room is still open, because I'm staying for a while."

Putting the keys into the ignition, he started the van. "Stay as long as you want."

"Thanks. Julieta is afraid and...are you sure you—"

"Damn it, stop asking me if I'm sure about what I'm doing!" he shouted. "I'm sick of it. *You* didn't know what the hell you were doing, and you seemed to have done all right."

Her eyes flashed, but her stiff response was controlled. "I didn't do well. And I was going to ask if you were sure you *wanted* to take on this challenge, not if you were *able*."

"Of course I want to," he said, glaring at her even if her concern made her only human. A good person. Everyone was doing what they thought was best. Damn it, he had to stop being so defensive.

She lowered her gaze. "Julieta is so little and she needs...a mom."

What the hell could he say to that? "You want to take her back with you?"

Isabel's head snapped up and she frowned at him. "Just Julieta?"

"Yes."

"I can't do that. They have to stay together. And Sandra needs a woman just as much as Julieta. How would she feel if I took her sister and not her?"

"Then leave them all. Rosa . . . promised to help me."

Isabel nodded. "Good. Rosa is wonderful."

"Yes." He didn't have anything to add. Admitting to being in love with her best friend wasn't relevant.

The kids opened the side doors of the van and climbed inside, sitting quietly as if going to another funeral. Ramiro turned the radio on loudly, then called over the music. "Smile—you're not going to jail. Tonight we're having a party. And tomorrow we pick up your puppies."

They all looked at each other. Sandra met Isabel's gaze and raised an eyebrow. Damn, she looked so much like Brenda, and her skepticism reminded him of Andres. He smiled. They might not like it, but they were his family, and he told himself again that he'd made the right decision.

Isabel got settled into a guest room. She called Stephanie to check in at work. "I'm not sure how long I'm going to be here this time."

Stephanie promised that everything was under control. Isabel wanted to call Nick, but she knew he wouldn't talk to her. Still, she needed to hear him say he forgave her. She dialed his number and got his voice mail. "Nick, it's me. I'm sorry." She was about to hang up but couldn't. "I'm here with the kids, and I'm staying for a while to make sure they get settled in okay. I wish you'd call me...." She swallowed hard and took a deep breath. "I love you," she said just as a beep cut off her words. Disappointed, she hung up.

When Ramiro said he was having a party, he wasn't kidding. He'd invited a bunch of friends, some with kids, some without. Never mind that his nieces and nephew were tired and felt uncomfortable in their new environment. Never mind that they didn't know anyone, even him. Still, he asked them several times why they weren't playing with the other children or what the long faces were about. Even though they were still angry at her, they pretty much stayed by her side.

Julieta sat on her lap and eventually fell asleep. Rosa came to sit beside Isabel. "How long do you plan to stay?" she asked Isabel.

"I don't know."

"I love you and you know how much I like having you around, so don't take this the wrong way, but you're not doing Ramiro and the kids any favor by prolonging the separation."

She didn't want to do Ramiro any favors. "He's insane. No one but him feels like partying. And don't you think he's had enough to drink?"

"Isabel."

"What?"

"He'll do fine, but you've got to give him a chance. If

you're here, how are they going to bond with him and start building their relationship?"

"I've only been here half a day. Is it okay if I give them a chance to get settled in? Or am I just supposed to drop them off and wave good-bye as I hightail it out of here?"

Rosa shook her head and held her hands up in surrender.

But Isabel knew she was right. The children had to get used to their new life, and she had to return home. One week. She just needed a little more time.

Ramiro took them to pick up the puppies the next day, and Isabel stayed behind. They seemed thrilled when they got back to the ranch and spent the rest of the day playing with the dogs. Ramiro went out on the ranch to work. Isabel was bored stiff.

The following day, he took them with him to do his chores. When she decided to go for a walk, she saw Adelmo riding around on a motorcycle and her heart almost stopped. When she questioned Ramiro about it later, he basically told her not to question him. Angry, she went out for a nighttime stroll to blow off some steam. Alone, she thought of all she'd been through lately. Somehow in the past six months, she'd managed to fall in love with three kids and her ex-husband, when she'd wanted nothing to do with any of them. And unbelievably, she'd managed to lose them all.

She found a fallen tree and sat on the old trunk, pulling her knees up to her chest and hugging her legs close to her body. It was cold outside. Fall was gorgeous in Mendoza, but the air whipped through the openness of the farm and chilled her. She lowered her forehead onto her knees and sniffed as tears began to fall. She didn't want to go home alone and leave behind her family. "Oh God," she said, and began to cry in earnest, like a child, like she couldn't cry when she heard about Brenda's death, like she never cried about losing Nick. She sobbed in deep mourning until she had no tears left and her throat hurt and her stomach ached.

After this rush of grief passed, she wanted to curl up in a ball and sleep, but she had no option but to stand up and go back to that damned ranch. She wiped her face and made her way through the wild grasses, past the chicken coop and barn. On the porch, Ramiro sat on a chair, apparently waiting for her, because the second he saw her, he stood and demanded to know where she'd been. "You had me worried. You can't just leave like that without telling anyone where you're going."

Was this man for real? "Shut up and give me the keys to the truck. I want to go for a ride."

"My keys?" He gazed harder at her face. "What's wrong? Have you been crying?"

"Give me the damned keys!"

He dug in his pockets, a frown on his face. "I can take you wherever you—"

"I want to go alone."

Hesitantly, he held out the keys. She snatched them from him and turned away. Mostly she wanted to get away from him for a while, but she also had this crazy need to go see her old house. The vineyard where she'd grown up.

She drove with tears beginning to fall again. For years she couldn't cry at all, and now she couldn't stop. She let them fall and wound her way out of Ramiro's private road, then onto the small two-laner that led to the larger highway. There was only one way out, so she couldn't get lost. Once she got on the highway, she had no problem heading in the direction of the wineries. There were even signs leading tourists to the wineries, just like back home in Temecula.

Home. Funny that she thought of Temecula as home. Though maybe it wasn't funny at all, but logical. Temecula *was* home now. As much as she missed some parts of Argentina, she'd lived her entire adult life in America, and Adelmo was right—she was more American than Argentine now.

As she reached the winery an hour later, her chest constricted and she almost turned around and left. But curiosity made her stop the truck and get out. Up close, she saw that the vines were still there producing grapes. Her father had sold their property and business to a competitor who wanted to expand. The lump in her throat was impossible to swallow away. Selling their winery here had allowed them to open up in America, but she wished she'd been able to keep both.

There were no gates or barriers to keep others out, only a grand entrance that once had said *Gallegos* and now had no name at all. This was just a vineyard. She didn't think anyone lived in her childhood home. She made her way to the house, and when she got there, she noticed it had been kept up. They hadn't allowed it to rot away the last twenty-six years. She ran her fingers along the brick walls. Timidly, she knocked on the door.

A man, probably in his sixties, opened the door. "Bueno?" he said.

"Hello," Isabel said. "I'm sorry. I used to live here. I...just wanted to see the house and the vineyard."

He nodded, although he seemed distrustful at first. "You lived here? When? I've been here for almost twenty years. I take care of the vineyards for the winery down the road."

"My parents owned the property."

"Are you the Gallegos girl?"

Isabel smiled. "Yes."

He nodded again. "I knew your father."

"Really?"

"Come in," he said.

She stepped inside and looked around. From the doorway, she could see the kitchen and the living room. On that small counter that had never been redone, she'd learned as a teen to make empanadas with her mother, sangria with her father.

"Are you visiting?" he asked. "Can I get you a drink?"

"No, thank you, and yes, I'm visiting family."

He picked up a pack of cigarettes that sat on top of his nineteen-inch television and lit it with a yellow Bic lighter. "Your father and I used to stand out in front of the Perez kiosk and smoke," he said, blowing out smoke as if that breath held the memory. Isabel watched it circulate with the air in the room. "He always talked about his business out here. We were all surprised when he decided to close down and move away. You know, once a winemaker, always a winemaker. It's in your blood."

Isabel listened to him, and the way he said *your* made her feel he was including her. "We reopened in America. The wines are different but... good."

"That's wonderful," he said. "Wonderful. How is your father?"

"He passed away a few years ago."

"I'm sorry. But he died living on a vineyard. Good. That's the way it should be. Right?"

Isabel nodded. "Yes." Her eyes filled with tears again. "The way it should be."

"You want to walk around?"

"Do you mind?"

He waved his arm, giving her permission. She walked back to her old bedroom that now seemed to be an office of sorts. It held a desk, messy with paperwork, and boxes stacked in a corner. She remembered the shelves of ocean books she'd had, posters of teen idols, and the warm light-blue rug that took the cold off the hardwood floor. All that was gone now, but it was still there in her memories.

She didn't look in her parents' old bedroom. It was this man's home now, and she didn't want to impose more than she already had. "Thank you," she said as she made her way to the front door.

"De nada," he said. "Take care of yourself and that vineyard."

"I will." She stepped outside into the dark. Pulling a twig off a vine, she brought it to her nose and let it scratch her face. "It's still here, Papi. Your vines," she said. Kissing the tiny leaves, she tossed the twig into the air to let it fall back to the soil it came from. The same soil where she'd been born. But now it was time to go home.

When the weekend arrived, Ramiro took them all to Tía Dominga's house. Over the weekend, Isabel told the kids it was time for her to pack her things and go, and they seemed to accept it. They knew it was coming. Julieta lowered her eyes and chin.

"I'll be back in a month or two." She reached across and raised Julieta's chin. "And you can call me on your cell phone every day if you want."

Julieta didn't look any happier, but she nodded.

When they returned to Ramiro's ranch at the end of the weekend, she headed to the airport.

She gave each of them a hug and held on to Sandra for a second longer. "You can come visit me, too, Sandra. We can still be close."

Sandra pulled out of her arms. "I love you, Aunt Isabel," she said sadly. "I want to hate you, but I don't."

Unbelievable, but she'd given Isabel a huge gift. "If you need me for anything, call me. I mean it."

Sandra nodded.

"And take care of Julieta."

"I will."

Going back to life before kids was remarkably easy. After all, working fifteen-hour days was what she'd trained herself to do long ago. The week she returned, she called Nick every day but he didn't call her back. Stephanie said he hadn't been back to work.

Had he gone back to Beth? Gone back to drinking?

Neither scenario seemed possible, now that she knew him better.

On Friday, Gallegos held a small celebratory dinner party with the new owners and local clients. But instead of rushing off to host the festivities, Isabel sat in her office, alone. She tried to reach Nick again, and this time he surprised her by answering his phone.

"What is it, Isabel?"

"I've been calling you for days."

"I've heard the messages."

"Why didn't you call me back?"

"You know why."

She sat behind her desk. "Nick, I apologized for not telling you my plans, but they were my plans to make. Not yours." She sounded tough, but it was bullshit and she knew it. She'd allowed them all to play house, then had snatched it away. She was guilty, but it was done now, and as much as she wanted, she couldn't make any of it different.

"Fine. Whatever you say, Isabel. I'm eating cheese and drinking soda water with our clients. Are you coming down?"

"Oh." She stood. "You're here?"

"I'm here."

"I'll be right there," she said, standing as she spoke. "Don't leave."

She crossed the grounds to the gallery where they held wine tastings and special events. The evening views were amazing: when it got completely dark, the stars sparkled in the night sky, and the cool, fresh air gave no indication that Los Angeles smog was only two hours away.

As soon as Isabel walked into the gallery, Stephanie handed her a glass of wine and pointed her in the direction of the future owners. Yet, her mind wasn't on the party or its guests. As she walked through the room, Isabel found herself searching for Nick. She finally found him outside, chatting with a client on the garden patio. Here, the flavors and scents of the wine seemed to mix in the air as everyone drank and spoke and laughed.

Stepping up beside Nick, she greeted the client and joined in the conversation. Eventually, she and Nick were standing alone. "Where have you been?" she asked. "No one has seen you around here for weeks."

"I moved out and rented an apartment in Del Mar. There's no need for me to hang around here."

"Oh, well..." Isabel wasn't sure how to finish her thought. He looked good and healthy, but his face lacked the joy and positive spirit that she'd become accustomed to seeing.

"I'll mingle a little more, then get out of here." Nick turned on his heel and started to leave.

"Nick, wait. I want to talk to you."

"There's nothing to talk about."

Isabel bit back a curse. She was tired. Tired of her life. Tired of apologizing to Nick. Tired of apologizing to everyone.

"You know, I'm not going to beg for forgiveness. You pushed yourself back into my life. I didn't ask you to. In fact, I warned you not to. And if it didn't turn out the way you wanted it to, I can't help that." She hated how ungrateful she sounded, but being defensive was better than breaking down and crying, which was what she felt like doing.

Nick only laughed. "I would say I hope it turned out the way *you* wanted, but it didn't, did it, Isabel?"

No, it didn't. Angry, she kept her mouth shut.

"But congratulations." He smiled. "You now have what you wanted. No more obligations." He waved his arms out to the sides. "And today I signed a stack of papers, giving you complete control of the winery. You—"

"What? Why?"

"It's all yours to sell and do what you want with. We have no more ties to each other." He shot her a look of disgust. "Now you're alone, just like you wanted."

She reached out and gripped his arm. "Is that so wrong?"

"Is what so wrong?" He frowned.

"Wanting to live my life my way. To have time for myself." Her voice cracked. "Don't I deserve just a few years for me after all this?" She gazed around, and her heart filled with a combination of sadness and pride and pain.

"That's not the point. Why couldn't you have been honest with all of us? Why make us all believe that what we had was real?"

"It *was* real."

"No, Isabel, not when you knew all along that you weren't going to build a permanent home for them. I was wrong about you. I thought . . . you had a heart."

"Please, don't start that again."

"No, this isn't like you telling me you want a divorce. This person that you've become, that you hide behind, I don't know her."

Isabel's heart ached—it simply ached—because she understood what he was saying, even if her mind didn't want to acknowledge it. Tears sprang to her eyes. "Neither do I." Turning away, she set her wineglass on a nearby table and, instead of going back inside to the party, headed out the back of the courtyard.

"Isabel," Nick called.

But she didn't stop for him. She ran to her car, got in, and headed to the beach house.

Speeding down the I-5, she tried to put Nick out of her mind. A gentle rain started to fall, and she turned on her wipers. Tears from her eyes, keeping time with the rain. She no longer had control of her emotions; looking back, maybe she never had.

She couldn't help the person she'd become. Maybe she was driven and focused, and maybe those weren't always great qualities. When she'd flown to Argentina after Brenda died, her goal had been to fix the problem without it affecting her. This was true. She'd been focused on selling the winery, and she thought she'd handled a tough situation the best she could. Not that she didn't feel guilty about her decision, not that she hadn't questioned if trusting Ramiro was smart. She had. But she'd had to make decisions based on what was best for all of them, not on emotions.

When she got close to her house, red flares and police blocked flooded roads. *Damn it. What now?* All she wanted was to get to the beach house and sleep. Following the signs marked DETOUR, she carefully drove down the slick streets, her mind drifting back to Nick. What had really baffled her was what Nick had said about her hiding. Hiding from what?

A horn startled her, and before she had a chance to react, a silver streak shot out from the right and hit the front side of her car. The Lexus slipped and spun but came to a stop fairly quickly. Dazed, but full of instant adrenaline, she looked around for the other car. It, too, had slid on the slippery street and sat behind her in the middle of the road.

Her heart hammering, she got out of the car and ran to see if the other driver was okay. The driver, a woman, was turned backward, talking to two children in the backseat. Isabel stared at them, noticing the scared looks on their faces. One child was crying. What had happened? Had she crossed the intersection without looking, distracted over her argument with Nick?

"I'm sorry," Isabel said when the woman rolled down the window. "Are you okay?"

"Yes. Were you in the car I hit?" the woman said. "I tried to stop, but my brakes. They just didn't work."

Isabel thought maybe she'd been the one to cross the intersection out of turn. Some of the guilt over being distracted faded. Still, she was shook up over not seeing this woman, over not focusing on driving.

The woman got out of the car. "We should exchange insurance information, but let's get out of the rain." She looked around and there was no shelter.

"I'll go get my information," Isabel said. "Stay in the car with your kids."

"Thank you."

Isabel called the police to get the needed report filed, gave the woman her information and took down hers, and waited for the police to come. By the time it was all over, two hours had gone by.

"Again, I'm sorry," the woman said when they were ready to leave.

Isabel glanced at her sturdy sedan. There was a large enough dent that she'd need the front panel replaced, but no serious damage had been done. The woman's car, on the other hand, was going to be towed to the dealership to get the brakes repaired, and the tow truck driver was going to drive her and the kids to the nearest Starbucks to wait for her husband to get off work and come pick her up.

"Why don't I drive you and your children home?" Isabel offered, ignoring the uncomfortable way her rain-soaked clothing stuck to her side.

The woman looked surprised. "I don't want to put you out anymore. My husband gets off work in"—she checked her watch—"another hour. Not long."

"I don't mind. Really."

"Well"—she smiled—"I do want to get the kids in bed."

"You should. Let's go."

She called her husband to let him know the change in plans and then rode with Isabel the twenty minutes it took to get her home.

"I can't thank you enough," the woman said as Isabel pulled into the driveway of the cozy Laguna Beach home. "Nor apologize enough for tonight. I hope you didn't have anywhere important to go."

Isabel shook her head. Nowhere important to be, and no one important to be with. "I'm just glad you all weren't hurt and that you'll be getting your brakes fixed."

The woman gazed at Isabel with a look of gratitude,

then ushered her kids out of the backseat. "Well, thanks, and my insurance will take care of everything. I promise."

"I'm not worried."

The woman got out and hurried inside her house. Isabel turned her car around and made her way to the beach house, where she parked on the wet driveway. Exhausted, she dug the keys to the house out of her purse. Stepping out into what was now a light drizzle, she shivered and unlocked her front door. The house was dark and smelled damp. Isabel turned on the lights. Her wet clothes caused a chill to seep through her skin and into her bones.

Heading straight to the bathroom, she took a long, hot shower. The day had finally come to an end, and she hurt from the inside out. She stayed under the stream of hot water until it began to cool, then shut it off. She'd already moved plenty of her clothes to the beach house, so she slipped into a pair of comfortable olive-green sweats and went into the kitchen and made a cup of chamomile tea.

Rain fell softly outside. It was the only sound, other than her own breathing. From her perch on the couch in her small, freshly painted light blue and white living room, she looked around at the place where she'd chosen to grow old.

And all of a sudden, she questioned *why* she'd chosen to grow old at such a young age. To give everything up and disappear to this tiny house. "My hiding place," she said aloud to the empty room, remembering Nick's words from earlier.

Rising abruptly, she went back to the kitchen and tossed the rest of her tea into the sink. Getting used to living here would take some time, that's all. It had been a stressful night, and now it was time for bed. Besides, there was nothing for her to do anyway.

Chapter Twenty-Three

*A*delmo shoveled horse shit as flies circled around his head. He was soaked in sweat. He tossed the shovel onto the ground and stomped away.

"Hey, where are you going?" Ramiro asked.

"Inside. Do this yourself."

His uncle Ramiro's face turned red, but he looked like he was trying to control himself. "We talked about this, remember? Each of you has chores. You all have to help out."

"Yeah, well, I didn't sign up to work like a dog in this barn."

"Adelmo." He paused his own work. "This is part of owning a farm. We have to take care of the animals. You're responsible for helping out."

"All we do is work," he shouted. "Mow the grass, feed the animals, collect the stupid eggs."

"That's not true." Ramiro raised his voice and Adelmo tried not to cower. "You go to school in the morning."

Just like before when his parents were alive, he went to school during the morning session, from nine to noon; then he did nothing but homework and chores when he got home. "Whoopee, school, life with you is full of excitement." He turned away.

"Come back here," Ramiro shouted.

"Kiss my butt," Adelmo yelled, and took off running.

He didn't want to look back, not that he thought Ramiro would chase him, but Adelmo didn't want to see the look on his face. He kept running until he got to the house. When he got inside, he went straight to his room and started packing.

Sandra peeked in at him. "What are you doing?"

"Leaving."

"What do you mean leaving? Where to?"

"Grandma's."

Sandra entered his room with a frown on her face. "You can't do that. What's wrong?"

He felt like crying and had to fight not to. But his high-pitched voice gave him away. "I hate it here. I hate Ramiro. All he does is make us do chores."

Sandra sat on his bed and nodded. "I miss Isabel."

"And Nick. I should call him and ask him to come get me. He would."

"No, he wouldn't, Adelmo. He can't. He's not related to us. There's nothing he can do."

Adelmo stood and kicked his backpack. He kicked it again and again and again. Then he started knocking books off the bookshelf.

"Stop it!" Sandra shouted. "This isn't helping, and he's going to make you clean it up."

Now actual tears fell from his eyes. "I don't care."

Sandra walked to him and hugged him. She understood how he felt. How alone he was.

"I wish Dad was here," he said, pulling back. "He'd kick Ramiro's ass."

Sandra smiled. "Maybe." She sighed. "Why don't you go play with Toby?"

His dog was the only good thing about living here. "How's that going to help?"

"Might not help, but Toby likes to play with you, and I bet he's tired of being on that chain."

He nodded, because playing with Toby usually did help. Somehow, it felt like he had a friend.

Ramiro appeared at the door, breathing heavily. He took one dark look at Adelmo's room and at the two of them, and without a word turned around and left. The front door slammed shut a few seconds later.

Isabel had never been this sick. She spent three days in bed with a high fever. The cold and being wet for so long had left her with the worst flu she'd ever had. Finally, she went to see a doctor, who filled her full of antibiotics. She angled a chair so she could stare at the beach through the sliding glass door and sat there under a pile of blankets for the rest of the week. She drifted in and out of sleep, not paying attention to the time of day. Stephanie had called every day, concerned about her health, and Isabel kept telling her she'd be in the following day. She'd threatened to stop by, but Isabel had managed to convince her to stay away. The last thing Stephanie needed was to catch the flu and take it home to her kids.

But there was no putting her off forever; she told Isabel she would be there to see her that evening. As miserable as she felt, Isabel wasn't interested in company. However, she was tired of being cooped up in the house, so she decided to venture outside in the afternoon. She walked a short distance, then sat on the sand to watch the surfers and thought of Sandra.

She hadn't called them. Not once. Part of her wanted to let them get used to Ramiro like Rosa had suggested. And part of her just didn't know what to say.

"Isabel!"

She lifted her head and saw Stephanie silhouetted against the setting sun, walking toward her across the sand with her high heels in her hand. "What are you doing out here?"

"I needed some fresh air."

Stephanie looked at the sand with distaste but carefully lowered herself beside Isabel. "How are you?"

"Better."

"You look horrible."

Isabel gazed at the ocean, folding her arms across her knees.

"When are you coming back to work?"

"I don't know."

"What do you mean, you don't know?" She paused. "Nick's gone, you know."

"I know."

"We need you back. If you're feeling better, and even if you're not, you should come back to your own home on the vineyard."

"Just tell me when it's time to sign on the dotted line, and I will."

Stephanie reached across and placed her hand on Isabel's shoulder. "What are you doing, Isabel? I know you want to leave, to finally be finished with the business, but this is no way to go out."

Isabel had no energy to argue. She had little energy for anything.

"Is it the kids? I don't understand what's going on. Why did you take them back to Argentina?"

"I had to."

"Why?"

She shrugged. "I can't talk about it."

Stephanie squeezed her shoulder and lowered her hand. "You know what I've always admired about you?"

Isabel didn't answer or look at her.

"You always do the right thing."

"Not always."

"You do what needs to be done. You do what is sometimes difficult or unpleasant so that other people won't suffer."

"Someone always suffers, Stephanie," Isabel said, rubbing her hand on her face. "No matter what you do. That's the shitty thing about being in charge. Someone is always unhappy."

"I'm not talking about pleasing everyone all the time; I'm talking about you finding the strength to think of others when life is falling apart around you. When your parents died, you didn't drop everything and leave. You wanted to, I know. But you kept things going for all of us who depended on you and the business. You've thought of us the entire time you've been negotiating the sale. And what about our clients? They love us because of you. You make sure we're offering the best products at the best prices. And you were there for Nick when no one else would have been."

Isabel angled her head and glanced at Stephanie. "Don't."

"You could have forced him out. You could have left him without anything."

"Stop," Isabel warned.

"I don't know what happened with the kids, but I know you . . . so don't you sit here and feel guilty about whatever happened."

Isabel straightened her back. "Do you realize that everything you've mentioned has to do with the business? I put the business first. It's a fabulous success. But what about my personal life?"

"What about it?"

"I don't have one! My husband was a raging alcoholic and what did I do? I ignored it. I wasn't there for him. I pretended it wasn't true until it was too late. How the hell was I going to throw him out when I did nothing to save him or my marriage? And the kids!" She shook her head. "Stephanie, I wasn't thinking about them. I was thinking about selling the winery and being free of it. I was . . ." She couldn't speak past the sobs threatening to choke her.

Stephanie shook her head. "You're not going to convince me that you're a horrible person. You took care of business; you took care of the children's welfare. You may not have chosen the best way to do it, but, honey, no one is perfect."

Isabel wiped tears from her face.

"So what do I do? What do I tell people who are calling to talk to you? Your attorney is driving me crazy. He's got things that need your attention. The future owners call a hundred times a day. Isabel, I'll tell them all to go to hell if that's what you want, but—"

Isabel laughed through the tears. "You wouldn't."

Stephanie put an arm around Isabel and pulled her against her side. "Only because you wouldn't."

"What if this time I can't save it? What if I don't give a damn?"

Stephanie sighed and leaned her head against Isabel's. "Then it's been a good ride. Just give me one hell of a good letter of recommendation for my job hunting, will you?"

Isabel smiled. "That was not fighting fair. Now, help me back to my house. My head is killing me. I need to take some painkillers and think about all this."

"All right." Stephanie stood. "Just don't think too long."

Or it would be too late.

Rosa watched and listened to Ramiro rant and rave about Adelmo's attitude, and Sandra locking herself up in her room with her music and cell phone, and Julieta's crying.

"I try to make them happy. I mean, I don't know what that kid is talking about," Ramiro said. "I bought him a bike, and a dog, and he's got a computer loaded with everything a boy could want. He's going to a good school, has clothes on his back. He should be so grateful he can't stand it."

Rosa shook her head.

"Why not?" he shouted.

"First of all, stop yelling," she said. "And second of all, you have to understand that they're kids."

"What does that mean?"

"Kids aren't grateful for clothes and school. If you're expecting them to be, you're going to be disappointed for a long time."

He dropped onto her love seat and ran a hand through his hair. "I'm trying to do what Andres would want, you know. Make them responsible by giving them each some work to do around the house, making sure they do their homework, eat right, go to bed on time. I...I don't know what I'm doing wrong."

Rosa placed a hand on his back and rubbed up and down. "Honey, they're just getting used to living with you, and they've been through so much. Laying down the law is probably more than they can handle. Why don't you spend some time getting to know them? Don't worry so much about what Andres would want, and do things your way."

He gazed at her. "Well, I want them to grow up to be responsible people too. I don't want them to be like I was as a kid."

She smiled. "I bet you were pretty cute."

"A cute pain in the ass. Like that boy. Son of a bitch, does he have a mouth."

Rosa raised an eyebrow. "Must run in the family."

He offered a lopsided grin. "I'm sorry. So, what do I do?"

"Try something fun."

"Fun?"

"Yes, something you like that you think they'd like."

"Fun, huh?" He seemed to think. "Okay, I have an idea. Will you help me?"

In answer, she leaned across and kissed him.

Isabel found the business card Alex Hewitt had given her for his public relations firm. She wasn't really sure why she wanted to call him, but she did. He seemed happy to hear from her and came out to the beach house to see her. Isabel ordered dinner from a local seafood place and prepared the back patio table so they'd have a view of the beach.

He gave her a kiss on the cheek when he walked into her house. "I was surprised you called. But before I get excited, was it a business call?"

Isabel smiled as she led him back to the patio. "I think so."

He laughed. "You think so?"

"I'm not sure about anything these days. I don't want to return to Gallegos. And I don't seem to be interested in pursuing anything else."

They each took a seat at the table.

Alex gave her a strange look. "I'm not sure I understand."

"I want to learn to surf. Like my little cousin. I should have learned with her. Will you sign up with me?"

"You want me to take surfing lessons with you?" He looked amused.

She smiled, feeling her spirits lift for the first time in weeks. "Will you?"

Leaning back in his seat, he smiled. "Why not?"

Ramiro booked a reservation for him, Rosa, and the kids to go on a horseback-riding excursion. A local guide got Julieta all strapped down on the saddle. She wasn't nervous at all, and practically giggled with giddiness when she saw her horse. Even Adelmo seemed excited. Sandra accepted that this day was going to happen but didn't display any emotion.

Their guide, Don Pedro, led them moved slowly uphill on a path through thick brush. Parts were steep and forced them to climb carefully. Rosa hadn't been on a horse since she was a teenager, but she appeared to enjoy the ride as much as the children. A beautiful cloudless sky allowed the sunshine to warm their backs.

Since the mountains were the precordillera of the Andes, they crossed many streams caused by the melting snow high above. Even with the sounds of running water, birds chirping above, and horses clip-clopping on dirt below, there was a calming silence in the air. "Imagine," their guide said, "General San Martin crossing these same cordilleras with his soldiers. What might he have been thinking?"

Adelmo looked high up at the Andes.

"Let's pretend," Don Pedro continued, "that we are those soldiers here to liberate the Americas."

Ramiro let himself be led into the story. Forgetting for a few moments that he was here for family bonding and instead identifying with the grand general who fought for Ramiro's great-great-grandparents. They'd become a proud independent nation, and Ramiro nodded, glad the kids were hearing this after being exposed to all that American nonsense.

Ramiro played along with the guide as he led the children through the game of pretending to be victorious granaderos. Once he had them excitedly participating in the illusion, he chuckled. "You would have made fine soldiers."

Ramiro continued along the path. The sights were amazing. Rosa rode up beside him. "This was a great idea."

"I think so too." He smiled, happy that he'd convinced her to begin dating him. His heart gave a little skip as she sat on the horse looking as perfect as a woman could look.

The guide led them to a ravine, where he stopped. Rosa breathed in. "Ah, flowers."

"Wild roses and all kinds of other flowers," he agreed.

The guide encouraged them to get off the horses and stretch their legs. "We will build a fire and eat." He got the kids ready to start looking for firewood. "But first, I have to warn you," he said, calling them close. "Wild pumas live among these hills. A friend of mine was once stalked by a puma, and just when he became aware that the cat was hiding in the brush, the puma lunged at him. They became engaged in a fierce battle. Cat against man." Don Pedro made wide arcs with his arms. "They rolled and fought. The cat sank his teeth into my friend's back, and he thought he was gone, terminated." The guide made a flat movement with his hands. "But then he remembered his knife, the one we always carry to cut the beef we eat on our excursions." He pulled a sharp knife out of his belt.

Ramiro, who had been mesmerized by the tale, stiffened at the sight of the knife.

"My friend grabbed his knife and stabbed at the wild beast repeatedly on his neck, puncturing the main artery and spilling the cat's blood all over himself and the earth."

"Okay," Rosa said. "I think the details are much too vivid for our little group."

Julieta's eyes were as wide as a fifty-centavo piece. But Adelmo grinned. "Is it true? Did it really happen?"

"Of course," the guide said as if insulted by the idea that he'd fabricate such a story. "So look for wood, but stay close."

"Ah, very close," Rosa said.

"Here." Don Pedro handed Adelmo the knife. "Just in case."

Rosa was about to protest when Ramiro grabbed her arm. Adelmo proudly took the knife and told his sisters he'd protect them.

"I don't like the idea of an eight-year-old with a knife," Rosa protested, and took Julieta's hand and helped her gather wood.

They started a fire and helped to salt the meat. Pretty soon, they created a makeshift grill and cooked their lunch outdoors, rustically. The guide pulled out a bottle of wine. "No meal is complete without a bottle of some of the best wine in the world."

Ramiro sat on the ground and smiled. "You're right there."

Adelmo knelt beside them. "My cousin Isabel makes the best wine in the world."

"What?" Ramiro said. "No California wine is better than a good Argentine wine, boy."

"Hers is," he insisted in the absolute tone of a kid who wanted to argue.

Rosa placed an arm around his back. "That's because Isabel learned from her parents who were the best wine-makers in Mendoza."

Adelmo sat down. "Did you grow up with Isabel?"

Rosa nodded. "We were best friends."

"You should have convinced her to stay here." He

glanced at Ramiro. "At least you were smart enough to stay in our country."

Ramiro laughed and caressed the boy's head. "This is where I belong. And where you belong. You're Argentine. Don't ever forget that."

Adelmo squinted from the sun shining on his face and seemed to think about that. "I'll never forget."

They ate under the midafternoon sun, and Ramiro realized he was happy. Truly happy. Maybe this would work out after all. Maybe he could allow himself to relax and get close to the children without having to prove something to his deceased brother.

Chapter Twenty-Four

I sabel was thrown from the surfboard and carried by a relentless wave. She swam to shore, fighting one breaker after another. When she made it to shore, she dropped onto the sand, out of breath.

"I'm going to die," she said.

Alex sat beside her in his wet suit, breathing heavily. "Think we're too old to learn this?"

"Hell no," she said.

He laughed.

"Though I think I prefer a Jacuzzi and a facial to being thrown by waves."

"How about dinner? Do you prefer dinner?"

"Yes. Dinner would be lovely." They dragged themselves to their feet and hauled their surfboards with them to the public bathroom where they changed out of their wet suits. They could shower and dress for dinner at the beach house. Isabel laughed as they approached her house, both complaining of sore muscles.

As they walked up to the front of the beach house, her smile faded when she saw Nick standing by her front door.

"Hi," he said, his eyes only glancing at her before locking onto Alex.

"Nick." She shouldn't be so happy to see him, but she was. He looked good. Professionally dressed in a suit.

While she stood there in a pair of shorts and a spaghetti-strap top, her hair stringy and wet.

"We need to talk," he said.

She glanced at Alex. "This is Nick."

"Her husband," Nick added.

Alex raised an eyebrow.

"Ex-husband," Isabel corrected, frowning at Nick. That was no slip of the tongue; they'd been divorced a long time.

Alex nodded. "Nice to meet you."

"We were actually going out," she said to Nick, though her stomach felt like it had dipped into another wave, and she wouldn't be able to eat a thing. "We've been surfing for about four hours and are starving."

Nick shook his head. "You know, Stephanie told me you'd flipped out, but I didn't believe her."

Alex looked uncomfortable, and Isabel didn't want him to be in a position where he felt forced to listen to her personal drama. "Maybe we should call it a day and have dinner another night," she said to him.

Alex seemed uncertain. "You'll be okay?"

Nick's faced hardened. "She's not okay; that's why I'm here. Just in case you need to know, the president of Gallegos Winery doesn't take the day off of work to hang out at the beach, blowing off a business she spent her entire life creating."

"Maybe some time off is exactly what she needs," Alex said.

Isabel stepped between them and opened the door to her house. "I'm fine. I'll call you, Alex." She turned to Nick. "Come in."

The moment the door was closed, he seized Isabel's arm and pulled her close. "Who the hell is that guy?"

Isabel didn't mind having Nick hold her so close. In fact, she wanted to wrap her arms around him. He'd come to see her. On his own. Or at Stephanie's request. But he was here, and he seemed jealous.

"He's a friend. I realized while sitting here alone that I don't have any friends. And I never dated anyone but you."

"So you're *dating* him?" Nick's distress caused his voice to crack.

"Not really. But I'm thinking about it."

He cursed and let her go. Turning away, he faced the sliding glass door that looked out onto the ocean. "Stephanie said you won't go back to the winery. If you don't keep up your agreement, the sale will not go through, Isabel. You're supposed to be there until their people officially take over and then you're supposed to be a consultant for a year."

"I know that. But I'm not ready to return."

He turned to gaze at her with a frown. "What does that mean?"

She shrugged and thought about the consequences of not returning. "I think it means I really don't care. And you can't imagine how free I feel."

Dropping his backside on the arm of her sofa as if he were straddling a bike, he stared at her without speaking.

"I'm always trying to save everyone and everything, and where has it gotten me?"

He watched her, wide-eyed, and the bewildered look on his face pleased her.

"I went to Argentina and had to decide what to do with the kids. I had the business to think about and everyone's jobs and you, and it was all on my shoulders. It's always on my shoulders. You've never been able to see that."

"I see it," he said softly.

"No, you don't." She stepped closer to him. "You think it's so easy to just do what you *feel*, and to hell with being responsible. Leave it all to me to take care of everything, then blame me when it all falls apart."

"Isabel, I know you were thinking of Gallegos when you agreed to transfer custody to the kids' uncle. I didn't see it when you told us about it, because all I could think of was that the kids were going to be gone."

"Well, they are." The room stirred with uneasy silence. "Look, I'm done being everything to everyone. You're right. Blowing off your responsibilities is the easiest thing in the world."

"Isabel." He held out a hand, but she slapped it away.

"Leave me alone."

"Can't you do this after the business is officially sold and all the paperwork is signed?"

"No."

"So then what the hell are you going to do? Hang out here and play at the beach day and night?"

She smiled. "Yes."

He shook his head. "The buyers are going to back out. You're going to end up with the winery again."

"I'm not going back until I'm ready. Doesn't matter what happens." She angled her head. "I have an idea— why don't you take charge for a change?"

"I signed everything over to you." He ran a hand through his hair. "And I can't do what you do."

They stared at each other. Finally, she said, "Then the hell with it."

Looking lost, he headed to the front door and opened it. "Isabel, come on. We get it. *I* get it. I'm sorry. Come back, please. I don't want you to lose your opportunity to sell; I know how much you want to unload the business."

"You know, the funny thing is, I was actually starting to feel sorry that I was selling the vineyard when the children were here. I remembered growing up in a vineyard and thought it would be nice for them to grow up in one too. Everything was so . . . perfect. Wasn't it?"

"Yes," he said softly.

Her anger and confusion suddenly lifted, along with the ambiguity she'd been feeling. "I just can't go back there without the kids . . . without you."

"Oh, Isabel." Nick closed the door and followed Isabel into the living room.

"I made such a terrible mistake." She lowered her tired body onto the couch. "Nick, how could I have been so wrong about what I wanted?"

"If you feel that way, then . . . go back to Argentina and get them."

Tears filled her eyes. "I can't. Ramiro won't agree to relinquishing custody."

Nick walked up to her. "Then fight."

She shook her head.

He knelt down and gripped her arms. "Isabel, you've always fought for what you wanted. Always. Go back and get the kids."

She shook her head again. "I'd probably have to go to court. It will cost a lot of money. Money I wouldn't have without selling the business, which, as you've pointed out, might not be possible thanks to my behavior these past few days."

"I'll take care of the business. Stephanie will help me. Everyone at the winery will. You go get our kids."

She gazed into his eyes. "You told me when you traveled to Argentina with me that you were going to be there for me when I realized what I had done."

"Yeah," he whispered. "I'm not all that good at being there for you, am I?"

She reached across and fit into his arms. "I realized what I'd done right after we made love the first time, but I didn't know how to tell you. I wanted to fix it. I knew our fragile new world was going to tumble apart and that it was all going to be my fault, but I was helpless to do anything about it. I'm sorry, Nick."

"Me too." He kissed the top of her head and held her close. "And this time I'm with you no matter what. I promise."

Isabel drove her rented car onto Ramiro's property, the wheels producing plumes of dust on the dirt road leading to his ranch. She parked in front of his house and looked out at the expanse of his ranch. Five horses stood lazily in their pen. A couple turned their heads to look at her. A long barn off to the side had an open door. She headed that way.

She heard Adelmo's laughter, and her heart picked up speed. She told herself that if she got there and the children were happy, she'd let them stay put. She and Nick would move to Argentina to be close to them. Nick would agree immediately.

Adelmo walked out of the barn with a pail of milk in each of his hands. He stopped when he saw Isabel, his eyes wide, a smile growing on his face. "Cousin Isabel!"

She smiled. "Hi, honey."

He put the pails down and ran to her, wrapping his arms around her waist.

Ramiro walked out, then leaned against the barn, pulling off a pair of gloves. "Back so soon?"

Adelmo pulled back and glanced at Ramiro. Then he stepped farther away from her. "Where's Nick?"

"He couldn't come. But he said to say hi."

He nodded. "Tell him I learned to milk a cow."

Isabel smiled, then started to chuckle. "You are one dirty little boy. Look at you."

Adelmo came forward again and gave her another long hug.

Isabel wrapped her arms around him, happy for the affection he was so willingly offering. "Where are your sisters?"

"Rosa picks Julieta up from school and brings her home in the afternoon so I can work," Ramiro explained. "Sandra goes to afternoon classes. She'll be back later."

Adelmo picked up his milk pails. "I'll take these inside."

"You can start on your homework then," Ramiro said.

Adelmo nodded; then he smiled at Isabel. "You're going to stay for dinner?"

"Sure . . . if it's okay with you, Ramiro."

"Of course," he said. He waved her into the barn. "Know how to brush a horse down?"

"Not really."

"Come here, earn your dinner."

She stepped closer, not dressed to work with a horse, but what the hell. "Is that what you do, make everyone earn their dinner?"

He grinned. "Absolutely. So what are you doing here?"

She entered the barn. He had stalls on both sides. "I wanted to see the kids."

"And?"

"And what? I missed them."

"Hmm." He handed her a brush. "I'll clean the hooves first; then you can do the rest."

The horse he planned for her to brush was secured by ties attached to his halter. Ramiro stood beside the horse and ran his hand down the front of his left leg until he reached the hoof. The horse offered his foot to receive his pedicure.

"How has it gone the last few weeks?" Isabel asked.

He held the hoof confidently in his hand and used a pick to take out all the gunk. "Great. How else would it have gone?"

She placed the hand not holding the brush into her sweater pocket and leaned on the gate of the stall. "No problems?"

Finished with one leg, Ramiro moved on to the next foot. "What problems? There's nothing to it."

Isabel doubted it had been that easy. "Adelmo can have an attitude."

"Hmm," was all he said as he continued to work. He

finished with all four legs, then gave the horse a treat. "Stand here," he barked, and Isabel wasn't sure if he was talking to her or the horse. Then she realized he spoke much more kindly to the horse. "You'll start up here by the mane. Use gentle, circular motions. Follow the direction of hair." He grabbed her arm and pulled her toward the horse, showing her what to do with the brush. "Go from the neck to the chest, then over the shoulders, like this."

He stood back, crossed his arms, and watched. "Long flight to check up on me," he said.

"Is that what you think I'm doing?"

"I know that's what you're doing. Now move down his back, work your way along the sides. Finish by brushing down the legs."

Isabel followed his instructions, murmuring to the beautiful horse. "How did you learn to do this?"

"When I decided to have a farm, I learned everything about it until I was an expert. That's the way I do everything. I don't fail."

Isabel stopped brushing. "This isn't a contest between the two of us, you know."

"Keep going," he said.

"I want the kids to be happy, that's all."

"Life isn't all about being happy."

She thought about that. And actually, he was right. Life wasn't at all about always being happy. She'd learned that. Sometimes life was about doing what was right regardless of whether it made you feel good. Life was about loving those you had beside you while you had the chance.

He took the brush from her and moved her aside, completing the job.

"Ramiro, I'm here to give you a chance to back out of our agreement," she said gently.

He stopped brushing.

"Now that you've had the chance to see what parenthood is really like, it's not failure if you decide you don't want to do it."

"Are you crazy?" He tossed the brush down onto the ground and advanced toward her. "Get this through your head. I'm going to raise those kids," he said, pointing toward the house, his voice cold.

"I just wonder if you're doing this out of some kind of misplaced loyalty to your brother rather than a real desire to want to share your life with them."

"Don't come here to *my* home—"

"I have a right to ask." Isabel's own temper began to rise.

"Bullshit."

"I have a *responsibility* to make sure that you asked to raise them because—"

"No, you don't."

"Because you want them, not just because you want to belatedly connect to your brother."

"Get out," he said through clenched teeth.

"I won't."

He grabbed her arm firmly and started to lead her toward the exit. "Leave. I won't have you here saying idiotic—"

"It's not idiotic. I *love* those kids." She yanked her arm loose and fought to catch her balance.

"And you think I don't?" He reached out to steady her, but she jumped back out of his way.

"I don't know, you son of—"

"That's enough!" Rosa walked into the barn. "I can't believe you two are fighting like children." She faced Ramiro. "You are not the only family member those niños have, so you'd better accept the fact that other people *do* have a right to offer their opinion and concern." She spun around to shake her head at Isabel. "And you can't keep changing your mind from week to week. You made your choice—now live with it."

Both Ramiro and Isabel stared at Rosa. At first, Isabel was too angry to reply. Rosa should be on *her* side, not his. She found her voice as that realization sank in. "I guess we'll all see each other in court."

"Bet on it, sweetheart," Ramiro shouted as Isabel stormed out of the barn.

Ramiro let out a string of curses when Isabel left. When he faced Rosa, she didn't look happy or sympathetic. "Did you hear her?" he asked, stretching his arm out and pointing in the direction of Isabel's exit. "Did you hear what she had the nerve to ask and insinuate?"

She crossed her arms. "I heard it and saw it all. And after seeing your reaction to her question, I have to wonder if she isn't right."

The injustice of Rosa's words wounded him. "But how can you say that?"

Rosa's eyes filled with compassion. She reached out and placed a hand in his. "Because from day one you've said that you wanted custody because you owed it to your brother, because they were your blood, because they *should* live with you. You never said anything about wanting them because you loved them."

"That's not fair. How could I love them when I'd never met them?"

"How about because you love kids?"

"I've never had kids. But who doesn't love children?"

"Well, now you have your brother's hijos, and now you know them. Do you love them?"

His jaw tightened as he clenched his teeth and thought about her question. He drew in a deep breath and looked away from Rosa. The hell with her and Isabel. The kids were his family. And he'd fight them all if he had to. "Love doesn't really matter, does it, Rosa?"

"I think it matters a lot."

"Does it matter to you enough to stand by me on this?"

"It matters enough"—she pulled her hand out of his— "that I'm going to be on the side of the children."

Hell. As Rosa headed to the house, he knew one thing for sure—he didn't want to fight with her. She was the best thing that ever happened to him. So, what the hell did she mean she was going to be on the side of the children?

He was the one who was right. Standing by the children would be standing by him, because he was doing the right thing. Yet . . . damn it, he just didn't feel as sure as he once had, and that bothered him. It bothered him enough that he was afraid, because he suddenly felt like he had when he'd taken his mother's money without permission. Sometimes doing good, doing the right thing, wasn't clearly spelled out. And all the good intentions in the world didn't reverse a painful mistake.

Chapter Twenty-Five

*I*sabel walked into Ramiro's house looking for Julieta. She found her in the kitchen eating a pastry and drinking a glass of milk. Dressed in her little white school uniform, she was kicking her legs as she enjoyed her snack at the kitchen table. Isabel watched her with a flood of emotion. How had she imagined that it would be easy to turn away from these beautiful children?

"Cousin Isabel," she shrieked when she looked up from her plate. She jumped out of her seat. "You came back! You came back!" She leaped into Isabel's arms. Isabel caught her and picked her up. Julieta buried her face in Isabel's neck, and Isabel closed her eyes and rocked her back and forth.

Rosa walked into the house. "Wonderful," she said. "Now you've come into his house, uninvited."

"He and Adelmo invited me to dinner."

"Cousin Isabel is back," Julieta said with a smile.

"Yes, she is, honey."

Isabel put Julieta down. "I wasn't trying to antagonize him, but he refuses to have a rational discussion. If living here with him is what's best for the kids, then fine, but if not, then I want them to come back home with me."

"Isabel, how can you do this? I warned you not to sign any paperwork—"

"I know. I was wrong."

"Yes, and because you realized you were wrong doesn't mean the kids should play musical houses."

Rosa was right, of course. And Isabel wouldn't pursue her legal rights if they wanted to stay with Ramiro. She promised herself that.

Ramiro walked inside and glanced at Isabel and Rosa. For a second, Isabel wasn't sure what he would do. But he offered a tight smile at Julieta. "Aren't we lucky tonight? Isabel flew all the way from America to have dinner with us."

Julieta giggled.

And Rosa seemed beyond happy with his response. "I'm going to go buy some ice cream for dessert. Who wants to go with me?" she said.

"I do," Julieta said.

"I don't," came Sandra's voice from the door as she put her book bag down on the ground and eyed Isabel.

Isabel couldn't control the smile that came instantly to her face. "Hi, sweetheart."

Sandra's chin lifted and she blinked a couple of times. "My hair's grown back," she said.

Knowing what to say was difficult for an adult, and Isabel figured it was even more difficult for a young girl who'd been through as much as Sandra had. "I can see that. Looks good. And you want to know what I've been doing?"

Still standing by the front door in her white uniform that matched Julieta's, she nodded. "Okay," she said with a thickness to her voice.

"I've been learning to surf. I'm hoping we can go out together sometime."

Ramiro cleared his throat. "Sandra, get your school stuff in your room and change. Then you can chat with Isabel."

Sandra nodded and obeyed.

Later, Isabel went for a walk with Sandra. "I made a lot of mistakes," Isabel said as they circled the horse pen. "But probably the biggest was acting more like your friend than a parent."

Sandra smiled. "But you are my friend. You're my cousin."

Isabel wrapped an arm around Sandra's shoulder. "But if I'm going to raise you, I have to be more than a cousin, Sandra."

"But you're not going to raise us, are you?"

"I came back to see if your uncle and I can come to an agreement. My other mistake was not honoring your mother's decision and not realizing what an honor she'd given me."

"My mom was a pretty smart mom."

Isabel found a spot to stop and watch the sun set over the far-off mountains. She leaned on the wooden beams of the corral, thinking of Brenda and the hundreds of letters she'd written that she'd only briefly read and almost never responded to. "Oh, honey, she was such an amazingly wonderful person, and I'm so sorry...so sorry that she's not here for you and that I'm here instead."

Sandra blinked away tears and bit her bottom lip.

Isabel leaned forward. "But I promise you, Sandra. I'm going to be the person your mother wanted me to be."

"Does that mean I'm going to live with you again?"

This was the complicated part. "I don't want to fight with your uncle, and we both want to raise you kids, but I just want you to know that no matter what happens, I'm not letting you guys out of my sight again."

Sandra ran into Isabel's arms, and they held each other for a long time. And Isabel knew that if Brenda could see them, and she was sure she could, she finally would be smiling.

Ramiro hated the idea of dropping the pibes off at their grandmother's house over the weekend as he'd been doing since they arrived from America. The woman had never said thank you, and now that Isabel was staying there, he had less desire to be gracious. But he also was really looking forward to spending some time alone with Rosa, so when Saturday morning arrived, he told them to pack their overnight bags and off they went to Grandmother's house.

For a change, Doña Dominga invited him inside. She kissed her grandkids, told them treats awaited them in the kitchen, and sent them off to play when they were finished.

"Sit down, Ramiro, Isabel," she said. "I want to talk to the two of you."

He didn't want to hear what was on her mind. Nothing she had to say would benefit him, but he sat on her couch.

"First, I want to congratulate you. You're doing a good job with my grandchildren and so is Rosa. You're lucky she decided to date you, by the way. Don't lose her."

Grinning, he nodded once. Good advice even if it was unsolicited.

"But what I really want to ask you is to take Isabel to Brenda and Andres's house to help her clear it out."

Isabel appeared surprised by the request. "Clear it out?" she asked.

"They left the house to you, mi amor. Probably because they expected you to take care of the children. But it can't stay vacant forever. You should figure out what to do with the items in the house and then...sell the condo."

"But...I don't know what to do with her things. Don't you want them?"

"I've been to their home, and I took the things I wanted. Some pictures of the kids, a few things that belonged to Brenda. I don't want her furniture or clothes or...other things. And Ramiro should help you. Ramiro, you can decide what to do with Andres's belongings and help Isabel donate the furniture."

He shifted uneasily. "I don't want anything that belonged to Andres."

"Nevertheless, you'll do it out of respect for your brother."

He sighed and stood, wanting to say he'd do nothing of the sort. Who the hell did she think she was to give him orders anyway? But having lost his mother so long ago and not having any family left made him look at Doña Dominga as he would have his own mother. "Bueno," he said. "I'll do it for you, señora."

She smiled. "Gracias, Ramiro. Okay, you two go. Let me enjoy my grandkids."

"You want us to go *now*?" Isabel asked.

"Sure, or do you have another important appointment?"

Like him, she caved in. And so they drove to Brenda and Andres's place in a neighboring suburb. Ramiro had never been to Andres's home, but Doña Dominga gave him the address, so he knew where it was. Isabel had a key. They entered the large condo and he felt strange, like he was invading Andres's personal space. "What do you want to do with all this stuff?"

"Well, maybe donating to a church or the needy would be a good idea. Are there organizations we can contact?"

"I don't know." He walked around the living room and made his way down the hall, glancing into the rooms. The kids' rooms. Andres and Brenda's room. He paused and looked inside.

Isabel followed him down. "Is there anything you'd like to have?"

"I wouldn't take anything from here. Hell, it's . . . eerie."

"Maybe the kids would like mementos of their parents."

He nodded. "You can bring them by and let them take what they want." He walked inside the bedroom and opened the closet. Inside was the usual—clothes and shoes. Boxes filled one side of the closet. He pulled a few out that had gloves and scarves. Then he noticed a box with his name on it, stuffed in the back.

"What is it?" Isabel asked. He opened the lid to the large box, which had probably been a boot box. Inside were things he'd had in his bedroom as a kid. Motorcycle magazines, a couple of his favorite books—*The Cabin Boy* and a leather copy of *Martín Fierro*—soccer flags that he used to take to the games, even his report cards from school that his mother had saved.

"Why did they have your things?" Isabel stood close, looking at the pieces of his childhood that he'd abandoned when he never returned home.

"Maybe when my mom died . . . he saved it from her house," he said quietly. He pulled out a picture that his mother had taken of him and Andres. They had their arms around each other's shoulders, smiling at their mother. They looked so much alike. Except that Andres looked older, thinner, and not as cocky as Ramiro. "Why did he save this stuff?" he asked himself.

"Maybe he hoped to give it to you someday."

"That son of a bitch," Ramiro whispered. Andres had never reached out to him. All those years he'd held a grudge. He dropped the picture back. Maybe Ramiro hadn't been easy to find. Inside the box was also an envelope with a letter Ramiro had written to say he was sorry and that he hadn't meant to lose their mother's money. Heavily creased, it appeared to have been read and reread many times.

"I'll leave you alone," Isabel said, and headed out of the bedroom.

"No. Wait." He gazed at her over his shoulder. "You were right about something."

She looked down and waited for him to continue.

"I've carried this poisonous guilt around for a long time. And anger. But when I heard he and Brenda had died..." He shook his head and swallowed. A tightness in his chest prevented him from continuing for a few seconds. "I wanted to make sure Andres's pibes were taken care of, you know. I had to make sure of that."

"I know."

"I didn't know you, and there was no way in hell I was going to let you raise my relatives in a foreign country. I didn't think Andres would really want that. I thought I owed it to him to...you know...be responsible and take care of the kids. They are the only ones left of our family." His voice cracked and he cursed.

She walked back into the room and stood close to him. "I understand how you feel."

He nodded and closed the box. Then he stood and looked around the room. He picked up a framed picture of Andres and Brenda and placed it under his arm. Maybe he'd take a few things that belonged to Andres after all. For his children. "The kids should come and take what they want," he said.

"Okay."

"And, Isabel. You and I are family. Let's work things out without lawyers, huh?"

She nodded. "If we can."

"We can."

"I'm not so sure. I love the children and want to raise them."

He cleared his throat and nodded. "Let's see what they want to do, and really look at what would be best for them."

"We might not agree on what's best for them. I think living with someone who really wants them is best. You think the fact that they share your DNA is reason enough. I'm not even sure you really want them."

He did...but how much of it was simply a feeling of obligation, he didn't know. "Let's talk. No more yelling, I promise."

She smiled.

"Now, bring them by this weekend while they're at Doña Dominga's, and once they take what they want, I'll have the condo cleared out. You can put it on the market in a week or two."

She arched an eyebrow. "Do you want it? I could—"

"No," he said. "Sell it. Put the money into a savings account for the pibes to use when they grow up."

They left the condo. He dropped Isabel back at Doña Dominga's and went to see Rosa.

Rosa noticed that her normally enthusiastic and highly animated lover was quiet as he sat in her living room. She brought him a beer and sat on his lap. He wrapped his arms loosely around Rosa's waist.

"Think you'd ever want to marry me?" he asked.

"Is that a marriage proposal? Because if it is, then the answer's no. That was terrible."

He smiled. "No, it wasn't a proposal. I was just curious what your plans were."

She ran her fingers through his long, silky hair. "I don't have a plan."

"What about kids?"

She arched an eyebrow. "What about kids?"

"Do you want more?"

Rosa whistled. "Ah." She slid off his lap and onto the

couch beside him. "I love children, and I miss not having mine around. But...I'm not sure I'd want to start again, if that's what you're asking."

He nodded and frowned. "Yes, I'm asking. I love you, Rosa. Do you love me?"

"I love you, yes...but—"

"No, there shouldn't be a but. I'm either going to be a package deal—me and my brother's hijos, plus a couple of my own—or I'm off the market."

"It's one thing to raise Andres's kids, and another to get pregnant and have my own. I'm too old for that." Her tone softened. "I'd love it, but women don't have babies at forty-six."

He took her hands. "Rosita, you're still young. Wouldn't it be nice to have a couple of babies and raise them on the ranch? Our kids could play with my brother's. It would be a nice life, no?"

It did sound nice. And living with this man permanently would be an adventure. Much like it had been with her ex-husband, except that Ramiro was responsible and a take-charge kind of guy. "I don't know, Ramiro. But what about your nieces and nephew? Are you planning to hear Isabel out?"

"I'm willing to do what's best for my brother's kids, like you said. If that means letting them go"—his Adam's apple glided up and down—"I'll be involved in their lives as an uncle rather than a father. But I've been thinking that no matter what, Rosa, I want you in my life."

"You crazy man." She caressed his face gently. "I don't want to get married, but I would be very happy to be with you for the rest of my life."

"I'm okay with that." He leaned toward her and kissed her. "But I think you'll marry me one day. Assuming I ask." He grinned and she did, too, leaning in for a kiss. As they reclined across the couch together, she reminded herself she hadn't planned on getting involved again with a man. But Ramiro was sweet and he offered her hope that her life didn't lie just in the past. Her life wasn't almost over; it was just beginning.

Ramiro and Isabel sat the children down in a circle in the living room. They'd had dinner and had moved to the living room to play a card game. When the game was over, the cards now stacked in the center of his round redwood coffee table, Ramiro told them to stay put.

He and Isabel had decided they were going to approach the topic of their future as united friends. As family members who loved them. But she was nervous, and she could tell Ramiro was too.

"The three of you know that Isabel and I both want to raise you."

A seriousness took over their young faces.

He sat on the couch, his arms resting on his legs as he leaned forward. "Isabel brought you back to Argentina because I didn't give her much of a choice. I wanted you raised here in Argentina."

Adelmo blinked, then cast a look down. She knew he'd felt the same way. An eight-year-old staunch patriot. She wondered if he still felt the same.

"But she didn't want to bring you back."

"That's not what you said," Sandra challenged Isabel.

"You said *you* wanted us to come back because you didn't want to be a mom."

Isabel reached for Sandra's hand and covered it with her own. "Everything I told you was the truth, but I didn't say I didn't *want* to be a mom. I said I didn't feel capable. Originally, I agreed with Ramiro. I thought you all would be better off here. But after the time we spent together, I've changed my mind. I can be a parent. I'm confident that I could provide a good life for us all."

"And," Ramiro said when she finished, "I still want you to live here with me. I think you'd have a better life here."

"My idea was that you come back to California with me. After the vineyard sells, I'll have unlimited time to spend with you. And there's nothing I'd rather do."

Ramiro nodded. "So you see that you are very much wanted. Your father was my brother and you are my family—that's important. And Isabel shared a special closeness with your mother. We both want to be here for whatever you might need."

Isabel nodded. He'd said that beautifully, and she had nothing to add.

"Though the decision is ours to make on where you'll be living, we are willing to listen to your input."

The kids all looked at each other. Finally Sandra spoke up. "What are we supposed to say?"

"Whatever you want," Isabel said. "Tell us what you like about living here, what you liked about living in California. What you didn't like."

"I didn't like the schools in America," Adelmo said. "Or that I had to speak in English."

"Okay," she said, feeling her heart sink.

"But I liked my soccer team. And learning baseball with Nick. And not having *chores*."

Ramiro chuckled. "Didn't your dad make you do chores?"

Adelmo shook his head.

"Yes, he did," Julieta said.

"Well, I had to take out the trash and clean my room, but that's *all*," he emphasized.

Sandra cleared her throat. "I liked school better in America. And surfing. And being with you, Cousin Isabel." Her eyes met Ramiro's and she added, "I'm sorry, Tío."

He shook his head. "Don't be. Nothing you say is going to hurt our feelings."

"No matter what, the two of us are going to be around for you. If you live with me, you're going to visit Argentina often to see your grandmother and your uncle. And if you stay here, I will live here part of the time, too, and you can come visit me in America."

They were now smiling. Having a little of both worlds probably appealed to them.

"What about me?" Julieta jumped up on her knees. "No one asked me."

"You're right," Isabel said. "Shame on us. Tell us what you think."

"I need to take care of my dog, Charlie. He needs me."

Isabel hadn't thought of taking three dogs home with her. She tried to keep her smile. "Well, Charlie is lucky to have you taking care of him."

"So, Cousin Isabel, I think I'm going to have to stay here, even though I miss your stories."

She smiled. "Losing out to a dog, huh? I guess I can understand that."

Ramiro cleared his throat and rubbed his hands together. "Okay, you all go get ready for bed. Isabel and I will talk."

They stood and hugged and kissed both Isabel and Ramiro, but Adelmo paused. "Uncle Ramiro?"

"Yes."

"Do you remember things about my papi?"

Ramiro leaned back and gazed at the boy. "Oh yeah," he said softly. "I remember a lot."

"Will you tell me some things sometime, whether I live with you or Isabel?"

"Well, flaco, my memories of your dad are all from when we were pibes."

"That's okay."

"He was always the kid who did the right thing. And I was always the troublemaker. We fought a lot."

"That's okay. I still want to hear what you remember."

"Okay, since you like soccer so much, I'll tell you one story about your dad and me, and then you go to bed."

"Okay."

"When I was nine and he was fifteen, we went to the soccer stadium together. He didn't want to take me, but I bugged him and my mom so much that she made him take me. Then halfway through the game, I got lost in a mob of angry fans."

He had Adelmo's attention, and Isabel's.

"Andres was supposed to take care of me. But I got away from him, and when he tried to capture me, I called him a wimp and ran off. There were punches flying, food being tossed over my head; it was great. But when the police broke it all up and detained me, they wanted to know where my parents were and I had to tell them I ran away from my brother. They helped me find him; then Andres kicked my butt all the way home."

Adelmo laughed.

"He swore he'd never take me anywhere with him again." Ramiro smiled. "It's funny. I was a lot like you when I was a kid. Opinionated, rebellious, you know—a pain in the butt."

"Hey," Adelmo said.

Ramiro reached for him and put him in a headlock. Adelmo giggled and socked at Ramiro's arms and chest to get loose. Ramiro chuckled and let him go. "Go on. Go to bed."

Ramiro watched Adelmo round the corner to the hallway that led to his bedroom. "You know, we're just now starting to get along. He's acted like he hates me since he got here."

"Don't feel bad. He made me feel the same way."

Ramiro nodded. "So . . . how do we make this decision that will affect all our lives forever?"

Isabel wasn't sure. She'd felt trapped so much of her life and had so wanted to be free. But right now, all she wanted was the opportunity to share her life with these wonderful little individuals fate had placed in her path.

"I'm younger than you," Ramiro finally said.

Isabel found that humorous. "I'm not planning on dying anytime soon, so the few years I've got on you won't make that big a difference. And, being older, I've got the financial ability to give them anything they want or need."

"Sometimes it's best not to have everything you want. To learn how to be happy with what you have."

"Is that why you stocked their rooms with stuff and bought them dogs and motorcycles, and—"

"I'm just saying, money isn't everything."

"I didn't say it was."

"Fine, here is another reason. This is their birth country. Staying here should count for something."

"I don't think that should matter at all. Aside from you and Tía Dominga, what do they have here?"

"Their culture, their language, their history, their friends."

"They had friends in America too. And as far as history, they'll always have their past; that will never go away. But where will they have a better future?"

"Here," he said.

"I disagree."

He shrugged. "Of course."

"I'm not denying that they could have a good life with you, Ramiro. In fact, we could probably both provide for them equally well." She decided to lay it all on the line. "But those little guys opened up a nurturing part of my soul I didn't know existed. They forced me to return to the world of the living. To spend time with them because I cared about them, not because I had to." Her hands shook on her lap so she gripped them together. "And...I want to share the rest of my life with them. I want to watch them grow up. I want to be with Sandra when she goes out on her first date." She paused to take a shaky breath and looked into Ramiro's eyes. "I couldn't figure out why Brenda wanted me to raise her children. I thought I was completely the wrong person. And I know it was probably because she didn't have a choice. Who else was there?" She shook her head. "How she must have hoped it would never happen that I'd be in control of her children."

Ramiro listened with his perpetual frown.

"But it happened. And I can't help feeling that her choice was the right one. For me. For the kids." Those short months together had brought her back from this ever-shrinking box of a life that included nothing but the winery and her personal pill of bitterness. Being with the kids taught her, maybe for the first time ever, what was really important. Family, and those who loved her.

He studied her. "I wonder," he said, his voice deep and contemplative, "what choice she would have made if Andres and I had had a better relationship."

"I don't know," she said honestly. Maybe Brenda wouldn't have chosen a cousin who lived in America, no matter how close they had been once. "But the facts are that you and Andres didn't have a relationship at all."

"No," he agreed. "And even if we had, they still would have chosen you."

Surprised, she lifted an eyebrow. "Why do you say that?"

"You're a determined woman who goes after what she wants in life." He leaned forward. "And you don't give up, do you?"

"I've given up on some things from time to time." Her marriage for one.

"But not on your responsibilities. Your cousin knew that."

"Except that I was willing to give up *this* responsibility, Ramiro. I'm not proud of that. But now I don't want them because I need to fulfill a responsibility...I want them because I love them."

"And if I still say no? That I won't tear up that guardianship agreement? You'll go back to the lawyers?"

Her heart sank. "No, no lawyers. I'll have to live with the stupid choice I made."

"Just like that?"

"You'll just have to get used to me hanging around a lot."

He chuckled. "That's something I don't want."

"So, is that what you've decided?" she asked, not able to share in his amusement.

"I've been asking myself how accurate you were when you said I just wanted to repair my past with Andres. And of course you were right. But I'm glad I've gotten to know his hijos. Like you, I feel a new appreciation for family, and being there for them when they need me."

"I'm glad." And she meant that.

"But I'm willing to continue to build that relationship as an uncle, not a permanent guardian."

Relief washed over her, like one of those strong waves. If she hadn't been sitting, her knees might have buckled. "You mean that?"

"Yes, I do. As a single man, I didn't realize how difficult raising kids could be. And I have no desire to watch Sandra go on her first date."

Isabel laughed.

"I think you want this more than I do," he admitted,

almost in defeat. "Don't get me wrong, I want to be part of their lives. They *are* my only tie to my family."

"I'll send them to visit you as often as you'd like, I promise. And, Ramiro, thank you."

"No thanks necessary. When I decided to become responsible for them, I didn't even know you existed. And once I met you...I was sure Brenda had lost her mind. But I was wrong."

She stood and gave him a hug.

He patted her back awkwardly, as if uncomfortable, then stepped back. "It's too bad that the choices we make can lead to irreversible paths, isn't it?"

She was so happy, so relieved, she could barely focus on what he was saying. "What choices do you mean?"

He shrugged. "I mean, you chose to leave the country. I chose to take my mother's money without asking. Andres chose to stop being my brother. We might have all grown older together, laughing and enjoying each other at one family gathering or another all these years. Watched those kids grow from babies to who they are today. Yet, here we all are, strangers."

Isabel's eyes grew misty. She'd never thought of it quite that way. "Not anymore," she said. "Somehow, tragically, fate has brought at least the five of us together. And we'll make up for lost time."

It wouldn't be the same. That, they both knew. The two missing people would always be missed. There would be that void—mostly for the children. So, especially for them, they had to try to be a family.

A week later, after Ramiro called in another favor to get new tourist visas rushed through, and Brenda's lawyer had begun the more permanent paperwork, everyone sat around the table at Tía Dominga's house. Isabel, the kids, Rosa, and Ramiro all joked and laughed as if they had always been close. Isabel happily grasped on to the thought that they really could make up for lost time and she could rebuild her family unit with this discordant group of people. Related by birth, marriage, and friendship, family was what one made it.

Chapter Twenty-Six

In a year filled with choices, deciding not to sell the winery was simultaneously the most difficult and the easiest choice. Difficult, because it was the final closing of those dreams Isabel had spent a lifetime wanting, but easiest because she no longer wanted the same things. Those days she'd spent on a surfboard or sitting at the beach house staring at the ocean brought home the truth. She was no longer the person who craved that life. A vacation, yes. But now she recognized that the life she had lived wasn't all bad. She'd been lucky to spend all the years she had with her parents. That never would have happened if she'd followed her original plans.

The winery was her home, and when she returned and had a closed-door meeting with the buyers and lawyers to complete the deal, she remembered all the times the kids had told her how much they loved living on a winery, how happy they were playing on the grounds. How much she herself had loved growing up in a winery in Argentina. And she just froze. She could not sign the final paperwork.

Immediately, she began interviews to hire a CEO to run the day-to-day affairs of the business. She didn't want to put in more than a few hours a day. All her time had to belong to the children. This was what she was in the middle of doing when Julieta barged into her office.

"You have to come outside now, Cousin Isabel."

Isabel apologized to the prospective new hire. "Honey, I'm in a meeting."

"But you have to come. Now. It's in the vines."

Isabel stood behind her desk. "What's in the vines?"

She shook her head. "Please." She ran and grabbed Isabel's hand. "Let me show you."

"I'm very sorry," Isabel said to the man sitting in her office. "I'll be right back."

Julieta ran out ahead, and though Isabel hurried, the girl disappeared into the vines. Isabel cursed. "Julieta. Wait."

But she didn't. Isabel carefully walked into the vines in her high heels. And she saw four square tables in the middle of the vineyard. Each of the kids and Nick were sitting at their own table.

"What's going on?" she asked, slightly out of breath.

Julieta reached in front of her table, where there was a large, white, movie-poster-size board. She turned it over and it said WILL.

Adelmo was next, reaching for his board and turning it over with a gleam in his eyes. His board said YOU.

Sandra's board said MARRY.

Isabel's rapid heart rate increased as Nick smiled and turned his board over. It said US.

All four of them waited expectantly for her answer. But her throat seemed to have sealed.

Julieta whispered loudly, "You have to say yes."

She laughed through the tears in her eyes. "Yes." She

nodded and moved forward to hug and kiss each of the children. When she got to Nick, she gazed into his eyes. "Again?"

"Only if you really want to this time," he said. "Not because of the winery or your parents or the kids, but because you actually love me."

She walked into his arms. "I actually love you and would be proud to be your wife." They shared a kiss that felt like coming home.

The children cheered and whistled. And Adelmo finally said, "All right, that's enough. Jeez, there are kids watching."

And both Isabel and Nick ended the kiss to smile and bring the children into their embrace.

Isabel and Nick were married one month later in an intimate ceremony at Tía Dominga's house, surrounded by everyone who mattered. And Isabel, who had taken flowers to her cousin's gravesite early the morning of the wedding, knew that somewhere in heaven her parents and Brenda and Andres were watching.

They had been blessed with a warm, sunny day that turned into a cool evening with a million shining stars. Isabel and Nick sat alone on the back patio staring at those stars, their heads resting against each other. This life that they'd shared full of hope, and pain, and broken dreams had come full circle. Here they were in Argentina again, as they had been when they met twenty-six years ago, dreaming of their future in America. A future full of possibilities as they raised their children together. Nick would run a restaurant, which they were going to build on the winery grounds. And Isabel would oversee the winery and attend school events and go surfing with Sandra on the weekends. Years from now, the children would go away to college and get married and search out their own dreams. By then, Nick and Isabel would be very old. They smiled. This was a great plan. Only fate knew if it would happen like this, but they were hopeful. Very hopeful.

Reading Group Guide for
Say You'll Be Mine

Discussion Questions

1. Losing a relative is never an easy thing. Isabel not only loses her close cousin, but also is entrusted to care for Brenda's children, all of whom she barely knows. Do you agree with Isabel's initial feelings about raising the children? What would you have done if you were in her place?

2. Do you think Isabel was selfish for being so adamant about pursuing her freedom? Was it realistic to think she would be happy trying to live out a childhood dream? Do you have a dream of your own? If given the chance, would you try to make it a reality?

3. Alcoholism is a serious addiction that Nick overcame, but that doesn't erase the painful memories that Isabel has of their marriage. Do you blame her for being hesitant of Nick's sincerity about the children? Do you feel that his efforts can make up for his past mistakes?

4. It seems like everyone has made up their minds about Ramiro based on who he was as a young man. Do you think people can truly change? If so, were they too hard on Ramiro? Would you have given him a chance to raise the children? Why or why not?

5. When events like this happen, often the needs of the

children are lost. Do you think the adults in this novel kept the children's interests in mind? Do you think their ending up with Isabel was best for them? Why or why not?

6. Given the hurdles that both Nick and Isabel have overcome in their lives, do you think they will be good parents for the children? Why or why not?

Choosing to Become a Mother

Some people who know me personally know that I adopted two children, and this prompts me from time to time to write stories that pull from my experience. To ask questions like, What does it mean to be a mother? What does it mean and feel like to children who must live with adults who are not their biological parents? Are we all cut out to be parents? Is it okay to NOT want children or to decide they will have a better life with a different family?

Since there are no easy or right or wrong answers, I can only explore possibilities through characters. Isabel, for example, didn't choose to become a mother, and she didn't *want* to be a parent—because the way the children came into her life was accompanied by pain (the loss of her cousin) and because she had "other plans." She changes her mind, of course; otherwise this would have made a terribly sad book. But in real life, I think it takes great insight and courage to know you're not interested or able to be a parent, and to make the decision not to be.

For me, I chose to become a mother through adoption and feel very blessed to share my life with two beautiful, amazingly bright, and loving kids. They are, by far, the best part of my life. Still, when people ask me if I think they should adopt, I always say that it depends on why they want children. It would be the same if they asked if they should give birth to a child. If they want to help another person grow, learn, contribute to society, if they have love to offer someone else without expecting anything in return, then having a child is a great idea. Birth or adoption—it makes no difference.

I have to say that I never refer to my kids as my "adopted children." They don't like the reference either. I think because it puts a qualifier on a relationship built on love. Adoption means "to take and make your own." However, this isn't the way I look at parenthood *at all*. My children are not *mine*, whether I gave birth to them or adopted them. They are individuals with their own personalities and personal gifts and goals that I try to help them develop. But they *are* my children—part of my family. We share experiences and family events, holidays and vacations; we worry about sick family members and grieve together when someone dies; we cheer each other on when something wonderful happens and try to console each other when life disappoints us. We share our lives with each other and we love each other, and all that creates a bond between parent and child.

This is part of what I wanted to portray in *Say You'll Be Mine*—the characters become a family by the end of the book, because they chose to accept and love each other. Personally, I think this is what being a family is all about.

Thanks for reading and being part of my "book family."

Ten Days in Argentina

Last year, my mom and I decided to take a trip together to Spain. I spent a long time trying to decide how to go about it. Did I want to spend all my time in the major cities? Did I want to let a tour group plan it for me and decide where I would go and how long I would stay in each city, or try to build a personalized trip myself? In the end, I chose a ten-day organized tour that took us through southern Spain, because this would allow us to see the most in a short amount of time. I had my doubts about what we'd get out of such a rushed trip, and worried that I'd be exhausted and unable to enjoy what I *did* see. But I was happily surprised at how much fun it was to take in the mixture of historical sites, museums, cathedrals, beaches, and vibrant city nightlife, all in one nicely arranged package!

So, I began to wonder if it would be possible to do the same in Argentina. What are the must-sees of Argentina, and can they be visited in ten days? Where would I take *you* if I were going to plan my own tour? Since this land is so vast and the temperature differences from the very southern tip to the northern border are huge, I decided a choice had to be made about seeing the north or the south. My decision was to start with the traditional north, where the majority of Argentines live, and come back for a second visit to see the dramatic, unique, and otherworldly landscapes of the Patagonia.

Are you ready? Let's take an imaginary ten-day trip to Argentina together...

Day one: We begin with our flight to Buenos Aires. I leave from LAX and have about a sixteen-hour flight. I've packed plenty of books, so I'm ready to enjoy the flight!

Day two: We arrive in Buenos Aires and check into Hotel Colón. We have the afternoon at leisure to recover from our flight but meet up in the evening to stroll down the lively pedestrian Calle Florida, where Argentine writer Jorge Luis Borges, who lived at the north end of the street, used to enjoy walking. There are many upscale stores for picking up the evening dress you forgot to pack or a soft leather jacket. We'll end with dinner at one of the many parrillas (steak houses).

Day three: This will be our first full day in Buenos Aires. I can't imagine going to Buenos Aires and *not* seeing Plaza de Mayo for its historical importance. In the center is a small obelisk commemorating Argentina's independence from Spain (great picture spot). Around the plaza you'll find the Cabildo (town council) Museum; the Catedral, which contains the tomb of General Jose de San Martín, Argentina's most loved liberator; and probably of most interest, the Casa Rosada, the presidential palace, where Juan and Eva Perón addressed their public (and where I got swept into a group of fanatics to cheer for President Raúl Alfonsín in the late 1980s while visiting family). The afternoon we should spend in multicolored, bohemian La Boca to go shopping for typical Argentine goods (like a mate gourd) or for original art created by local artists, and enjoy the local flavor of street vendors and performers. After returning to the hotel to change, we'll go to a tango dinner show.

Day four: For a taste of the Pampas Argentina (a large stretch of flat land that has been romanticized in gaucho books such as *Martín Fierro*), we'll visit an estancia on the outskirts of Buenos Aires. We'll go back in time to witness the Argentine gauchos in action as they display their horseback riding skills. Just in case you haven't had your fill of Argentine beef, the estancia will provide a typical barbecue, an asado cooked out in the open on iron grills over wood coals. We'll return for an evening at Teatro Colón (which is across the street from our hotel)—even if you don't like opera, this opera house is so gorgeous that it's an event just to be inside.

Day five: We are finally ready to leave Buenos Aires and, after a buffet breakfast in Hotel Colón, we'll fly to Iguazu Airport and transfer to our hotel—Iguazu Grand Hotel Resort and Casino. No longer will you feel like you are in what is characteristically thought of as Argentina when you enter Iguazu National Park and visit the Argentine side of Iguazu Falls. From the visitor's center, we will take an open train to Cataratas Station, where we'll get off and walk wooden paths to gorgeous lookouts of the 275 waterfalls. Not only will the breathtaking falls make you want to pitch a tent and stay there for the rest of your trip, but also the variety of local flora and fauna will probably use up your camera's memory card. Butterflies and birds of all colors fly from ferns to wonderful-smelling orchids and begonias. Later we will return by train to the visitor's center and back to our luxurious hotel. Here some of us will relax with a book at the pool (me!); others can choose to golf at the eighteen-hole, seventy-two-par golf course or visit the European-style casino.

Day six: Taking our winnings from the casino, we're ready to fly out of Misiones and travel to Mendoza (Isabel's home). From the airport, we'll transfer to the Park Hyatt hotel. Here we begin our walk through *Say You'll Be Mine*. The rest of our day will be reserved for winery tours. Mendoza produces 70 percent of the Argentine wines, and you'll get to walk through peaceful vineyards and visit wine cellars to see how wine is produced. We will, of course, sample many of the finest Argentine wines during our tours.

Day seven: After breakfast at the hotel, we'll take a full-day excursion to the Andes mountains. We'll travel along mountain roads, enjoying the landscape and panoramic views on the way to Aconcagua Provincial Park to view Mount Aconcagua, the highest mountain in the Americas. We'll make stops at Potrerillo, where we'll raft down the Mendoza River and have lunch, and visit Uspallata Village. Finally we'll come across Puente del Inca, which is an amazing sight because it was formed by thermal erosion caused by the sulfurous waters of the Las Cuevas River.

Day eight: After breakfast at the hotel, we'll check out and go on a morning bike tour of Mendoza city. Starting at Plaza Espana—one of the most beautiful plazas in Mendoza with its Andalusian motifs—we'll ride through Parque San Martín, then stop at Old Town Historical Mendoza, where we'll turn our bikes in and have lunch before we get on the bus that will take us to Mendoza Airport. We'll arrive at the Sheraton Mar del Plata Hotel (249 miles from Buenos Aires), and we'll spend the rest of the afternoon at La Perla Beach either paragliding, jet skiing, windsurfing, or simply relaxing under the warm sun. That evening we'll head over to Constitution Avenue, where the best dance clubs are, and dance until morning.

Day nine: The morning will be free for sleeping or enjoying more of the twenty-nine miles of beaches. After a late lunch at the hotel, we'll travel by bus back to Buenos Aires, where we'll check back into Hotel Colón and have the night free to pick up last-minute souvenirs.

Day ten: Fly home.

I hope you enjoyed the trip! It's only a glimpse of the beauty of Argentina. Check my website for part two—the Patagonia tour!

Q & A with Julia Amante

Why did you decide to set your novel in a vineyard?

Vineyards have always felt so romantic to me, and I've taken many wine tours in the Temecula Valley and Napa Valley in California. My mom visited the wine country in Mendoza, Argentina, and came back with stories of how much she enjoyed it, and recently we went together to a bodega in Spain to sample the strongest sherry I've ever had. When I started researching the business, I knew that Isabel had to be the owner of a vineyard, because it would be a business where she could take her expertise from Argentina and transfer it to California with ease.

How much research was involved? Did it take a long time to write?

I've had bits and pieces of this novel floating around in my head for a long time—probably three years. I did a lot of research and spent a lot of time visiting wineries, which sounds like a lot of fun—*and it was*—but what I was looking for was to see not only how wine is produced, but also what else happens on the premises (weddings, concerts, dining) and how difficult a business it actually is. I'm by no means an expert now, but I learned a lot!

Where did the plot of Isabel becoming responsible for three children and having to put her plans on hold come from?

My very favorite Christmas movie has always been *It's a Wonderful Life*, and I watch it every year. One year as I sat through the entire movie yet again, I had a different feeling. Instead of the usual, pleasant happily-ever-after at the end, I felt bad for George. Even though the angel showed him how important he was to the community and that by him being alive the entire town was a better place, George *still* didn't get to live out his dream. I wanted to explore the fact that life doesn't always turn out exactly as we want. Sadly, this is true more often than we wish. And I wanted to do it without an angel—since we don't usually get one in real life. I wanted readers to learn about a character whose life spun in a direction she didn't expect and she still managed to have a great life. Our initial life's dream doesn't have to be the only way to be happy, and I wanted to remind people (and myself) about that.

Isabel had to learn to balance motherhood and her career. How do you balance the two?

I'm not sure there is such a thing as balance. Usually I feel like I'm not parenting well enough, and I'm not doing as much as I want for my career. At times, I'll focus more on one and less on the other and try not to feel guilty about how I divide my time. But unlike Isabel, who saw children as an impediment to her goals, my kids *are* a very important part of my personal goals in life. I chose to become a mother; it wasn't dropped on me like it was on Isabel. So, though I have my days of frustration and feel totally incompetent at times, I think I handle things as well as most women with kids, a job, a husband, a house that refuses to stay clean, dogs, clubs . . . well, the way most women with busy lives do.

Do you enjoy being a mother?

Motherhood is complex. The days when kids sit in their bouncers and strollers and are happy to do anything you want don't last long! Very soon they grow up and have their own plans and ideas and likes and dislikes that usually are the opposite of yours. So I think as long as you can adjust well to the constantly changing demands of motherhood, it is an amazing experience. I LOVE to see the world through their eyes and to observe how they handle friendships and school, and life in general. I can't imagine having gone through life without them. But yes, there are days when I need a break and go somewhere where I'm not someone's mother, but just me.

Did you grow up in Argentina or ever live there? And did you include any of your own Argentine experiences in the book?

I didn't grow up in Argentina, but when I was seventeen, I got to spend a year there with my family. It was life changing. Prior to that, I didn't really know who Argentines were. I met wonderful people and amazing friends. The only part of the book that reflects my life in Argentina actually comes from Nick. While I was in Argentina, I had to go to high school (an all-girls school) and my classmates were all so, so wonderful to me. In *Say You'll Be Mine* the girls all love Nick, because he's a cute American guy. My experience wasn't quite the same since there were no males in the school—but I found an immediate acceptance and curiosity from girls who welcomed me into their lives and made me feel a part of the school. I also tried to include in the book a few cultural tidbits that I witnessed, like the slower pace of life and the freedom children have to come and go as they please—because it is safe for them to do so.

Why did you make Nick an alcoholic?

The simple answer is that I was creating a romanticized picture of a vineyard and winery, and I wanted to show another perspective—the very real effects of alcohol. Isabel becomes rich with this industry, after all. So I wanted to show the other side of the picture. There is a scene in the book where Nick is being interviewed about the winery and wants to point out the dangers of drinking too much, and Isabel cautions him not to make the winery look bad. Even after his alcoholism destroyed her marriage and almost her husband's life! Nick is a reminder, to her and to us, of what can happen if we aren't responsible drinkers. Obviously since I decided to set the book at a winery, it's because I love wineries, enjoy all kinds of wines, and often go out with friends for social drinks. I did want to show that I understand it's not all fun. But the deeper, plot-related answer to why Nick is an alcoholic is that I realized early on in character development that Nick and Isabel are very similar. Her "addiction" was making the business a success—

even when she saw that the environment was toxic to her husband. She was addicted to the success of the business; he was addicted to the product of the business. It all made logical sense to me when I was writing it—hopefully it turned out well.

Is there anything in particular you want readers to take away from this book?

Yes—that you have to be flexible enough in life to see the good in what you've been given. It's incredibly easy to feel disappointed that you don't have your dream career, dream family, dream relationships, that you didn't have the dream childhood—and to miss seeing the wonderful things you *were* given. I think being open to love changes the way you look at life, and that is probably the second thing I'd like people to see in the book.

About the Author

JULIA AMANTE had the misfortune of growing up away from the extended family that is so valued in the Latin culture, but she missed out on very little of what it means to be Argentine. Asados were sacred meals shared together on weekends. Cheering for the Argentine soccer team was a must, as were the pilgrimages to the Argentine Club in Los Angeles, where the young Americanized kids hid under the tables and watched the adults dance tango until the wee hours of the morning. Julia giggled right along with the rest of the kids at how geeky the parents looked, but secretly she was intrigued by the romantic culture and passionate music.

Julia lives in California with her husband, son, daughter, and two pampered pound puppies. She is hard at work on her next novel.

Want more of Julia Amante?

Then check out her first novel, *Evenings at the Argentine Club*

Available now from Grand Central Publishing

This poignant novel follows the interwoven struggles of two Argentine families trying to achieve the American dream.

"By turns touching, funny, tragic, and triumphant, it's the story of an endearing group of people in search of their own American dream...A delightful feast for the reader."

—*New York Times* bestselling author Susan Wiggs